ANDREW LOWE
TENDER IS THE NORTH

By Andrew Lowe

The Jake Sawyer Crime Thrillers

Creepy Crawly
Stronger than Death
The Dying Light
Pray for Rain
Chase the Devil
The Skeleton Lake
Cruel Summer
Fear of God
Tender is the North

Vinci Books

vinci-books.com

Published by Vinci Books Ltd in 2025

1

Copyright © Andrew Lowe 2024

The author has asserted their moral right to be identified as the author of this work in accordance with the Copyright, Designs and Patents Act 1988. This work is a work of fiction. Names, characters, places and incidents are the product of the author's imagination or are used fictitiously. Any resemblance to actual persons, living or dead, places and incidents is entirely coincidental.

All rights reserved. No part of this publication may be copied, reproduced, distributed, stored in any retrieval system, or transmitted in any form or by any means, including photocopying, recording, or other electronic or mechanical methods, nor used as a source for any form of machine learning including AI datasets, without the prior written permission of the publisher.

The publisher and the author have made every effort to obtain permissions for any third party material used in this book and to comply with copyright law. Any queries in this respect should be brought to the attention of the publisher and any omissions will be corrected in future editions.

A CIP catalogue record for this book is available from the British Library.

Paperback ISBN: 9781036703608

Printed and bound in Great Britain by Clays Ltd, Elcograf S.p.A.

For Tom and Josh

Prologue

JULY 1988

FRANCES HORTON LAY BACK and settled her head into a cushion of long grass. 'Dad doesn't think he should pay for the whole thing.' She pulled down the brim of her straw hat, shading her eyes from the fierce afternoon sun. 'He says it's an old tradition. Times have changed.'

Duncan Gibbs peeked into his salmon paste sandwich. 'What's he offering? A minicab to the church? A backhander to your brother to take the photos?'

'He says it's the principle. It's our joint decision to get married, so both families should contribute.'

'The old romantic. Maybe we should go to Lake Windermere instead of Lake Garda.'

Frances reached across to the portable CD player and skipped the track. Ecstatic yowling segued into a drowsy backbeat.

Duncan flung the sandwich into a bush and stood up, dusting down his shorts. 'We should just swap parents' numbers. Let 'em sort it out between 'em.' He gazed down at her for a moment. 'Let's go for a wander. Find a nice pub.'

Frances lifted the hat off her eyes but didn't move. She lay there, tapping her fingers on her shoulders as she sang along to the music.

Duncan scowled. 'This song is confusing. Why does he want to be her girlfriend?'

'He doesn't. He's just imagining their relationship if the roles were reversed. It's funny.' She switched off the CD player and stood up. 'And sexy.'

They kissed: lascivious, unhurried. Duncan's hand strayed to Frances's lower back.

Giggles from the edge of the field.

Frances held the kiss, but shifted Duncan around so she could see over his shoulder. A group of uniformed schoolgirls watched from the other side of a low dry-stone wall. They caught Frances's eye and ducked away, laughing, scuttling towards the medieval church on the edge of Wardlow Mires village.

Duncan broke away and turned to catch sight of the girls. He laughed. 'Nice to provide the entertainment.'

Frances smoothed out her dress. 'Not much going on around here.' She gathered the picnic things into a large biscuit tin, which she shoved into a cooler bag and handed to Duncan.

He shrugged. 'I read there's a big rock over the hill or something.'

Frances grinned. 'I'm sure there is.' She snatched up the CD player, then grabbed Duncan's hand and led him away to the opposite edge of the field. 'Let's find a quieter spot.'

A dog barked, further along the lane that curved away from the field into a verdant cluster of ash trees.

'Not that way, then,' said Duncan, as Frances sat up on the wall and swung her legs over. He vaulted over a stile and followed as she hastened down a shallow verge onto the lane below.

Frances stopped in a patch of shade from an overhanging tree. She turned off the music and listened.

The dog sounded closer than it had seemed up in the field. It barked and barked and barked, without pause. Hoarse and urgent.

Duncan caught up. 'Someone's not happy.'

Children's voices. Shouts.

Duncan tugged at Frances's wrist. 'Let's go up to Whitehouse Farm. It's not far.'

She pivoted. 'Are you seriously suggesting a roll in the hay?'

'Yeah. We're young and free. That's what you do on a day like this.'

'In porno films, maybe.'

A woman screamed, from the direction of the barking dog.

'Jesus Christ!' Frances startled so violently she dropped the CD player into the grass at the side of the lane. The jolt restarted the music.

Duncan set down the tin and sprang away, as the woman screamed again. He sprinted around the curve of the lane, disappearing into the trees.

Frances followed, away from the music.

Away from the tin filled with cakes and fruit.

The woman screamed again.

The dog stopped barking.

She ran, along the straight, narrow lane, under the ash trees, sunlight strobing through the leaves.

The woman. Screaming, crying.

Duncan up ahead, brandishing something. A stick. Branch.

Frances called to him.

'Stay back!' he shouted. To someone up ahead?

No. To her.

'Fran!' There was a tone in his voice she hadn't heard before. Jagged, animal.

But she didn't stay back. She stumbled forward, shielding her eyes, squinting at the sight of Duncan clambering up the verge, pushing into a field of long grass. Giving chase. Then turning and spotting her and falling, dropping the stick, picking it up again, running for her.

'Fran! Don't look.'

She made it to the patch of grass at the foot of the verge.

She didn't want to see, but she looked.

Bodies. A dog, a young boy. Not moving.

Another young boy, crawling, trying to raise himself upright.

The grass, gleaming with fresh blood.

A distant figure in the field above, running into woodland.

'Fran!' Duncan was with her now, holding her, trying to turn her away. 'I couldn't… He got away…'

Frances stared ahead, unblinking. 'Up there.' She waved an arm back at the field behind, towards a farmhouse with outbuildings. 'Get help.'

Her words were measured, quiet. She fought against her thumping heart, trying to steady her breathing.

And again she looked. Down and around, at a nightmare in motion.

A woman's body lay at the foot of the verge.

Black hair scattered.

Her face: a cavern of gore.

The grass around her head was flattened by a bloom of blood spatter: deep crimson at the centre, lighter at the edges.

'Oh my God,' said Frances. 'Oh my good God.'

Duncan held Frances's head, trying to find her eyes.

But she kept looking: at the woman's bright orange summer dress, soaked and blackened; at the dog's twitching paws; at the smears of red on the unconscious boy's socks.

'Get help,' she said again, and crouched, to the other boy. He was the younger of the two, his black hair matted by blood.

He tipped back his head and wailed into the air above.

Shouted in her ear as she held him.

Screamed for his mother.

Frances turned to Duncan. *'Go!'*

He looked up over the field, to the woodland. 'But—'

'He's gone. Get help, Duncan. *Please.*'

Duncan bolted.

Frances held the boy tight, let him howl into her breast. He pulled back and she shifted position, blocking his view of the bodies, shielding his vivid green eyes from the sun.

'Shh,' she said. 'You're safe now. Hey...' She moved around, face to face. 'Listen. My name is Frances. What's yours?'

The boy settled but kept staring ahead, his breathing snatched and shallow. He raised his gaze to Frances, and she gently shifted his hair to the side and wiped the blood and tears from his cheeks.

'Jake,' he said, then let his head drop.

'It'll be okay, Jake,' she said, stroking his hair. 'You'll be okay.'

Part I

NO SURPRISES

Chapter One

PRESENT DAY

THE MAN SAT on an orange-and-white exercise mat in the half-lotus position, head bowed, hands resting in front with fingertips touching.

He had positioned himself between two tall black speakers that sat either side of a double casement window: wide open but covered by a closed Venetian blind that blocked the morning sun.

Soft sounds wafted from the speakers: single notes, patterns of twos, threes, fours. Chimes, bells, distant washes of synth chords. Circling, cycling, overlapping, with each note sustaining until the very end of its fade.

The room was large but modestly furnished: single bed in the far corner; sliding-door wardrobe; grey armchair facing a sizeable TV and smoked-glass coffee table with a compartment for a games console, games and DVDs. A rack of dumbbells sat beneath a full-length mirror beside a sturdy wooden pillar with protruding limb-like struts.

A deep-set bookcase held a dense line of books, a slim turntable and CD player, and a rack of vinyl records.

The room adjoined a small kitchen with table and chairs, and a boxy bathroom.

The man kept his eyes closed, filling his lungs with deep breaths through his nose, holding for a few seconds, then releasing through his mouth in long, slow exhales.

Five taps on the ajar door.

He opened his eyes. They sparkled green in the diffuse light that leaked in between the slats.

'Sorry to interrupt.'

The man frowned. 'Visitor, Rob?' He turned his head to the bulky orderly in light green scrubs.

Rob nodded. 'I have to ask.'

The man shook his head.

Rob took a breath. 'It's police.'

'Definitely no, then.'

Rob opened the door wider and hovered in the frame for a moment, listening to the music. 'I like this. It's putting me to sleep, though.'

The man smiled. 'Eno will do that.'

'His name is Darryl Bentley. Detective Chief Inspector. Seems decent. He says five minutes and he'll be gone. He says he thinks you'll want to know.'

'He thinks wrong.'

Rob paused. 'He says it's about William Caldwell.'

The man turned back to the window. 'Send him through.'

'Really?'

He nodded. 'Would you make sure it is five minutes, though, Rob?'

'Of course.'

'Leave the door open, please.'

Rob retreated. The man rose to his feet and half-opened the blind. He was tall, long-limbed, slim but evenly muscled, with untamed raven-black hair that gathered at his neckline. He was barefoot, in loose white T-shirt and jogging trousers, and walked across to the CD player with a sway to his gait but no swagger.

He switched off the music and sat on the edge of the bed.

Rob reappeared with a short, wiry character in a well-fitted grey suit and carrying a chocolate-brown shoulder bag. Fortysomething build but mid-fifties features.

Rob nodded and held up five fingers before retreating again.

The man stepped in without being invited and held out a hand. 'Detective Sawyer. I'm DCI Darryl Bentley—'

'Is he dead?'

'Caldwell?' said Bentley. 'No.'

Sawyer stood, shook Bentley's hand. 'You could have at least brought me some good news.'

'Right,' said Bentley, lowering himself into the armchair. 'He's a fucking wreck, if that helps.'

'In what way?'

Bentley opened his shoulder bag and squinted at Sawyer. 'Big C. Pancreas.'

Sawyer sat again, closed his eyes. 'How long?'

Bentley sighed. 'I'm not his doctor, but I'm told it's late stage. Six to twelve months. Given his age—'

'So, does he want me to put him out of his misery?'

Bentley took out a white folder and handed it to Sawyer. 'Your man says I've got five minutes. He's a big lad so I'm not going to argue.'

Sawyer set the folder down on the bed. 'Straight to it, then? No pleasantries or platitudes?'

Bentley shrugged. 'Well… How are you doing?'

Sawyer made a show of settling himself. 'Thanks for asking. Not too bad, considering.'

'You've been in here almost a year.'

'That's right.'

Bentley looked around the room. 'What have you been doing with yourself?'

Sawyer thought for a second. 'Upgrading.'

Bentley nodded to the wooden contraption in the corner. 'Is that an exercise thing?'

'It's a wooden man dummy. I train in Wing Chun kung fu. The dummy simulates the human form. Limbs. Target areas. It helps to practise offensive and defensive techniques. Ingrains them so they become muscle memory.'

Bentley nodded, impressed. 'Do they still do kung fu? Isn't it all mixed martial arts, these days?'

Sawyer opened the folder. 'I also train in the system that began all that. Bruce Lee devised it. He's the father of MMA.'

'Bruce Lee. The movie star?'

'Yes.' The folder contained a sheaf of smudgy photocopies: missing person forms, pathology reports. Sawyer slipped out three A4-sized headshots of young women and laid them out on the bed. 'He was more of a philosopher, though. Ahead of his time, really.' He looked up. 'I suppose I should call you sir.'

Bentley scoffed. 'Let's keep it informal. I'm from Staffordshire CID. The girls are Deborah Wade, Julie Saltwell and Simone Heath. Sex workers. Back then, we called them prostitutes. All three worked the streets in the same area of Stoke in the early to mid 1980s. All three went missing in a three-month period back in 1986.'

Sawyer studied the women. Similar style: heavy eyeshadow in blue, green, purple. Shiny red lipstick for Deborah and Julie; pink for Simone. They were all brunettes with big hair, sprayed and back-combed: Julie and Simone permed, straight for Deborah. They held their heads high, tilted back slightly, glowering into the camera with a mix of dignity and contempt.

'I worked the cases,' said Bentley. 'I was a freshly minted constable. Basically, a DC of the time.'

Sawyer raised an eyebrow. 'Teacher's pet.'

Bentley gave a grim smile. 'I was one of the youngest, yes. There was a fourth sex worker from the same area. Sharon Wright. She went missing in early 1987. Some kids heard shouting from Bolehill Wood near Hathersage. They reported it, and we found Sharon's body dumped in a clearing.'

Sawyer slid out a separate envelope marked *SW*.

'Scene photos,' said Bentley. 'Black-and-white but not pretty.'

'No, thanks.' Sawyer laid the envelope down, unopened. 'He didn't have time to hide the body. Maybe the kids spooked him.'

Bentley nodded. 'He left us a bit of DNA, but this was the dark ages. We'd only just started analysis. No national database for another ten years. The scene location brought the case to Buxton, but we were involved because Sharon lived in Stoke.' He paused. 'We had to ID with dental. Couldn't do family. Not much to identify.' Bentley lowered his gaze. 'The killer used a hammer.'

Sawyer braced for the flash.

Nothing.

He ran his fingers through his hair. 'Did you not check the DNA trace later? Pick it up as a cold case?'

Bentley shook his head. 'Not enough to work with. And what we did have was too degraded. Also, the disappearances stopped, and it was pushed a long way down in the backlog.'

'Low-grade victims. Low priority.' Sawyer glanced at his bedside clock. 'You're almost out of time here. Rob is a stickler.'

Bentley edged the armchair forward a couple of inches, scraping the wooden floor. 'Detective Sawyer. Three weeks ago, an excavation near Hollow Meadows unearthed Simone Heath's body. Her skull had been shattered by blunt force. Probably a hammer. No preserved DNA, but when the discovery was made public, something really unusual happened.'

'You got a confession.' Sawyer gathered the items back into the folder.

Bentley sat back. 'Caldwell gave us detail on the clothes Simone was wearing. That was never made public. He also admitted the Sharon Wright murder, along with Julie Saltwell and Deborah Wade.'

Sawyer closed the folder. 'He's using it as leverage.'

'He is. His lawyer had already appealed for clemency due to his condition. Now he's pitching for compassionate release. The Heath and Wright families want him to die in prison. But the Saltwells and Wades are desperate to find out the locations of Julie and Deborah's bodies.'

Footsteps in the corridor outside.

'They couldn't just set him free,' said Sawyer. 'You're talking about two new murder investigations, with a potential for two more.'

Bentley leaned forward, elbows on knees. He locked in on Sawyer's eyes. 'He's offering to reveal the locations of the bodies, provided we grant the compassionate release. He's in the prison hospital now, and his lawyer is arguing he'll effectively be immobile in a matter of weeks. So the deal is on a clock. The brass see this as a way to squeeze something positive out of a rotten case. Nobody could claim that Caldwell is a danger anymore. He's skin and bones, Sawyer. Looks like something out of a horror film. I met him last week.'

Sawyer's eyes went to his own hand.

'I didn't touch him.'

Five taps on the door.

Sawyer sat up, holding eye contact.

'You're going to ask what this has got to do with you,' said Bentley.

Sawyer smiled. 'Come in.'

Rob eased the door open but hung back in the corridor.

'No, I wasn't. I was going to apologise for your wasted journey. Caldwell says he'll only reveal the body locations to me. Yes?'

Bentley gave a slow nod. 'Detective Sawyer. I can barely imagine the pain this man has brought to you and your family. But he'll be feeding worms before we know it. These families... You would be freeing them from their pain. The limbo of it. You would be letting them finally bury their loved ones. Deborah Wade's mother is on her last legs.'

Sawyer stood up; Bentley did likewise.

'I'm not asking you to be happy to do this. I'm asking that you see the bigger picture. It would be a gift to the families, not a concession to Caldwell.'

Rob walked into the room and stepped aside, holding the door open. 'Mr Bentley.'

Bentley ignored him. 'Detective Sawyer. Jake. You just have to hold your nose one last time. Close two cases in one go. He'll soon be dead and gone, and you can—'

'Move on?' Sawyer handed him the folder. 'It's a power trip. A final act of cruelty and control. A game. And I'm not playing. Sir.'

Chapter Two

LEON STOKES GAZED up at the yellow-and-red Auerbach and slurped his protein shake. 'You ever tried your hand at art?'

'I took a few life drawing classes at college,' said Boyd Cannon, parked in his usual spot on the purple sofa. He snapped his laptop shut.

Stokes turned. 'A cheeky eyeful of the models, eh?'

'I wish. They were all blokes. Older blokes. Fat fuckers.'

'Now I know why you stuck to numbers.'

'My dad was arty. He played the saxophone in a band. I didn't get it. Just sounded like a racket to me. He tried to get me into the guitar, but it didn't stick.' Cannon grinned. 'I was more interested in money.'

Stokes studied him, smiling. 'I don't suppose many kids go on to do what their parents picture them doing. My mum wanted me to be a lawyer.'

Cannon barked a laugh.

'I know. When she started to lose it, I just told her that's what I did. She doesn't know any different. She barely knows who I am now. I see a little flash of happiness, though, when I talk about my cases. You get about ten minutes with her, then it's like she reboots. She called me Adrian last time I was there.'

Cannon squinted. 'You're not an Adrian. What about your dad? Did you disappoint him, too?'

'Oh, he was a twat. Didn't matter either way. He was a twat to me, a twat to my mum. Used to knock her about. It only stopped when I got big enough to get between them. Seventeen, eighteen.' Stokes laughed. 'He pulled a knife on me once. I caught him on the nose, split his lip. He dropped it and stormed out. I don't remember seeing him again.'

Cannon's phone buzzed; he checked it. 'They're here.'

Stokes walked to the coffee table and turned to face the hall doors, tilting his head left and right, cracking his neck muscles. 'Need to know, Boyd. And that isn't much.'

He picked up a fluorescent bottle from the coffee table and sucked on the spout. The protein shakes were bulking him out, expanding his turning circle. He was still workout-shaped, but fleshier, insulated.

The doors opened, and a powerfully built man in a fitted suit strode through and stood aside to admit two hefty characters in designer leisurewear. They flanked a third: short and sinewy, in jogging trousers, his face obscured beneath the brim of a sky-blue Manchester City baseball cap. The man in the middle loped over to Stokes and pulled him into a hug with backslaps.

He stood back and raised his chin, revealing a black patch over his left eye. 'Leon the fuckin' lion. Still on the youth potions, then?' He nodded to Cannon. 'I heard that stuff just gives you the shits.'

'Wesley fucking Peyton. That's sort of the idea. How's life on the NCA Most Wanted list?'

'Dull as dishwater.'

'It's ditchwater,' said Cannon.

Peyton flashed him an unfriendly glare. 'How's business?'

'Better,' said Cannon.

'I hope you're not suggesting things have improved since I dropped out of the frame.'

Stokes flopped onto the sofa and spread his arms across the backrest. 'Don't confuse causality with correlation. Business is more like a business now.'

Peyton paced. 'Now Uncle Dale's the top boy, eh?'

Stokes nodded. 'Strickland stepped in, kept the bigger noses out. Doesn't hurt to have friends in high places.'

Peyton froze, mid-pace, turned to Stokes. 'I'll tell you what does fuckin' hurt. *This.*' He pointed a finger up to the eyepatch. 'I was planning on having two working eyes for the rest of my life.'

'Until you called Malecki by his name and you had to clear up the mess.'

Peyton stepped in, too close to Stokes. 'Yeah. And that fuckin' copper lost his shit.'

'He lost his shit,' said Cannon, 'because you were about to pop his missus.'

Peyton walked to the polished dining table and took a seat, leaning back in the chair until he was almost horizontal. 'There's books need balancing.'

'Sawyer's in the loony bin,' said Stokes. 'The cash is flowing outside, and your brother is shifting a ton of spice inside.'

'The University of Crime,' said Cannon.

Peyton sneered. 'Yeah. And he's graduating soon.' He sprang up and wandered over to a drinks cabinet beneath the painting. He poured a glass of whisky and gazed up at the wall. 'You paid too much for this.'

'Been dabbling in art dealing in your safe house, Wes?' said Cannon.

Peyton kept his back turned. 'I want him.'

'High risk, low benefit,' said Cannon. 'He'll keep.'

'He's *kept* for nearly a fuckin' year now.' Peyton paused. 'I know he came here. The day he attacked me. And Strickland.'

'Malecki fucked up,' said Stokes. 'Trying to track down Mavers. Taking it to Sawyer direct. Sawyer made the link to us.'

Peyton turned and headed back to the dining table. 'Like I say. Books need balancing.'

Stokes slurped at his drink. 'He's a fucking shell, from what I hear. He almost killed Strickland, who used it as a moral springboard. Never one to miss an opportunity. Sawyer made a mess of you, Wes, and I'm sorry that happened. But he's off the board. And off the list.'

Peyton sipped his drink, tapped the glass on the table. 'You think when Eddie comes out, there won't be changes?'

'Not his shout,' said Stokes.

Peyton scoffed. 'Fuckin' shot-caller inside.'

'This is outside.'

Peyton strolled over to Stokes and lifted the patch. His upper and lower eyelids had been stitched together, protecting the socket. The skin around the eye was pale and bloated, and the lids had shrivelled, but the line of fusion was neat. 'The beating gave me an orbital fracture. It pushed my eye back into the socket. Trapped and tore the muscles. They had to suck my own fuckin' eyeball back out of my skull.' He drained the glass and clanked it down on the coffee table. 'I could have had a false eye. Look like a

Bond villain. But I thought, fuck it. Close it up. Let it go. I have to use a magnifier for reading and my field depth is fucked. *I'm* fucked, okay?' He replaced the patch. 'I've done a serious shift for you, Leon. I want my time with this cunt.' He leaned in closer, pushing his face inches from Stokes. 'You've heard of an eye for an eye, yes?'

Stokes didn't flinch. 'You'll get your time. But it isn't now.'

Chapter Three

A SLATE-GREY PORSCHE Cayenne crunched along an expansive gravel drive and slowed at the side of a three-storey detached house. Before it had fully come to a halt, two young boys scrambled out of the same back door, tumbling over each other.

A short, elegant woman stepped out of the passenger door and brushed down her fitted skirt, unperturbed by the commotion as the boys flailed and grappled in the baize-like grass at the edge of the drive. They broke free of each other and raced up to the portico facade, laughing and shouting.

The woman bent down and spoke to the driver. 'Will you be long?'

A short but solid-looking man killed the engine and climbed out of the driver's seat, smoothing down his thinning blond hair. 'Just an hour or so. I have to catch up with one thing. The stakeholder meeting was fucking epic.'

The woman froze. 'Lyndon…'

The man closed the door, opened the boot. 'They hear worse at school.' He took out a large wheeled suitcase.

'Yes.' She smiled at him. 'Passed on from potty-mouthed parents like you.'

He grabbed at her. 'You love it, really.'

She made a show of dodging his advance. 'In the right context, yes.' She kissed his cheek. 'Don't be long.'

He sighed, closed the boot. 'I won't. I have to be in early at the agency tomorrow.'

'Anna's made cannelloni.' She lowered her voice. 'Me for dessert?'

Lyndon Wilde raised an eyebrow, held his wife Rebecca's gaze for a second, then extended the suitcase handle and spun away, down a winding side path that led to a modern garden office, constructed to blend with the house's rustic honeyed gritstone. He lingered at the solid core hardwood door, waiting for the commotion with Milo and Jamie to die down.

He steadied his breathing, listening to Rebecca's voice as she chided and cajoled the boys. Then, the slam of the front door and silence.

Wilde closed his eyes, switched to meditative breathing. Four seconds in, six seconds out. He repeated the rhythm for a minute, then swiped his thumb across the biometric panel. The heavy-duty deadbolt lock clunked open, and he pushed the door and stepped inside.

Recessed overhead lighting flickered for a moment then settled, casting the room in a sepulchral shimmer. It was a bare space: soft whites, greys, natural wood tones, with an abundance of natural light from floor-to-ceiling windows. A brushed metal desk sat at the far end, with a desk lamp, bright yellow iMac and two neat piles of books and documents. Wilde closed the door, locking it automatically, and flicked a wall switch, closing the window blinds.

He clicked on the lamp and lifted the suitcase onto the desk.

His heart fluttered, and he shifted back to the meditative breathing pattern again.

Four in, six out.

Four in, six out.

Wilde unzipped the suitcase and opened it out. One compartment contained several packets of Plaster of Paris, compacted tightly, a large pot of Vaseline, strips of gauze, a plastic litre bottle of water, various bowls and stirring implements, brushes, scissors.

The other compartment contained a three-dimensional representation of a woman's face, sealed in polythene and held in the centre by tightly packed bubble wrap. He carefully peeled the polythene aside and took out the mask, holding it in cupped hands. It was pale white, with a smooth matte finish which highlighted every contour and nuance of the nose shape, closed eyelids, curve of the lips, pores, subtle wrinkles.

He held it up to the light from the lamp. The surface carried a barely perceptible grid-like pattern from the gauze reinforcement. That still bothered him. Cheesecloth smoothed it out, but gauze delivered better detail and durability.

Four in, six out.

Four in, six out.

His heart raced, pushing against the breathing pattern. He tilted the mask from side to side, letting the light glide across its milky surface.

The woman's expression: frozen, forever serene. The existential weight lifted. The tension of living released. All that worry and pain swept away.

Wilde set down the mask and walked to the wall behind

the desk. He swiped his thumb across a second biometric panel and pushed at a door in the side wall. He retrieved the mask and walked into an adjoining room, then closed and locked the door. Low overhead lighting revealed a long, narrow space, with a padded leather chair in the centre, facing the featureless far wall.

Four in, four out.

Four in, three out.

Six out.

But now his heart hurried.

He reached into his pocket and pressed the button on a small remote, setting off a soft whirring from the far wall.

A panel high in the wall slid open, left to right, revealing a single line of white face masks, evenly spaced. The features—all female—stared out with expressions similar to the mask in his hand: liberated, unburdened.

The opened panel exposed a line of clips alongside the masks, arranged into square groups of four. Wilde raised the new mask and fitted it to the first available space, then eased himself into the chair.

He squeezed a lever in the arm and the seat dipped into a slight recline.

Two in, two out.

Two in, two out.

Lyndon Wilde placed his shaking hands on his knees and stared up at the masks.

One in, one out.

One in, one out.

Four in...

He let out a long, full-throated scream—a howl of anguish—swallowed by the soundproofing.

Chapter Four

'GOOD MORNING, CAMPERS.'

DSI Robin Farrell crashed into the conference room at Buxton MIT and took his seat at the head of the table. He tapped open a canister of breath mints and tossed one into his open mouth. He wiped his touch screen with his sleeve and fell silent as he accessed the case file system.

An image of a smiling young girl appeared on the wall-mounted screen behind him. She wore a yellow-and-black cardigan, and her blonde hair was gathered into two short bunches. She smiled for the camera: uncertain, curious.

'We're now almost three weeks into the Phoebe Gray disappearance,' said Farrell, smoothing out his over-dyed black hair. 'I'll let DS Walker take up the story.'

Walker looked up from his screen. 'Shouldn't we wait for DI Shepherd, sir?'

Farrell sighed, keeping his eyes on his screen. 'DI Shepherd knows the case, and I gather there isn't much in the way of progress or development, anyway.'

Walker stayed silent long enough for Farrell to look up.

'Well?'

'Sir. Phoebe Gray, nine, left Hartington Junior School to walk home alone on 18th April. She never got there, and we haven't had a single credible sighting since. A road CCTV camera picked her up at 3:37pm crossing the B31 by the overhead bridge. From the other side, she could have followed several routes to her house, but we have no further pick-ups. Her father Orlando says that Phoebe is a sensible, mature girl who never went anywhere without letting him know first. Phoebe has type 1 diabetes and her father has a strong concern over her access to medication.'

'I have a golf partner whose daughter has type 1,' said Farrell. 'If someone's keeping her alive, they'll need to be following her insulin regime.'

'We've checked with pharmacies. No unusual patterns. You can get insulin online and we've trawled all the major site purchase records, but for the quantity required, it's practically impossible to track. Phoebe carried a refillable pen, but according to her father only had enough for a few days.'

Farrell banged the desk. 'Whoever's taken her... this is a big problem for them.'

Walker sighed and swiped at his screen. A picture of a balding middle-aged man in a cheap-looking blue suit appeared on the main screen. 'Her father is a handyman at Cavendish Hospital. His wife died last year, so he's a single parent.' Walker looked around at the other detectives. 'There has been a development, though, sir. I'm surprised you're not familiar.'

Farrell crunched his mint. 'There are some things even I don't know, DS Walker.'

Walker continued. 'Orlando Gray is in a cell downstairs. He was arrested after an allegation of gross indecency.

Anonymous tip-off. One of his responsibilities is the hospital mortuary.'

'Jesus Christ,' said DC Myers, his head jerking up from his screen.

'Fiddling with the stiffs?' said Farrell.

Walker forced a smile. 'A co-worker backed up the allegation, saying that Gray's shift patterns made it easy for him to engineer plenty of alone time in the mortuary. Frazer Drummond oversees the post-mortem process at Cavendish. He's conducted further tests and has discovered clear evidence of wrongdoing in the individuals that tally with Gray's schedule.'

'Circumstantial, though, surely?' said Myers. 'I assume he's denying it.'

No answer from Walker. All eyes turned to him.

'He is,' said Walker. 'But—'

'Go on, then, Sherlock.' Farrell leaned back in his chair and dug a little finger into each nostril in turn. 'What's your hunch?'

Walker looked up at the on-screen image of Gray. 'It's the background work we've done, after Phoebe's disappearance. Enhanced DBS check was solid. There's nothing to suggest this in his background.'

Farrell waved a hand. 'The darker the perversion, the harder the pervert has to work to hide it.'

A female DC, Beverley Swift, shook her head; it was subtle, but Farrell caught it.

'DC Swift?'

'Sir?'

'You disagree?'

Swift looked around the table for help, but all eyes were down. 'No, sir. It's just—'

'Oh, I get it,' said Farrell, 'You don't like the word

pervert? How else would you describe someone who touches up dead bodies? I haven't been on that particular sensitivity course, I'm afraid.' He drummed his puffy hands on the tabletop. 'Gray's arrest isn't a complication. It's a breakthrough.'

'How so?' said Myers.

Farrell squinted. 'Do you need me to spell everything out for you? We double down on the questioning about Phoebe's disappearance. If he can do dead bodies, then he can surely—'

'That just doesn't follow, sir,' said Walker. 'Paraphilias are specific and usually isolated.'

Farrell pushed himself to his feet. 'Not always. There's overlap. Comorbidity. Gray could have been getting busy with dead people and also knocking off his daughter. Maybe even his dead daughter. Maybe he's stashed her away somewhere for his pleasure? Look at his movements since Phoebe's disappearance. Where has he been? Any abandoned houses nearby? Relatives' places? Keep it plausible. He's hardly loaded so I doubt he's hiding a second home. He might have a caravan somewhere, though. Or a shepherd's hut. We might have a case of necrophilia and paedophilia.' He squeezed out a mirthless grin. 'Two for the price of one.'

Swift groaned. 'There's no evidence of—'

Farrell faced her down, raising his voice. 'Then find me some. This is what we do here, yes? Evidence. Interviewing people. Arresting them if we think they've broken the law.' He sat down again. 'Maybe you've all got a bit sloppy. Too dependent on our absent friend.' He crunched up the mint, swallowed it, then lowered his voice close to a whisper. 'Well. Other detectives are available. Am I right? Walker, work with Shepherd on this. Let's build a case nice and quick. Fast-track the forensics. Gold star if you can get a confession from Gray. That'll help us with the lack of progress on the Phoebe disappearance.'

'I've heard he's frozen up,' said Myers. 'Won't say a word.'

Walker scoffed. 'He's traumatised. Not all recalcitrance is wilful.'

Farrell raised an eyebrow, looked around for solidarity, didn't get any. 'DS Walker. We're detectives at the heart of a serious enquiry. Not contestants on bloody *Countdown*. Lay out the body photos in front of him. Look for his reaction.'

'Old school,' said Walker, nodding.

Farrell rolled his eyes. 'Yes. Old school. Because old school works. It's quicker than shipping in specialist interviewers. It's what I pay you for.'

'Press are on it,' said a slender, Nordic-looking character in a tailored suit, standing behind Farrell. 'It's on the *Derbyshire Times* website.'

'Already?' said Farrell.

Stephen Bloom shrugged. 'Families of the victims. They've probably got someone in the hospital on a retainer. They get names from the mortuary roster. Cross-ref with medical records. Trace the families and throw some money at them.'

'Get Shepherd,' Farrell said to Walker. 'Talk to Gray. He's looking at two or three years for Offences Against a Corpse. Multiply that by the number of victims.'

'Four,' said Walker.

'And if he has done something with Phoebe—'

'Circumstantial for the mortuary bodies will stick harder,' said Myers.

Farrell spun his breath mint container around on its side, pondering.

'We already have a specialist interviewer,' said Walker, 'with a shitload more empathy than the ABE guys.'

Myers glanced at Swift. 'Achieving Best Evidence. One of the standard techniques.'

Swift smiled. 'I was aware.'

Farrell pocketed the container and stalked to the door. He threw it open. 'Shepherd and Spark. Sounds like a shit cop show.'

Chapter Five

DETECTIVE INSPECTOR ED SHEPHERD tapped twice on the sitting room door.

'Come in.'

Shepherd eased the door open and stepped inside, greeted by the sound of a clattering keyboard.

Maggie Spark sat at her desktop computer, facing the vast window that overlooked the Roaches ridge. An extra-large yellow candle burned on the desk beside her, presumably the source of the lemon tang in the air. She gave a brief look over her shoulder. 'One second, Ed.'

'Take your time. Justin let me in. Your daughter is setting up some tea and cake. I'm on a plan, but she insisted.'

Maggie laughed. 'Mia is deep in a baking phase.' She reached for a matte black walking cane with an ergonomic handle and raised herself from the chair. 'I think it's her nurturing instinct. Or she's trying to make me so heavy I can't leave the house again.'

Using the cane for support, Maggie walked over to the chocolate-brown futon in the centre of the room. Her rust-red hair caught a shaft of sunlight from the window as she smiled up at Shepherd, who carefully pulled her into a hug.

'She's not doing a good job,' said Shepherd.

'Of what?'

'Filling you out. I mean that as a compliment.'

She gave a rueful smile. 'My mother isn't so diplomatic.' She gestured to the futon and Shepherd took a seat. 'She says I'm wasting away.' Maggie manoeuvred around the other side of a low glass coffee table and eased herself down into an armchair, facing Shepherd. 'She's been saying that since I was seventeen, though.'

A teenage girl—tall, with tinted blonde hair tied into a neat ponytail—backed into the room with a tray loaded with mugs, teapot, and a plate of cakes. A middle-aged man held open the door for her and waited at the entrance as she set the tray down on the coffee table.

She grinned and flicked out her AirPods. 'Vanilla custard cream squares. They're messy, but that's okay. It's part of the fun.' She leaned down to Shepherd and whispered. 'There's a bit of rum in there.'

Shepherd reeled in mock shock. 'Mia. I'm on duty.'

Mia looked back at the man. 'Dad?'

'I'm confident Detective Shepherd can execute his duties without fear of court action,' he said.

Mia spun away to leave. 'Enjoy!'

'Thank you, darling,' said Maggie.

Mia paused at the door as her father retreated into the hallway. 'I'm going to Joshua's after lunch, Mum.'

'Okay.'

'Mr Shepherd, you can take a few cakes with you if you

like…' She glanced at Maggie. 'Can you get one to Uncle Jake? I mean, Detective Sawyer?'

Shepherd smiled. 'Save one for him.'

'Oh, he'll love them,' said Mia. 'I thought my brother had a sweet tooth, but he—'

'Takes the cake?' said Shepherd.

She frowned at him, re-inserted her AirPods, and headed out, closing the door behind her.

'Boyfriend?' said Shepherd, pouring tea.

Maggie took a cake. 'She says *friend* friend, not boyfriend, but who knows? Joshua was one of the boys held at the Harrison Briggs house. They've started an organisation to help children who have been the victims of trauma. Online group therapy, mainly. Justin has been helping her jump through the legal hoops.'

Shepherd hesitated, then reached for a cake. 'Don't tell Mia, but I've been on this strict sugar-free diet for a few months now. But there's no joy in it.' He took a bite, catching most of the pastry flakes in his palm, and chewed slowly. 'Wow. It's true what they say. There is a rush. You sure she hasn't bought these from M&S?'

'Mia does things her own way. She's not the shop-bought type.'

Shepherd sipped his tea. 'And how are you?'

'I've been better. Also a lot worse. I still have muscular pain and a few balance and coordination issues, but I'm working with a good physio. The cane is useful for getting seats on busy trains.'

Shepherd looked out of the window at the colours of the rolling moorland: yellow and white wildflowers; purple heather; green bracken; the multicoloured jackets of the climbers dotted across the distant gritstone rocks. 'How about up top?'

She grimaced. 'Memories can be foggy. Moods not so stable. The hardest part was just… rediscovering the world. The confusion, disorientation. Relating to a reality I'd been cut off from for so long.'

'It'd be nice to have you around the office. Bit of sanity.'

'How is Farrell working out for you?'

He wrinkled his nose. 'He's an arsehole. You know that. But Keating had served his time, and our esteemed mayor took office on a serious sympathy kick. Bought himself a lot of direct influence.' Shepherd set down his mug and plate and shifted across the futon to where he could lean over and rest a hand on Maggie's. 'Have you remembered anything else about the station attack?'

She looked up, held his eye. 'It's still just flashes. This and that. No identifiable detail. I know the men Jake attacked at the hospital were coming for me, though.'

Shepherd nodded. 'That ship has well and truly sailed. Wesley Peyton is the last man standing. As the phrase goes, we remain keen to eliminate him from our enquiries.'

Maggie slid her hand away. 'Any sign?'

Shepherd shook his head. 'He'll be holed up somewhere in a prison of his own choosing. He knows we know about his role in the attack now, so I'd say you've been crossed off his worry list. Farrell is still insisting it was all about the Fletcher fella.'

Maggie closed her eyes. 'He helped me.'

'Yes. But he's keeping his head down, too. That leaves one other man who brass want to speak to about the hospital carnage. But he's also unavailable.'

She opened her eyes. 'Jake…'

'Strickland used the assault as leverage with the Home Office to restructure everything. Derbyshire and Staffordshire are pretty much outposts of Greater Manchester Police now.'

'With Robin Farrell as his Sheriff?'

'Absolutely.'

Maggie took her time over another sip of tea. 'Ed, I'd like to work. That's why you're here, isn't it? But it's too soon for me.'

'I thought it would be. But I just wanted you to know we've kept your seat warm.'

She smiled, stared down into her mug. 'Anything new from Jake?'

Shepherd waited until she looked up. 'He still won't see people. Turns down visits.'

'Have you spoken to his brother?'

'Yes, but he won't pass on anything.'

Maggie set down the mug. 'It's wise. He's recovering. Michael has been through it himself.'

Shepherd took out a piece of paper and unfolded it. 'The unit manager gave something to Michael four months ago. He said it's all Sawyer wanted to communicate for now.' He read from the paper. '*With bodily and mental seclusion, distraction does not arise. Therefore, upon renouncing the world, one should renounce discursive thoughts.*'

Maggie blew out a sigh. 'In other words, leave me alone.'

'It's Buddhist. I tracked it to a meditation book.'

'It's good for him. As long as he's safe.'

'Medium-secure. Private. Hard to get into. Harder to get out. If he's gone full Zen, won't he be renouncing possessions, too?'

Maggie followed Shepherd's gaze out of the window. 'Buddhists normally work on understanding the impermanence of possessions and focus on spiritual development.'

Shepherd nodded. 'That's a shame. I've got a present for him.'

'Cake?'

'Sweeter than that.'

Chapter Six

DR HARRIET MARTINEZ swished a finger across her tablet screen then wrote something with a stylus. 'We started on quetiapine. It seems extreme in hindsight, but the presentation was extraordinary. You refused lithium and aripiprazole. Why was that?'

'Extensive research,' said Sawyer.

Martinez glanced up from the tablet. 'Google?'

Sawyer nodded, and leaned forward on his chair, resting his elbows on his knees.

Martinez was the unit's lead consultant psychiatrist, and her office was regarded as the hot zone: for some, the antechamber of release and rebirth; for others, a seat of judgement, prolonging incarceration. It was a roomy and welcoming space, blessed with natural light from broad windows overlooking the gardens at the back of the grounds. All was mild blue, cosy cream, diluted yellow. At the back, three teal armchairs sat around a low coffee table with a tray of brochures and an undersized snake plant.

'Lorazepam,' said Martinez, returning to her tablet. 'Benzodiazepine...'

'For sleep,' said Sawyer.

'Promethazine...'

'That one gave me a runny nose.'

She smiled. 'I remember.'

'It did feel like you were just cycling through drugs but didn't really know what would work.'

Martinez slotted the tablet into a charging station. 'Well, that's exactly right. We still have no way of looking into your brain and seeing what isn't working. It's all pretty much trial and error.'

She took off her blue-framed glasses and clasped her hands together on the desk. Martinez was mid-forties, and, like most of the Trafalgar Lodge clinicians, pleasant but a little pompous. In his previous life, Sawyer would have read her contradictions as performative: mumsy with designer heels; natural and unstyled chestnut-brown hair with painted eyebrows and nails; family photos but sporty car; Mexican background but a taste for bland British salads.

Her eyes drifted to the side as she contemplated. The silences were part of her rhythm: never loaded or deployed to intimidate.

'Your tattoo,' she said at last. 'Across your back. *True to his own spirit.*'

Sawyer slumped. 'We have talked about that.'

'Oh, of course. *Spirit.* The alternative translation of *demon.* We used to think that mentally unwell people had been possessed by demons.'

'That's just religion. Religious metaphor. And scientific ignorance plus confirmation bias. The usual toxic brew.'

'Sure,' said Martinez, refocusing. 'And we still suffer from expectations around this idea. A disease of the system.

An invasion that can be repelled. Cured. Did you ever feel taken over in this way? The aggression you displayed before admission… A guard at the hospital referred to your behaviour as "like a wild animal".'

'I was in control. But making poor choices.'

Martinez closed her eyes for a moment. 'Do you worry if this was your *true spirit* running the show, Jake? And did you submit to our care to reduce its potential for harm?'

'I submitted to care for more complex reasons than that.'

Martinez opened her eyes. 'Do you feel cured, Jake? Have we at least… mitigated this part of you that makes poor choices?'

Sawyer ran his fingers through his hair. 'I'm ill, but hopeful.'

She laughed. 'Correct answer.'

'The worst thing anyone can do in here is to insist they're feeling better.'

Martinez unhooked the tablet and wrote something with her stylus. 'You've clearly learned a lot, Jake. So… What if I reframe the question? Would you say you're the same person who came to us around a year ago?'

'Categorically not.'

Martinez looked up from the tablet with a raised eyebrow. 'You reported hallucinations. Phantom insects. Manifestations. And delusions. I remember an intense session where you talked about our concept of time and how it relates to quantum mechanics.'

'You can blame Carlo Rovelli for that.'

'The theoretical physicist?'

Sawyer nodded. 'And no more hallucinations. The version of me who came here a year ago… He'll always be in me. But I have him under control now. So, I've been focusing on moving myself further away from him.'

'And this is your interest in meditation? In Buddhism?'

'That's a part of it, yes.'

Martinez looked up and to the left: a familiar tell. She was building to a conclusion. 'So, when do you think you might feel sufficient distance from that version of yourself to move on from our care?'

'Trying to get rid of me?' said Sawyer quickly.

She smiled. 'Trying to formulate the beginnings of a care plan. Jake. It makes sense that you're reluctant to leave. Outside, the world is chaos. In here, it's knowable, predictable. Constructed around routine. You've suffered greatly. You've endured a lot.'

'Death by initialism.'

'Sorry?'

'CBT. EMDR. ACT. MCT.'

'Yes, but by your own admission, you've travelled a long way. You've *changed*. And you've refocused on this meditation. This self-discovery. Self-work. Perhaps now, you need a new focus. A new project. Something outside of the self.'

Sawyer stayed silent, studying the wood patterns in the floorboards.

Martinez got up, walked to a window. 'Remember. Unlike most of our service users, your presence here is entirely voluntary.'

'Maybe you should see it as a comment on the service.'

Martinez perched against the window sill. 'So, when you do leave us, what will you miss? What feedback would you leave?'

He looked up. 'I do like the way it feels more like a vocational college than a psychiatric institution.'

'How so?'

'It's light on medical detail. No bleeping machines.' He surveyed the office. 'Maybe lose the stylised nature scenes, though. And there's too much Formica in the rec room. The right middle pocket on the pool table sticks. Pudding portions are too small. Also, a bit of humour might help.'

Martinez frowned. 'In what way?'

Sawyer smiled, activating a dimple in his right cheek. 'I can see a sign on the dining room wall: *YOU DON'T HAVE TO BE MAD TO EAT HERE, BUT IT HELPS.*'

Martinez laughed. 'Nobody could fault your defences, Jake. But I do have concerns about your engagement.'

'You heard about my visitor.'

'Can we call that a breakthrough?'

'Did Bentley see you before seeing me or after?'

Martinez walked back to her chair. 'Bentley?'

Sawyer smiled. 'Nobody could fault your effort.'

'At what?'

'Lying. But you're forgetting who I am. What I am.'

'So, a year in here hasn't dulled your professional instinct.'

Sawyer fixed Martinez with clear eyes. 'I don't go back.'

She nodded slowly. 'You don't go back?'

'If it feels like going back, I don't do it.'

Martinez clicked her fingers. 'And at last, we circle to our recurring theme. Avoidance. How it keeps us safe but can also be detrimental to healing.' She wrote on the tablet. 'Did you know that Freud never maintained a patient for more than two years? And Lacan would cut sessions short if he felt the patient was just wasting time. In fact, he charged a lot to discourage that. Jake, I relish our work. You keep me on my toes. I'm always excited to see you. But for me, you've moved as far forward as I can take you. And to stay here any longer is, as you say, to go back.' She hit him with her signature move: rolling her chair around the desk and joining him up close, knee to knee. 'You've set up your life here in a perfect stasis. But I suggest that you're experiencing something new and unusual: fear. To leave your room, you know you'll have to be different. You'll have to keep changing. Re-engage with relationships. Make decisions. I know that you're too smart to be in denial about this. For me, you're in deferral.' She paused and put on her glasses. 'Humans are unique in that we have a long childhood. We're plastic and we learn and mould ourselves around formative experience. Your formative years were arrested by your mother's murder. So, now you have to rediscover that plasticity. Learn again how to change and develop. Professionally, your cases have arrived as problems to be solved. And you've solved them, marked them as finished, moved on. But outside of the therapy room, outside of this institution, everything is fluid and ever-changing, and that's okay. Some business will always remain unfinished.'

Chapter Seven

ALFIE REDCLIFFE MADE a third trip from the desk to the door and back again. 'We've had the full set now. *Too quirky. Counterintuitive. The science isn't sound.*'

Redcliffe was long and leggy, and he covered the distance from desk to door in four heavy steps. Dale Strickland observed his deputy with practised patience, framing him in the space between his dual desktop monitors.

Redcliffe was a degenerate gesticulator; he could barely order coffee without sending something flying. 'The pivot is too radical, Dale.'

Stop. Pause. Turn. Here he comes again…

'Tabloid tycoons don't set the agenda any more. But anyone close to executive political power will always err towards risk aversion. And a platform of drug decriminalisation is risky.'

Strickland dragged and arranged his solitaire cards. 'The Ancoats trial shows it's all hearts and minds. Once you crack the prejudice, the resistance starts crumbling.'

Redcliffe arrived back at Strickland's desk. He gave him a look, then...

Pause. Turn. Off he goes.

'Ancoats is not London, Dale. Greater Manchester is not England. This can't scale. It's maybe generational. But you started the Ancoats initiative when you were way down the ladder.' He stopped mid-step and spun. 'And this is how power changes things. When you're on the outside, railing against the system, you're a radical. Shouting for change. But once you're in the tent, you can't keep pissing out. You have to be pragmatic. Work with increments. This idea is useful for highlighting waste and overspending in local civic structures, but it's too out there to stand alone at national level.'

Redcliffe bared his teeth; some of them still milk. He wore his youth like a provocation, as Strickland had hoped. He was a provincial community leader gifted a stage to match his ego; a shabby student firebrand upcycled in Paul Smith and Burberry. Best of all, he darkened the office colour palette, as Strickland had planned but could never admit.

Strickland took off his oversized black-framed glasses and puffed air onto the lenses. 'Would it help if I attended the meetings? Backed up my ideas with physical presence?'

'God, no,' said Redcliffe. 'You're the top boy. You don't see presidents jetting in and using their mighty stature to browbeat ceasefires. They send their stuffed shirts to secure the deals, then they show up for the glory and the photo ops.'

Strickland wiped his lenses with a sleeve and replaced the glasses, then returned to his game. He sighed and dealt a card from the stock, then another.

Restless, he stood and strode over to the window. His tailoring was bespoke, from Dooley & Rostron, reviewed monthly. Handmade woollen suits in grey and navy. Fitted pastel shirts: Twill, Jersey, Oxford, pleated for civic evening functions. The glasses: Gucci, with the brand name rendered along each arm in large type. His white hair had retreated so far he now buzz-cut it to a natural stubble pattern, which he tinted for a silver shadow effect.

He lifted the window, speckled by the Deansgate drizzle, and looked down on the morning clamour. Redcliffe was still talking somewhere.

'Bottom line, Dale. This is a conservative country. The tendency is towards punishment. Political rivals call anything else soft. And soft loses you the middle ground. And the middle ground is—'

'What's the closest you've been to death, Alfie?'

'Sorry?'

Strickland looked at him. 'Death. Have you ever been in a situation where you thought, "This is it. This is my time."'

Redcliffe stopped his pacing near the door. On the other side, a young man in a remote headset pointed through the glass into the office. Redcliffe shook his head and held up his index finger.

He turned to Strickland. 'I had a motorbike when I was… too young to have a motorbike. The back wheel got clipped at a junction and I came off. It wasn't high speed, but I was lying in the middle of traffic, curled into a ball. Luckily, it was early morning and nothing hit me. But I do remember thinking—'

Strickland snorted. 'Well, you've upstaged my story.'

'I know the story. The detective attacked you, right where you're standing. Tried to throw you out of the window. It's always puzzled me, though.'

The young man outside tapped on the door. Redcliffe held up a palm.

Strickland slid the window shut and went back to his desk. 'What has?'

'You're the mayor of Greater Manchester. You could take any office in this building. Why stay in the one where you were attacked by a madman?'

Strickland shifted a king of clubs into a new column. 'Sawyer's not mad.'

'He was fucking furious that day.'

'And a shiny new office would help me get over it?' He gave a slight nod, keeping his eyes on the cards.

Redcliffe signalled to the man outside, who opened the door.

'Mr Strickland...'

'Thank you, Oliver. Please send him through. We're finished here.'

Redcliffe headed out. 'Christie fundraiser tonight, Dale. Kimpton Clocktower. Probably a late one.'

A stocky man with a thick black moustache pushed into the room, not waiting for Redcliffe to fully exit.

Redcliffe nodded at him. 'Mr Abadi.'

Oliver saw Redcliffe out, and Abadi closed the door behind him.

Strickland continued with his game. 'Farouk. How goes the hunt?' Abadi didn't answer, and Strickland looked up. 'You're smiling.'

'He went to see Stokes.'

Strickland pushed his chair back from the desk. 'It was definitely Peyton?'

'Definitely.'

'And you tracked him?'

'No. We forgot.'

Strickland shot him a dark look, then grinned.

Abadi checked his phone. 'Appley Bridge.'

'Jesus Christ. The badlands of Preston. I bet the locals love a scumbag like Peyton rattling round up there.' He scowled. 'Strange choice. Just outside the GMP border. Does he think he's dodging an extradition treaty or something?'

Abadi gave a phlegmy laugh. 'He wasn't with Stokes for long. Barely an hour.'

'We should extend a cordial invitation.'

'Is that wise?'

The dark look again. 'Yes. It's wise. Any whiff of our smoky friend?'

Abadi shook his head. 'Feels like we're chasing a ghost. I even tapped up an old *Mukhabarat* colleague. GIS.'

'So... Subcontracting?' said Strickland.

'You said whatever it takes.'

Strickland rolled back to his desk, resumed the game. 'We won't find Fletcher until he's ready to be found.' He shifted cards around, letting the silence hang.

Abadi cleared his throat. 'Dale. Do you ever think about how it might be better... to let it all go? You have all you'll ever need. Wealth. Power. Status. A fine son.' He hesitated. 'A hot wife.'

Strickland continued playing. 'Farouk. Do you ever think about how it might be better... to not talk so much? Give your jaw a rest.'

Abadi scoffed. 'It still clicks.'

Strickland spun away from the desk. 'You know what my hot wife says? She says I've won. She says I've escaped the mistakes of my past. Righted my wrongs. And now I should relax. Graze on the fruits of my labours. But here's the thing, Farouk. Just because you've built a castle, it doesn't make you safe.' He lowered his voice, causing Abadi to lean forward. 'The wise general concerns himself more with his enemy's plans than with the lay of the land.'

Chapter Eight

WES PEYTON POUNDED the heavy bag chained to the corner rafter of the outbuilding. He worked through his usual circuit of basic combos: jab-cross, hook-uppercut. Three minutes each, with thirty seconds of rest. Then, the power drills: heavy crosses, explosive hooks. Then footwork, endurance.

The rafter creaked as the bag swung under the impact. Peyton kept his breathing pattern regular, puffing out with each punch, sucking in oxygen for the follow-up.

During rest breaks, he moved in to get a clear look at the wall-mounted flatscreen TV, where Manchester City were toying with some lower league side.

The connecting door swung open and an ogre in an electric-blue soft shell jacket and Moncler joggers marched in.

Peyton clocked him, nodded to the TV. 'This had better be a fuckin' cricket score, Remmel. Why has he got a DM on as a CAM, though?'

Remmel handed Peyton a white hand towel. 'Trying things out against lesser opposition?'

Peyton towelled off his head, then raised his eyepatch and dabbed around the socket. He let the patch snap back into place and glared at Remmel with his good eye. 'What have you been readin'?'

'Eh?'

'I've never heard you say, "lesser opposition". That's a lot of fuckin' syllables in one go. You'll have to give your brain a break now.'

Remmel scowled and gazed down at the scuffed stone floor. The comeback wouldn't come. Instead, he held up a phone. 'He's on in five.'

Peyton took the phone and jerked his head towards the door. Remmel exited and Peyton switched off the TV. He sat down at his corner desk and slotted the phone into a charging station which held it upright.

He took off his baseball cap and smoothed out his matted hair, then stared at his shadowy reflection in the lock screen.

Lesser opposition.

When they were younger, Peyton's older brother got the bigger food portions. He broke his best toys. Later, he took his girlfriends.

In one of his earliest memories, his brother took him to Moss Side, for his first match at Maine Road, bought him a steak and kidney pie and a bottle of fizzy orange.

'This is the little 'un.'

One of his brother's friends called him *Half Pint.*

The phone rang and Peyton connected the call instantly.

A scowling face filled the screen, already scrutinising.

Shaven head; borderline monobrow; short, sculpted beard with a cheek-to-ear fade. The man grinned, baring perfect white teeth.

UK-accented hip-hop hammered and ranted in the background.

'Alright, Eddie,' said Peyton.

'Our kid.' The face ducked to the side for a moment then reappeared, filling the window with vape smoke. 'You're looking buff, bro. Not a puppy no more, eh?'

'Never been one.'

More vape smoke. 'So, how've ya been, little bruv? Watching my business out there?'

'Y'can do that yourself soon.'

Eddie laughed through his teeth. 'Mindin' your *own* business, eh? When you're not down the fuckin' gym. You still set up?'

'Yeah.'

'Dibble no wiser?'

'Too fuckin' right.'

Eddie nodded, unblinking. 'Me neither.'

'Leon's out of the loop, too. Best way. Nothing personal. Need to know, yeah? Not saying you'd say 'owt. But you never know who's listening in.'

Eddie considered this, doubtful, then nodded. 'Speak up, then. I've got a couple of minutes. Took me five to get this phone out of my skivvy's arse. Daft cunt ordered the wrong size. Made his fuckin' eyes water, I can tell ya.'

Peyton steeled himself. 'Need some info.'

'Do ya now?' A slow bloom of vape smoke. 'Should have done this earlier, but... When a man and a lady love each other very much...'

'Fuck off, Eddie.'

Laughter at the other end. Eddie wasn't alone in his cell.

Tender is the North

He waited for quiet. 'Who's fucked you off this time, then? You talked to Leo?'

Peyton stayed silent.

'Right, right. Mum says no, so you've come to Dad, yeah? Wesley, lad. You're already down an eye. What are you steamin' in on now?'

'Sick of hangin' about.'

'We've just got settled again. We're not doin' coppers. The juice isn't worth the squeeze.'

'The cunt took out one of my eyes.'

Eddie moved in closer to the camera. 'I don't care if he had both your bollocks. We're settled. I'm sweet for release next year. I've got *plans*.' He pointed. 'You can be part of 'em. Don't fuck this up now.'

Peyton glanced at the TV screen. Man City players aggressively celebrated a goal, urged back by stewards.

'Sometimes it's like Leon's the real boss,' said Peyton.

Eddie stared, seeping vape smoke. 'He is. While I'm still in here.'

'He's knockin' on.'

A grin slowly took shape on Eddie's face. The teeth again. 'Not a puppy no more, little bruv.'

'No.'

'Wesley Peyton 2.0.'

Peyton stifled a flash of irritation. 'What about Billy Rice's fam?'

Eddie sat back, shrugged. 'Still choked for 'em. Good soldier, though. It was a shitshow, but we took out two dibble.'

'Fletcher,' said Peyton. 'Austin Fletcher. The fella in the cells. He shot Billy. I can set that right.'

Eddie shook his head, smiled. 'Fuck me. From puppy straight to mad dog.'

'Stokes has done fuck all. If I deal with Billy's killer, I get a boost with the crew.'

'*Company*.' A voice off-screen.

Eddie nodded. 'Gotta get back. Any last requests?'

Peyton snatched up the phone, got closer to the screen. 'This Fletcher. He's gone dark. Light him up for me.'

Chapter Nine

SHEPHERD CHECKED the DVR was running and took a breath as Walker settled in beside him. The man opposite looked like he'd been dragged in from a battlefield. His skin was dirty, greasy and streaked with sweat, and he wore an ill-fitting blue suit jacket over a stained white shirt.

A well-groomed older man sat beside him, leafing through a neat pile of documents. He pushed his chair away at a slight angle. 'Before we start, DI Shepherd, I have a short statement, composed by myself in collaboration with my client. If you'd indulge me.'

'Of course, Mr Davies.'

Davies read from a document. 'My client acknowledges the current situation and the accusations that have been made against him. But they are merely allegations at this stage, and my client strenuously denies any wrongdoing. I have advised my client to exercise his right to answer police questioning without comment until formal charges are made. We understand the serious nature of the allegations and are fully cooperating with the authorities in the investigation.'

Shepherd gave Davies a curt nod and leaned forward on the table. 'Are we gonna hear what you sound like today, fella, at least?'

Orlando Gray kept his eyes on the wall behind Shepherd and Walker, and lifted himself upright, tilting his head back a little. 'No comment.' His voice was faint, wavering, but he kept his eyes rigid on the wall.

'You can look at me, Orlando. I'm your advocate. It's what I'm paid for. Getting you justice. I'm the civil servant, not the judge.'

Nothing.

Walker took out four headshots and laid them on the table: three young women, one middle-aged. 'Can you give us a brief overview of your role at Cavendish Hospital, Orlando?'

'No comment.'

'I'll help. I checked with HR. You're a maintenance assistant. Regular checks on hospital systems, equipment and infrastructure. Repairs. Electrical, plumbing, structural. Conducting safety checks for H&S compliance. Equipment set-up and breakdown. Working with contractors. Keeping records. Adhering to hygiene standards. Emergency response. Now, I don't know if you got your wires crossed when you did your job interview, but I couldn't find anything about the sexual violation of the dead.'

Shepherd studied Gray. His breathing rate seemed to increase slightly, but he kept his eyes fixed on the wall.

'Is that why you took the job, Orlando?' said Shepherd. 'Access to the bodies? Privacy? On your terms and in your own time?'

'No comment,' said Gray.

'But you weren't careful enough, were you? The Senior Pathologist received an anonymous tip-off about the scheduling of your shifts and how they coincided with fresh transfers from the hospital to the mortuary. The tip-off also said how you made inappropriate comments about two recently deceased young women brought into the mortuary. The pathologist found evidence of sexual violation on the bodies of these four women. Were you responsible for that, Orlando?'

'No comment.'

'We've seen CCTV footage,' said Walker, 'of you entering the mortuary basement level carrying work tools and clipboard, doing routine tasks like checking fridge temperatures. But there's no CCTV in the post-mortem room. So, we can't see what you're doing. But we can look at how long you spend in there.' He took out a document. 'On five occasions, over a three-week period, you enter the main mortuary via the outer corridor doors, and you don't re-emerge for two hours. Does it really take you that long to execute your tasks?'

'No comment.'

'There is an exterior entrance to the mortuary, a bit deeper than basement level. But there's no CCTV there, either. So, unless you're going in, covering your work, and then going for a walk for an hour or so, you can hardly blame us for putting this together. The tip-off, the internal CCTV.'

Gray screwed his eyes shut, then opened them again. He pawed at his face, stretching the skin. Davies watched him, frowning.

Shepherd edged his chair closer. 'We understand that you're under a lot of stress, Orlando, with your daughter's disappearance. But the silence isn't doing you any favours.

We're doing everything we can to find Phoebe, but with little progress, this is only going to throw the attention on you.'

'Have you hurt Phoebe?' said Walker.

Gray's eyes darted around, then fixed on Walker, raging. He raised his voice. '*No…* comment.'

Now Walker moved in closer. 'Where is she, Orlando?' He pointed to the photos. 'These people are gone. You'll be prosecuted for what you did to their bodies, but that doesn't have to be the end of your life. But if you know where Phoebe is, and you're not telling us—'

Gray's eyes shifted to Shepherd, then back to Walker. He muttered something under his breath.

'What's that?' said Shepherd.

Gray stared at him. 'You're wasting time.'

SHEPHERD AND WALKER headed out and sat side by side on an empty bench in the custody suite.

Shepherd slumped forward, elbows on knees. 'There's enough. Forensics already looks strong. But unless he confesses, it'll be a slog.'

Walker stared. *'If you want to understand the artist, look at his work.'*

'Oh, very good,' said Shepherd. 'So, what about Gray's work? What do we understand?'

'Nothing. There are no red flags in his past. And do we really think he's abused and murdered his daughter, then moved on to necrophilia as… What? Self-soothing?'

'Maybe he's taking something out on the bodies. He's not the killing type, but there's anger and frustration over Phoebe. He gets easy access to the bodies as part of his work… But then he gets rumbled. It might be separate from Phoebe's disappearance.'

Myers hurried down the central corridor, turned towards the cells, but then saw Shepherd and Walker on the bench. 'Bloom got a call. From Dean Logan at the *Derbyshire Times*. He wants a comment.'

'What about?' said Shepherd.

'Gray sent the *Times* a phone. He'd recorded a video on it just before his arrest.' Myers shook his head. 'Logan says it's a courtesy call, and they're running it whatever we say. It won't stay local for long.'

Chapter Ten

BRAD SINGLETON TUCKED his vapour-grey Volvo SUV into a leafy lay-by at the top of the road that coiled down into Dovestone Valley. He stepped out of the car and retrieved a small backpack from the boot. He checked the contents: night vision scope, long lens camera, GPS handheld, tactical hunting knife, Kronos electric lock-pick gun and tension tools.

The fading light threw long shadows across the drystone wall and gate, as Singleton crouched and looked through the scope, down across the valley.

He surveyed the vast seventeenth-century farmhouse.

No sign of life. No vehicles out front. Lights all off.

Singleton shouldered the backpack and headed down the steep lane. He'd gone full ninja: black sweatshirt, black Lycra trousers, black sneakers. Awkward for any chance meetings with late-night walkers, but he had the peripheral awareness and skill to avoid them, and, worst case, he could spin some bullshit about nocturnal birdwatching.

Planning had always been his thing. Logistics. But he'd

drifted into driving for the hands-on experience. Then the IED had checked his ascent.

In quiet moments, he could still sit and watch the events play out, second by second, with abysmal clarity.

Supply line security recon near Basra. Two armoured vehicles; Singleton was in the first, driving. The second vehicle took most of the explosion, killing its occupants and two of Singleton's colleagues in the back of his vehicle.

His own injuries led to a lengthy rehab, then a turn before the Military Medical Board, and medical discharge from fieldwork. After that, he'd pivoted to consultation, training, pen-pushing, chair-warming. All talk, no action.

Singleton slowed as he approached the side door of the farmhouse, conscious of every footstep now. He ducked behind a tree, listening.

Distant cattle. A trilling blackbird. Restless leaves. The rumble of traffic on a back road at the edge of the valley.

Singleton checked the scope, focusing on a door at the top of a short external staircase. From the website imagery, he'd spotted a Yale padlock, estimating access time at five to ten minutes.

He put on a pair of latex gloves, took one last survey for movement, then crouch-walked at speed across the courtyard and up the steps.

The padlock was easier than expected: older, with a worn mechanism. He took out a small torch and held it between his teeth, as he used the Kronos to open the lock.

He slipped inside, closing the door behind him.

Singleton pivoted his head slowly from side to side, getting a torchlit aspect of the enormous open-plan kitchen, reflecting the spaciousness of the original barn.

He looked up, to the exposed wooden beams, then across to the polished stone central island.

The tall, uncovered windows admitted the last of the day's light, and Singleton squinted into the far corners: one with a high-grade stove and oven, the other with a wardrobe-sized fridge.

He waited, listening.

Nothing but the low drone of the fridge.

He crouch-walked to the interior door, and opened it a few inches, then paused, listening for noises deeper in the house.

Nothing.

He turned off his torch for a moment and squinted across to a closed door on the far side of a connecting hallway. Was there a faint light underneath it?

He closed the door and edged back into the kitchen.

A light flared up from the lane.

Car.

But by the time he reached a side wall window and peered round the edge of the frame, the light had faded, and the engine had fallen silent.

Passing car.

He turned the torch back on and scuttled over to the far wall.

Ceramic sink beneath a row of cupboards, all empty.

Nothing in the sink.

He edged over to the fridge and opened the door.

Salad drawers: lettuce, tomato, cucumber, sealable sandwich bags of grapes, mango.

Bottom shelf: packets of cooked deli meats, cheese.

Middle shelf: multi-pack of organic strawberry and blackberry juice. Small cartons with attached bendy straws. Colourful design and cartoon fruit characters.

Top shelf: glass container with sealable lid. He peeled away the lid, revealing a syringe pen with refillable cartridge. A second container held several vials marked *INSULIN, HUMULIN-N, U-100*.

Singleton yanked open the freezer compartment.

Burgers, frozen pizza, ice cream.

He closed everything and looked around the kitchen, thinking, listening.

He took out his phone. No service.

He could search deeper, with potential unknown danger and a possible confrontation.

Or he could get back to his car. Find service. Call it in now. Safety first, glory later.

Singleton walked out of the kitchen and resecured the padlock.

Focus on the mechanics.

He hurried down the steps.

Slow and steady.

He passed the tree and walked back up to the Volvo.

Walk, don't run.

At the car, he took out his phone. Plenty of service.

He made the call, keeping eyes on the house.

Voicemail.

He tried to keep his voice low and calm, but he stumbled over his words.

'It's me. I, uh… I'm here. I finally tracked him to a place. By Dovestone. Definite evidence inside. But this is beyond us both now. I'm calling this in. I'll try you again later. *Call me.*'

Singleton hung up and dialled 999.

He took a big breath, looked up and saw the other car for the first time—a Porsche—parked higher up the road, almost out of sight.

Rapid footsteps from the other direction.

His face crashed into grass, ears ringing from the impact.

A scorching agony spread across the back of his head.

He scrambled to turn, but another blow smashed into his cheek, from something rough and heavy.

Another blow.

And another.

Chapter Eleven

SAWYER TOOK a coffee and sandwich to a corner seat in the Harmony Café and gazed out at the unit's sensory garden, segmented into themed sections: lavender and roses in the calm zone; marigolds and daylilies in the stimulation zone. He caught the fragrances through the open window: rosemary, mint, jasmine.

His eye wandered to the wider grounds, with their walking paths, benches, blended water features, art stations.

Beyond, the ten-foot security wall was subtle but sturdy. Enough to discourage unauthorised exit but not imposing or impervious. At the top, the stone was curved, to make foothold purchase difficult but not impossible. As a self-admission, Sawyer was free to come and go as he pleased, but he was expected to inform a care worker or therapist of any planned prolonged absence.

He opened his book: *Call for the Dead*. Another crack at le Carré.

The café was quiet: only three other service users, all older men. One sat reading a newspaper a couple of tables over, while the other two slumped into the corners of a couch, watching a television playing at low volume.

A young woman in a light green regulation polo shirt cleared a few cups from a nearby table. 'Running today, Jake?'

'Always running, Abbie. That's why I'm free.'

She laughed. 'Piss off.'

'I'll go later today. Might keep going.'

Shouts and commotion. Rob and another worker entered, supporting a chunky, wide-eyed man who flailed his trembling arms and shouted towards the TV.

'Oh. Here we are again... Here we go again...'

They sat him at a table and spoke in hushed voices. Rob encouraged the man to drink from a glass of water, while the other worker tried to distract him from the television.

After a few minutes, they all got up and walked along the side corridor towards the rooms.

The man with the newspaper watched them go. 'Poor bleeder. He's off for electric shock treatment, probably.'

He looked over, and Sawyer obliged him with a grim laugh. 'Constant obs.'

'Sorry?'

'Constant observation. A worker will park a chair at his open door and sit there watching him until they're relieved by another. Self-harm risk. It's the second highest level.'

The man whistled. 'What's the first?'

Sawyer sipped his coffee. 'Arm's length.'

His ear cocked to the TV. A news programme. The studio reporter faced the camera, looking grave, explaining that some people might find the following scenes upsetting.

The image changed to a jerky, self-filmed video of a balding middle-aged man. He spoke to the camera, but the audio and video were edited with contextual voiceover.

'I'm going to be arrested. Something vile. I… did some wrong things. But this isn't me, okay? It *isn't me*. Please believe me…'

Sawyer got up and sat at the centre of the sofa.

'Mr Gray's daughter Phoebe has been missing now for almost three weeks. He maintains his innocence in the face of the current allegations.'

The footage segued, as the man pointed at the camera. 'My girl. *My girl…*' He bowed his head, sobbing. 'I've tried my best.' He loomed in close. 'You've got to believe me. This isn't my choice. I didn't have…' He paused, gathering his breath. 'A choice. I didn't *have one*.'

Another clumsy edit found Gray facing the camera, head in hands. 'This is nothing to do with my girl, okay? Please. I did everything right. I just made a mistake. I want people to know that I'm the victim. I've suffered so much. I'm not responsible for my choices now… I made a *mistake*, okay? I wasn't careful enough. I had nothing to do with my girl going missing.' He was sobbing hard, choking out his words. 'I'm the only one who should… who should suffer. Not her. Please don't hurt her. I'm a stupid, stupid man but I don't have a choice now, okay? This isn't my choice.' He wiped his eyes.

Abbie came over and stood by the TV, watching. She held a hand over her mouth.

Sawyer reached across to the remote and tapped the volume increase button a few times.

The man held his head back and stared down the camera. 'I've been in a dark place, okay? A private hell. But the truth will come out soon. There's light ahead.'

Chapter Twelve

MARCH 1994

THREE GENTLE KNOCKS.

'What?' Angry.

Harold Sawyer slid the door open a few inches and pushed his head into the gap. His younger son sat crouched in the corner by the old fireplace, hugging his knees to his chest. Harold forced a smile. 'Jake. Come on. You can't keep this up.'

Harold entered and crouched, leaning his back against the wall, lowering himself to Jake's eyeline. He was a tall, rangy man who had recently switched his clean-cut look to a wilder style: leonine hair, lightly tamed beard.

Jake looked up. 'He won't give me the bear. He says I'm too old for it now. He always takes that.'

Harold fumbled in his pocket. 'Michael knows it's dear to you, Jake. It's his way of getting your attention. Your brother's going through a funny age.'

'I hate him.'

'No, you don't.'

'He won't talk to me. He took the bear, and he locked his door.'

Harold took out a paper bag. 'I'll do the talking. I'll get the bear back later. I have someone coming over and I need to know you're okay. Will this help?' He held out the bag: boiled sweets, lemon, orange, blackcurrant.

Jake reached out and took a lemon sweet. Harold stood up and put the bag on the shelf above the fireplace.

'Can I leave them here, Jake? Can I trust you not to eat them all?'

Jake unwrapped his sweet, nodded.

'Also, most children hide in their own room when they're upset.' He looked around, at the desk, the shelves of books, record player and records. 'What's the fascination?'

Sawyer squeezed the sweet into his mouth. 'What did Mum study in here?'

'It was just a private space. They call them studies, but that just means somewhere you can be alone.'

'Like the cave?'

'Yes.'

'Mum has a book called *No One Here Gets Out Alive*. Why is it called that?'

Harold looked up at the bookshelf. 'It's a line from a song she liked by The Doors. The book is all about the lead singer. I suppose it's saying we should all remember that we won't be around forever.'

Jake sucked on the sweet. 'Me and Mike say a thing. He started it, though.'

'Go on.'

'We say, "There's always death to fall back on."'

Harold winced. 'Jake…'

'It's true, isn't it? No matter how bad things get—'

'Can you please come up with some happier things to say?'

Jake lowered his head, sulking. 'Mike doesn't hardly say anything.'

'Your English teacher might have a few thoughts about that sentence.'

'Dad?'

Harold closed his eyes, braced. He knew the tone. 'Go on.'

'The man who killed Mum. Why did he do that?'

'Jake, we've done this a thousand times. I don't know.' The doorbell rang. Harold stood up, checked himself in Jessica's old wall mirror. He ran a hand through his hair, smoothed out his beard. 'We'll probably never know. He was very sick.'

'In the brain?'

Harold moved out. 'In the brain, yes. Seriously, don't eat all those sweets. I won't be long.'

Jake listened to his father's familiar stair-descending rhythm. The front door opened.

He crawled over to the study door, opened it slightly and listened to the deep voices of his father and another man as they carried from the front door through to the sitting room below.

The conversation began loud—although he was too far away to hear anything—but then quietened down.

Jake sucked on the sweet, pondering for a moment. Then he crawled out of the room to the top of the stairs.

From the voices, he could tell that his father and the other man were at the kitchen end of the sitting room, and he could only catch snatches of their conversation.

'*…it's too clean…*'

'*It's just a bloody moustache, Harold. Not a disguise.*'

The other man asked Harold how he'd been, and Harold told him he'd started to paint.

'I'm thinking of moving. Not too far, but away from Wardlow. Staying in the area for the boys.'

There was a lull. Jake shifted position.

The other man replied but he didn't catch it. Harold was closer to the door at the bottom of the stairs and his reply was clearer.

'I'm not sure I can come back, Ivan. Things have changed too much.'

Footsteps, as his father moved around. Jake missed the next bit of conversation, but then…

'You'll laugh, but I'm feeling a higher calling. Something bigger than me. Bigger than just criminal justice.'

'You're getting this from Kelly.'

'I used to feel so sure. But now it's all… uncertainty. And that day at Bolehill—'

The other man interrupted, replying in a low hissing whisper, inaudible.

Then he spoke in a normal voice. *'You're letting your emotion direct your suspicion. It's faulty reasoning.'*

More whispered exchanges.

Heavy footsteps, out of the sitting room.

The front door opened and closed. No goodbyes.

'Jake…'

The voice from behind made him jump.

Michael had half-opened the door of his room. His shadowy face peered through the gap. 'What are you doing? What's going on?'

Jake put his finger to his lips. 'Shh.'

Footsteps from below. Harold, climbing the stairs.

Jake backed away and scurried into his bedroom, closing the door quietly behind him.

Harold reached the top of the stairs and stopped.

He pushed open the door of Jessica's study: ajar.

No Jake. The bag of sweets was still on the shelf above the fireplace.

He closed the door and paused, his nose twitching at something sharp, lingering on the landing near the top of the stairs.

Lemon.

Both boys' doors were closed.

Harold gave a wry smile and headed back downstairs.

Chapter Thirteen

PRESENT DAY

WES PEYTON TAPPED in his regular program and set the treadmill moving. Three-minute warm-up walk, then 10k run in two chunks with a three-minute rest walk in the middle. He pointed the remote at the wall TV and fired up the NBA channel. Peyton had always been too short to play basketball, but he loved to watch, loved the way it all looked like a pack of wild animals scrapping over a kill.

He had no patience for current teams or leagues. He stuck to the classic reruns for guaranteed drama. First up today: Celtics vs Lakers from the 1980s. Bird, Johnson. He'd watch for a while, then shift forward a few years and catch a Pistons vs Bulls game, for the joy of early Jordan.

But the Knicks were his team, his basketball equivalent of City. His comfort game was the 1970 Lakers classic, with Knicks captain Willis Reed scoring two baskets with a torn thigh muscle.

Peyton finished his warm-up and upped his speed, breaking into a trot.

During his year in the wilderness, the Knicks had set his heart on Manhattan, as a fantasy city. He craved the relentless energy. The life. The noise.

He would live there someday.

The gym door flew open.

'Visitors.'

Peyton turned, to find Remmel in the doorway, arms folded. He kept running. 'Friend or foe?'

Remmel lumbered over and held his phone in front of Peyton, showing an image of a white Mercedes S-Class parked off the connecting road at the front of the safe house. 'What do you think?'

Peyton hit the emergency stop on his program. 'Well, it's not the fuckin' Amazon delivery, is it?'

He turned off the TV, towelled himself, and slipped on a grey-and-white Knicks hoodie, then screwed on his sky-blue City cap and walked out to the main door.

'We've got it covered,' said Remmel. 'I can go see.'

Peyton patted his immense shoulder. ''Salright. I'll take this one.'

He opened the door and strolled along the path, triggering the security lights. The house was planted in low-lying moorland stretched thin over the dead zone between Lancashire and Greater Manchester. It was quiet in daytime, and silent at night. The unfathomable depth of the silence freaked Peyton, and he needed a thunderstorm sound-effects app to get to sleep, switching to the chatter and clink of coffee shop ambience during the day.

A burly man with a bushy moustache stood by the back door of the Merc, holding it open.

'*Wesley!*' A male voice from the back seat. '*Step into my office.*'

Peyton ducked down and looked into the car.

Dale Strickland beamed out at him and patted the seat. Peyton climbed in and Abadi closed the door behind him. The interior smelt bleachy, with a hint of rich cologne.

Strickland opened a pull-down cabinet in the back of the passenger seat, revealing a bottle of Glenfiddich and two tumblers.

Peyton shook his head. 'I'm good.'

Strickland closed the cabinet. 'Sorry it's a bit late. But, as the *boss of the cunts*, as you called me when we last met, I sometimes have to operate in the dark.'

Peyton took off his cap, scrubbed up his hair. 'What do you want?'

Abadi stepped into the passenger seat and closed the door.

'How are you finding things out in the West Pennines, Wes? Not exactly the Wild West.'

Peyton shrugged. 'Keepin' me head down.'

'By visiting your boss in his big house in Greater Manchester?'

'Stokes isn't me boss.'

'I expect he'd disagree.' Strickland caught Abadi's eye in the rear-view mirror. He leaned forward, studying Peyton's eyepatch. 'And how are you coping with the visual compromise?'

'I'd rather have two eyes but I'm getting by with the one. Look, what the fuck do you want? I can't see you turning up here to offer moral support.'

'I'm curious about a couple of things. And as a fellow victim of Detective Inspector Jake Sawyer's wrath, I was hoping you could help.'

Peyton kept quiet, turned to the window.

'My main question is, why?'

'What do you mean?'

'Why was Sawyer so angry? He was hell-bent on killing me, and you.'

Peyton scoffed. 'You really don't fuckin' know?'

'Really.'

'I can help, but I need something from you in return.'

'What's that?'

Peyton turned. 'Protection. I've been warned off Sawyer. But there's another thing I want, and I'm not in the mood to ask permission from old Leon.' He lowered his voice. 'Y'know, I think we might want the same things, Dale. Because here you are. Billy Big Bollocks. King of the North. In the middle of nowhere. In the middle of the fuckin' night. You've been stewing, haven't ya? You can't relax.'

Strickland glared at him. 'What's the other thing you want?'

Peyton beamed. 'Your old mate, Austin Fletcher. He killed my own mate, Billy, who had a shitload of respect with Stokes's crew. Slotted a couple of coppers that day. I've heard you've fallen out with Fletcher, and I bet you're still watching your back, eh? Worried he might pop up at some fundraiser. I bet he knows where your bodies are buried, right, Dale? Don't you just love it when you click with someone over a shared interest?'

'You know where he is?'

'I don't, but my big brother's better connected, even though he's banged up. He's picked up a lead.'

Strickland re-opened the cabinet and took his time pouring a glass of Glenfiddich. He sipped it at first, then knocked it back. 'What about Sawyer?'

Peyton nodded towards Abadi. 'Is he alright?' Strickland nodded. Peyton turned to the window again. 'So, Boyd Cannon is Stokes's right-hand man. He calls him his *consignore*.'

'*Consigliere*.'

'That's the one. Stokes watches too many fuckin' films. He thinks he's the Godfather. So, Cannon always has his laptop when he's with Stokes. And he obsessively records everything. Now, you came over that day, boss of the cunts, and riled Stokes to attack the station. Remember?'

Strickland nodded, cautious.

'I think Cannon recorded you. And I know Sawyer went to see Stokes on the day he attacked us.' Peyton grinned, holding his moment.

Strickland's gaze hardened. 'And Stokes played the recording to Sawyer.'

Peyton slapped Strickland on the shoulder, making him cringe. 'You're fuckin' getting it. So, here's my dream deal. I get my bump from taking down Fletcher. You pop in to see Stokes again, get that recording out of the mix. Then, you're a pig in shit, because you've cleared off a couple of niggles, and you can see to it that I don't need permission to settle the books for *this*.'

He raised the patch, revealing the horror show of scars and welts.

Strickland didn't flinch. He kept his eye on Peyton, a sly smile slowly forming. 'I'd tagged you as an entry-level toerag. But if you can tick all these boxes, then I guarantee by the time Eddie gets out, you'll be telling him what to do.'

Chapter Fourteen

FARRELL FLOPPED into the chair at the head of the MIT conference table and swivelled to look up at the face of Orlando Gray, staring down at the detectives from the main screen.

He popped out a breath mint. 'Putting his video aside for a second, did we get *anything* out of him at interview?'

'No comment,' said Shepherd, 'apart from a grumble about wasting our time.'

Farrell placed the mint on the back of his fingers and snapped it into his mouth with the tip of his tongue, chameleon style. He raised a finger towards the group at the back of the room but didn't turn. 'Mr Drummond?'

A hulk of a man taking up most of the space around the far corner of the table raised his head. He took off his semi-rimless glasses. 'Present and correct, sir.' He gave a little salute. 'Would you care to review my findings?'

Farrell spun his chair round. 'Unless you have any other reason to be here?'

Frazer Drummond looked up to the left for a moment,

then turned his icy blue eyes back on Farrell. 'I can't think of a single one, sir.' He grinned and opened a document folder. 'I hope you're sitting comfortably, and your breakfasts are fully digested. The four victims in question... I found clear evidence of vaginal penetration on three. One, anal. Nothing oral. Small mercies, eh? Muscular lacerations in all cases. The anal penetration was probably responsible for the two small fissures I found in the anal canal lining. There's no evidence of immune response or localised pooling or clotting, so I'm confident that the injuries weren't inflicted ante-mortem. And there's no inflammation or swelling. No attempt by the body to heal. The dead don't heal.'

'He must have lubed 'em up,' said Farrell.

Drummond grimaced, then glanced over at the middle-aged woman with short peroxide blonde hair sitting in his shadow beside him.

'He did indeed *lube them up*, sir,' said Sally O'Callaghan. 'He also used polyisoprene condoms, which would suggest a latex allergy. We found plenty of silicone-based lubricant on all four victims.'

'Any rogue DNA?' said Shepherd.

'There's plenty from Mr Gray. A few unidentified hairs and fibres, probably from the clothing of the people who'd handled the bodies on their journey to the mortuary. We're busy with elimination but it'll take time. Quite a few people involved in that process.'

The room fell silent for a moment. Farrell crunched his mint. 'Semen? Saliva?'

O'Callaghan shook her head. 'I have hair and skin cells that match to Mr Gray. But also others I suspect will be from previous handlers and workers. He was... efficient with this.'

'Is Gray allergic to latex?' said Walker.

'He says he is,' said O'Callaghan. 'We've requested medical records to check. Doing the legal dance as we speak.'

'But no fingerprints,' said Myers. 'So, he *was* wearing gloves.'

'This is why you're here, DC Myers,' said Farrell. 'Vision. Insight. That Sherlock Holmes type of clarity.'

'Actually,' said O'Callaghan, 'we do have fingerprints. Gray's. On all the victim's torsos and shoulders. A few around the buttocks and lower regions.'

'And you can get non-latex gloves in Boots,' said Walker. 'They're hardly specialist. Why would he be careful not to leave sexual DNA by using condoms, but not worry about fingerprints?'

Farrell sighed. 'Same old story. He thought he was smarter than everyone else. He thought he wouldn't get caught. He's in, he's out. The bodies go to the crem. Evidence burned. Job done.'

O'Callaghan continued. 'I also found small traces of Plaster of Paris around the neck and face of two of the victims. It could be contamination from handling but it's worth analysis with X-ray diffraction. Plaster of Paris is a form of gypsum, so we should be able to break it down to identify a brand or batch. It could help with elimination or match up with a suspect later.'

'Have we identified the source of the tip-off?' said Walker.

'It was anonymous, DS Walker,' said Farrell. 'By definition, that's unidentified.'

Walker just about stifled an eye roll. 'I meant since.'

Shepherd shook his head and turned to a skinny, flat-headed detective with a moustache groomed so neatly it looked stuck on. 'Karl. Anything on Gray's computer? Devices?'

Karl Rhodes, the station's digital media advisor tapped his fingernails on the table. 'Either he's got secret devices or flash drives in storage somewhere, or he's all about the moment. The hands-on kicks. Not a sausage on his phone, work computer or laptop.'

Shepherd smoothed out his goatee. 'David Fuller was an electrician at the Kent and Sussex Hospital. He was convicted of two 1987 murders after a cold case review. He also got twelve years for abusing the bodies of over one hundred female corpses during his time at the Kent and Sussex, and another nearby hospital. He's on a whole life order in Frankland now, with Michael Stone and Wayne Couzens.'

'Hell of a coffee morning,' said O'Callaghan.

'Fascinating, DI Shepherd,' said Farrell. 'Your point being?'

Shepherd checked a note on his phone. 'Sussex Police found around fourteen million images and four million videos in his home office and loft. There were one hundred hard drives, over two thousand floppy discs, thirty sim cards and mobile phones, thirteen hundred CDs and DVDs and thirty-four thousand photos, slides, negatives, prints. He's the poster boy for this kind of crime. It's high risk and so the perpetrators don't linger. They usually film or photograph themselves so they can enjoy the moment again later.'

Farrell sprang to his feet. 'We have circumstantial, fingerprints. He even made us a bloody video saying he was about to be arrested, he's made bad choices, he wasn't careful enough.' He headed for the door. 'He's obviously in a bad way, and I'm sorry about his daughter, but we can't consider any of that when we're trying to get a charge. We'll go again with him later, and I'll conduct the interview this time. We need something clear from him, on police record, by the end of tomorrow, when our extension runs out. Myers. I want you focused on finding his daughter. I'm going to review the case and then Shepherd, Walker, I want you both in with me later. I've done my fair share of specialist interviewing, so we'll see how he holds out once I get started on him. Class dismissed.'

He left the room, loosely followed by most of the other detectives. Shepherd, Drummond, and Walker hung back.

Once the room had cleared, Drummond spoke up. 'Did you see the comments on the video?'

'I try not to read them,' said Shepherd, checking his phone messages.

'Fuck,' said Drummond. 'Me neither. My eyes just drifted down there, for some reason. Some wag calling him "The Vulture".'

'What?' said Walker.

Drummond nodded. 'If it wasn't so fucking awful it'd be quite good. The sicko who feasts on his victims when they're freshly dead.'

'Jesus Christ.' Walker stood up, went to the window.

Shepherd handed his phone to Drummond, who read the on-screen message to himself, then looked up to a smiling Shepherd, then across to Walker. 'Fuck me. Say what you like about Sawyer, but he does know how to make an entrance.'

Walker moved over, snatched up the phone and read the message.

HE DIDN'T DO IT.

Chapter Fifteen

LYNDON WILDE ROLLED over and ran his hand along Rebecca's shoulder, then slowly down, into the groove at the small of her back. She arched, just enough, and he lifted his leg up and over her thigh.

He reached back to the bedside table and found his smart lighting pre-set, steeping the room in midnight blue.

Rebecca threaded her fine blonde hair into a ponytail and swished it over her shoulder. She rose onto all fours, keeping silent.

Wilde clasped her ponytail at the root and wrapped it around his fist. Rebecca gasped and Wilde reached forward with his other hand and covered her mouth.

Nothing.

She curved herself up further, presenting for him. Passive prey.

Her back muscles rippled as she tried to steady herself under Wilde's weight. He raised himself higher, squatting over her, almost slipping off the bed.

Wilde swept the sheets away, giving him uninterrupted

access. He gripped Rebecca's ponytail harder and pushed her head down into the pillow.

Still nothing.

He took his hand off her mouth and stroked her thigh, balancing himself, spiking at the connection.

Rebecca turned her head slightly, but Wilde gripped her hair tighter, keeping her faced forward. She yelped in pain.

Wilde turned away, fixated on the window.

Double-glazed. Low-emissivity glass. Argon insulation.

uPVC frame. Farrow and Ball 'Vert de Terre'.

Motorised Roman blind. Linen blend.

Still nothing.

As Wilde turned back, he veered to the right, unbalancing them, and Rebecca had to slap her hand on the side table to stay in place.

But it wasn't enough, and Wilde toppled over, pulling them both onto the hardwood floor.

Wilde stumbled to his feet and pulled on a pair of Calvins.

Rebecca turned, caught his eye.

He snatched his gaze away, focused on the clothes draped over the wicker armchair.

Luca Faloni chinos. Olive green.

White silk vest.

Lacoste mid-layer.

And the woman's eyes, wide. On him. In him. Roiling with terror and contempt.

He inhaled, puffed out a sigh. 'Sorry, sorry…'

'It's fine.' Rebecca climbed up and sat on the edge of the bed. 'You've got to laugh about that.'

'Yes. Sorry.' He dressed, fell into the chair, pulled on his trainers.

'It's okay. Don't apologise.'

'Don't tell me not to apologise.'

'Sorry.'

Wilde sprang up. 'Gonna get some air. Won't be long.'

Rebecca sprawled across the bed, dragging the sheets back in place.

Toned calves, from her elliptical trainer.

Blonde. Caramel tan.

Nothing.

She covered herself. 'It's late. Are you driving?'

'Might go to the twenty-four-hour place. Find some chocolate.'

Rebecca tidied her hair. 'We have chocolate.'

'Not the stuff I like.' He leaned in, kissed her, turned to go.

'Lyndon. I read about someone who could help.'

He scooped his things off the dresser. Wallet, keys.

'She's good. Not like the other one. She'll get it.'

He nodded, stared down at her.

'We'll take a holiday. Costa Rica. Barbados. Richard can cover.' She shrugged, smiling. 'It's all stress. There's just… too much at the moment. Too much going on.'

The woman's eyes again. Reddened. Shimmering with fury, disbelief.

Her frozen expression. The grunts of protest.

'I won't be long.' He swept out of the room and hurried down the stairs, out the front door and into the Porsche.

WILDE FLICKED on the light at the top of the uneven staircase. He pulled on a half-mask respirator and a pair of blue nitrile gloves, then hoisted the duffel bag over his shoulder and side-stepped down, keeping one hand on the rough stone wall.

At the bottom, he dumped the bag on the flagstone floor and took out a roll of thick plastic sheeting, opening it out and spreading it beside the man's body. The mask's combination filters shielded him from the worst of the smell, but his nose still twitched at a hint of sickly-sweetness from the early-stage decomposition.

He took a large white bath towel from the bag and laid it out on top of the sheeting, then gripped the man by his legs and shoulders and slowly rolled him onto the towel. He wrapped the body in the towel, avoiding sight of the face, then covered it in a further layer of heavy-duty polyethylene refuse bags, secured with duct tape.

Wilde repacked and shouldered the bag, then gripped the feet, bundling them into the plastic sheeting. He edged back up the stairs backwards, dragging the body behind him. The sheeting beneath the body made the movement easier, but the head still clunked on each step as he climbed.

He'd parked the Porsche as close to the basement door as possible, with the boot open and another length of plastic sheeting laid flat. He hauled the top half of the body into the boot, then the bottom half, then paused for a moment, bent double as he caught his breath.

Wilde turned off the light at the top of the stairs and locked the basement door.

He stuffed the mask and gloves into the duffel bag and slipped a fresh pair of gloves into his pocket for later. He tossed the bag into the boot and slammed it shut.

'Fuck,' he said to the trees, then dropped his head back and stared up at the night sky.

Ten-minute drive.

Back tomorrow for a thorough clean-up.

He opened the driver's door and hesitated, listening to a

distant lorry squealing its way along the Greenfield road just over the rim of the valley.

Wilde closed the door, locked the car and walked back towards the house, across the courtyard.

He let himself in, turned on the light, and headed through the kitchen and out across the hallway that connected to the rest of the house.

He stopped at the door. No light from underneath.

Four in, six out.

Four in, six out.

He carefully eased the door open, stepped inside, and closed it behind him, blocking the light from the kitchen.

More meditative breathing as he stood there in the dark.

Four in, six out.

Four in, six out.

He was dealing with an unwanted interruption.

Rethinking after an unexpected setback.

But now, his eyes adjusted to the darkness, and the moonlight sneaking through a gap in the curtains revealed a much bigger problem: the small shadow of an unwelcome guest.

Chapter Sixteen

SAWYER CAREFULLY PEELED AWAY the pastry around the edge of his Danish and dropped the apricot onto his plate, like an abandoned yolk.

Shepherd watched, sipping his latte. 'Are you leaving the pastry or the fruit?'

'What do you think?' He dipped one half of the pastry crust into his coffee and bit off a chunk.

Shepherd looked round the quiet café. 'Seems a well-named place.'

'Hmm?'

'Relatively harmonious.'

'Usually, yeah. There's a games room. Most of the aggro kicks off in there. Everyone in this place is suffering in some way, but the men still have that kernel of competition. Like a primal override.' Sawyer dipped the other pastry half into his coffee and swirled it around. He glanced up at Shepherd. 'You shouldn't be through here, really. The boss is out, though.'

'The manager?'

Sawyer shook his head. 'Consultant psychiatrist. They run the show.'

'So, can you give me the full tour?'

'I would, but they're doing a cell spin.' He held Shepherd's eye and smiled, giving him the dimple. 'How's the big man?'

Shepherd spluttered on his coffee. 'A pain in the arse, that's how he is. Took him a while to settle. He spent the first three weeks in the broom cupboard. But now he's bringing in a mouse a day. One hid under our bed last week. That was a fun night.'

Sawyer smiled but stayed quiet, finishing his pastry.

Shepherd scrutinised him. 'Thanks for letting me in. So, why the change of heart?'

'I only just found out that I get extra confectionery privileges for accepting visitors.'

Shepherd sighed. 'And how's the healing?'

'Not for me to say. That's one for the boss.'

'So...' Shepherd sat back. 'How much is this place costing you?'

Sawyer eyed him. 'If I told you, I wouldn't have to kill you. Because you'd have a heart attack.'

'Your dad's legacy, though, right?'

Sawyer gave a grim laugh. 'In more ways than one.'

Shepherd watched a dumpy fiftysomething man in a Rush T-shirt. He surveyed the sugar station like a passenger forced to land a plane getting his first view of the flight deck. He had unkempt grey hair that hung around a gleaming bald patch and wore grubby white jogging trousers and black slippers. 'Do you know the other patients by name now?'

Sawyer looked over his shoulder, following Shepherd's eyeline. 'They call them service users, not patients.'

'Do all the service users know about each other's situation?'

'Privacy first. Boundaries. Adherence to treatment protocols. Unsolicited probing is discouraged. It causes friction if one person shares what another told him without their permission. There's a strict system of rewards and sanctions, and using knowledge as currency would lose you access to off-ward activities. You might even get something personal confiscated. I do know the Rush guy, though. Ernie. BPD. APD. Self-harm. He's been here around four months.'

Ernie sifted through the sugars and sweeteners and looked up, catching Shepherd's eye. He looked away quickly.

'Maggie would love to hear that you asked about your cat before her.'

Sawyer nodded, stared into his mug. 'Mike told me she was out. Don't tell her about the pastry thing.'

'She sends love. She'd like to see you.'

'I've caused her enough pain. She needs to get on with her life.'

Shepherd squinted at him. 'As do you.'

Sawyer ignored him, kept staring into the mug.

'Okay, so tell me about your message.'

Sawyer swirled the mug round. 'Orlando Gray? I saw his video, ended up watching a news item on him. He's in a bad way.'

'He is indeed. We're still looking for his daughter.'

Sawyer sucked in a big breath, frowning. 'Necrophiles are rare. What's the history?'

'No criminality. No mental health issues.'

'Kept that quiet, then.'

Shepherd leaned forward. 'This really doesn't feel like

the time or place, but… Go on, then. Why do you think he didn't do it?'

Sawyer gazed down at the tabletop, then raised his eyes to Shepherd. 'Mainly the video. I watched the whole thing. There's something in his eyes.'

'Don't say this is a hunch.'

'He says, "You've got to believe me."'

'So?'

Sawyer found the tabletop again. 'It feels personal. His eyes are locked into the camera all the way. Usually, in confession videos, they're darting around, desperate, looking for respite. And he doesn't say, "Please believe me." He says, "*You've* got to believe me." As if he's addressing someone.'

Shepherd pondered, then sat back. 'And that's it?'

'He also says, "This isn't my choice." Don't you think that's strange? He's been reported by someone. Caught abusing dead bodies. So, whose choice was that, if not his?'

Ernie shuffled past with his coffee and took a seat near the TV. Shepherd watched him go and looked around at the other service users: reading, using their phones, talking in small groups. 'You shouldn't be here.'

'Because I'm better than them? I'm not.'

Shepherd lowered his voice. 'Because Strickland put you here.'

'He didn't.'

'He certainly played a big role. As I'm sure you've seen, he's doing pretty well for himself. While you're stuck in what Farrell calls the funny farm.'

Sawyer smiled. 'How's life under Farrell?'

'He's surprisingly hands-off. Keeps briefings brief, like he's always got something else to get back to.'

'He really is Strickland's puppet. I almost feel sorry for him.'

'Wesley Peyton lost an eye.'

Sawyer nodded. 'Michael told me. Any sign?'

Shepherd shook his head. 'That's one Christmas card you don't have to worry about.' He took a long drink of his coffee. 'A fella came to see Farrell. DCI Bentley. Staffordshire CID. They called me in. Farrell said he didn't have the resource to help him persuade you to take on the Caldwell thing.'

'Means nothing to him. And he wouldn't want a part in anything that would make me look good.'

'Bentley collared me in private after the meeting. Asked me to have a go on you.'

Sawyer chewed his lip. 'It's too neat. Caldwell will never show us where he's buried the women. It's a blatant power trip.'

'You're thinking of Ian Brady. Stringing police along, never revealing little Keith Bennett's body.'

'Yes. Also, Bundy.'

'That was just death-row bargaining. Standard.'

'It's all from the same place. Power, control, manipulation, attention. Nothing to do with giving the families relief. Caldwell wants to torture me one last time, and then he wants the thrill of withholding the information, watching me fail, savouring the families' anguish.'

Shepherd smoothed down his goatee. 'That'll just send him straight back inside. I know he's the devil to you but imagine the human being underneath that. He doesn't want to die in the prison hospital. His missus is still alive. Surely he wants to come home.'

Sawyer stayed silent.

'Bentley is running out of time. He reckons he can take it higher.'

Sawyer laughed. 'What are they going to threaten me

with? The Home Office are more interested in softening the embarrassment of Caldwell than giving any relief to the families.' Shepherd started to speak again, but Sawyer leaned forward. 'Doesn't matter how high up the chain they go. I don't do it anymore.'

'What?'

'Go back. That's my truth now.'

Shepherd propped his elbows on the table, rested his chin on his hands. 'So, you're all about moving forward now, yes? Excited about what tomorrow might bring? I bet every day is full of surprises round here. All these people, busy avoiding their suffering.'

'You're thinking you could have been one of them.'

'Of course I am. You know the mantra. Every day, in every way, I'm getting better.'

Sawyer winced. 'Say that out loud here, they extend your stay.'

They shared a few seconds of silence, soundtracked by the low chatter of the TV.

Shepherd dug into his pocket. 'Got you something. Don't get excited. They were out of lemon sherbets at the garage.' He took out a business card, with handwriting on the flip side. 'After the hospital... confrontation, GMP traced Curtis Mavers to a flat in Deansgate. I did an off-the-books ANPR check and clocked a visit there a few days earlier.'

'Strickland,' said Sawyer.

'Ten points to Gryffindor.'

Sawyer eyed him.

'Sorry. Just started on the *Potters* with Theo.' He handed the card to Sawyer. 'The address of the flat. Could be something to build on. Awkward questions for our esteemed mayor. Why was he visiting a known murderer? Wouldn't take much to connect up Strickland's affairs to the property, cross-ref his movements with Mavers's release, then—'

'It's old news,' said Sawyer, turning the card over in his fingers. 'Doesn't help me.' He put the card on the table and rested his hands in the centre, one on top of the other.

'Not while you're in here, no. *Sir…*' Shepherd planted his palms on the table, too loud. A few service users looked over; he lowered his voice. 'If you've found Zen or Buddhism or the pursuit of nirvana or your truth or whatever, and it's helped you heal, then I'm happy for you. Really. But…' He grimaced, dragged his palm across his beard. 'But here's *my* truth. I miss you. I miss the old you. DI Jake Sawyer was direct. He had integrity, a strong moral compass. He worked out what was right and hunted it down with no fear. He was a difficult bastard at times. But he was never boring. Or passive. And, you know what? Despite all this detachment and distancing, I think he's still in there somewhere.'

Chapter Seventeen

SADIE FLETCHER UPLOADED a batch of new photos into the Wix Studio back end. She navigated to the site editor dashboard and scrolled through the project to-do list on her phone. Class schedules, levels, instructor profiles, registration and payment system, testimonials, photo gallery and videos.

For the first time, she considered rewriting the business plan to make room for a digital assistant. Maybe someone who could cover social media, too. That would let her focus on the sessions, the people, customer retention…

The doorbell rang.

She glanced at the clock. Late afternoon. Nobody expected.

Sadie got up from the back-room corner desk and wriggled into a black hoodie with a gold monogram at the lapel: *S&G*. She was mid-twenties, short but robust, with chestnut-brown hair gathered into a neat French braid.

Out in the hall, she paused and listened.

Male voices on the other side of the front door. Talking, laughing. Charity cold-callers?

Sadie walked to the door, glancing at the trophy shield hanging beside the full-length wall mirror.

She opened the door to two men: one short, the other taller, bulky. The tall one had a Middle-Eastern look, with a bushy black moustache, while the short man wore a sky-blue baseball cap and a black patch over his left eye.

He tried on a smile. 'Alright, love? Sadie, yeah?'

She eyed them both. 'What can I do for you?'

The man's smile wavered. 'Just a quick chat, yeah? Can we step in for a second?'

'No.'

Sadie tried to close the door, but the shorter man had wedged it in place by planting his foot near the hinge. The moustached man raised a handgun with silencer, holding it at his hip.

'How about now?' said the eyepatch guy.

Sadie looked at the gun, then up to the moustached man's droopy eyes. 'Still no. Move your foot.'

The gunman shouldered the door open, and his friend pushed through into the hall. He reached for Sadie, wrapping an arm around her neck, trying to get a hand over her mouth. She stepped away from his grip and lashed out a fearsome right cross. But he saw it coming, and weaved back, out of its range. The burly man bundled his way inside and closed the door behind him, holding the gun higher, aimed at Sadie's face. She froze, then backed away, holding her hands out at hip level, palms up.

'Easy now, darlin',' said the eyepatch guy. 'We're not planning to hurt you. The gun's for our protection. I mean, you're hardly Snow fuckin' White, are ya?' He looked up at the trophy shield. 'What's this for?'

Sadie kept her eyes on the gunman. 'BMMA tournament. British Military Martial Arts. I won the Taekwondo section when I was eighteen.'

'Right, right. We'll be quick. No nonsense, yeah?' He held up a hand. 'Before you ask, I'm alright for tea. Wouldn't say no to a blow job, mind.'

An inscrutable look crossed Sadie's face and she clenched her fists.

He laughed, wheezy. 'But I don't want this dirty fucker watching us, so we'll leave it for now. Let's go in there.' He nodded to the back room. 'Do me a favour, darlin'. Pop your arms down by your side.'

They moved into the room: functionally furnished with the computer desk, a couple of bookshelves and an old sofa bed.

Eyepatch dropped onto the sofa and browsed through a pile of books and documents on a side table.

The gunman hovered at the door. He jerked the barrel towards the desk. 'Sit down there.'

Sadie retook her seat.

'I'm Kyle,' said Eyepatch. 'This is Kevin.'

Sadie spluttered. 'Kevin? Fuck off.'

Kyle looked up at the gunman, doubtful. 'Yeah. You're right. Let's go with Bernardo.'

'Man City players,' said Sadie.

Kyle took off his cap and grinned, scrubbing up his hair. 'Bang on.' He nodded at the monogram on Sadie's hoodie. 'What's that, then? *S&G*. Same logo on your screen, yeah?'

'Strength and Grace,' said Sadie. 'It's the name of my self-defence brand, for women. I'm opening my own centre in a few months in Castleton.'

'Good for fuckin' you,' said Kyle. 'Proper little entrepreneur, yeah?'

'Women can't run businesses,' said Bernardo.

Sadie frowned. 'Why not?'

He shrugged. 'Too emotional.'

'Fucking hell,' said Sadie. 'What year are you living in? 1970?' Bernardo scowled, but Kyle hissed a laugh. She glared at him. 'So, how long have you been supporting City? Since they got bought out and started buying all the best players?'

Kyle sighed. 'Ah, there you go. I thought you might be alright, Sadie. But now you're bringing the same old tired shite.'

Sadie shifted in her chair. 'Look. I'm busy. What do you want?'

Kyle sat back in the sofa and spread his arms across the back. 'We don't want you or your little women's fighty shit. We're interested in your dad. We know he's been near here in the last few months. So he must have dropped in, and we wondered if you might know where he got off to.'

'I haven't seen him in a long while.'

Kyle leaned forward, studying her. 'You know what? I'm having that.' He glanced up at Bernardo. 'I don't think she's bullshitting.' He stood up, walked over to Sadie. 'I'm a bit sad you didn't use your chop-socky skills to disarm Laughing Boy back there. Swift kick in the bollocks.' He demonstrated a few exaggerated martial arts moves. 'Take me out with a roundhouse kick.'

Sadie smiled. 'Tell him to put the gun down and I'll show you a few moves.'

Kyle moved in on Sadie and grabbed her neck, lifting her up out of the chair. Bernardo stepped close and held the gun on her, two-handed, staying just out of her range.

Kyle shoved her back into the wall, knocking over the

chair. She held onto his forearm, trying to push him away, but he was stronger than he looked.

He leaned in close and hissed in her ear. 'Fuckin' bull dykes. Those women are for us men, yeah? A good hard curing normally sorts your type out. I reckon you're too far gone, though.'

Kyle nodded at Bernardo, who reverted to holding the gun with his right hand only. He pulled out his phone with the left and took a picture of the distressed, red-faced Sadie with the hand around her neck, keeping Kyle out of frame.

Sadie wriggled free and collapsed in the corner, holding her neck, breathing hard.

Kyle nodded to the door and Bernardo backed into the hall, keeping the gun on her.

'Think on,' said Kyle to Sadie. 'We'll be back to ask again soon. Not so fuckin' nicely, second time round. I need a clear answer on Daddy's whereabouts, yeah? Otherwise, I don't give a fuck which way you swing. I'll do something to you downstairs that'll put you out of action for months.'

He followed Bernardo out of the front door, slamming it behind him.

Sadie scrambled to her feet and bounded up the stairs, still gasping. She hurried into the street-facing bedroom, keeping low, then peered over the lower edge of the window.

The men had parked a black SUV on the corner of an adjacent side street. As they climbed in, she lifted her phone above the window, zoomed in on the car number plate, and took a picture.

Chapter Eighteen

FARRELL SET the tape running and sat back in his seat in the interview room, flanked by Shepherd and Walker. He stared Orlando Gray down for a few seconds, then tapped out a breath mint, offering the canister. Gray shook his head and lowered his gaze to the tabletop.

Farrell opened his mouth wide and tossed in the mint. He looked over to Gray's solicitor, pointing. 'Casper Davies, isn't it?'

Davies looked up from his case file and nodded, curt and efficient. 'DSI Farrell.'

'I had you with that grooming gang in Bury. Few years ago. Got 'em in the end, eh? No thanks to you.'

Davies eyed him. 'Your case fell short on evidential requirement.'

'Not on public interest. But you don't care about that, though, do you?'

'Burden of proof on prosecution, DSI Farrell. With respect, we're here to discuss my current client.'

Farrell nodded, rolled the mint around his mouth. He

picked up the canister and tapped it on the table. 'How long have stiffs given you stiffies, then, Orlando?'

Davies held up a hand. 'For the tape, I object to the phrasing of DSI Farrell's question. It's inappropriate and prejudicial. It assumes a fact not in evidence. That my client has a sexual interest in the deceased. I urge him to rephrase the question in a neutral manner that pertains to the specifics of the case.'

Farrell grinned at him. He turned to Shepherd and Walker. 'He's good, this one.'

'We've seen your video, Orlando,' said Shepherd, maintaining a neutral expression. 'You said, "This isn't my choice." What did you mean by that?'

'Detective Shepherd,' said Farrell. 'Let's stick to one interviewer, thank you very much. Mr Gray is confused enough as it is.'

Gray raised his head. He looked haggard, the bags beneath his eyes dark and deep like fresh bruising. 'No comment.'

His voice had lost the low end. It was now faint, reedy, as if his vocal cords had been stretched too thin.

Shepherd shuffled his chair closer to the table. 'What choice were you talking about, Orlando? The offence you're accused of, or something else?'

Gray shifted his eyes over and Shepherd held his gaze.

Farrell pivoted his chair. The legs ground loudly against the floor, causing everyone to flinch. 'Detective Shepherd. I'm leading this interview. One more interruption of this nature and—'

Gray muttered something.

Farrell turned back to him. 'What was that?'

Gray looked across to Davies, who shook his head. He

turned back, addressing Shepherd. 'Where is my daughter? Have you heard anything?'

'We're doing everything we can to find her,' said Farrell. 'Unfortunate as it is, her disappearance isn't the reason for the interview today.'

'She hasn't disappeared,' said Gray, emphasising the word. 'You just can't find her.'

'Are you afraid that someone is holding her, Orlando?' said Walker. 'If that's true, then anything you say today will remain confidential. Nobody will know what you tell us.'

Farrell glared at Walker, then back at Gray, who looked around the faces in turn: Davies, then Walker, then Shepherd. His haunted eyes fell on Farrell, and he tilted his head forward, as if studying him.

'Well?' said Farrell.

Gray opened his mouth, about to speak, then lowered his head again. 'No comment.'

'On the video, you say you didn't do it,' said Farrell, crunching his mint. 'But our forensic evidence tells us otherwise. We have a principle you might have heard of. Means, motive, opportunity. Means and opportunity is pretty clear-cut here. Let me tell you what I think about the motive, Orlando.' He sat up, held an overlong moment of silence. 'Your expertise could have taken you anywhere. You could have set up as a private contractor, got work with a corporation, joined an agency. But you chose a job that gave you access to a mortuary.'

Davies sighed. 'DSI Farrell—'

Farrell held up a finger. 'Bear with me, Casper.' He leaned forward, trying to get Gray to look up. 'So, why did you choose that route?'

'No comment.'

'We know your marriage didn't pan out.'

Gray's eyes lifted to Farrell.

'I know it's not your fault that your missus died. But people can suffer profound behavioural changes as the result of sudden bereavement.'

'Naomi had a heart condition,' said Gray, his voice low and steady. 'It wasn't sudden.'

Farrell nodded. 'No, but it doesn't lessen the shock when it happens, eh?' He screwed up his face, twisted his hand around in the air. 'Did it break something inside you, Orlando? Make it hard to get your kicks with living women? Did you keep seeing Naomi's face in your mind? And when you couldn't get it up with living women, with adults—'

Gray sprang to his feet.

Davies held an arm across him. 'For the tape, I am formally requesting that this interview be terminated at this point. I have serious concerns regarding the nature of the questioning and the conduct of this interview, which I believe are prejudicial and potentially harmful to my client's rights.'

Farrell pushed closer to Gray. 'Did you turn to young girls, Orlando?'

'No comment,' said Gray, eyes burning into Farrell.

'And did you turn to the young girls you had easy access to? Your daughters?' Gray looked across to Shepherd and Walker, who had also got to their feet. 'And did you take it too far with Phoebe?'

'The line of questioning has been leading and suggestive,' said Davies, raising his voice, 'and it is my view that it is not being conducted in a fair and impartial manner—'

Farrell ramped it up, raising his voice above Davies. 'And when she threatened to tell someone, you had to stop her getting out, didn't you? I think you know where Phoebe is, Orlando. Don't you? I think your wife's death pushed you over the edge. As you say in the video, into a "private hell". And when you couldn't get your kicks that way, when that didn't touch the sides anymore, you had to go up a level. You indulged yourself in a fantasy that had been in you all along, but you could never tell anyone about. You thought those poor women in that mortuary could get you out of this private hell, while your daughter lies dead or locked up somewhere. Dead by your own hand.'

Gray lunged forward and grabbed Farrell by his lapels. Shepherd stepped between them and wrestled him away, as Farrell backed into the far wall. Walker filled the gap as Shepherd settled Gray back into his chair.

Shepherd found his eyes. 'Orlando. Look at me.'

Davies gathered his documents. 'This is appalling, DSI Farrell. It's a violation of the standards expected in police interview and could impact the integrity of the legal process.'

Farrell stepped away from the wall and addressed his comments to Davies. '*For the tape*. The interviewee Mr Gray has physically assaulted me. We have taken immediate action to restrain the interviewee and ensure the safety of everyone present. I do not require medical assistance, but I am leaving the interview room for my own personal safety. This incident will be treated as a separate criminal offence and I formally request that the second most senior officer, Detective Inspector Ed Shepherd, place the interviewee under arrest for assaulting a police officer.'

Farrell spun away and left the room.

Gray stood with his back to the opposite wall, trembling with rage, head in hands. Shepherd stayed close to him, trying to get eye contact. 'Orlando… Look at me. Please.'

Gray slowly edged his hands aside and held Shepherd's eye.

'Orlando, I want to help you. And I want to help Phoebe.'

Gray's features crumpled. Tears trickled down his cheeks and spattered down onto the floor. He looked to Walker, then Shepherd. 'Phoebe has her pen.'

Walker stepped forward. 'For her diabetes?'

Gray nodded. 'I didn't hurt her. I didn't... do the things he says I did. I don't know where she is.' His wild eyes darted from Davies to Walker, back to Shepherd. 'Do you know where she is?' He pushed his palms together, as if in prayer. 'Do you know where she is? Have you heard anything yet? Has anyone contacted you?'

Shepherd held his shoulders. 'Orlando. Please answer me one thing. Have you told us everything you know about Phoebe?'

Gray sniffed, wiped his eyes, then nose. He glanced at Davies, then back at Shepherd. 'Yes, I have.'

SHEPHERD CRASHED out of the lift, side-stepping through the still-opening doors. He barrelled across the main MIT floor, followed by Walker.

Unusually, Farrell's office door was ajar. They found him semi-reclined in his chair, feet up on the desk.

Shepherd stormed up to the desk, looming over him.

Farrell flashed him a wry grin. 'Don't start.'

'Well, that was certainly fucking old school,' said Shepherd.

'Watch your language, detective. It wasn't pretty, but sometimes old school just *works*.'

'Doesn't work too well for his mental well-being.'

Farrell waved a hand, as Walker entered. 'What about his daughter's mental well-being? Or the relatives of the victims he's abused? The people, dead and alive, he might go on to abuse if we don't stress him out of the "no comment" nonsense and actually get something useful out of him? Did you make the arrest for the assault?'

Shepherd didn't answer. He turned away and walked to the window, looking across to the Tarmac Silverlands Stadium, home to Buxton FC.

'It's done, sir,' said Walker.

Farrell swung his feet around and planted them on the floor. 'Good. Now we have more time with him. More time to build a CPS pitch they might actually go for. It also keeps a sick individual off the streets.'

'More press this morning,' said Shepherd, watching a group of players in fluorescent bibs work through a training session. 'This Vulture thing is sticking. As if he's some kind of Marvel villain.'

'Yes,' said Farrell, 'when he's really just a dirty pervert.'

'You sound like one of the headline writers yourself,' said Walker, earning a glare from Farrell. 'Sir.'

Farrell gripped the edge of his desk and leaned forward. 'Once everyone has calmed down, I think you'll both admit that we've just learned a lot. I feel a good deal more confident about securing a charge.'

'What did we learn?' Shepherd said, walking back to the desk.

'I looked into the eyes of a guilty man,' said Farrell. 'I've done this for long enough to know when a suspect is holding something back.'

'The toughest sell is his history,' said Walker. 'Or the lack of it. That kind of specific… perversion has to start somewhere. There would be signs of it in his past, and we've rooted around pretty deep.'

Farrell grinned again and patted his unnaturally black

hair. 'Like I said to him, he's suffered a lot of loss. People react in strange ways to loss. One person might grieve by withdrawing from the world, while another might... flip, in ways that seem incomprehensible to normal people like you and me.' Shepherd scoffed; Farrell ignored him. 'I know you want to keep drawing from your serial killer files, DI Shepherd, but you can't cross-reference everything with case history. New precedents are set all the time.'

'Yes,' said Shepherd, 'including new precedents that conveniently align with a pre-decided idea of a case. It can lead to confirmation bias.'

'Inductive thinking,' said Walker.

Farrell looked between the two of them, tapping on the desk. 'I spoke to Drummond. Apparently, we had a message from Mr Jake Sawyer. Interesting that you both worked closely with Sawyer, and you seem to share his thinking that Gray is innocent.' He closed his eyes, opened them again. 'So, here you both are, judging me for a little robust police work, and yet you *conveniently align* with a man who recently beat a murder suspect half to death and allowed him to escape, then attacked a senior politician so badly he required hospital treatment. A man currently receiving residential psychiatric treatment. So, let's stop weeping over Orlando Gray's well-being and work on getting a charge. And if you really don't think he did it, then find me someone who did. Bring me the real Vulture.'

Chapter Nineteen

MILO AND JAMIE WILDE chased each other down the central aisle, shouting. Jamie, the eldest, ducked into the *Beauty & Skincare* aisle, and by the time his brother had reached him, Jamie was holding up a pink canister of VO5 Mega Hold Gel Spray.

Milo grinned. 'Dare you.'

Jamie aimed the can at the face of a model on a life-size display card.

'*Boys!*' Their mother, Rebecca called over, stuck at the self-service tills.

Jamie turned the can towards Milo, who lowered his head, offering his thatch of curly brown hair.

'You're too scared,' said Milo. 'You won't.'

Jamie wavered.

'Double dare,' said Milo. '*Triple.*'

A heavy hand snatched up the spray can and placed it back on the shelf. Lyndon Wilde roughly shoved his son into the central aisle. 'Get back to your mother. No PS5 for a week.'

Jamie scuttled away and Wilde turned to Milo. He crouched, eye level.

The young boy winced, dropped his head. 'Sorry, Dad. Sorry.'

Wilde reached over and hitched a thumb under Milo's chin, tilting back his head, forcing eye contact. 'I don't want to hear you daring people to do things, Milo, okay?'

The boy nodded, flinching.

Wilde edged his face closer. 'It's horrible.' He screwed up his face. 'And if I ever hear you do it again—'

'Okay, Dad. Okay.' Milo shook his head, closed his eyes. 'I'm sorry. Really. Please don't... Please.'

Rebecca arrived, with Jamie. '*Boys*. It would be nice if we could all just go shopping like normal people without having to manage you all the time.' She grabbed Milo's arm and tugged him away. 'You're old enough to know this now. And, you know what? No McDonald's.'

Loud protests as she led them away.

'I have to get a few things,' said Wilde.

'Don't be long,' she called over her shoulder. 'I need a coffee. See you in Starbucks?'

'Sure.' Wilde walked around to the *Pharmacy & Health* section. He studied the ingredients of the sleep aids Nytol and Sominex.

Diphenhydramine hydrochloride.

Promethazine hydrochloride.

And the snake oils: Valerian root, lavender, Bach flower remedy. Friendly packaging with reassuring fonts but, essentially, overpriced placebos. It was all too *soft*. He might have to go online, risk leaving a trace.

He headed round to the *Men's Grooming* section. As he browsed, his eyes drifted up to a young woman in a full-length fur-collared coat, sashaying down the central aisle.

She tossed her head, swishing back her long, thin blonde hair, then raised her sunglasses as she picked out a few items from a rack of make-up products.

His stomach fluttered and he kept his eyes on her, over the top of his section, as she marched to the self-service tills, heels clicking. She tapped at the screen and waited, using her phone to pay.

As the woman slipped the phone back into her coat pocket, she turned her head towards him, caught his eye, then tore away her receipt and strutted out of the shop.

Wilde took a moisturiser to the same self-service till. He could still smell the woman's scent: perfumed but not too sickly or synthetic. The shop was quiet, and he lingered for a moment, savouring her essence.

Four in, six out.

As he turned to leave, he noticed a small black purse resting on the bag platform at the side of the machine. He picked it up. It was leather, with the words *KATE SPADE* and *NEW YORK* embossed in small letters on the front.

Wilde stole a casual look over his shoulder, then unzipped the purse. Two ten-pound notes, a London to Manchester train ticket, compact lip balm, mirror, AirPods case, packet of gum.

He ran his thumb along the card slots and slid out a UK driving licence.

The woman's face stared out at him, expressionless.

Wilde read the details: Ms Hannah Lewis. Thirty-three. Her signature was a large letter 'H' which blended into the left stem of a letter 'L' and swept out to the right in a wavy line.

She lived at 5 Cole Lane, Hayfield.

Wilde slid the card back into its slot and zipped up the

purse. He took the receipt for his moisturiser and headed for the exit.

At the door, he smiled at the male security guard. 'Excuse me. Someone must have left this on one of the tills.'

'Ah, I'll get that to Lost Property. Thank you, sir.'

Wilde nodded. 'No problem at all.'

Chapter Twenty

LUKA STRICKLAND STABBED a wooden fork into a large section of sausage and mopped one end through the currywurst sauce. He bit off the end and chased it with a couple of chips.

'Good?' Dale Strickland looked up from his full-size kebab.

Luka nodded. 'Really nice, yeah.' He ran his fingers through the messy crop of blond hair gathered at the top of his head. 'I like that it's a secret kids' menu. Bit weird they bring it on a paper plate.'

'It's German street food, darling.' Eva Gregory took a sip from her glass of red wine. 'They're just trying to be...'

'Authentic,' said Strickland, draining his glass of whisky.

Luka shrugged. 'It's an affectation.'

Eva eyed Strickland with a small smile. Sultan & Spice, in Manchester's Corn Exchange, was hardly fine dining, but with his mayoral profile, they were always obliged to dress for an occasion: Strickland in a tailored navy blazer with purple paisley tie, while Eva had gone for an Oscar de la

Renta floral fitted minidress. Luka was Mr Designer Sportswear, but more CK than JD.

It was a mild evening, and they sat out in the garden bar, in a corner partially hidden by hanging greenery and neutral fairy lights. Three stern-looking suited men shared a table at a discreet distance.

Luka slurped on his chocolate milkshake and nodded to the men. 'They're new.'

Strickland shook his head. 'You just haven't noticed them before. That's their job, really.'

Luka leaned forward, whispered. 'Are they *strapped?*'

'The bald guy has an AK-47 up his jacket, yeah,' said Strickland.

'They're all bald.'

'I think Reece calls it a wide parting.'

Eva took off her dark brown Tom Fords and polished the lenses. 'Talking of hair...' She nodded at Luka. 'What do you think?'

Strickland chewed his food, pondered. 'Cropped around the sides. No flop on top. Very grown-up.'

'I am grown up,' said Luka. 'I can get married in three years.'

'Four,' said Eva. 'And no, you can't.'

'Alright, then. I can have sex in two.'

Strickland grinned. 'As if you haven't already.'

'*Dad.*' Luka tutted and took out his phone, searched for something. 'I can drive in three. Well, get lessons.'

Strickland's phone rang in his pocket. 'Let's talk about the present. Did you enjoy the football museum?'

He checked the Caller ID.

Abadi.

Eva gave him a look. 'Is this work?'

'I might have to check, yes.'

'I loved the memorabilia stuff,' said Luka. 'The 3D stadium models and interactive exhibits were cool, but I really liked seeing how football was played in the past. It's mad to think that people were playing it before I was even born. All those shirts and trophies, passed down.'

'Representing the achievements,' said Strickland.

'Yeah! That's what it's about, isn't it?'

'How do you mean?' said Eva.

Luka scraped the milkshake round his cup with a straw. 'So, lots of the players have died now but what they did and won has sort of made them immortal.' He went back to his phone. 'It does my head in. Like, all those decisions they made. To try and shoot instead of passing or whatever. It all added up and now they have a... what's the word?'

Strickland got to his feet. 'Legacy. I do need to take this.' He held up a hand, stifling Eva's protest. 'Five minutes. Promise.'

Luka was still rolling. 'That's what it's all about, isn't it? What you do, not what you say you'll do.'

One of the suited men got up from the table and followed Strickland to a small private lounge at the side of the restaurant's open kitchen. A manager nodded to him and unclipped a velvet rope, letting Strickland walk through to the empty lounge while his bodyguard hovered near the rope, chatting to the manager.

Strickland threw himself into a padded banquette seat and answered the call. 'Farouk. I hope this isn't bad news. I'm out with family.'

Abadi hesitated. 'Don't shoot the messenger, Dale.'

Strickland poured himself a glass of iced water from a jug on a nearby table. 'I hate that phrase. Go.'

'We sent the picture of the daughter.'

'To Fletcher?'

'To the number you gave us.'

Strickland sipped the water. 'Is this a pause for dramatic effect, Farouk? Like a reality show?'

'We said we'd come back if she didn't tell us where he was. All of that.'

'And did he bite?'

Abadi sighed. 'Yes. Well, we assume so.'

Strickland closed his eyes. 'You *assume* so?'

'We put two guys on her place. Surveillance. Lost contact with both. I went over and they were both dead. Single headshots. One through the eye.'

Strickland opened his eyes. 'So—'

'All gone,' said Abadi. 'I dealt with it.

'Tell me more about the guys.'

Wes Peyton spoke up. 'Dale. On speaker. They were fuckin' good guys. Lower level. Young lads from our crew.' His voice caught; he was clearly struggling to stay measured. 'It was a shitty job.'

'Turned out even shittier,' said Strickland. 'The daughter?'

'Abadi went back to her place. No sign. These were fuckin' good lads, Dale. Bit wet behind the ears but not lightweights. His daughter was into her martial arts shit. She might have taken 'em out herself.'

Strickland gave a bitter laugh. 'Fletcher has moved her somewhere safe. This isn't good. This is really fucking not good.'

'At least we now know he's around. We try new angles. I can go direct to the lad who gave Eddie the lead on Fletcher… He's the one who heard a fella who looked like Fletcher got his plates done up near Leeds.'

'Near to the daughter's house.'

'Yeah. He's a top boy. He's got a link to Middlesbrough.

We can get him to check on Fletcher's ex up there. Marla Jacob. Sadie's mum. Then, when Fletcher—'

'Wes, Wes, Wes,' Strickland interrupted. 'Give me a second.' He looked over at his table: Luka showing Eva something on his phone; Eva pretending to be interested but keeping her eye on Strickland. He took a slug of water, shivering at the chill. 'We were too soft.'

'You what?'

'We should have gone in harder. Waited for him. Held on to his daughter. Now, the ball's in his court. And we're stuck holding our dicks instead of a racket.'

'So, now Fletcher will come for us,' said Abadi. 'Yes? We just have to be ready. He is one man.'

'We were too *soft*,' Strickland hissed. 'Too subtle.'

'So, what's the story?' said Peyton.

'The story is, no more clever shit. Waiting for people to come to us. Letting them make a move. Reactive. Now, we act. We go to them.'

'Yeah,' said Peyton. 'We fucked up. Everyone fucks up.'

Strickland got to his feet. 'You win or you learn.'

'And what did we learn?' said Abadi.

'We hold back now, we pay more later. The future doesn't just turn up someday. You create it with your actions in the present.'

Chapter Twenty-One

MAY 1997

HAROLD SAWYER LET himself into the house and turned back at the foot of the stairs, facing the door. His eldest son followed him in, and immediately squatted by the phone table, prising off his shoes.

Michael had grown: up, but mostly out. In the words of their family doctor, he had always been "big-boned", but since his seventeenth birthday, there had been a dramatic uptick. He'd covered his bedroom mirror and taken a razor blade to his shoulder and bicep, scoring lines so deep Harold had wondered if he was trying to cut away the excess. But the side effects from his tricyclic anti-depressants easily compensated for the excised flesh.

He'd pushed his black hair up into a vertiginous quiff, but neglected to cut the back and sides, rendering the style dangerously close to a mullet. The quiff wilted as he bent to slot the shoes into the shelf, and he swiped it back with chunky fingers.

'Do you fancy spaghetti, Mike?' said Harold. 'Ready at six-thirty.'

Michael gave a brief, wincing smile and nodded, then nudged his way past Harold and scaled the stairs, heading for his PC.

His younger brother crashed through the door, in bright yellow goalkeeper kit, scraping his fingers through his long black hair.

'Jake. You're dropping half the pitch in the hall. Do that outside.'

'Lost my headband.' Jake leaned out of the front door, shook off his head. 'I'll have a shower in a bit.' He ran inside, shouted up the stairs. 'Mike! Can I watch you do *Command & Conquer*?'

A door slammed. Heavy footsteps thumped across the floor above their heads.

Jake sighed, looked at Harold. 'Dad…'

'Give him his space.'

He sat on the stairs and stripped off his socks. 'You always say that.'

'He needs it at the moment, big man. You'll be seventeen one day.'

Jake scoffed. 'There's years to go.'

'About two and a half,' said Harold, heading for the kitchen. Jake hung up his football bag and followed.

Harold lifted a couple of pans from the hanging rack and caught Jake slipping a Fruit Pastille into his mouth. 'Hey! Not before dinner.'

'It'll be ages yet. I'll chop some onions.'

Harold smiled. 'We're not bartering. I'm the boss, remember?'

'Of what?'

'The household.'

Jake slid into a seat along the side of the wooden dining table. 'Mum always let me have sweets.'

'Yes, and if she was still around, I'm sure she'd regret it.'

Jake frowned. 'That doesn't make sense.'

Harold pulled a bag of vegetables from the cupboard and turned to face Jake, mock stern. He lowered his voice. 'I need you to set a good example for Mike. We need to help him with his food at the moment.' He turned back, slid a knife from a block.

Jake took out a handheld game console and muttered something.

Harold turned again. 'What was that?'

'He doesn't *say* anything.'

Harold shrugged, prepared the onions. 'But meanwhile, I can't shut you up. Is that Mike's Game Boy?'

'Game Gear. He said I can use it. He doesn't like it anymore.'

'So, he did say that, at least.'

Jake started up a game. 'He wouldn't copy me, anyway. If we want to help Mike lose weight, then you should let me eat loads of sweets. That would make him not eat them.'

Harold began chopping. 'I get all kinds of wrong'uns trying that all the time.'

'Trying what?'

'Reverse psychology. You forget what I do. Look, Jake. Just promise me you'll cut down on the sugar.'

'I promise to try.'

Harold sighed. He reached across to the radio and flicked on *The Archers*.

'Mike's room smells bad,' said Jake, deep into the game.

'He says the same about yours.'

He looked up. 'Does he?'

'Of course not.' Harold started to chop.

'Are you going out tonight?' said Jake.

'Not for long.'

Jake tutted. 'You always say that, too.'

'I'm busy, big man. *Commit your work to the Lord and your plans will succeed.*'

A long huff from Jake. 'And is the Lord always checking on you? Making sure you're working hard?'

'I think so. If you respond to His will and guidance.'

'What are you doing, anyway, Dad? It's the weekend. Sunday. Isn't that supposed to be a day of rest?'

Harold paused. He set down the knife and took a brown envelope out of a drawer, then walked over and sat opposite his son. 'Stop your game for a second.'

Jake flicked off the Game Gear and tossed it onto the table. 'It's crap, anyway. *Rise of the Robots.*'

Harold tipped a slim brochure out of the envelope and laid it flat on the table. Jake leaned in as he turned the pages. 'This is a property portfolio, from an agency that specialises in detached homes. Mostly places that need a bit of work.' He turned to a page with a selection of photographs of a large house with outbuildings, perched on high ground above a reservoir.

Jake skimmed the bold sections in the sales copy. *Historical elegance… serene waterfront living… original details…*

'It was built in the eighteenth century,' said Harold.

Jake chewed his sweet and flashed his green eyes at his father. 'That's even older than you.'

Harold scowled. 'It's in a place called Upper Midhope. Not too far from here.' He tapped a page. 'That's the Langsett Reservoir. Beautiful, isn't it?'

'Is it the reservoir Mum used to go to?'

'No. That's Fernilee.'

Jake surveyed the pictures. 'Are we moving there?'

'I don't think so. It's just a private project. A retreat. That's what I've been working on. It'd be somewhere to relax. Maybe do some fishing. I'm setting up a studio there, for my painting.'

Jake went back to the Game Gear. 'So, we're not allowed to go?'

'Not yet.' Harold furrowed his already-deep brow and studied the top of his son's head. 'The future might seem a long way away for you now, Jake, but you and Michael will move on soon. And so will I. Life can be hard, as we all know. But we all need a purpose. A project. Something bigger than ourselves. I'm sure you'll find yours one day. For now, this is mine.'

JAKE LAY on his single bed, staring up at the messy collage of posters and postcards that almost covered the back wall. Bands, movie stars, footballers, fighters. Massive Attack, Leftfield, My Bloody Valentine. Robbie Fowler celebrating a goal, arms aloft in 'V' shape. *Trainspotting, Pulp Fiction, Scream.* Winona Ryder, Cameron Diaz. Scully perched in front of Mulder, arms folded. A scuffed and scarred Bruce Lee facing a hairy-chested Chuck Norris.

He flipped onto his front and ran through his rack of CDs. *Loveless, Second Toughest in the Infants, The Bends, In Utero.*

It was late. 11pm. As usual, Michael had retreated and locked his room, and Jake assumed his father had gone to bed.

But then, as he flipped open the CD player lid, he paused.

A familiar rumble from downstairs: his father, talking on the phone, the volume rising and falling. Long pauses. Short exclamations.

From the distance and texture of the sound, Harold wasn't taking the call on the landline by the front door. He was in his workroom at the far end of the kitchen, on his new mobile phone.

It was out of character. And therefore irresistible.

Jake slipped off the bed and padded out to the landing. He crouched at the top of the stairs, straining to hear, but the conversation was muffled and inaudible.

He crept down the stairs and headed through the hall into the sitting room, where he reached out and opened the connecting door to the kitchen a few inches. A faint light from the oven hob seeped through.

Jake looked down at the shoe shelf. His father's boots weren't there. Going out this late?

His nose twitched at the smell of fresh coffee.

Jake leaned his head out of the sitting room. Harold's voice carried better here, but he could still only catch the moments where he raised the volume.

'Yes, I know he's a fucking DCI…'

'I visited because I wanted to see for myself, but he wouldn't accept the visit.'

'How should I know? Dead in a ditch somewhere, I hope.'

'After Bolehill, I wouldn't be surprised.'

'It's not my place to judge him.'

A long silence.

A chair scraped the floor of the workroom. Jake slipped out of the sitting room, quietly closing the door behind him. He just made it to the stairs as his father's workroom door opened and his weighty boots walked across the kitchen.

Jake lurched up the stairs as the connecting door opened. He tiptoed across the landing back into his room.

He rolled back onto his bed and lay there, staring up at

the collage, listening to his father moving around, coughing, opening the front door, closing it again.

The clock radio ticked over to 11:23pm.

Jake closed his eyes, whispered it out loud, over and over.

'All shall be well… all shall be well…'

Chapter Twenty-Two

PRESENT DAY

FIVE TAPS ON THE DOOR.

Sawyer lay on top of the bed in orange T-shirt and joggers. He hitched himself up and rested the book flat on his chest.

'Jake?' A male voice from outside.

'I'm doing my forms in a minute, Rob. Can it wait?'

The door opened a few inches and Rob stuck his head in, smiling. 'Your mate is back.'

'It's like Piccadilly Circus in here. Which one?'

'The policeman. Bentley. With a lady friend.'

Sawyer's stomach flipped. 'Red hair?'

'No. Blonde.' He whispered. 'I think you've pulled.'

Sawyer sat on the edge of the bed. 'Also police?'

Rob shrugged. 'Dunno. Thirty-odd. Well dressed. Posh-looking.'

'IC1? IC2?'

'What?'

'Never mind.' He pondered for a moment, listening to Jim Morrison singing about a crystal ship.

'Five minutes?' said Rob.

'Five minutes.'

Sawyer got up off the bed and slipped into his canvas training slippers. He muted the music as DCI Bentley entered.

'Detective Sawyer.' Bentley shook his hand. A young woman, a few inches taller, followed. She was early thirties with evenly cut natural blonde hair that brushed the shoulders of her designer peplum jacket. 'This is Leona Fullerton. Apparently, you know each other.'

Fullerton stepped forward and shook Sawyer's hand. She smiled. 'I remember those green eyes, Detective Sawyer. The last time I saw them, I was the one in a bad way.'

Sawyer squinted, then smiled in recognition. 'Nice to see you again, Leona. Have you taken over from your father as Home Secretary now?'

She laughed. 'God, no. He stepped down a couple of years ago. I do work for him, though, as a lowly civil servant. Joint Committee on Human Rights. Asylum seekers, security measures, civil liberties. He's the chair. Still an MP. He sends his regards.'

Rob brought in a couple of chairs, then exited.

'Have you told DCI Bentley how we know each other?' said Sawyer.

'Lanzarote,' said Bentley. 'Few years ago. Leona was the victim of...' He faltered.

'I was raped,' said Fullerton. 'And my boyfriend, Kyle, was attacked by my rapists and abducted. He's never been found.'

Sawyer sat on the edge of the bed. 'Don't hold anything back for our benefit.'

She smiled, with a grimace, and took out a small notepad. 'It was awful, but you were wonderful. I don't know where I'd be now, mentally and emotionally, without you.'

'This sounds like flattery.'

'That sounds like your ear is off-key.' She looked around the room. 'Maybe something to do with this place? I mean it, Jake. No irony or excess sincerity. I do have a teeny bit of an agenda, though.' She sat down.

Bentley stayed on his feet. 'Deborah Wade's mother is going downhill, Detective Sawyer.'

'Straight to it, eh?' Sawyer set the book down on his bedside table.

'*The Go-Between*,' said Fullerton. 'Love that.'

'It's my mum's old copy.'

Bentley took a seat. 'Julie Saltwell's father wanted to come with us. I knew you wouldn't see him. I'm not saying I blame you for that, but…'

'This isn't an official project for me,' said Fullerton. 'My father got wind of it from DCI Bentley, through the local brass.'

Sawyer looked between the two. 'And he suggested I might listen to you because of our previous encounter.'

Fullerton side-eyed Bentley. 'Well, yes. It's an angle, isn't it? What would you do if you were the father? I'll tell you. Anything you could. You'd be desperate. I'm married now, Jake. I have a young daughter. But I think about Kyle a lot. There's a part of me that's still out there on that island, and until I know what happened to him, I'll never quite be whole. And that's what these families feel. Their daughters were murdered by Caldwell, so he claims. He knows his life is coming to an end. He doesn't want it to end in prison. He's also desperate.' She paused. 'I can barely imagine how much you must despise him. But have you considered the possibility that he might just be willing to reveal the locations with no drama? He might have had the desire for mind games or power plays kicked out of him over the years.'

'So, why insist on only working with me?'

'He might want to feel there's some kind of atonement,' said Bentley. 'Giving you a win. You know how it works. People who do terrible things often try to overcome the guilt by compensating. Think of Savile and his marathons and charity work. When I last spoke with Caldwell, that's the impression I got. I know you'll be cynical about this, but I've been a copper for a long time, too, and I can spot gameplayers. However you feel about him personally, maybe he wants to go out doing something decent. And you're the key to making it happen.'

Fullerton reached over and took Sawyer's hand. 'Jake. Don't make me bring my father in here. We're pretty much at the top of the chain. Julie Saltwell's father is totally alone. He still holds a vigil for her at their family church, by himself, every year on the day of her disappearance. Back on that balcony in Lanzarote, you took my hand like this. Do you remember? And you said that I shouldn't be defined by my pain. That I would discover what I needed to do to survive. I decided I would try to bring some good into the world. Some light. My daughter represents that most strongly now. I'm sure you know the old line about how it's better to light a candle than curse the darkness. Look at you, in here. You've been through darkness yourself. And now you can deliver some light, some clarity, to these desperate people. Don't let them be defined by their loss.'

Sawyer eased his hand away. 'Caldwell wants to see me suffer before he checks out. He's a psychopath, and psychopaths lie to get what they want. They're good at it. He's certainly fooled both of you.'

Bentley scoffed and got to his feet, paced.

'How much more could he make you suffer?' said Fullerton. 'I read that article about you, where you talk about your faith in Stoicism. Think of that quote attributed to Marcus Aurelius. *You can commit injustice by doing nothing.* Whatever's in Caldwell's mind, you can't control it. But you can choose to not let him have control over your thoughts. Don't let his actions in the past define your future.'

Sawyer held her eye. 'Caldwell will know you're doing this. He'll enjoy the thought. He also knows this will give the families hope, and he'll be enjoying that, too. If you want to free the families from limbo, you should be straight with them. Tell them this isn't a path to easing their pain.'

Bentley turned, unable to keep his frustration in check. 'I spoke to Caldwell's doctor again. He's going downhill fast. He might only have weeks. This isn't some devious ploy from a dying man. It's medical fact, Jake. We're running out of time.'

The raised voice brought Rob to the door; Sawyer shook his head at him.

Bentley barged in front of Fullerton and crouched, staring Sawyer down. 'Listen. You're a world-class detective. And you're sitting in a jumped-up Travelodge listening to old records. You've lost your way. But I don't think you've lost your mind. So, frame it how you want… Turning evil to good. Finding light in the darkness. That's what you do, Detective Sawyer. So, get yourself out of this place and go and do it.'

Chapter Twenty-Three

COLE LANE WAS a steep and narrow side road that kinked away from the main route through the centre of Hayfield. Most of the houses were terraced pairs, tumbling into each other as they rose up the slope, while some stood detached, with dividing entryways.

Lyndon Wilde sat low in the Porsche, a few doors up from Number 5: the detached end terrace. He glowered up at the properties.

Local stone. Early 1900s.
Small windows with stone mullions.
Slate roofs.
Exposed beams, inglenook fireplaces.

His estate agency had shifted two of the big ones for half a million each in the last year, rounding up from £460k by leaning on the period features, the rustic charm.

A quintessential country living experience.

He pulled on a pair of neutral-coloured nitrile gloves, took the duffel bag from the back seat and got out of the car. Wilde was dressed in nebbishy work-wear: navy jacket, dress shirt, neutral tie. Muted enough to blend into the dusk, but not memorably dark.

Four in, six out.

Four in, six out.

He fitted the duffel bag over both shoulders, then opened the boot and lifted out the wheeled suitcase.

Number 5 hadn't been one of the properties he'd handled personally, but the houses were uniform enough to know what layout to expect inside. From the street, the lower level was dark, but a soft light glowed behind a blind in the first-floor back room: probably a home office.

He lowered his head and moved quickly, walking up the short stone path and ringing the doorbell.

Four in, six out.

The sound of movement on the stairs.

Hannah Lewis opened the door, nice and wide. She wore a loose pink hoodie and jogging trousers, and her hair was tied back in a long ponytail. She reached up and turned on the porch light, but Wilde stepped in and flicked it off again, closing the door behind him.

'Hey!' Lewis made a grab for the door, but Wilde swatted her away.

He stepped in close, grabbing the ponytail with one hand and clamping the other over her mouth. She tried to wrench her head away to shout something, but he held her chin firm as he slammed the back of her head once, twice, into the wall, yanking back the ponytail for extra impact. Her arms flopped at her side, and he carefully and quietly lowered her to the floor at the foot of the stairs.

Wilde took the man's tactical hunting knife from his inside pocket and stood over the body, braced in the fluttering light from a candle burning on a shelf in the hall, and faint glimmer from the room upstairs.

He listened, looked around.

No masculine-looking shoes by the door.

No pet smell; just the scent of the candle.

Four in, four out.

Slow it down.

Lewis was alone; he was sure of it.

He had seen her enter the house an hour earlier, when no lights were on. She had switched on the sitting room light, then the upstairs office.

Four in, six out.

Wilde opened the front door and retrieved the suitcase.

He closed the door and, with a firm grip on the knife, climbed the stairs. Step by step, slow and silent.

He checked the rooms: small spare with the light on, main bedroom, bathroom. The spare had a corner desk with a laptop.

New York cityscapes cycled on the screensaver.

He stopped to listen again.

Silence around the house and outside.

He shrugged the duffel bag off his shoulders and took out the man's torch, turning it on as he clicked off the spare room light.

He went back down the stairs and checked the sitting room, kitchen, small dining room.

Empty.

Four in, six out.

Four in...

Lewis stirred, groaning. He fell onto her, kneeling on her upper arms, restricting her movement. She gasped in pain and shock, opened her eyes wide and flapped at him as he gripped her neck with both hands, squeezing.

She fought hard, kicking her feet, bucking, trying to

wrench her upper body back and away, making it harder for him to hold her neck in place.

He didn't have the strength.

He couldn't do it with his hands.

Wilde yanked open a small cupboard under the stairs. Lewis hit out at him, her nails grazing his cheek. He grabbed her forehead, bashed the back of her head into the floor again, subduing her.

He reached into the cupboard and pulled out a small vacuum cleaner, tipping it over as he yanked away the power cord and wrapped it around Lewis's neck. He gripped both ends and pulled.

Her eyes opened wide, bulging in panic. Wilde turned his head away as he squeezed, staying out of range of her flailing arms. She gave up trying to attack him and clawed at his gloved hands, then the cord, trying to prise it away from her neck.

He kept up the pressure, compensating for her thrashing and convulsing, until she weakened and slumped.

Wilde turned, loosening the cord slightly, and Hannah Lewis, playing dead, made one last lunge for life, thrusting her open hand into his face. He ducked clear of the hand and tightened the cord again, turned away, holding her back with his knee as she steadily wilted and, at last, stayed still.

He fell back, panting, and lay there for a while.

Two in, two out.

Two in, three out.

Wilde raised himself onto his knees and reached for the torch, shining it over the length of Lewis's motionless body.

He shuffled in close, and ran the torchlight around her face, tracing the contours, checking for damage, discolouration.

He lifted her wrist, feeling for the radial pulse.

Nothing.

Then her chin for the mandibular. Nothing.

There was still the faintest trace of carotid pulse: usually the last to go. But it slowed and stopped as he waited.

Now, he would take his pleasure.

Then, he would capture her. The late Hannah Lewis would be rendered immortal.

But the clock was ticking.

Chapter Twenty-Four

SAWYER STROLLED through the unit's sensory garden, inhaling the aromas of lavender and mint. The bamboo wind chimes tinkled in the mid-morning breeze.

On the pavement outside the main gate, he warmed up by running on the spot as he waited for traffic to pass, then jogged across the road into the vast public park.

He settled onto the main path, keeping his pace light on the uneven inclined section, then turned into the grassy cut-through and emerged at the edge of the boating lake. Here, the path was smooth and wide and well tended. He could keep to the left, hugging the lake, leaving room for cyclists and walkers on the right.

At the first touch of his foot on the lakeside path, he lifted an old-school stopwatch out of his pocket, and clicked it. One mile per circuit. Three circuits then back to the gate for a 5K. PB: twenty-six minutes dead on.

He made his first pass of the familiar markers that formed the limits of his world: a fleet of moored paddle boats, bobbing and scraping; a group yoga session on the buzz-cut lawn by the café; young mothers with their lattes and high chairs.

Sawyer dodged a meandering poodle and pivoted onto a short wooden bridge, then joined a section of path lined with benches in the shade of drooping willows.

A short figure in a black hoodie stood at the edge of the lake, scooping breadcrumbs from a sandwich box and sprinkling them over the water. A mob of ducks and swans swept in.

The figure turned as he passed, and flipped down the hood, revealing a young woman with braided chestnut-brown hair. 'Mr Sawyer?' She fell into step with him, easily matching his pace. 'Don't worry. I'm not a fangirl.'

Sawyer smiled and studied her face as they ran. 'For a minute there, I thought you were an ex-girlfriend.'

'A vengeful one? Do you have many of those?'

'Not anymore.'

No laugh. 'Can I get a few minutes for a chat? Bench over there.'

'You'll have to go through my agent.'

She held out a hand, and he shook awkwardly. 'I'm Sadie Fletcher. You know my dad.'

Sawyer slowed. 'I assume you're not aware of the full history.'

She shook her head. 'I honestly don't want to know.'

'You really don't.'

Sadie dropped her pace to a fast walk and led the way to a spare bench. 'You're in hospital, right?'

'Sort of. Voluntary admission. I had a bit of a turn last year.'

They sat.

'So, do they let you out like this regularly?'

'There's no letting,' said Sawyer.

'But there's a process, right?'

'I'm still under the care of the unit, yes. So I need to tell them what I'm doing, when I'll be back. There might be therapeutic implications. I check out and check in again. RUR. Review Upon Return.' He nodded at the monogram on Sadie's lapel. 'What's S&G?'

'Strength and Grace. Women's self-defence. It's been pop-up so far. Church halls, leisure centres. I'm opening my own centre in Buxton soon. MMA. You trained in Wing Chun, right?'

'And JKD. Listen. No offence, but in my experience, an unsolicited visit from a Fletcher is rarely a good thing.'

She nodded. 'Dad couldn't be here, but he's briefed me.'

'Briefly, I assume.'

At last, a smile. 'He wanted you to know a few things. In case they come for you.'

Sawyer frowned. 'Come for me?'

'The last person to ask me about my monogram threatened me with a gun. Wesley Peyton. Horrible little bastard with an eyepatch.'

'I've had the displeasure. Was he alone?'

'No. There was a guy with him. Middle Eastern-looking. Moustache. He had the gun.'

Sawyer sighed. He watched the birds squabbling over Sadie's bread for a moment, rewinding his mind. 'That sounds like Farouk Abadi. Another charmer.'

'Peyton called himself Kyle, while his friend was Bernardo.'

'Man City players. It's theatrics, though. They knew you'd find out who they were. They just wanted you to think they didn't want you to know.'

She squinted. 'You what?'

'Never mind. What did they want?'

'My dad.'

'Did they hurt you?'

A shrug. 'They roughed me up a bit.'

'At your place?'

Sadie nodded. 'They wanted to know where my dad was, and said they'd be back again soon. Peyton threatened to rape me if I didn't tell him.' She scoffed. 'I'd pull his fucking dick off before he could get a semi.'

'Like father, like daughter.'

She shrugged. 'It's a family tradition.'

'How did your dad find out and ID Peyton?'

'He guessed. Asked if he was wearing a baseball cap. He was.'

'Sky-blue.' Sawyer toyed with the stopwatch in his pocket. 'They were using you as bait. Did they take a picture of you?'

'Yes. And I got a picture of their car as they left. Morons parked it in view of the flat.'

'They wanted you to do that, too. They wanted your dad to work out who they were. Power games. Did they come back?'

Sadie shook her head. 'They put two young guys out, watching the flat. Dad dealt with them and got me in a safe place.'

'Don't tell me where. What did he say when he found out who the main men were?'

She caught his eye. 'He said it's a clean-up. He told me to tell you that you're not safe.' She leaned forward on the bench, staring him out. 'He said you'd get it. He said they're just puppets, and you'd know who was pulling the strings.'

Chapter Twenty-Five

FAROUK ABADI CLIMBED out of the driver seat of a red-and-black Tesla Model S, followed by two imposing suited men from the back. Abadi walked out of the shadow of the double garage and led the men across the courtyard, through the glare of security lighting.

A tall, broad-shouldered man stepped out of the front door and stood on the porch, facing the visitors.

Abadi's heavies waited on the drive at the foot of the porch while he climbed the steps and stopped at the edge.

He grinned and bowed his head. 'Good evening. We're here to see Leon. Mr Stokes.'

The doorman glared at him, then leaned to the side, checking the two sidekicks. 'He's busy.'

Another smile. 'Wayne Torrence, yes? I'm told you're not stupid. So, do the clever thing.'

Torrence nodded, amused. 'What's the clever thing?'

'Play nice. There is a benefit for you.'

'And what would that be?'

Abadi paused, took a deep, slow breath. 'Your daughter gets to start her period before she loses her virginity.'

Torrence lunged for him, then froze as Abadi slipped the Glock from his inside pocket and held it low on his hip. He raised his other hand. 'No, no. That doesn't work. That's not the clever thing.'

His men stepped up onto the porch and flanked him.

Torrence stood braced, eyes blazing. 'If you go anywhere near my daughter—'

Abadi waved a hand. 'Yes, yes. I'll wish I'd never been born.'

'Behave yourself, Wazzer.' Wes Peyton walked over from the Tesla, skipped up onto the porch and ruffled Torrence's hair. 'You can stick around if you want. I won't blame you for doing your job. But it might get a bit feisty. You packing?'

'Yeah. G34.'

Peyton balked. 'Fuck's sake. Why didn't you pull it on this daft cunt first?' Peyton slapped Torrence across the cheek. 'Always show your threat early, remember?'

Torrence nodded, sheepish.

Peyton held out a hand. Torrence passed over the handgun. Peyton checked it. 'Jesus wept. Did you get this from the local shooting club? Leon is such a fucking tightarse.' He pocketed the gun and patted Torrence on the shoulder. 'Like I say, Wayne, I'd get yourself home if I were you. But I won't hold it against you if you hang around.'

Torrence looked from man to man, then back to Peyton. 'I'll see you in, Wes. He's watching a film with Cannon.'

Peyton shook his head. 'Bum-chums together.' He jerked his head towards the hall and Torrence led Peyton and Abadi into the house while the two heavies hung back. They walked past the sitting room to a door at the far end of the hall. Torrence opened it, and Peyton pushed past then paused on the top step of a steep staircase. He looked round at Torrence, who sighed and headed back to the front door.

Peyton turned to Abadi and pointed to the gun. 'Put that away.' He led Abadi down the staircase and opened the insulated door to Stokes's cinema room. The lights were off, and a film played on an enormous screen, beamed from a 4K projector mounted in the ceiling. He felt around the corner and spun the dimmer dial, bathing the room in bright light.

Stokes sat in a cushioned chair, with Cannon in a U-shaped sofa, ankles propped on a footrest. His laptop lay open on a low glass table between the seats.

Stokes sprang to his feet and spun to face the door.

'What the fuck is this?' Peyton stared up at the screen. Glowing monochrome imagery. A young man walking through the streets of Paris, then boarding a Metro train.

Cannon tapped something into his laptop and the film froze.

Abadi entered behind Peyton and stood at his shoulder.

Stokes squinted in the light, angling his head. 'What's going on, Wes?'

'Is this some old French shit?' said Peyton, still looking up at the screen. 'Subtitles.'

'It's Bresson,' said Cannon.

Peyton frowned, pondering. He nodded at Stokes. 'What's going on, Leon, is that I'm done with my place out in the country. I'm expanding my horizons.'

Stokes gave him a grave look. 'This isn't a good plan, Wes. Whatever it is. Who's your new friend?'

'Don't worry about him,' said Peyton.

Loud footsteps on the stairs. One of Abadi's heavies entered and stood aside to make way.

More footsteps on the stairs. Lighter.

'We having a party, Wes?' said Stokes.

'I hate parties.' Dale Strickland stepped in and walked over to Stokes. 'Too much expectation. Too many people. I get overwhelmed.' He extended a hand.

Stokes hesitated, then shook. 'I know the feeling, Dale. I can't work out who's throwing the party in here.'

'We're getting to that,' said Peyton.

Strickland shot him a dark look. 'Keep it cordial.'

'You look like you're ready for a covert mission, Dale,' said Stokes, nodding at Strickland's attire: black trousers and shoes; fitted zip-up navy polo; distinctive white hair concealed with an all-black Prada baseball cap.

Strickland smiled and looked up at the screen. '*Pickpocket*. His best, I reckon.'

'Not a fan of *A Man Escaped*?'

Strickland made a face. 'Too slow. But I suppose that's the point. How big is that screen?'

'Hundred and fifty inches. I can give you my supplier details if you like.'

'Perfect,' said Strickland. 'Hugely appreciated, Leon. I need to up my home cinema game. Not that I get much leisure time, these days.' He walked to the far side of the U-shaped sofa and sat down. 'Sorry about the dramatic entrance. I need to be careful.'

'These days,' said Stokes.

'Of course. And I hope this doesn't come back on your doorman. We didn't give him much choice.'

Stokes folded his arms. 'To what do we owe the pleasure? I thought we were keeping "geographically distant", as you put it.'

Strickland glanced at Cannon. 'I wanted to get a couple of things straight. Around a year ago, Jake Sawyer attacked me in my Manchester office, shortly after intercepting Wes here, during an ill-advised trip to the Manchester Centre for Clinical Neurosciences, which I think had something to do with Sawyer's colleague or girlfriend or whatever. Suffice to say, things got messy.'

'Too fuckin' right,' said Peyton.

'Now, two men were killed in that little debacle. An associate of yours and an associate of mine.'

'Mavers was full-on rogue,' said Stokes. 'He'd caused a massive beef between—'

Strickland raised his hand. 'I'm not here to mourn a puffed-up scally like Curtis Mavers. Or some Ukrainian sadist.'

'Polish,' said Peyton.

Strickland shrugged. 'Same difference. I don't really care about any of that. What is bothering me, though, is why?'

'Why what?' said Stokes.

'Why Sawyer would attack me.'

Stokes cast his eyes to Cannon, who kept his gaze on the table in front of the sofa, then back to Strickland. 'And you're asking me this, because?'

'It's an old interrogation trick, Leon. I already know the answer. I'm just gauging the level of goodwill. And if you choose not to offer the information I already know, then that tells me a lot about the trust between us.'

Stokes stayed silent.

'How about you, Boyd? Any thoughts?'

Cannon shook his head.

Strickland sank back in the sofa. 'I've been the Mayor of Greater Manchester for a year now, fulfilling all my executive responsibilities. Public engagement, strategic planning, policy development, transportation infrastructure, housing, policing, public services. Environmental fucking sustainability. And I am as bored as a blind kid, Leon. I tried so hard, I really did. But I've turned into a civil servant, and I've discovered something about myself. I'm not the serving type. You know the scorpion and the frog story? The scorpion asks the frog for a lift across the river on his back. The frog protests, says the scorpion will sting him. The scorpion promises he won't. And, halfway across, the scorpion stings the frog, who points out that now they're both going to drown, so why did he do it?'

Abadi spoke up. 'And the scorpion says, "Because I'm a scorpion."'

Strickland pointed at him. 'Exactly.' He leaned forward, propping his elbows on his knees. 'You are what you are. You can't change your nature.'

He nodded to Abadi, who moved to step forward. But Peyton stopped him and walked around to the back of the U-shaped sofa himself. He took out Torrence's gun and aimed it at Cannon's head.

Strickland smiled. 'And my nature is that I'm a scorpion.' He looked up at Abadi and waved a hand.

Cannon stiffened and sat upright as Peyton dug the barrel into his temple. Stokes kept his arms folded and his eyes on Strickland.

'So, here's my take,' said Strickland. 'Young Boyd here recorded me on the day I urged you to attack Sawyer's station. And then he played it to Sawyer, who didn't assault me out of some frustration with all the run-ins we've had over the years. It was darker than that. He was past caring.' He pointed to Cannon's laptop. 'So, let's hear the audio. Show me that goodwill. Or, I promise you, Leon, from a scorpion to a lion, you'll have to find yourself another bean counter.'

'This is ducking stool logic, Dale,' said Stokes. 'Boyd plays the audio, and you kill him for secretly recording you. He doesn't play the audio, and you kill him for holding out.'

Cannon swerved his head back, away from the gun, and aimed a punch at Peyton's good eye. Peyton turned just in time, and it glanced off the side of his head.

Cannon made a dash for a door at the back of the cinema room, but he'd barely covered two steps before Abadi aimed his own gun and shot him once in the back of the head. Cannon tumbled forward, clattering against a rack of Blu-rays, and lay still on a yellow-and-red-striped rug.

Peyton gathered himself and held his gun on Stokes, who rushed over and crouched at Cannon's side, checking his pulse.

He rose slowly to his feet and turned, breathing hard.

'Do the clever thing,' said Abadi, also holding his gun on Stokes.

Cannon's blood seeped over the edges of the rug's red stripes, staining the yellow stripes.

Strickland got up and stepped around Cannon's body. He opened the door Cannon had aimed for and looked inside for a moment, then closed it and turned. 'Isn't that sweet? You've got a panic room.'

Peyton snatched up Cannon's laptop.

'You did me a favour,' said Stokes.

Strickland strolled back to the sofa and sat down. 'Come again?'

'He showed his true colours. He was going to hide in there and leave me to your mercy out here.'

Strickland scrutinised him. 'Let's lose the weapons before someone crucial to this business gets hurt.'

Peyton and Abadi lowered their guns.

'You're a film man, Leon. You know the bit at the beginning of *The Departed?* Jack Nicholson's character says he doesn't want to be a product of his environment. He wants his environment to be a product of him. I can identify with that, and I'm sure you can, too.' He patted the sofa next to him.

Stokes walked over and sat down.

Strickland leaned in close as he spoke. 'You're knocking on a bit now. It might be time to think about taking lighter duties. Lions aren't kings of the jungle, anyway, are they? Come to think of it, they don't even live in the fucking jungle.'

Peyton laughed.

'Now...' Strickland wrapped an arm around Stokes's shoulders. 'You've upset me, Leon. But let's consider this a reboot of relations. I do need something from you, though. I want you to use all your conniving little street connections. From generals to cannon fodder. Call in your best men, leverage your environment and help me find someone who's upset me even more. As a matter of extreme urgency. And you're working with Wes on this.'

'*With?*' said Stokes.

Strickland nodded. 'Let's just say he's had a favourable performance review.'

'Are you talking about Sawyer?' said Stokes.

Strickland shook his head. 'Someone else. Wes will brief you.'

'So, what's the plan for Sawyer?'

'You said I'd get my time,' said Peyton. 'It's come.'

Chapter Twenty-Six

SHEPHERD PLUNGED the boxy mustard-yellow Range Rover into a pothole puddle at speed, dousing the roadside hedges in rainwater. Walker's shoulder slammed against his window with the impact, but he absorbed it without protest.

Shepherd glanced over. 'Sorry. Picked up some bad habits. I'll slow down.'

Walker gazed out at the metallic sky. First light glimmered through the freshly emptied clouds. 'It's a mistake.'

'What is?'

'Charging Gray.'

Shepherd eyed him. 'Pope also Catholic.'

'Farrell is a short-sighted arsehole.'

'Is this Bleedin' Obvious Hour? Next up, Tories hate taxes.'

Walker turned, grim-faced. 'He wants the collar.'

'He's damaged goods with the brass. He's only there because Keating knew he wouldn't have to deal with Sawyer. There was a fella from Sheffield. Another from Brum. I heard Keating insisted on Farrell.'

'So, what if Sawyer hadn't gone postal?'

Shepherd laughed. 'Haven't heard that one for a while. Dunno. The woman who comes in to clean the phones every Friday has more natural authority than Farrell.'

'I wouldn't cross her.'

Shepherd turned off the wipers and opened his window. He inhaled. 'One of the benefits of country living. The smell of grass and soil after rain.'

'Petrichor,' said Walker.

'Didn't he play left back for Spurs last season?'

Walker opened his own window. 'Maybe it was reverse psychology on Keating's part. Motivating Sawyer to return, knowing we had to put up with Farrell.'

'And that's going well.'

'Farrell's got a task force on the Gray case now. Press conference with the families. The victims of the sicko they call The Vulture. Demanding action from the NHS. Dignity for the dead.'

'Pushing at an open door. He wrote Phoebe off a long time ago.'

'We might have found her if—'

'We're not going there,' said Shepherd. He turned off, onto a smooth but narrow A-road, carving through a canopy of overhanging trees that thinned to reveal the undulating heathland of Sterndale Moor. Not a soul about.

'I don't know,' said Walker. 'Maybe Gray did do it. Someone took his daughter. It triggered something dark. Deeper than we can understand yet. At the moment, we have no hard evidence to the contrary.'

'Are you saying that Farrell might be right?'

Walker scrubbed at his stubble. 'Christ, I think I might be.'

'It's early. Your brain isn't fully online yet. Sharpen up, though. We're here.'

Shepherd slowed the Rover and eased it off the road onto a low verge, sodden with mud. He rumbled along the edge of the field and parked in a relatively dry spot near the Scientific Services Unit van. They got out and signed in with an officer at the cordon.

'Gentlemen.' Sally O'Callaghan, in turquoise Tyvek suit, looked up from a conversation with a group of white Tyveks. 'A shitty morning for a shitty job. Squelch this way...'

She turned and strode off towards a white forensic tent erected across the edge of the field.

Shepherd and Walker caught up.

'No inner cordon?' said Shepherd.

'Bloody hell,' said O'Callaghan. 'Priorities. We're closed off at all footpath entry points. Preservation next, then roads. Hardly a thoroughfare out here, though.' She handed over two pairs of latex gloves.

'What's the state of the body?' said Walker.

'Fresh, as bodies go. They don't get easier, though.' She glanced at Shepherd. 'You sure you're—'

'I'm fine.'

'Roadside ditch,' said O'Callaghan. 'It's more like fly-tipping than body-dumping.' She surveyed the sky, tracking the liquid warble of a spiralling skylark. 'Fuck this weather. It's washed away most things that could be useful to us. Tyre tracks, mainly. Although we would have found hundreds up here. Without the rain it might have been possible to separate the old from the new. But now...' She shrugged. 'Detail erosion. And the impressions will be filled with water. Oil and rubber particles will be washed away. We can try light scanners, 3D shots. But the hardy souls in the van will need to do the searches first. Line, grid, spiral.'

Shepherd stumbled out of a furrow. 'Any sign of the parasites?'

'Huh?'

'Press.'

'Not yet. If I were you, I'd set up blocks down at the Heath View intersection and the dirt roads in from Chelmorton and Hurdlow, maybe as far as the Royal Oak. But I'm not you. And these are the times when I give thanks for that. All I ask is that you take a look and get the party started nice and sharpish. There's more rain coming, and I want to ruin Drummond's day as soon as possible.'

At the tent, Shepherd nodded to the officer on guard. The man nodded back, just about managing a strained smile.

Shepherd and Walker stepped into shoe covers and followed O'Callaghan inside. The tent covered a patch of roadside ditch so shallow it was practically dry.

Shepherd nodded to the royal-blue canvas tarpaulin covering the midsection of the ditch. 'This yours?'

'Yes,' said O'Callaghan, with a flicker of exasperation. 'As I say, preservation. Discretion. It was raining when we first put up the tent.'

Shepherd crouched and rolled away the sheet with both hands. The body was naked, face down, with the right arm raised and the left squashed into the side. The areas of skin not mottled with muddy water were callow, almost translucent in the tent's LED lights, with a slight bluish discolouration at the extremities.

'Livor mortis,' said Walker. He crouched. 'It's ongoing, though. Hasn't been that long.'

Shepherd touched a gloved finger to the back of the

neck. 'Bruising. A few broken blood vessels. Can't see ligature marks. No obvious wounds on the back side.' He looked across to Walker. 'We need to turn her over.'

'Scene is fully documented,' said O'Callaghan, nodding.

Walker and Shepherd hitched their hands underneath the body and carefully rolled it onto its back, alongside its original position.

'Ah, she's light as a feather,' said Shepherd.

It was a young girl. A child. Her blonde hair was streaked with mud and coiled around her cheeks and forehead.

O'Callaghan crouched. 'Thank Christ her eyes aren't open. I hate that.' She ran a torchlight across the ground vacated by the body. 'No obvious items or fluids underneath her. We'll fully document when you're done.'

'No signs of injury on the torso,' said Walker. He leaned in. 'Lots of bruising around the neck. Looks like she was strangled.'

'It's Phoebe, right?' said O'Callaghan, standing.

Walker followed her up. 'Looks like her, yes.'

Shepherd stayed on his haunches. He lowered his head. 'Fucking bastard.'

O'Callaghan side-eyed Walker. She placed a hand on Shepherd's back, but he didn't get up.

Chapter Twenty-Seven

SAWYER ROSE from the teal armchair and walked to the windows at the far side of Dr Martinez's office. After a moment, he turned and walked back to the coffee table, thumbed through a copy of *Esquire*, looking at the pictures, then tossed the magazine back onto the table and made for the window again.

Martinez was scribbling on her tablet. 'This is new.'

'What's that?'

'Pacing. Animals do it in zoos. Zoochosis. Lack of space or stimulation. Suppression of natural behaviours.' She smiled. 'Are you trying to tell me something?'

Sawyer gave her a theatrical eyeroll. 'Honestly. Psychiatrists. Always overthinking.' He looked out at the gardens, at the resplendent flower beds. Marigolds, sunflowers, daylilies. Zesty yellow, radiant orange. 'My mum had a thing for orange.'

'I see a lot of the colour in your living space.'

'You're thinking it's how I keep her alive in my mind. How I hold on to her.'

Martinez sighed. 'Yes. I was. But also the colour's associations. The sun. The source of life. Significance with the natural world.'

'It's linked to asceticism,' said Sawyer. 'A renunciation of material life. But also compassion. Spiritual awakening. Enlightenment. The end of suffering.'

'Is that what you've done in your time here? Seek enlightenment?'

He turned and walked back to the chair, smiling. 'What else do you think I've been doing?'

'You were suffering when you came here. Are you still suffering?'

He sat. 'Surely you're not expecting me to mansplain the noble truths.'

Martinez set down the tablet. 'Desire causes suffering. Move beyond desire to ease the suffering. Accept that all things pass and nothing is permanent.'

Sawyer dropped his head, nodding. 'Achieved through meditation and mindfulness.'

'And how do you think you're doing?'

He thought for a moment. 'Things are clearer now. The version of me who came in here... He chose to suffer. He indulged his desire.'

'Which is?'

'Revenge. It was clouding everything I did. I had to blow away the fog.' He got up again, walked to a side window that overlooked the front path and main gate. 'I had to see what was on the other side of it. The desire to see enemies suffer forces us to act like them.' He rested his forehead on the window. 'But there's nothing on the other side but more revenge, more pain. My mum suffered greatly for a few moments, and then she was beyond suffering. I've been paying that pain forward ever since. Someone has to end that cycle. Be the grown-up.'

'And, of course, you were a child when she died. Perhaps that's been your fight, Jake. To break away from the infantile self. This version of you who chooses to suffer, to keep returning to that moment.' Martinez took up her tablet and stylus. 'So, do you feel you've reached a point of understanding? Of, dare I say, enlightenment?'

'In theory. But I'm not as done as I thought I was.'

'What do you mean?'

Sawyer turned, walked back. 'You said some business stays unfinished.' He flopped down in the chair, flailing his arms. 'But that's true of everything. It's all forever in motion. Change is the constant. My mum used to say that there would always be bad things in the world. Sin, as she saw it. Darkness. But *all shall be well*. I used to think that was trite, that she meant it would all come good in the end, and we could get on with living happily ever after. But my dad reminded me of a Bible quote. *There is nothing in darkness that will not be disclosed. Nothing concealed that will not be brought to light.* I'm not healed, but I've cleared the fog. And now I'm ready to work on that darkness.'

Martinez scribbled, taking her time. 'Have you heard of status quo bias?'

'No.'

'We tend to defend the way things are. We're loss averse. We believe that the pain we'll feel from a loss outweighs the pleasure we'll get from a similar-size gain.' She leaned forward. 'If your current situation was no longer the status quo, would you actively choose it? If not, then you're stuck in a bias. Because you're showing a preference for the status quo, over a potentially valuable change.'

'So, that would be the real breakthrough. The moment the risk to stay budded is greater than the risk to blossom.'

Martinez frowned. 'That's the poetic version, yes.'

'I stole it from a French writer.'

'Yes. Anaïs Nin. I've read books, too.' Martinez sat back in her chair, pondered for a moment. 'You say change is the constant. You do realise that the therapy you've taken here isn't a talking cure. It's not even a listening one. As I've said before, when you leave this place, you have to *act*. You have to be different, change your life, have new relationships, make dramatic decisions. You have to actively choose to not suffer.'

Sawyer was up again. Back to the window. This time, he turned. 'Have you ever had a real connection with someone? A partner, a relationship. But the responsibility of maintaining that connection makes it less and less of a pleasure. And so you snuff it out, even when the flame is burning brightly.'

Martinez nodded, curious. 'Before the other person does?'

'Yes. Because then at least you're the one who takes control. Who makes the change. I had that with someone. And I snuffed it out. Then, I had it again. And I snuffed it out again.'

'Of course. The first deep emotional relationship you had with a woman, your mother, ended terribly. So you take steps before that happens again. The trauma from the loss of your mother has bedded deep inside you, as loss aversity.'

'And so the cycle, the suffering, continued. And it was all down to my choosing.' He squatted down, with his back to the window. 'Hell isn't other people. Hell is yourself. Wherever you go, whatever you do, whoever you love… There you are, choosing the suffering over the change.'

Sawyer got to his feet, took his jacket off the back of the chair. He spun it over his head, twisting it and slotting in his arms in a single motion, then shrugged it up over his shoulders.

Martinez frowned. 'Are you going out?'

'Time to be the grown-up.'

Chapter Twenty-Eight

LYNDON WILDE WHEELED the suitcase over the winding side path and stood at the door of his garden office.

He closed his eyes, listened, tuning in to his sharpened senses.

Soft waves of occasional traffic on the overpass.

A child's shout of excitement, from one of the semis at the closed end of the cul-de-sac.

The waspy drone of a light aircraft engine.

The sting from the fresh scratch on his cheek.

Four in, six out.

Four in, six out.

He swiped his thumb across the biometric panel, releasing the deadbolt lock, then stepped inside.

The recessed lighting flickered into life, and the association stirred something primal: a swell of anticipation.

His heart accelerated, fighting against the quest for calm.

He paused, focused on the breathing.

Four in, four out.

Wilde walked to the desk and swiped the second biometric panel, then stepped through the unlocked door in the side wall, trailing the suitcase.

As the muted overhead lighting faded up, he closed and locked the door, then unzipped the suitcase and surveyed its contents.

Four in, three out.

He pressed the button on the remote in his pocket.

Whirring came from the wall as the panel opened, revealing the line of faces.

Wilde carefully lifted Hannah Lewis's mask from the suitcase and unpeeled the polythene. He held it up to the light, running his fingertips over the contours, admiring the serenity of her expression, captured so soon after the release of death. So pure and unpolluted by decay. Untroubled by gravity. Untethered from the leaden pull of living.

The grid pattern from the gauze was almost invisible this time.

A thought passed over him: he was more than a mere preserver now.

He was a fine artist, honing his craft.

Taking pride in improving his work.

He fitted the mask into the third available space in a grouping of four and stepped back, sinking into the padded leather chair.

Three in, three out.

Lyndon Wilde gazed up at his private gallery.

He rested his trembling hands on his knees and indulged in a smile.

One in, one out.
One in, one out.

He had conquered the interruption.
Found a way around the setback.
Evicted the unwelcome guest.

Part II

ALL APOLOGIES

Chapter Twenty-Nine

NOVEMBER 1995

'FUCK ME, Jaz. He's crying again.'

The biggest of the three older teens barged in between the other two and crouched down before their much younger blond companion. The big lad gripped the youngster's head between his hands and raised his face, forcing eye contact for a few seconds before easing his grip and turning to glare up at the other two.

'He's not crying, you twat.' Jaz turned back and shuffled closer, pushing his face forward until they were nose to nose. 'You're not crying, are you, Donny?'

Donny took a couple of sharp breaths and shook his head rapidly.

'He's stopped now,' said the thinnest of the three older teens. 'But he—'

'Shut your fucking mouth, Breezy,' said Jaz, quietly, keeping his eyes fixed on Donny. He pulled back, stood upright. The third older lad—short, heavy—stepped away to give him space. 'He's alright, our Donny.' He shot out his hand and slapped Donny across the face. 'Aren't you?' Another slap, harder. '*Aren't you?*'

Donny rubbed at his cheek and glared up at Jaz. 'I'm alright, yes.' The accent was sharper than the others. Higher born.

The heavy one spoke up. 'He's shitting out. He needs some special energy again.'

Jaz smirked. 'What d'ya reckon, Don? Pal or Pedigree Chum?'

Donny breathed in slowly, then out, taking his time before answering. 'I'm not eating dog food again.'

Jaz reached down, pulled him upright. 'Nah. I'm just messin'. We're going up a few levels today. I want to see if you've got any balls. How old is he again, Gandhi?'

'Thirteen,' said the heavy teen.

Jaz nodded, thought for a moment. 'We're going on an adventure, Donny.' He shielded his eyes against the low setting sun and squinted out to the two-storey house across the fields. 'Have you ever had sex?'

Breezy snorted. 'Course he fucking hasn't.'

Jaz turned and shoved him back. Breezy stumbled against the crumbling stone bench set at the back of the old bus shelter, and fell to the ground, immediately springing back up again.

Gandhi laughed.

'Fuck off,' said Breezy, trying to shove him. But Gandhi was too bulky and didn't budge. Breezy sat down on the seat, laughing. 'Fuck me. You wanna go easy on them poppadums.'

Jaz squatted back down before Donny, placing him just

below his head height. He softened his voice. 'You ever had sex, then, Donny?'

Donny shook his head.

'We might get you sorted tonight. Do you know what I mean?' He stood upright again and leaned his tall, powerful frame against the dry-stone wall at the side of the bus shelter. He pointed at the house. 'My brother's mate has done some labouring there. Fixing up a wood storage shed for the winter. There was a couple who lived there. They had a car crash and the bloke died, but the woman is still there. She's quite old, but they've got a daughter, too. She's only a bit older than you, Donny.'

'Plenty worth robbing there, I reckon,' said Breezy.

Jaz nodded. 'Yeah, they had a few quid. The bloke ran a business. Farm vehicles or something. Donny's done well with our dares, but if he wants to be a lifetime member, there's one more to do.'

'I heard they had an older son, though,' said Gandhi. 'Farmer.'

'Yeah, but he's not there now, is he, dickhead?' He pulled Gandhi over to the wall by his neck and pointed. 'There's only that little red car.'

'He'd have a four-wheel drive or a tractor or something,' said Breezy, coming over to the wall.

Jaz smiled. 'Exactly. So, you go down the little track, just off the lane back there. And that's how you get in the front way. But the back way is best. If we can pinch a few things, then my brother can sell 'em on and give me a cut.'

'And you're gonna share with us, yeah?' said Gandhi.

'Course I am. That's only fair. We can make a bit of cash.' He reached back and pulled Donny to his side. 'And Donny can have some fun.'

JAZ HUNG BACK with Donny while Gandhi and Breezy led the way across the field. They stuck to the edge, deep in the shadows of the threadbare birches that loomed over the low perimeter wall.

By the time they reached the house it was fully dark, with a sliver of moon barely piercing the starless sky.

They crossed the dirt road and crept round to the back of the house. Two lights on: one upstairs at the back, one downstairs at the front. Jaz pulled a torch out of his backpack and guided them to rough open ground beyond the back garden. A battered old stile marked the entrance to a walking track that wound uphill through a field of sheep and into a scruffy patch of woodland at the top of a ridge.

Jaz checked his watch: 5:20pm.

He jerked his head towards the house, and they all slipped through the narrow gate and scuttled over to a roofed wood store where a set of builder's tools lay under a thick canvas sheet, flapping in the wind.

Jaz held the torch up to his face and hissed at them. 'Stay here. Donny, come with me.'

Gandhi and Breezy lurked out of sight behind the wood store and watched Jaz hurry across the garden, closely followed by Donny. At the back door, Jaz turned back to check on them, then delivered three loud knocks to the door, making them jump.

After a few seconds, a light came on in the kitchen and the face of a middle-aged woman pressed close to the window. She opened it a couple of inches and called out, cautious. 'Hello?'

'Hiya, love,' said Jaz. 'Sorry to bother you but my little brother's got a nasty cut on his ankle. I think he's sprained it, as well. We were walking and got lost. Yours is the first house we've seen since he did it. Really, really sorry to bother you.'

The woman peered out at them. 'Is he okay?'

Jaz nudged Donny.

'It really hurts,' said Donny. 'I can't walk on it anymore.'

'Please, love,' said Jaz. 'He's only a young 'un, as you can see. We're desperate. If he can just give the wound a bit of a wash…'

'I'll call you an ambulance,' said the woman.

'Oh, blimey,' said Jaz, 'I don't want to bother the ambulance. My mum is a nurse and I know they're so busy with real emergencies. Please. We'll just be a few minutes. You'd be an absolute lifesaver, love. My brother is twelve. I'm only sixteen myself.'

The woman sighed. She closed the window and disappeared. The back door rattled as a heavy-sounding bolt ground free of its faceplate.

The door opened and the woman stood in the frame. She was short and slim, in a chunky Fair Isle-style jumper and jeans.

'Okay. Come through to the kitchen and I'll—'

Jaz lunged forward and punched her full in the face. She cried out and fell backwards, into a wall-mounted cabinet, dislodging several mugs that fell and shattered as she toppled down onto the stone floor.

Breezy ran through from the wood store and was on her before she could get up, forcing his hands over her mouth, muffling her shouts. Gandhi followed. He pushed the woman upright against the wall, forced her arms behind her back and bound her at the wrists with a length of thick rope he'd pulled from Jaz's backpack.

Donny froze at the door, breathing fast and hard.

Jaz reached out and pulled him inside, then slammed the door shut and slid the bolt back in place.

Breezy kept his hands over the woman's mouth. She lurched and twisted her head from side to side, trying to get her mouth free.

'Fucking get something,' cried Breezy. 'The gag.'

Jaz stood back, watching him, amused. 'Forgot to bring it.'

Breezy bellowed with pain as the woman bit his finger. He staggered back, and Jaz leaned in and punched her again, bang on the nose. There was a loud wet crack, and she shrieked in agony.

'Sort it out, Gandhi!' shouted Breezy, nursing his finger.

'No names,' warned Jaz. 'Not even nicknames.'

Gandhi yanked a tea towel from its holder and fell on the woman, bunching it up, tying it around her mouth.

She fought him hard, wrenching her mouth free, screaming over and over, spitting blood onto his face. *'Get out of my house! Get out of my house!'*

Jaz shoved Gandhi away and twisted the tea towel into a long tube. As he pressed it into her mouth and tied it tight at the back, she managed one last shout.

'Please! Don't hurt my—'

He stepped away and looked down at her, smiling.

She thrashed around on the floor, howling behind the gag, eyes squeezed shut.

Breezy turned on the cold tap and ran water over his bleeding hand. 'Nasty fucking bitch. She's taken half my finger off, Jaz.'

Jaz looked into the sink. 'Bollocks. It's fuck-all. Get that cleaned up and look around. Find a bin bag. Scoop up anything that looks pricey. Jewels. Ornaments.'

'Money?' said Breezy.

Jaz slapped him. 'Yeah, you dozy cunt. Money. That'd be alright. Gandhi. Check the rest of the downstairs. Donny. Upstairs with me.'

AT THE TOP of a short set of carpeted stairs, Jaz paused and crouched down to Donny. 'Stay here on the landing, Don. I'm going to have a look in the rooms on this side. Don't move. Give me a shout if you need anything.'

Jaz opened the door on the left and crept inside.

Donny waited, listening to the groan of the floorboards as Jaz clumped around. He spotted a framed family photo hung on the facing wall, and pushed his head close, studying the people and setting. A park. Bright sunshine. A late-teen boy and a woman sitting on a bench, with a young girl in the centre. The girl's head sat at a strange angle, resting on her shoulder.

'Hey, Jaz,' called Donny. 'That old slag nearly bit off one of Breezy's fingers.' He laughed.

Jaz poked his head around the door. 'Hey! What did I say about using nicknames? Keep quiet.'

'Sorry. What's in there?' whispered Donny.

'Fuck all. Double bedroom and bathroom. Just going to have a look through the drawers and wardrobe. Stay there and not another word, okay?'

Jaz disappeared back into the room.

Donny turned to the right of the landing. He leaned in and rested his ear against the closed door.

Rhythmic bleeping sounds. Repeating at regular intervals.

Donny turned the handle, slowly and quietly, then eased

the door open and stepped inside, onto a cushioned, non-slip vinyl floor. He reached up and switched on a muted overhead light, revealing a hospital-style bed with padded side rails.

The room was uncomfortably warm. In the far corner, a rack of compact monitors were mounted on a portable stand beside the bed. Their displays showed shifting, real-time data with rapidly updating, colour-coded readouts. Heartrate, pulse, respiration, blood pressure, EEG.

A deep shelf had been fitted to the wall behind the bed, which held medical supplies in labelled cabinets: gloves, masks, sanitiser, gauze, bandages. Beneath the shelf, in the near corner, a wheeled chair sat before a miniature desk which held neatly stacked documents and notepads.

Donny edged away from the door and walked around to the monitors where he could get a closer look at the bed's occupant.

It was the girl in the photograph. She wore a thin night-dress and was propped upright with pillows and wedges of foam. As he moved around the bed, she followed him with her eyes, but didn't turn her neck.

The girl's expression stayed fixed, but as he leaned in, her eyes sparkled with alarm and she jerked, holding herself rigid.

'Fucking hell, Donny.'

Jaz came in, but Donny kept his eyes on the girl, appalled and thrilled at the intensity of her outrage. He could almost feel the heat from her eyes.

A slap from Jaz brought him round. 'Why can't you do what I tell you? Eh?'

Breezy and Gandhi stumbled in, laughing.

'We found a drawer, Jaz,' said Gandhi. 'Plenty in there

we can flog.' He froze on sight of the girl. 'Ah, shit. Who's this?'

Jaz stood over the girl, looking down on her. 'She's called Melanie.' He kept his voice low and measured.

They walked round the bed and stood by Jaz.

'What's up with her?' said Gandhi.

Breezy squinted. 'Fucking spaz.'

Jaz smacked him across the back of the head. 'She can't move much by herself. Her arms and legs don't work but she's okay above the neck.' He reached out and rested a palm on Melanie's forehead.

She let out a shrill scream and twisted her head from side to side, crying out. *'No! No!'*

Jaz shifted his hand to cover Melanie's mouth and hold her head in place. He leaned in next to her ear. 'Hey, hey… None of that. Settle down. We've got your mum downstairs, yeah? If you keep that up, we'll kill her. Right?'

Her eyes fixed on him, pumping out fear and fury.

Jaz lifted his hand away from Melanie's mouth. 'So she *can* feel things.' He gave a strange little smile as he stroked her cheek. 'I've got a new dare for you, Donny.'

Breezy sniggered. 'He won't make her feel much. Probably got a dick like a—'

'Shut your fucking mouth,' said Jaz. He turned and crouched down by Donny, then rested a heavy hand on the back of his neck. 'You know what to do, don't you, son?'

Donny nodded. His breathing was too fast, too shallow.

'Shh,' said Jaz. 'Steady does it. Nice and easy. Breathe in for four seconds, Donny. Then out for six. It'll calm you down. Can you do it for me?'

He nodded again, and slowed his breathing just as Jaz had taught him.

Jaz reached over to Melanie. He lifted off the sheets and

shifted her towards the edge of the bed. She grunted in protest, and her body jerked and spasmed as her eyes shifted again from Jaz to Donny.

'Just a quick one, eh?' said Jaz. 'Get yourself ready, Don. She's on the edge of the bed so you can stay standing up. Do this one and you won't be a boy any more. You'll be a man.'

The girl's eyes blazed as Donny undid the buttons of his trousers.

'Shit. He's gonna do it.' Gandhi edged back, pulling Breezy with him.

Four in, six out.

Four in, six out.

Jaz rested a hand on the back of Donny's neck as he stepped towards the girl.

Breezy and Gandhi pinned themselves into the corner, watching.

They waited.

Melanie's eyes widened, and Donny looked away. But when he looked back, her expression hadn't changed. Her gaze stayed fixed on him: eyelids twitching, eyes brimming with revulsion.

Four in, six out.

Judging him. Marking him as unready.

Four in, six out.

Unworthy.

Jaz sighed and gently shifted him aside. 'It's alright, Donny, lad. Maybe a bit too soon for you, eh? We'll have another try somewhere else.' He unfastened his belt. 'But we can't leave this poor girl hanging on anymore, can we?'

And the room was silent, but for the trilling monitors and the steady sway of the bed springs.

And they watched.

Breezy and Gandhi watching Jaz.

Donny watching Melanie.

Melanie watching Donny with those searing, staring eyes.

Not resigned or submissive.

So righteous.

So alive.

Chapter Thirty

PRESENT DAY

FARRELL PUSHED through the conference room door and took the chair beneath the main screen. He tapped out a breath mint and surveyed his domain. It was a full house, with all the key detectives in their usual positions around the table, plus O'Callaghan, Drummond and Bloom. A few of the junior staff huddled against the far wall, grim-faced.

He gave a petulant sigh. 'Are we all on a group meditation or is someone going to talk? DI Shepherd?'

Like most of the others, Shepherd's eyes were fixed on the image at the centre of the screen: Phoebe Gray, in her yellow-and-black cardigan, blonde hair gathered in bunches.

Smiling.

Farrell thumped the table. 'Anyone home?'

Shepherd jumped and turned his eyes to the room. 'Sir. It's been two days since we discovered Phoebe Gray's body.'

Another sigh from Farrell. 'Can we skip the bits we already know?' He crunched his mint. 'What's new?'

Shepherd glared at him, letting the silence make his feelings clear.

'Phoebe was strangled,' said Drummond. 'The killer did it by hand. No ligature marks. Finger pattern bruising.' He checked a folder of notes. 'Heavy, thumb-sized bruise on Phoebe's Adam's apple. Petechial haemorrhage in the eyes and on the eyelids. You can get them in manual and ligature strangulation but they're more common in manual. Also, severe damage to the hyoid bone and thyroid cartilage. Hyoid bone practically fractured, actually.' Drummond closed the folder. 'I'd put TOD at no more than twenty-four hours before she was found. No sign of sexual abuse.'

'And no prints,' said O'Callaghan. 'Chemical residue shows non-latex gloves.'

Drummond nodded. 'Blood glucose and C-peptide levels were normal. Well, C-peptide was acceptable but low, which suggests she was receiving exogenous...' He glanced at Farrell. 'Externally administered insulin. Looking at the toxicology report, I'd say her last dose was twenty-four hours before her death.'

'The killer gave it to her,' said Walker. 'That takes planning. It confirms he must have known about her diabetes before he took her.'

'Phoebe was in decent condition,' said Drummond. 'He was feeding her well.'

Farrell squinted at him. '"He"? Aren't we assuming there?'

Drummond shrugged. 'If this is a woman, then I'm a fruitarian.'

'Women don't strangle,' said Shepherd.

Walker shook his head. 'That's a trend, not a rule.'

O'Callaghan twirled her pen. 'If I may... I have a piece of game-changing forensic evidence. Nothing at the scene, but we did find something on Phoebe's body. Right side of her neck.' She swiped at her touchscreen, changing the communal image to a magnified, brightly lit forensic photograph of an individual strand of hair. Another swipe, and the image switched to a heavily magnified version which looked more like a tree branch with sine-wave fibre patterns along the length. 'It's human, dark brown, and complete with, joy of joys, the root. So we pulled out a nuclear DNA profile, which is more detailed—'

'Yes,' said Farrell impatiently. 'I'm aware. ID?'

Shepherd swiped his screen and the image switched to a scowling shot of a scruffy-haired man in army fatigues, head tilted forward, glaring straight down the lens. 'Brad Singleton. Forty-four. Private security consultant. Ex-military. Did a tour of Afghanistan in 2001, and another in Iraq in 2004. Both as a vehicle operator with the Royal Logistic Corps. First as Lance Corporal. Second as Corporal. His truck hit an IED in Iraq. Six men killed. He survived, along with his co-driver. Singleton only suffered minor injuries, but they evidently compromised him in a way the army couldn't accommodate. He was discharged from service in 2006 when he was twenty-six.'

'How did we confirm the profile?' said Myers. 'Was he in NDNAD?'

'Happily, yes. We were spared a soul-crushing liaison with military intelligence. Singleton served a few months for a drug offence back in 2010. Nothing major but DNA swabs are mandatory for drug offences.'

'And this is definitely his hair on Phoebe Gray's body?' said Farrell.

O'Callaghan managed a sour smile. 'I checked really

hard, sir. Did all the sums. So, that's the good news. I'll let DI Shepherd give you the bad news.'

Shepherd took a breath. 'Singleton has been missing for more than a week now. He lives alone and his landlord says he missed a rent payment, which is unusual. His neighbour called the landlord when Singleton's dog was howling and barking.'

Myers spoke up. 'His fridge was full of fresh food, bought a couple of days before his neighbour last saw him.' He fell silent; the detectives' eyes stayed on him, expectant. 'The dog's fine. The Ark Animal Rescue Centre in Matlock is looking after him for now.'

'We only got Singleton's DNA confirmed today,' said Walker. 'But I'm looking deeper into him.'

Farrell pointed. 'See if there's any links to Orlando Gray.'

'Where is the poor bastard now?' said Drummond.

Farrell waved a hand. 'Off with the fairies.'

'Cavendish,' said Shepherd. 'The acute inpatient care ward. He had a full-on psychotic reaction to the news of his daughter's death. Screaming and raving. Trying to harm himself. He remains under arrest but is now under the care of the unit, on a twenty-eight-day section, under double guard. Given the press attention and his profile, we have officers posted at the unit's entrance and outside his room. He's stable but sedated.'

Farrell raised an index finger into the air. 'One. We need the dirt on Singleton. Any paedo history? How could he have gained access to Phoebe Gray? Why did he take the trouble to look after her so well, including dosing her with insulin?'

'Why did he choose to kill her now?' said a junior officer at the back.

Farrell nodded and raised a second finger. 'Two. Where the fuck is he? History of known movements. CCTV. ANPR data for his car. Stations, airports. Tally up with Phoebe's movements. Where might he have snatched her?' Another finger. 'Three. Time of death shows Gray couldn't have killed his own daughter. But he's still under suspicion for a serious offence. So we cannot lose sight of that.'

'Four,' said Shepherd. 'The presence of one of Singleton's hairs on Phoebe Gray does not prove that he killed her.'

Farrell rolled his eyes. 'No. But I'd say it does make him the prime suspect, DI Shepherd, don't you think? So, let's find him and...' He wobbled his head from left to right as he trotted out the familiar phrase. *'Eliminate him from our enquiries.'*

'The priority should be Orlando Gray, sir,' said Walker. 'We need to ask him about Singleton. There may be a connection. Getting it confirmed directly will help—'

'Way ahead of you, DS Walker,' said Farrell. 'I've sent word to our... FLO At Large, Maggie Spark, who I'm told has agreed to speak to Gray, when he's fit to talk.' He prodded another finger towards Stephen Bloom. 'And I'm sure I don't need to tell you that we need to control the media narrative.'

Shepherd and Walker exchanged a weary glance.

'The red-tops will be in a froth because, for them, this isn't just a bog-standard pretty young girl who's been murdered. This is The Vulture's daughter.'

Chapter Thirty-One

UMA LEARY STOOD BACK from the kitchen island and perched on a tall padded stool. 'Thank you so much for the grand tour.' She placed her palms together in a praying gesture. '*So* gorgeous.'

Lyndon Wilde took a stool opposite and produced a sleek black folder with an embossed silver logo in the corner: *Elite Estates International*. 'Oh, it's a pleasure. There's a great deal of interest from high-end rental companies, but I always feel better about private sales.'

Leary smiled. 'Where the house will be looked after like a home, rather than simply added to an existing range of assets?'

'That's always my preferred conclusion, yes.'

Leary slipped off the stool and walked to the centre-piece window that looked out on the undulating greenery of the Dovestone Valley. She bent forward slightly as she looked out. 'It's just picture-perfect here. Grade II listed, yes?'

'That's right.' Wilde's eyes drifted down her body. She

wore fitted high-waisted, wide-leg trousers, and her posture accentuated the sweep of her lower back into the curve of her lean backside.

Wilde's breathing quickened as she stood perfectly still for a moment, captivated by the view.

Leary sighed. 'If I do take this place, I'll set up my studio on the top floor. But the views are so extraordinary I'll need to keep the blinds shut to get any work done.'

She turned.

Wilde shifted focus to his folder. 'What sort of fashion do you design?'

Leary walked to the kitchen island. She tugged at her tailored blouse. 'I'm a walking advertisement for it, I suppose. Traditional and modern blend. Our focus is on sustainability. Eco-friendly materials. Ethical labour practices.'

She sat opposite. Wilde caught a hint of her perfume: floral but with a complex musky undertone. She jangled a set of intricate bracelets around her wrist.

'These are ours. I want to get into more jewellery, but I'd rather buy up one of the smaller online businesses that already understand the market. My favourite work is bespoke commissions for select clients. One-of-a-kind pieces for special occasions. Elton's company provides the e-commerce.'

The bathroom toilet flushed and a pale-skinned man with a mane of frizzy ginger hair stepped into the kitchen. He wore a short-sleeved cotton shirt with geometric, tribal patterns; the loose fit flattered his blocky frame. 'Prague is on,' he announced, sipping from a water bottle.

Leary angled her head. 'Are you reading emails in the toilet?'

'Everyone does. Leaving tomorrow morning. Just three days. Tech incubator event.'

Leary leaned in towards Wilde and mock-whispered. 'He wants to steal some ideas before they get patented.'

Elton Leary hitched up on a stool beside his wife and took off his glasses. 'Talent borrows. Genius steals.' He looked at Wilde, then his wife, then back again. 'So, are you buying the farm? Not metaphorically.'

Wilde's phone buzzed with a message. He turned it over. 'I have to say I'm detecting some interest.'

Elton grinned. 'Our place near Chatsworth suits me fine, but Uma's like a little girl hankering for a private playhouse. And our interior design tastes don't really converge. I'm minimalist. She's oldy-worldy.'

'It's called *rustic*,' said Uma, retying her long blonde hair into a side-hanging ponytail. 'Period features. A bit of soul. And this is hardly a playhouse.'

'You'd need staff,' said Elton.

Wilde nodded. 'I know some fine agencies. For a place like this, you could keep it simple. Take a housekeeper. Maybe someone to maintain the grounds. Perhaps even a gardener to make the colours pop.'

Uma gaped at Elton. 'Imagine the children leaping through the flowerbeds.'

Elton smiled at Wilde. 'We don't have any.'

'Yet,' said Uma. She smiled at Wilde. 'We don't have permanent staff at our home. Just housekeeping at weekends. And a caterer on call when we have guests.'

Elton looked around the room. 'Do you mind if Uma and I take a walk around alone, Mr Wilde? Just a few moments.'

'Of course not. Music to my ears, actually, as I have some paperwork to complete.'

'We won't be too long,' said Uma, grabbing Elton's hand and leading him out into the hall.

Wilde looked at his phone. Message from Rebecca.

First session tomorrow. I could only get an early appointment. Sorry. She's in demand because she's good. She can help us. Talk later? x

He replied with a thumbs-up emoji and opened the document folder. He dug out his appointment register and noted the Learys' current address, then located the property in Google Maps.

The image associated with the entry showed a robust wrought-iron gate flanked by stone pillars capped with ornamental finials. Behind the gate, a handsome red-brick Georgian-style house with a columned portico sat in generous grounds, surrounded by a high stone wall.

Wilde scrolled around the image. The Leary residence was deep into remote rural land a couple of miles south of the Chatsworth estate.

An unsolicited visit from their estate agent would be irregular, but not suspicious.

He just had to get the timing right.

Chapter Thirty-Two

SAWYER FELL BACK onto the bed, arms stretched, and lay there for a moment, gazing up at the ceiling. The room smelt stale and dry, and he'd opened the window to freshen it up. Birdsong drifted in, briefly muted by the chug of a passing tractor along the Kinder Scout road.

Shepherd called through from the sitting room. *'Your brother says he can get the van tomorrow. To pick up your nightmare sculpture... thing.'*

'Wooden man training dummy.'

'That's the one.' Shepherd stepped into the room and stood at the foot of the bed. 'I'll unpack the shopping while you have a lie down, if that's okay with you.'

Sawyer sprang up. 'We need to let the cat out of the bag.' He headed into the sitting room. Shepherd followed and watched as he crouched by the cat carrier and unhooked the door clasp. A muscular black-and-white cat stepped out, cautious. It sniffed the floor, then ambled over to the corner of the kitchen, where Sawyer usually kept the food bowls. It sniffed the floor again, then turned to face the two men as it settled into a compact sitting position with its tail tucked around the base of its body.

'Bruce wants you to feed him,' said Sawyer.

Shepherd scoffed. 'Theo said he gave him something a few hours ago.'

'That was then,' said Sawyer, rummaging through the shopping bags squashed together on the coffee table. 'This is now.'

'Is this a Buddhism thing?' said Shepherd, pulling out a box of food pouches. 'Y'know. All we have is this moment.'

Sawyer sprawled on the couch. 'That's not just a Buddhism thing. That's a true thing. Top left cupboard.'

Shepherd took out a saucer and squeezed one of the pouches into it, wincing at the smell. 'This reminds me of my old dentist's breath. Weird that, isn't it? Dentists always have bad breath.'

Sawyer got up and walked round to the back of the sofa. Shepherd set down the food and Bruce dived in.

They stood there in silence, in the centre of the low-beamed, L-shaped room, watching and listening to the wet chomping.

'Thanks for picking me up,' said Sawyer.

Shepherd nodded. 'I need to get back.'

'Has Farrell installed a punch clock?'

'Like I said, he's oddly hands-off. He saves the annoying stuff for meetings.' He scrubbed at his beard. 'So, what now?'

'I usually put down a few biscuits for the day, then feed him again before bedtime.'

Shepherd eyed him. 'I mean with you.'

'Occupational health overseeing the return-to-work programme. Part-time to start with. Status and rank retained, but they're putting me on a crime-management unit on some estate out of town.'

'Buxton?'

Sawyer grimaced. 'More or less. It's mainly desk work. Taking and reviewing reports, advising on what gets further investigation.'

'Admin,' said Shepherd.

'Back office. Low stress. Regular and predictable environment. I get a manager who assesses me on a weekly basis to decide if it's working for me. Fifty per cent hours to start with. Building to seventy-five for good behaviour.'

'Do you get a parking space?'

'I do, actually. Not the kind of place to leave a car overnight, though. On that note, where is it?'

'I took the Mini to the White Hart garage at Bradwell for a tune-up. Your brother sorted the MOT and insurance. I mean, I don't know what you'd do without me.'

Sawyer smiled. 'Thank you.'

'So, what about the hospital business?'

'NCA want a word.'

'About beating the shit out of Wes Peyton?'

'Enough about me.'

Shepherd squinted at him. 'Are you deflecting?'

'Of course I am.'

'What about the Caldwell thing? I'm glad you decided to do that. It almost shows maturity.'

'I'm starting in a couple of days, with Bentley babysitting.'

'At least you'll get to see the old fucker on his last legs.'

Sawyer shook his head. 'I know what he wants.' His eyes drifted from Bruce to the blank floor. 'How's work?'

Shepherd paused. 'Never a dull moment. On top of this

Vulture business, we've got a young woman dead in her house just up the road from here.'

'Hayfield?'

'Yeah. Her sister discovered her first thing today. Strangled with the vacuum cleaner cord, it looks like. No forced entry. We're checking boyfriends, dates.'

Sawyer's eyes found Shepherd's. 'Tell me about this Vulture business. Has Farrell singlehandedly solved it yet?'

'I'm not at liberty to divulge anything.'

'Of course not.'

Shepherd indulged in an epic, shoulder-heaving sigh. 'We haven't got anything out of Gray. He's in a state. Victimology are focused on his daughter's abduction and murder. We found DNA on her body. Sally got it from a hair root. Fella called Brad Singleton. Ex-squaddie.'

'Was she sexually—'

'No. Strangled. Hands on. No prints.'

'Singleton history?'

Shepherd frowned. 'Just a minor drug charge. He left the army after getting injured in Iraq. Got into private security.' He turned toward Sawyer. 'He gave her insulin for her diabetes. Fed her well. She was in decent condition when we found her, dumped in a ditch on Sterndale Moor.'

'Have you brought him in?'

'He's been missing for over a week. Still no sign. Probably gone to ground somewhere. Car missing, too.'

Sawyer leaned on the back of the sofa. 'So, this guy with no history of paedophile tendencies... He just decided one day to abduct a young girl, keep her alive for a few weeks, then murder her and dump the body without even—'

'He knew her dad. We found out late yesterday. They did basic training together, but Gray didn't make the grade. Singleton did. Walker says it looks like they were close at one time. The feeling is that he visited his old army buddy, clocked his daughter—'

'Even though he has no history of paedophilic tendency?'

'Singleton's not that old. Maybe it's been in him for a while, and she sparked it up. There's no evidence he openly abused her, but he might have chickened out, kept hold of her, building up his nerve. But then lost it and got rid of her.'

Sawyer studied Shepherd. 'Truly a gruesome twosome. A necrophile with no history of necrophiliac tendency and a nascent paedophile who goes to a lot of trouble abducting a child and keeping her healthy over a long period, but then decides he'd rather murder her than abuse her. And this is all based on the evidence of a single hair.'

'We don't have anything else. Maggie is hoping to talk to Gray. See if he can shed some light on where Singleton might go.'

They watched Bruce again for a while, as he sat in the corner washing himself.

'I know she'd like to see you, sir,' said Shepherd.

Sawyer dropped his gaze to the kitchen floor again. 'If Singleton did abduct Phoebe Gray, he must have been keeping her somewhere comfortable. You need to find his car. Triangulate ANPR pings and cross-ref with properties he might have access to. As ex-military he'll be resourceful, so maybe include abandoned houses, empty places he could get into. Maybe even show homes.'

Shepherd's phone buzzed on the coffee table. He turned and walked around the sofa.

Sawyer took a couple of shopping bags and shifted them onto the kitchen surface. 'Why would he take care of her so well but then dump her out in the open like that, with such little respect for her dignity?' He took out a few items and started to fill the cupboards. 'It's almost as if he's angry with her. Or with her dad.'

'Fuck!'

Sawyer startled at the volume of Shepherd's shout. He turned to see him staring into his phone, guiding himself down onto the sofa.

'What?' said Sawyer.

Shepherd closed his eyes. 'Orlando Gray.'

Chapter Thirty-Three

DALE STRICKLAND CLOSED down his solitaire game and leaned back at his expansive glass desk, facing his blank dual monitors. He gazed at his murky reflection, defined by the hazy morning light from the window behind.

'Know yourself and know your enemy, and you will never be in peril.'

'Sun-Tzu?' said Abadi, perched on the edge of the silvery grey couch on the back wall.

Strickland peered around his monitor. 'Plenty of scholars think he didn't exist, you know. *The Art of War* is the work the likes of you will know him for, but the doubters say it might just be a mish-mash of other generals' ideas.'

Abadi looked up from his phone. 'I know his ideas. But I prefer Salah ad-Din Yusuf ibn Ayyub.'

'Saladin?' said Strickland.

'Yes. A Kurdish Muslim. First Sultan of Egypt. He recaptured Jerusalem from the Crusaders in 1187. And he definitely existed.'

Strickland smiled. 'And you're a devotee?'

Abadi wrinkled his nose. 'Not really. The Egyptian generals and *Mukhabarat* bosses had Saladin drummed into them. So they drummed him into us. He was big on respect for the opponent. A code of conduct. He also stressed adaptability, resilience.' Abadi's phone rang. 'But he was cautious. Knowing your enemy is fine, but you also have to know when to attack and when to hold back. He said victories are dangerous because they feel too good. They give you a desire for more. You can get blinded by your thirst for shedding blood. He said that "blood never sleeps"'. Abadi connected the call. 'Wesley.'

'How are we, chaps?' Peyton's voice came over the phone speaker.

'You'd be a lousy poker player, Wes,' said Strickland.

'Yeah? Why?'

'I can tell you're pleased about something down a phone line. I bet you're the type of card player who might as well be wearing mirrored glasses.'

Peyton took a breath. 'Gambling's a dickhead's game. I'm more into certainties. Knowledge.'

Strickland smirked at Abadi. 'Oh, right. And how's that working out?'

'Very well, as it happens. Who's there?'

'Just Farouk and me.'

Peyton sniffed. 'We're getting warmer with Fletcher. Stokes's crowd have put some more flesh on the bones. Also, more info from Eddie's sources. Do you want the story?'

Strickland grinned and settled himself in his chair. 'I'm sitting comfortably.'

'Okay. Fletcher has links to Middlesbrough—'

'Sadie's mother, Marla, is from there,' said Strickland.

Peyton sighed, paused again. 'Do you want to hear this?'

Strickland raised an eyebrow at Abadi. 'Sorry, Wes. Carry on.'

'So, yeah. Feds checked her out straight after Fletcher legged it from Buxton station. No joy. But we think he was knocking around there or thereabouts for a while. The Moors. Dales. Probably bothies and abandoned buildings. Stealing cars. Then, a few months ago, a fella matching Fletcher's description got the plates of a car done near to Sadie's place. The lad who did it knows one of Eddie's mates. That's why we paid her a visit... And, yeah. Didn't go well. But we go again, right?'

'Right,' said Strickland.

Peyton cleared his throat. 'So, now there's no sign of Fletcher or his daughter. But one of Stokes's bitches came through with a solid sighting of a couple matching Fletcher and daughter in a little village called Wetley Rocks.'

'Staffordshire Moorlands,' said Strickland.

'Yeah. Even better, they tailed them to an out-of-town rental in the middle of bastard nowhere.'

Abadi looked quizzical.

Strickland read his mind. 'Are they sure Fletcher didn't see he was being tailed?'

'He's not James fuckin' Bond,' said Peyton.

Strickland bristled. 'You underestimated him before, remember?'

'Yeah, and we learned from the mistake. I'm setting this up right this time. Going in meself. If you want a job doing properly... I could use some wheels and back-up, though.'

Abadi nodded and held up one finger.

'Farouk will help, plus one other. Is that enough? Can you manage?'

'Yes, Dale. I can fuckin' manage. No balls-ups this time. No outsourcing.'

Strickland swivelled his chair and got to his feet. He pushed his face close to the windowpane and looked across the Victorian rooftops to the Spinningfields financial district. The metal and glass high-rises glinted beneath hurrying clouds. 'And the Cannon thing?'

'All good,' said Peyton. 'Clean as a whistle. Stokes has got a face on, but he's had his fun.'

Strickland's nostrils flared and he drew in a deep breath. 'It might be safer to send him on his way, once we deal with Fletcher.'

Another pause at Peyton's end. 'It'd be a fuckin' kindness. Like putting an old dog out of its misery.'

'Remember Saladin,' said Abadi. 'We shouldn't overreach.'

'Who's Saladin?' said Peyton.

Strickland kept his eyes on the distant buildings. 'A little birdy tells me Jake Sawyer is back in circulation. One of my staff recently asked me why I stayed in this office, after what happened with Sawyer here.' He turned, walked to the door and drew down the blinds, then took a bottle of Glenfiddich and a weighty tumbler down from a shelf. 'Redcliffe. A strategist.' He poured out a splash of whisky. 'I fired him soon after.'

'Why?' said Abadi.

'Because it's the stupidest fucking question I've ever heard. I gave Sawyer a pass back then because it worked for me at the time.' Strickland downed the drink in one. 'We know what they say about revenge.'

Abadi shrugged. 'It's sweet?'

'Nah,' said Peyton. 'It's a dish best served cold, yeah?'

Strickland poured another measure, wincing as he downed it in one. 'Yes. But that's bullshit. Revenge is something you want to keep hot.' He punched his chest. 'Keep it burning in your heart. That way, when you dish it out, it goes down so much smoother. As fresh as the day it was spawned. I stayed in this office because every time I look out of this window, it's a little flash of memory. A helpful trauma. A fanning of the flames.'

Chapter Thirty-Four

FARRELL SLUMPED OVER HIS DESK, head bowed. He ground his palm in a circular motion around his forehead, then jabbed a finger towards the two chairs.

Shepherd and Walker sat down.

'Detective Inspector Shepherd,' said Farrell, his voice low and calm. 'Detective Sergeant Walker. Please explain to me how a man detained under Section 2 of the Mental Health Act, under strict medical supervision and police guard, managed to take his own... fucking... life.'

Shepherd eyed Walker. 'The scene was preserved immediately. Initial findings suggest that Gray sharpened a metal clip dropped from a medical file. As a porter at the hospital, he would be familiar with shift changeover procedures, and he exploited a brief unsupervised period in the early hours.'

'He used the clip on both his wrists, sir,' said Walker. 'Long and deep lateral cuts. Looks like he did it under the bed covers, which is why it wasn't immediately apparent. By the time he was discovered, it was too late.'

Farrell looked between the two, wide-eyed, as if hoping for absolution. 'And what happens now?'

'IOPC enquiry,' said Shepherd. 'Since he was technically in custody. There will also be a hospital internal review, but that'll be focused on their practices and protocols. Also, a coroner's inquest, probably involving a jury since the death occurred—'

'In custody, yes. Is anyone not involved in the aftermath of this? Any chance the fucking fire brigade might want their say?'

Shepherd and Walker stayed silent and solemn.

'And who's likely to get the blame? Us?'

'It could be seen as police inaction, sir,' said Walker.

Shepherd shook his head. 'The coroner is focused on how and where the deceased came about his death. It's not about blame.'

'Yes,' said Farrell, raising his voice, 'but the IOPC will be shining a bright light on an already overexposed case.' He tapped his pen on the desk and stared into space. 'In one sense, you could see it as a good thing.'

'I'm not sure Gray's parents will feel that way,' said Walker.

'He's already a body-snatcher in the public's eyes,' said Farrell. 'Nobody outside his family is going to mourn him.' He shrugged. 'Gets him off the books. Saves the crown a bit of money in pursuing the case.' He pointed his pen. 'Did anybody get to speak with Gray before he did the deed? Maggie Spark? Anyone in the hospital psych team?'

'Sadly not,' said Shepherd. 'He just wasn't in a fit state at first. He seemed to settle a couple of nights ago, and Maggie was on stand-by. And then, this. She's overseeing family liaison.'

Farrell sighed and ran a hand through his oily hair. 'It's just…'

'Tragic?' said Walker.

'Embarrassing. Where are we with his daughter's murder?'

'Singleton and Gray met at the Army Foundation College in Harrogate in the late 1990s,' said Walker. 'Singleton excelled and moved on to the Defence School of Transport in Leconfield. Specialised training in land-based transport. I spoke to one of the training officers at the AFC, and he said the two seemed to be friends but not what he would describe as inseparable.'

Farrell sat back in his chair. He crossed his legs and twirled his pen around in the air as he spoke. 'Singleton gets injured. He's discharged, has the thing he really loves taken away. He goes a bit doolally. All that isolation. Watches a lot of porn. The normal stuff stops working and he has to go under the counter. Then the dark side. Barely legal. Then kids. He visits his old training college mate, sees his pretty blonde daughter. Then, because of all the coverage after Gray's arrest, he panics, kills her and legs it.'

Walker frowned. 'There's no evidence that Singleton visited—'

Farrell ignored him. 'Did we eliminate those hair and skin cells on the mortuary victims' bodies?'

'Sally matched them up to hospital workers,' said Shepherd. 'Apart from two profiles, which are probably cross-contamination from individuals not in NDNA. We have them on record, though.'

Farrell gave a snidey little laugh. 'For when you bring me an alternative suspect. Otherwise known as hell freezing over.'

'No note,' said Walker.

Shepherd looked at him. 'Suicide note?'

He nodded. 'To not even feel the urge to say goodbye or justify his actions... He must have been in absolute despair. Over what was happening to him, and then his daughter—'

'This is all irrelevant,' said Farrell, pitching himself forward onto the desk again. 'We laser-focus on Brad Singleton as the chief suspect in the murder of Phoebe Gray. Orlando Gray is dead and gone. Old news, along with all this Vulture rubbish. We need to tickle the likely press narrative.'

'Which is?' said Shepherd.

Farrell tilted his head from side to side. 'An undiagnosed mental health issue. Trauma, grief. The enquiries into his death are just background detail. I want everything we've got on finding Singleton.'

'We can't commit everything to that enquiry,' said Shepherd. 'We have another major crime. The murder up in Hayfield.'

Farrell made a face. 'The woman? Get Myers and one of the other DCs on that. Not in Phoebe Gray's league. We need to make up ground for the mess her dad has caused.'

'What if Singleton is responsible for both killings?' said Walker. 'Same method.'

Farrell sighed and smiled. He looked up to Shepherd for support, but Shepherd kept his eyes on Walker. 'Oh, yes. They're exactly the same. A nine-year-old girl and a thirty-four-year-old woman. One is the daughter of a man associated with our key suspect. The other, erm, isn't. One strangled by hand, the other with a cord. One sexually abused, the other one untouched... Like I say, get Myers on the woman's murder.'

'Her name was Hannah Lewis,' said Shepherd.

Farrell rolled with the slight. 'Get Myers on *Hannah Lewis's* murder, and, DS Walker, lend that high-powered deductive mind to DI Shepherd and find me a straightforward fugitive, if you'd be so kind.'

Chapter Thirty-Five

SAWYER CAUGHT an early morning cab to Bradfield and picked up the Mini. He drove out of the village and into the Hope Valley, wallowing in the abundant mosaic outside his open window: primary wildflowers bobbing behind yellow gorse bushes; ragged crags streaked with violet heather; the dew-soaked hedgerows shifting from emerald to lime green as the sun seeped through the morning mist.

The woozy sights demanded the right soundtrack, and he cued up Eno's *Apollo: Atmospheres and Soundtracks* album: one of his meditation standards in the unit. As he swung the car into the long, straight Rushup Edge road, the 'mother hill' of Mam Tor loomed on his left, and he squeezed the accelerator, smiling as the sighing synths of 'An Ending (Ascent)' complimented the familiar but unknowable landscape.

He parked up and climbed the rough flagstone path to the trig point at the Mam Tor summit. As ever, the spot was busy with early hikers and lingering insomniacs. His father had once hauled Sawyer and his brother up here in the half-light of a perishing winter predawn to gaze down on an otherworldly cloud inversion. Today, it was plain old morning mist that obscured the views across the Vale of Edale.

Sawyer was standing on rock that was over three hundred million years old, with the southeast face of the hill in a slow-motion landslide which had begun four thousand years ago. He headed back to the car, along the paved summit path, squinting through the haze. At the Great Ridge gate, he stopped and looked across the Hope Valley. The mist had thinned, and he could just make out the high moors of the Kinder plateau.

After so long in hiding, he had wanted to confirm what was out here; the eternal extent of it all. Did he still have a place in the picture?

THE CRIME MANAGEMENT Unit was shut away in a quiet corner of a liminal industrial estate on the edge of Buxton. It was a two-storey red-brick building with a flat roof and a blue-and-white *Derbyshire Constabulary* crest beside the reinforced steel door.

Sawyer punched in the keypad code and entered the small reception hall, overseen by a bullet-proof glass window with a pass-through slot and sign-in desk. A few cheap-looking fixed chairs lined the wall for visitors.

'Greetings!'

Sawyer finished signing in and turned to the slight man in a short-sleeved white shirt with a laurel wreath insignia on the shirt's epaulettes. He gave Sawyer a pat on the shoulder and reached down to take his hand, shaking vigorously.

'DCI Barry Creedon. Excited to have you here, DI Sawyer.'

'Happy to help, sir. "Excited" might be pushing it, though.'

Creedon studied Sawyer for a moment, clinging to his smile. His heavily lined face relaxed, and he forced a laugh, moving in for another shoulder pat. 'Of course. Step this way.'

He turned and led Sawyer across a thin grey carpet through a musty-smelling open-plan office. Basic modular desks lined up in rows, most unoccupied. A few eyes flicked from their screens to clock Sawyer as he passed. The windows were half-obscured by blinds, and the overhead strip lighting rendered the staff sallow and cheerless. It had the vibe of a temporary measure that had been hastily expanded; an incident room that had rumbled on long past the resolution of its inciting case.

'Here's where you'll live,' said Creedon. He ushered Sawyer into a tiny office with slim partition walls that wobbled as he opened the door. A slightly larger version of the modular desk sat at the far end, beside a basic filing cabinet. A corkboard clung to the facing wall at a slight angle.

'Compact,' said Sawyer, looking round.

Creedon smiled in sympathy. 'We were using this as an interview room, but it's not… really suitable. There's a properly soundproofed interview room on the top floor, where I take my office. We might sometimes have to throw you out if there's a need for a private meeting, but that'll be rare. There's a coffee machine at the end of the main floor, near a break room with table and chairs, kitchenette, microwave…' He trailed off.

Sawyer nodded to the desktop PC. 'Can I access HOLMES?'

'Ah. Not at the moment. The HOLMES system is installed on the computers, but your DSI Robin Farrell has advised me that you won't be assigned to any major cases during this transitional period. Although of course you do retain your rank. I'll get the IT chap to set you up properly later this morning. All the work is assigned through a local content-management system, and he'll show you the ropes. Any questions, just speak to one of the DIs or DCs on the main floor.'

Sawyer walked round the desk and tried out his wheeled seat. The chair had hard-edged, unpadded arms, and felt frail and unsteady.

Creedon hovered in the door frame. 'I'm aware of your history and your abilities, DI Sawyer, and I do understand that this posting may seem rather beneath your pay grade. But try to see it as an important part of getting you fit to return at a more appropriate level. How you tackle the tasks here will determine how fast that happens.'

He flashed a smile and exited.

Sawyer nudged the computer mouse, and the screen showed a custom VPN log-in. He checked an email on his phone, entered the details into the VPN, and navigated to the computer home screen, which featured a beach scene background image and various applications lined up on the desktop.

His user profile on the system's CMS was already loaded with casework. He worked through the welcome emails and, carefully, reclined the chair.

He swiped at his phone screen and navigated to the VLC video app, where he'd saved an offline version of Orlando Gray's video.

Sawyer lowered the volume to its minimum level and set the video playing. He propped the phone at the base of the computer monitor and shifted the mouse around as he watched. Creedon would have one of the DIs in the office outside compiling a report on Sawyer's daily activity, and it would just look as if he was getting on with settling in.

'I'm going to be arrested,' said Gray. *'Something vile. I... did some wrong things. But this isn't me, okay?'*

Sawyer glanced up. A seated female detective shifted her eyes from him just too late. She focused on her computer screen and moved the mouse around, but her gaze remained at a fixed point.

'My girl...' said Gray, sobbing.

Sawyer pinch-zoomed to get a close-up of his face.

'This isn't my choice. I didn't have one.'

He glanced up from his phone to the main screen and caught the female detective's eye again. This time, she gave a brief smile and returned to the screen. She was good. Probably realised Sawyer had noticed her attention and wanted to catch him again, as if the first time had been perfectly natural.

'I did everything right... I just made a mistake, okay?... I wasn't careful enough...'

Sawyer studied Gray.

Regular blinking. His camera eye contact was steady and unwavering.

'I've been in a dark place, okay?' he said. *'A private hell. But the truth will come out soon. There's light ahead.'*

Chapter Thirty-Six

LATER THAT EVENING, Sawyer sat in the half-lotus position at the foot of the bed, wearing joggers and T-shirt. The elongated chimes and arpeggios of Eno's *Reflection* played on his bedside speaker, beside a burning citrus candle.

His iPad sat propped open on the bed, playing a guided meditation from the actor Michael Imperioli, who sat on the floor in front of his sofa.

'May all beings have happiness and the causes of happiness,' said Imperioli in a quiet, steady voice.

Sawyer closed his eyes and bowed his head, hands resting in front, fingertips touching.

Imperioli continued. *'May all beings be free from suffering and the causes of suffering.'*

There was a light knock at the front door.

Sawyer opened his eyes and checked his watch. Just gone 9pm.

'May all beings not be separated from the happiness that has never known suffering.'

Sawyer paused the video and got to his feet. He took a deep breath, slowly bringing himself out of the meditation mindset, then pushed his feet into his canvas training slippers.

The knock came again.

He peered around the edge of the closed sitting-room blind, then stepped back, taking a moment to think.

He opened the door.

Leon Stokes held up a hand. 'I come in peace.'

The suited man behind Stokes was built like a linebacker, but with a wary look in his eye.

Stokes threw a thumb over his shoulder. 'This is Wayne.'

Sawyer stared Stokes out.

'Wayne Torrence. He works for me. He's solid, seriously. Look. It's late. I get it. I had to be a hundred per cent sure nobody saw me come here. We stuck the car down a side road.'

Sawyer still hadn't spoken.

'I... hope I'm not interrupting anything.'

'The four immeasurables,' said Sawyer.

Stokes eyed Torrence. 'Eh?'

Sawyer stood aside and Stokes and Torrence stepped in. 'Love. Compassion. Joy. Equanimity.'

'Buddhism,' said Stokes, closing the door.

Sawyer nodded and gestured to the sofa. He walked into the kitchen and opened the fridge door. 'Will this take long? Can I get you a drink? I've got Diet Coke.'

Stokes winced. 'You don't drink that shit, do you?'

'That's not the standard response to an offer of hospitality.'

Stokes took a seat. 'Sorry, it's just... Phosphoric acid leeches minerals out of your bones. And the sweetener seriously fucks with your microbiome.'

Sawyer hesitated, took a bottle of water from the fridge, then swung the door shut. He headed back to the sitting room and flopped down in the armchair. 'Are you down with this, Wayne? Does he give you nutrition lectures before you collect the dead drops?'

'What's "equanimity"?' said Torrence.

'Composure,' said Stokes. 'Calmness.' He kept his eyes on Sawyer.

Sawyer took in Stokes's freshly shaven head and slim-fit T-shirt that strained against his muscled upper body. 'Been on the weights, Leon? Is that why you didn't bring your baseball bat?'

Stokes leaned forward, propping his elbows on his knees. 'Like I said, I come in peace. Our last meeting was pretty fraught, so… Do you remember Boyd Cannon? The lad with the laptop? The one who played the audio of Strickland pretty much ordering the attack on Buxton station. And saying how much he wants you "off the board".'

Sawyer nodded. 'A lot has happened since then.'

'Indeed. Including a visit I received from Strickland and his new pet, Wes Peyton. Strickland has put it all together and he took the laptop. Peyton shot Cannon for good measure.'

'Dead?'

'Yes. Peyton has always been trouble, but he's been careful not to overstep. But now he's got Strickland's hand up his arse, and he's down one eye.'

Sawyer sipped his water. 'How does Eddie Peyton fit into this?'

'Like petrol on a bin fire. Peyton Jr is rogue. He's after Austin Fletcher, who killed one of the crew at the station. It'll give him major credit.'

'Strickland will want Fletcher gone, too.'

'Totally.'

'Does he know where he is?'

Sawyer caught a slight glance from Stokes to Torrence. 'He tapped us up for a few leads, but he's a slippery fucker.'

Sawyer thought for a moment. 'Strickland isn't an idiot. He'll assume there's a back-up audio from the laptop.'

Stokes gave a grim smile. 'Of course. But he might be arrogant enough to assume that I'm enough of an idiot to think the laptop audio business is concluded, and it's all about Fletcher. And you.'

'You think he'll come for you, too?'

Stokes nodded. 'Dead right. I'm a tricky one, because Strickland knows he'll need the nod from Eddie if he wants to keep control of the crews. But he's hell-bent on Peyton taking out you and Fletcher.'

'When is Eddie out?'

'Within the year, looks like.'

'And has he green-lit his little brother's revenge rampage?'

Stokes took a big breath in through his nose, pushed it out. 'No. Eddie is sharp. He's too close to release to risk an association with a direct attack on a senior detective.'

'Can't you leak it to him?'

'It's too risky. Too much detail. It'll be obvious it came from me.'

Sawyer frowned and dug a hand through his hair. 'Dale is a master at staying just outside the blast zone. He's using Wes Peyton to clean up the mess, letting him think he's the anointed one. But we both know that means he'll need to clean away Peyton, too. He's too volatile for Dale to work with long term.'

'So, what's his ultimate goal?'

'Given his influence, he can probably guarantee to Eddie Peyton that he'll pass his parole hearing.'

Stokes shook his head. 'And then Strickland and Peyton Sr rule the roost.'

'It's how I'd do it,' said Sawyer. 'That leaves him with a clean playing field. A perfect balance of legitimate political power, which is useful for status, but I doubt he enjoys it, and plenty of skin in the crime game, which is lucrative and he does enjoy.'

'Makes sense. He can't fucking stand the mayor work. He had a fine old rant about it at my place.' Stokes watched as Sawyer drained his glass of water. 'So, what now?'

'I need that copy of the Dale audio,' said Sawyer. 'The one where he ordered you to kill me.' He stood up. 'And... No hard feelings. But I also need you both out of my house. Busy day tomorrow. Early night.'

Chapter Thirty-Seven

DCI DARRYL BENTLEY eased his black BMW X3 off the narrow approach road and slid into a space in the main car park of Bathpool Country Park. It was early, and the car park was empty apart from an unmarked Ford Transit van in the far corner.

Bentley switched off the engine and pointed to the van. 'Secure transport. Discreet on the outside but tooled up inside with steel cage, compartments, video. Caldwell also travels with a clinician from the prison hospital. Looks like a makeshift fucking ambulance in there.' He winced. 'State of him, though. He couldn't escape if they opened the doors and gave him a two-week start.'

Sawyer lowered his head and looked through the fully fruited ash trees at the edge of the car park. He studied the small group milling around off the central path. 'So, who's who? How does this work?'

'Just essential staff to avoid attention. The park authorities are aware. There's a plain-clothes DS from Nottinghamshire, couple of uniforms for scene control and security, two prisoner transport officers. Two CSIs with kit bags and more on call if needed. Coroner on stand-by. Once he gives us a nod for the general area, they'll cordon it off and the detectives will assess for the best excavation plan, assisted by the CSIs.'

'He was moved from Wakefield recently, yes?'

'To Nottingham. Late last year. Back when his symptoms became unmanageable as part of the everyday routine. Wakefield is Cat A, and a more hardcore set-up. Given his age and low flight risk, Cat B Nottingham made more sense. Better medical facilities, too.' He took a folder from the glovebox, opened it. 'According to his statement, Deborah Wade was the first woman he murdered. He says he picked her up at a kerb-crawling spot down in Kidsgrove and brought her to this park. It's a decent size. About a hundred and eighty acres. Back in 1986 it was more rough and ready, but these days they have colour-coded walking and cycling trails. There's a lake in the middle. Fishing and picnic spots. Even a ski slope on the western edge. Caldwell says he took Deborah into the woods, where they had sex. He killed her, then buried the body in a shallow grave he'd prepared earlier and concealed.'

Sawyer caught sight of an emaciated figure standing near two larger men who were probably the prison officers. 'Was that the case for the other murders?'

Bentley took a breath. 'So he says. He hasn't given much detail on the Sharon Wright killing at Bolehill Wood, because her body was found at the time. But we think he was interrupted, as you said, and so dumped the body in the clearing.'

'This is when he was a DCI at Buxton?'

'Stoke. He was a DI at this time. Transferred to Buxton later that year as DCI.' Bentley checked his notes. 'Ranks were different back then. His next bump would have been DSU, Detective Superintendent. They didn't have DSI. He stayed at DCI in Buxton for ten years until his… disappearance in 1997.'

Sawyer watched as the figure bowed his head, hands behind his back. 'Is he cuffed?'

'No point. You'll see why.'

Sawyer opened his door. 'The first four women were serving his need. He changed his MO for my mother.'

Bentley nodded. 'No prepared grave.'

'That one was personal. The years might have withered him, but he's still a narcissistic sexual sadist at heart. Whatever he's negotiated, he should be cuffed on principle.'

'Is that a problem for you?'

'No. Let's get this done.'

THEY WALKED TOWARDS THE GROUP. The sky was electric blue and cloudless, and both men shielded their eyes from the sunlight as it strobed through the ash trees.

'If this goes smoothly,' said Bentley, 'Caldwell has promised to identify the location of Julie Saltwell's body by the end of the week.'

Sawyer glanced at him. 'It'll be smooth. I've thought it through. I don't think he's interested in stringing us along.'

'Really?'

'He'll enjoy the power while it lasts, but that's not the sole reason he wants me here.'

'DCI Bentley.' A man in his mid-thirties stepped away from the group to greet them. He was tall and trim, slightly overdressed in a tailor-fit charcoal suit with white shirt and striped tie.

'DI Sawyer,' said Bentley. 'This is DS Kwame Boateng. Nottinghamshire CID.'

Boateng treated Bentley to a fulsome handshake but hesitated as he turned to Sawyer.

Sawyer held out his hand. 'Jake Sawyer.'

Boateng shook. 'DI, yes?'

'Nominally.'

Boateng shot a nervous glance at Bentley. 'Of course. Our hierarchy hardly matters here. Not a pleasant task. I assume DCI Bentley has—'

Jake.

The emaciated figure hobbled out of the shade, flanked by two men with HM Prison Service pin badges on their lapels.

He stopped a few feet from Sawyer and looked him slowly up and down, then grinned, exposing a set of chipped yellow teeth. 'So glad you could make it.'

William Caldwell was literally half the man Sawyer had last seen in his father's makeshift prison basement. He was cadaverous, impossibly gaunt, with hollowed and skeletal eye sockets. His jaundiced skin stretched taut over the protruding bones of his jaw and cheeks, with only a faint padding of flesh. His hair was ashen and patchy, and his heavy eyebrows had receded to wisps of white. The familiar bushy moustache was an uneven scrub above thin, cracked lips.

The prison officers moved forward, between Sawyer and Caldwell. The elder of the two rested a hand on Caldwell's shoulder, and as he stepped back a pace, the movement dislodged the hang of his jacket, accentuating the unnatural looseness of the fit.

Caldwell rubbed at his eyes with spindly fingers. 'Don't worry. I won't get close. I doubt my breath is too sweet. The chemotherapy has made me pretty sick, and I stopped bothering with dental hygiene.' He shrugged his bony shoulders. 'I suspect my French kissing days are long behind me.'

He stood there for a moment, eyes fixed on Sawyer. His breathing was shallow and laboured, with a slight background rattle.

'How are you, Bill?' said Sawyer. 'Keeping well?'

Caldwell grimaced. 'The morphine keeps the pain down. Thirty milligrams morning and evening. Liquid in between if I need it. And I always do. They tell me I'm developing ascites. That's when cancer cells irritate the lining of the stomach, causing it to make too much fluid.' He paused, gathered his breath. 'Lymph nodes in the stomach become blocked and the fluid can't drain properly. It's pretty much the body announcing the arrival of that bastard with the scythe. We're down to weeks, not months, now.' He coughed and spat phlegm onto the grass. 'Thanks for asking.'

Sawyer surveyed the audience of grim-faced officials. All eyes were on him. Only Bentley watched Caldwell, with a look of appalled fascination.

He took a step forward. 'Where did you bury Deborah Wade, Bill?'

Caldwell nodded. 'Follow me.' He turned and shuffled along a slim, overgrown trail that led away from the main path. The two officers stayed at his side. Caldwell stopped and looked around at the group. 'Just him.' He pointed at Sawyer. 'Anyone else and we're not doing this.'

Boateng stepped forward but Bentley raised a hand, blocking him.

'We can't just let this man wander off into the woods like this,' said the older prison officer.

'Yes,' said Bentley. 'We can. I'll be shadowing them, keeping them in sight at all times.'

Caldwell sighed and glared at Bentley.

'Come on, Bill. You know the score.'

Caldwell turned and walked on. 'Keep your fucking distance, though.'

SAWYER FOLLOWED CALDWELL SILENTLY along the trail, crowded by the tall, straight trunks of the ash trees. The canopy was dense, almost completely blocking out the sun. They passed through a clearing with wooden picnic tables, and Caldwell paused beside a tree.

He lowered his head and placed a hand on the trunk. 'I can't take ten fucking steps now without stopping to get some oxygen into my wretched lungs.'

Sawyer sat down on a nearby bench. He took a look behind and spotted Bentley lurking with the two prison officers a few hundred paces back.

'I was reading about that case,' said Caldwell, rising to his feet. 'The Vulture.' He cackled, then coughed again. 'Fucking hell. I'd love to have got my teeth into that one, back in the day. Hardly got any left now, though.' He turned to face Sawyer. 'Necrophilia. Honestly, Jake. Some people are just sick.'

Sawyer remained impassive. 'Where did you bury Deborah Wade, Bill?'

Caldwell held up a hand. He spread his fingers, gnarled like pipe cleaners. 'I've started to smell like death. It's like it's seeping over me. You know the smell. It's like nothing on Earth. Just a slight whiff seems to stick to your nostrils for days. It kicks in during the early stages of putrefaction. The body produces a compound called ethyl mercaptan. They add it to gas to make leaks detectable by scent.' He leaned his back against the tree and lowered himself slowly to the ground. 'In California in the 1930s, workers noticed vultures circling the thermal drafts around pipeline leaks. So, they tested the gas to see what might have attracted these creatures who are famously lured by the odour of decay.' He paused, caught his breath. 'They found tiny trace elements of ethyl mercaptan in this gas they were pumping out to customers. So, they added more of it. That way, humans could smell it, too. So, these birds that were seen as portents of doom... They actually helped us save lives.'

Caldwell lowered his head, regaining his breath.

Sawyer waited, watching the monster who had visited such a savage death on his gentle and loving mother, now so wrecked and rotted. 'Why the hammer?'

Caldwell sighed. He pondered the answer for a long time. 'The judgement. I couldn't stand them looking at me, judging me.'

Sawyer got up from the bench. 'You've had your time. But you can still try something new, even this late in the day. You've taken so much from so many. It's time to *give*.'

Caldwell raised his barren eyes, staring straight ahead. 'Deborah... I remember thinking she was too pretty to be a prostitute. More like a model. Long, straight black hair. What was she? Twenty?'

'Nineteen,' said Sawyer.

He shrugged. 'We had a bit of fun in the car park. She didn't want to come out here, but I offered to pay double. I'd already dug the hole, filled it with leaves and branches. Covered it up. I got what I wanted. She asked for her money, but I gave her a backhander. Bashed her head into the tree.' He shook his head. 'Knocked her clean out. Then I got to work.' Caldwell's eyes found Sawyer's. 'Hell of a way to wake up, eh? Having your face bashed in with a hammer.'

Sawyer walked over to him, crouched, within touching distance. 'Where did you bury her, Bill?'

He pointed. 'Just through there, in those trees. They were saplings back then. Like you, eh? *Little Jake.* That's what Jess used to call you.' Caldwell's eyes clouded over, but he kept his gaze locked on Sawyer. 'I fucked up, didn't I? If I'd done the job properly, we wouldn't be here right now. You wouldn't be here. I ended your mother. I should have ended you.'

Sawyer stared back, unblinking. 'Nothing really ends, though, does it? Things just take on different forms. Endings spark new beginnings. The ripples fan out, fade away. But they inspire fresh ripples. And so it goes on.'

Sawyer turned, and beckoned Bentley and the others. He stood upright.

Caldwell did likewise, with difficulty, using the tree trunk to steady himself. He faced Sawyer, panting. His arid lips cracked a tiny smile. 'I'm sure you've heard all the clichés. Dying gives you urgency. Clarity. You see the things you take for granted in a different light.' He tapped his forehead. 'You think you know so much, don't you? *Little Jake.* You think you've seen the full picture. You think you're *enlightened.*' He leaned forward, his putrid breath contaminating Sawyer's nostrils. 'But you're still in the dark.'

Chapter Thirty-Eight

MARCH 2004

HAROLD SAWYER CROSSED the dirt track and walked to the top of the ridge. He dug his hands deep into the pockets of his canvas jacket and gazed down into the valley. The Langsett Reservoir shimmered under the moonlit sky.

A long, tall shadow fell across his back, then slipped over the edge as its owner exited the house and crunched across the track.

'You're going to ask me how much,' said Harold.

His companion stood by his side. 'The car? I would never be so gauche.'

Harold turned to the young man with scruffy black hair that curled at his jawline. '*Gauche*. That's a university word, Jake.'

'Most of my other language stayed true to my roots.'

Harold laughed. 'What do you think of the house?'

Jake looked down at the water, and the moonlight flashed in his green eyes. 'Bit out of the way.'

'Oh, well spotted. It's an old mining cottage. Eighteenth century.'

'Old.'

Harold raised a finger. 'Vintage. And you say, "out of the way," but I say peaceful.'

Jake nodded. 'You told me it was your "project".'

'Did I?'

Jake unwrapped a yellow boiled sweet and slipped it into his mouth. 'Yeah. Ages ago. I remember. You said it would be somewhere to relax. But I bet there's a lot of work to do on the outbuildings. Or you could just use them to store junk or have prayer meetings. Or whatever.'

Harold reached out a hand. Jake pushed the sweet wrapper into his palm, and he scrunched it up then stuffed it into his jacket pocket. 'You'll spoil your dinner.'

'No, I won't. What are we having?'

'Spaghetti.'

Jake smiled, rolled the sweet round his mouth. 'That's all we ate for, like, five years. After Mum died.'

'That's not true. We also had your omelettes. Michael's strange risotto thing.'

Jake winced. 'I can still taste that.'

'I've honed the spag bol over the years.' He leaned in, whispered. 'I use a secret ingredient.'

'Heroin?'

'Honey. The sauce is rich, so I lighten it with sherry vinegar, smoked paprika, couple of drops of hot sauce. But the honey in the sauce keeps it just on the right side of sweet.'

Jake nodded. 'Have you been painting?'

'Yes. Made a start on the studio. I'll show you.'

Jake stepped forward and sat on a large flat stone at the

edge of the dirt track. He reached into his pocket and pulled out a neatly rolled cigarette.

Harold sat beside him. 'Oh, don't tell me you've started smoking.'

'Dad, I've just spent three years at university. It's practically compulsory. And this isn't a cigarette.'

He took out a disposable lighter and lit the spliff.

Harold watched with a mixture of disbelief and curiosity as Jake took a puff and offered it to him.

'Jake, I haven't smoked marijuana since—'

Jake laughed, coughing out smoke. '*Marijuana.*'

'What do you call it, then?'

'Weed.'

Harold took a drag. He inhaled, waited a few seconds, then released the smoke into the crisp evening air.

He turned to his son. 'That's really good.'

Jake laughed again. 'How would you know?'

'Hey. You don't know what I know.' He took another toke and passed the spliff back to Jake.

'Are you sure this isn't against your religion?' said Jake.

Harold shrugged. 'It's God's bounty, I suppose. It'd be like outlawing broccoli or something.'

'Now, there's a creed I could get behind.'

They sat smoking for a while, listening to the water lapping against the shore.

Jake leaned forward. 'Are they frogs?'

Harold listened to the distant chorus of croaking. 'Yes. Breeding season. I come out here a lot, enjoy the nature. There are some lovely walks down in the valley.'

'Show me tomorrow.' Jake tapped off some ash. 'How's Michael doing?'

Harold's shoulders rose and fell. 'He's... Michael. Doesn't

seem to have many friends. But he's found a bit of work in the Yondermann Café at weekends. The Bull at Foolow on week nights. He looks after the old house surprisingly well. Although I do get the impression he's recently tidied up when I arrive.'

Jake smiled. 'Fresh smell of detergent. All the dishes drying.'

'Oh, yes. I'm there Friday to Monday.' Harold thought for a moment. 'He's hard work, though, Jake.'

'Does he talk?'

Harold furrowed his brow. 'I don't think I've heard his adult voice. Maybe once. I remember he got frustrated with a game he was playing a few years ago and shouted something. I thought there was a stranger in the house. His voice was so much deeper than I remember.'

Jake took a deep drag on the spliff. 'We need to get him right. I met someone. She wants to be a therapist. I was telling her about Michael.'

Harold narrowed his eyes. 'Wait. You met someone?'

Jake sighed. 'Yes. Maybe she could talk to him.'

'He won't talk to anyone.'

'I'll go and see him. Take him somewhere.' He offered Harold the spliff.

He waved it away. 'I need to get the sauce moving soon. That requires a clear head.'

Jake turned back to look at the house, and the Volvo parked out front. 'What colour is that car?'

'It's a sort of laurel green.'

Jake nodded. 'It's big.'

'I'm big.'

'Yeah, but—'

'I might get a dog. Maybe two. They'll need the space. So, am I going to meet this therapist?'

Jake shot him an impish grin. 'Depends how loopy you

go all on your own up here. Oh, yeah... By the way. I've applied for police training college. Hendon. Bramshill. Finals this summer, then I'll take a break. Course starts next year. Twenty weeks of training, then two-year probationary period.'

Harold beamed at him. '"By the way?" Jake... This is *everything*. That would give me so much joy.' He bowed his head. 'Your mother would be so proud of you, big man. Even if you don't go on to—'

'I'll be CID in five years.'

'Not if you keep smoking that.'

'Six, then.'

Harold turned back to the water. A hooting bird call drifted up from the valley. He pointed. 'Tawny owl.'

Jake nodded. 'What's the story with your old boss?'

'How do you mean?'

'I was reading about him. He's been missing for a while now. Years.'

'Ah, yes. A real mystery. He was a bit of an odd character, though.'

'Did you know him? I mean, socially?'

Harold shook his head. 'Kept himself to himself. We heard his marriage wasn't too good. Probably taken himself off somewhere exotic with a woman half his age.'

'What happened at Bolehill, Dad?'

Harold ran his hand through his long grey hair. 'Bolehill Wood? Up near Hathersage?'

'Yeah.'

'I've been fishing up there a few times with Ivan.'

'Your police friend.'

Harold nodded. 'Why do you mention it?'

'It just stuck in my head. I remember hearing you mention it a few times. Always meant to ask you. In the thing I was reading about your old boss, it said he had a place there. A cabin or something. It just pinged my memory.'

'Maybe he's gone native,' said Harold, grinning. 'Hiding in the woods. It's the beginning of a local legend. Sasquatch of the Peak District. It could be your first case when you qualify.' His knees cracked as he hauled himself to his feet. 'For now, though, I need you focused on the present, not the past. Stub out your weed, or whatever you call it. We need a *soffrito*. You're my sous chef.'

Chapter Thirty-Nine

PRESENT DAY

LYNDON WILDE STEERED the Porsche onto a shallow grass verge and reverse-parked it in the shade of a clump of trees. He sat there for a moment, looking back down the long, meandering road he'd joined after turning off at Hassop.

He was on alert, certain he'd caught sight of a red car turning in behind him as he crested a hill. The road was a dead end, tapering at the house's main entrance. He lingered for a few minutes, but the car didn't appear. The driver must have made a mistake and doubled back.

Wilde got out of the car and walked to the stone wall: more than twice his height. He looked through the wrought-iron gates and surveyed the red-brick house, set back behind a gravel drive separated from a footpath by a neatly trimmed boxwood hedge.

An elegant home set amid beautifully curated gardens.

The Learys had owned the house for five years. Wilde had researched the property via the local conservation office and found no planning application for a modern security system: a requirement for a Grade II building. Online images—still live from the previous exchange—also showed no external security.

He covered his thumb with a jacket sleeve and pressed the entry buzzer.

Four in, six out.

'Hello?' Uma Leary's voice over the intercom. Friendly but wary.

'Ah. Ms Leary. It's Lyndon Wilde from Elite Estates.'

'Oh!' She brightened. 'Yes. Mr Wilde. Is everything okay?'

'Absolutely. I'm terribly sorry to call on you unannounced but I met with a client earlier this morning just round the corner in Bakewell. As I was finishing up, I received a message from the owners of the Dovestone property. I was hoping to speak with Mr Leary about the finance. It won't take more than a few minutes.'

She hesitated. 'Oh, dear. Elton's not available at the moment. Could I help? What's the issue?'

'A local farm has submitted planning permission for a children's play centre near the property. I need to make you both aware of the extent and potential timings. I wanted to show you in person because it's easier to lay out—'

The gate lock buzzed as it disengaged.

'Not a problem at all,' said Leary. 'Come through and I'll take a look.'

As the gates slowly opened, Wilde walked back to the Porsche and took the duffel bag from the back seat. It would look strange if he arrived at Leary's door with the wheeled suitcase, so he left it in the boot for later.

He shouldered the duffel bag and walked through the gate, then diverted onto the footpath, lined on the far side by mature wisteria and climbing roses.

Regal charm.

The tall double doors opened, and Uma Leary stepped out onto the portico, dressed in black Lycra trousers and a green-and-black jogging top. 'Mr Wilde. Lovely to see you. Please excuse the attire. I was about to go for my morning run.' She ushered him into the hall. 'I normally like to go earlier but I find my sleep patterns are disturbed when Elton is away.'

'Oh, I'm the same. If my wife and children aren't around, I seem to turn into a teenage boy.'

Leary laughed and led him through a tall-ceilinged hall into a kitchen and breakfast room that ran along the entire west side of the house. An indigo-blue, two-oven Aga sat in the centre, surrounded by matching hand-painted timber cabinets and a vast stone worktop.

Exquisite decorative plasterwork.

Well-proportioned rooms.

She turned towards a large, industry-standard black-and-silver Jura espresso machine. 'Will you stay for coffee? Freshly ground.'

Wilde held up a hand. 'Ah, no. I couldn't possibly. This will only take a few minutes. I have another meeting in half an hour, and you're ready for your run. I'd appreciate a glass of water, though, if that's okay.' He set down the bag and unzipped it.

'Of course.' Leary turned her back and took down a tumbler from a cupboard. 'I wouldn't be taking coffee before running, I can assure you. Elton is in Prague, but the time difference is only an hour ahead. We could get him on a video call?'

'Well, that would be helpful, if you wouldn't mind.' Wilde put on a pair of neutral-coloured nitrile gloves and took out a short length of nylon rope, wrapping the ends around both fists. 'I'd like to show you both some documents related to the planning permission.'

Leary pressed the tumbler into a recess in the fridge door and it dispensed a few cubes of ice.

Wilde stepped towards her. He reached his arms up and over her head, pulling the rope against her neck. The glass fell from the fridge recess and shattered on the stone floor.

Wilde pulled the rope tight. Leary pushed herself away from the fridge, almost overbalancing him. He tried to compensate by planting his right foot in place, but his heel caught an ice cube, and he slipped back and tumbled to the floor, with Leary on top of him.

The fall loosened his grip and Leary managed to cry out, but she was no match for Wilde's strength, and he pulled the rope tight again.

Leary writhed and jerked, thrashing her hands behind her head, trying to get a hold of Wilde. But he dug his chin into his chest, keeping his eyes out of reach, and her fingers only brushed at his hair.

He'd hit the back of his head in the fall. It was only a light blow, but he would need to check the spot for potential blood and clean it up.

Wilde's arm muscles strained as he held the rope tight, until Leary fell limp against him. He stayed in position for another minute before loosening the rope and gently shifting Leary's body off him and onto the kitchen floor, where her head slumped to one side.

He got up and closed the window blinds. The low light from the hall was enough to see without his torch.

He gazed down at Leary's body, concentrating on his breathing.

Three in, three out.

As Wilde walked back to Leary, he froze.

Her position had changed since he had turned away to close the blinds. She now lay slightly twisted, with her head facing up.

He approached, slowly, and crouched down by the body, then checked her pulses.

Nothing.

The upper half of Leary's body lay in a patch of shadow at the foot of the worktop. Wilde took the torch out of his bag and shone it onto her face.

Her eyes were wide open.

Two in, two out.

'No, no, no...'

He fell to his knees, into cold water from the ice cube spillage, and held Leary's head in both hands. Her neck felt unnaturally stiff, and he recoiled, as if he'd touched something hot.

Wilde moved in closer. He reached a hand out to her face and pressed his fingertips on her eyelid.

It was fixed in place. Frozen.

He clawed at it but couldn't find enough purchase to close it.

He used both hands and pinched at Leary's eyelashes, trying to force the eyelid shut. It complied for most of the way, but then he lost his grip, and it sprang back open.

Wilde recoiled again and scrambled to his feet.

Trembling, he aimed the torch at Leary's face.

Her lifeless eyes stared ahead, reflecting the light.

One in, one out.

One in, one out.

Wilde staggered back, feeling for a surface to keep his balance.

He dropped onto one knee, pushed the palm of his hand over his open mouth, and released a muffled roar of fury.

Chapter Forty

THE BLOND-HAIRED BOY received the ball on the half-turn at the edge of the opposition penalty area. The nearest defender closed him down, but his approach was too eager and obvious, and the boy used the outside of his foot to tap the ball past him. The other defenders were all too high up the pitch, and the blond boy found himself one on one with the goalkeeper.

Dale Strickland leapt up from his pitch-side folding chair, shouting. 'Bury it. Go on, Luka!'

The goalkeeper rushed out, but Luka saw the challenge coming, and quickly side-footed the ball towards the corner of the goal. It glanced off the post and rolled into the net.

Luka ran to the corner flag, where he was mobbed by his teammates.

The small clique of parent supporters went wild, leaping and embracing. It had been a tight game, with Luka's team conceding an early goal and clinging on for the rest of the game, with few chances of their own.

Dale Strickland took off his black baseball cap and waved it in the air. 'Get the ball! There's still time.'

The opposition trudged back to the centre circle and restarted the game, passing the ball carefully between themselves, creating space for risk-free returns. Luka's team chased them for a couple of minutes before the referee blew full time.

Strickland ran on to the pitch and hugged his son. 'Brilliant, Luka. Nice finish.'

Luka smiled and fell into the arms of another teammate, who teased him. 'Nearly missed it!'

'Didn't, though,' said Luka, stumbling away to shake hands with the scowling opposition players.

Strickland turned and headed back to side of the pitch. He had tipped over his chair in the celebrations, and as he bent to correct it, he spotted a familiar face waiting by a grey Audi in the stadium car park.

'That's cost you, Dale,' said a man from the group of celebrating parents. 'What's your lad's goal bonus? McDonald's?'

Strickland smiled, keeping his eyes on the man by the Audi. 'I wish. Nothing less than an Honest chicken burger, these days.'

He held up a hand to a hefty man with a suit, watching from the back of the dugout. 'Two minutes, Reece.'

Strickland passed through the old turnstile gate and strolled out to the Audi. The driver was now in the driving seat, and a tall, broad-shouldered man in a tight-fitting suit stood behind the open back door.

Strickland nodded.

The man smiled. 'Mr Strickland.'

He slid onto the back seat, and the man closed the door behind him, then stood off the car.

Classical music played at low volume.

Leon Stokes took off his shades and caught Strickland's eye in the rear-view mirror. 'Nice goal.'

'He doesn't score many. Did his fucking best to miss.'

'His movement was good, though. Anticipating the play. He reads the game. Doesn't follow the ball.'

Strickland looked out of the tinted back window. 'My boy says tinted windows look suspicious.'

Stokes laughed. 'I'm thinking about the UVA and UVB rays. You can get sunburnt when you're driving.'

'In Manchester?'

'Even weak sun can get you, in regular doses. I read that ninety per cent of fatal skin cancer is down to UV radiation over-exposure. Particularly for pale faces like us.'

Strickland pondered for a moment. 'I admire your optimism, Leon. Thinking long term. What's this?' He nodded to the music.

'"Cavalleria Rusticana". *Raging Bull* soundtrack.'

'Of course. Business good?'

'Excellent. Dotting the i's personally now.'

'It's a fucking nightmare, isn't it? Filling vacant positions. You have to do some jobs yourself. To make sure.' Strickland took out his phone, navigated to the Voice Recorder app and tapped the *RECORD* button. He laid the phone down on the seat beside him and smiled. 'Mutually assured destruction.'

'I'm not wired up.'

Strickland shrugged. 'You can hardly blame me for the caution, after last time. So, why the interest in grass roots football?'

Stokes cleared his throat. 'I wanted to give you a personal nod. The Fletcher leads look solid.'

'I hoped as much. I trust Wesley has passed on my appreciation.'

'Of course he fucking hasn't. So, what are you thinking?'

Strickland angled his head from side to side. 'Next day or two.'

'Insurance?'

'An associate of Farouk's. Ex-Egyptian military. It'll be clean. Once Fletcher is down.'

'And Peyton goes out a hero.'

'In his own little world, yes.' He shook his head. 'But I can't have him fumbling another shot at Sawyer.'

'Skying it over when he's one on one.'

Strickland smiled. 'He's too emotionally invested. And he's damaged.'

'A walking time bomb.'

Strickland picked up his phone and opened the door. 'I see him as more of a suicide bomb.'

Chapter Forty-One

SAWYER PUSHED out his desk chair and turned to the pile of folders that had greeted him on arrival that morning. Creedon had put him on case file review, with an initial batch of offline reports to cross-reference with data within the CMS.

The folders—both live and recently closed cases—were heavy cardstock, weighted with hundreds of individual documents. They were standardised and colour-coded: red for violent crimes, blue for thefts, green for drug-related. Each was labelled with case number, lead detective, type of crime, and the date the case was opened.

He lifted one off the pile, browsed through. Summary sheet, divider cards separating out incident reports, witness statements, evidence logs, photographs, forensic, legal. He was to apply a standardised workflow to each: familiarise with the case; review and verify the timeline; check for inconsistencies; confirm the chain of custody for each piece of evidence. Some of the cases required collaborative review, where he would call a team meeting and discuss the details, focusing on disputed elements. But he was mostly expected to compile his own report of findings, feedback, recommendations.

His phone rang on the desk.

Bentley.

Sawyer slammed the folder shut and took the call.

'Good news,' said Bentley. 'The GPR team found the soil anomalies soon after you left. Forensic archaeology excavated the remains. The lab got nuclear DNA from the bones. They can't confirm for a few days, but they found Deborah's shoes. Heavily degraded, but they were distinct enough for her mother to ID. There was a necklace, too, also confirmed by her mother.'

Sawyer wheeled his chair to the left and looked through the ajar door, clocking the backs of two men signing in at the front desk: one tall and burly, the other slim and short. 'Did they find the skull?'

'Yes. Not in one piece. Do you really want the detail?'

'No.' He turned his back to the door and gazed up at his empty corkboard. 'So, when do we go again?'

Bentley hesitated. 'That's the thing. Caldwell's brief says he's exhausted after the first outing. The specialist has advised him to rest. I don't think he's stalling. I hope not, anyway. He should be fine in a couple of days.'

Sawyer stayed silent, watching the men make their way to his office.

'What did you talk about, in the clearing?'

'Old times.'

Bentley covered the phone, and his voice muffled as he spoke to someone at the other end. The line cleared again. 'Sit tight, DI Sawyer. You did good. A few more days and you never have to worry about the old bastard again.'

He ended the call.

Three taps on the door.

Sawyer turned. 'Come.'

Shepherd stepped in, followed by Walker. 'That had better be ironic. It's what Farrell says.'

'He knows,' said Walker. He nodded to Sawyer. 'Sir. Good to see you.'

Shepherd looked around. 'Nice place you've got here. Handy for the postal depot. And there's a lovely logistics hub next door.'

'How did it go with Caldwell?' said Walker.

'As well as you could expect. Finale in a few days, up at Padley.'

Shepherd raised an eyebrow. He pointed to Sawyer, then at himself. 'That's where we came in, with Crawley.'

'Take a seat,' said Sawyer, gesturing to the single chair. He looked at Walker. 'It's not ideal, but Shepherd's lap will be comfy enough.'

'We're not stopping,' said Shepherd. 'A quick heads-up. A couple of NCA spooks were in with Farrell yesterday.'

'I know. The chat about Peyton. The big boss here has them on my schedule for later today.'

'DCI?' said Walker.

Sawyer nodded.

'Sounds like he's more of a PA.'

'He's okay. Probably flew a bit too high, realised he wanted an easier life. Oversee the bureaucracy instead of juggling the bodies.' He saw Shepherd eye Walker. 'Another one?'

Shepherd nodded. 'Young woman. Uma Leary. Similar type to Hannah Lewis, the Hatfield murder I mentioned. Bobbies found her yesterday after her husband said she didn't return a call, which was unusual.'

'Too early for full details on Uma, but it looks like both were strangled with a ligature.'

'Drummond has also found post-mortem abuse on Hannah Lewis's body. Uma Leary is with him now.'

Sawyer nodded to the door; Shepherd closed it. 'You shouldn't be telling me this.'

'Probably not,' said Shepherd. 'But I'm pretty sure you didn't do it.'

Sawyer looked up at Walker; he was keeping his eyes low. 'And Orlando Gray took his own life?'

Shepherd nodded. 'Cavendish. Cut his wrists with a sharpened metal clip.'

'He used to work there,' said Sawyer. 'So, he'd know the rhythms, changeovers.'

'Yes,' said Walker. 'IOPC are on it. Farrell's feeling the heat.'

'We also have Phoebe Gray,' said Shepherd. He puffed out his cheeks.

Sawyer thought for a moment. 'What about the guy whose DNA you found on Phoebe?'

'Brad Singleton,' said Walker. 'No joy. It's like the ground has swallowed him up.'

Sawyer wheeled to his desk and opened an application window. 'Are you sure the NCA spooks weren't there to question Farrell?'

'Could be,' said Shepherd. 'It's a mess.'

Sawyer looked between the two. 'If it ain't, it'll do till the mess gets here.'

Shepherd frowned. 'What's that from?'

'*No Country For Old Men*,' said Sawyer. 'And Singleton is still your chief suspect for Phoebe Gray?'

'Yes,' said Walker. 'Although we got his medical recs through today. He doesn't have a latex allergy. So, that complicates any connection to the mortuary victims and the women.'

Sawyer nodded. 'Anyone in the frame for Hannah Lewis?'

'Myers has been on it,' said Walker. 'Nothing yet.'

'We're getting a picture of Singleton's movements from ANPR and phone data,' said Shepherd. 'Matching with places he might have held Phoebe.'

Sawyer smiled. 'Good idea. It might be nothing to do with him. Cross-contamination from the killer. Maybe they crossed paths, worked together…'

'Singleton knew Gray,' said Walker. 'Old army buddies.'

Sawyer frowned. 'Spicy. Could still be cross-contamination. You checking their recent contact?'

'Yes,' said Walker. 'And Sally found traces of Plaster of Paris on the mortuary victims and also on Hannah Lewis.'

'You should check Singleton's flat for that,' said Sawyer. 'Does he make models? Is he doing any decorating work?'

Shepherd paced. 'None of this helps. It relies on too many things syncing up.'

'Post-mortem sexual abuse on Hannah Lewis is interesting,' said Sawyer. 'Is there any link to the mortuary abuse Gray was accused of?'

Shepherd looked at Walker. 'In what way?'

'Have you checked if Singleton's DNA is a match for anything you found on the victims?'

Walker nodded. 'No good.'

Sawyer shrugged. 'You could set up an alert on calls involving women who are a similar type to Hannah and Uma…' He stared into space. 'I don't see how much more I can do.' He glanced at Shepherd. 'With secondary information.'

Shepherd gave a pained smile. 'It's fine. We just wanted

to see how they were treating you.' He walked to the side of Sawyer's desk and looked at his screen: the HOLMES database home page, with blank input boxes awaiting username and password entry. He turned and nodded to Walker.

'Sir,' said Walker to Sawyer, and exited.

Shepherd followed him, looking over his shoulder before he closed the office door. 'Stay away from that coffee machine. Looks lethal.'

Sawyer wheeled to the side and watched them through the window in the door, as they walked to the reception desk, signed out and left.

He turned back to the folders, and something on the floor caught his eye: a plain white business card.

He picked it up. Shepherd's name andrank were printed on the front, with a mobile number.

On the back, Shepherd had added a note in his own handwriting.

Edshep
dixiedean383

Chapter Forty-Two

REBECCA WILDE SLID into the Starbucks booth and set down two black coffees. She tied her hair into a tight ponytail and took out a mint-green compact mirror.

The woman opposite kept her eyes on Rebecca as she tore open a sachet of sweetener and sprinkled it into her drink. She was early forties, lean and fit-looking, with flecks of grey in her neatly styled brown hair.

Rebecca checked herself in the mirror.

'You can't tell,' the woman said.

'I haven't been crying, Marcia. I'm past that now.'

Marcia blew on her coffee, surveying the room.

Rebecca snapped the mirror shut and stuffed it back into her bag. 'Are you going to tell me, then?'

'He's been around and about a lot, obviously. That's his work. But there are two outings that don't add up for me. Just over a week ago, he visited an address over in Hayfield. Cole Lane. Anything?'

She shook her head.

'It wasn't the kind of place I could surveil up close

because the road is too small, and he would have spotted me. I parked up on the main road below and got a long-lens shot of him, but it's murky because the light was poor. Early evening. He was there for a few hours, and he took in a black shoulder bag and a large wheeled suitcase.'

Rebecca sighed and closed her eyes. 'Why?'

Marcia winced. 'I don't really want to let my imagination run with that one. Then, a couple of days ago, he visited a nice little country pile near Chatsworth. I kept back because the approach road was a dead end, but he was only there for about an hour.' She took a drink. 'I can't confirm or deny the shoulder bag and suitcase.'

'He was in his Porsche both times?'

She nodded. 'I couldn't see which address he entered in Cole Lane, but it was down the lower end of the street. The second place is owned by a Mr Elton Leary. Tech entrepreneur. He sold up his software start-up a couple of years ago and now has stakes in a bunch of tech firms. Lives there with his wife, Uma. Fashion designer. Lots of detail about her on her website.'

Rebecca sipped her coffee. '*Uma...*'

'As in Thurman. The Learys' house isn't on the market, and I couldn't find anywhere on Cole Lane that would qualify for Elite Estates.' Marcia watched Rebecca as she pondered. 'They could still be clients, looking to buy.'

Rebecca shook her head. 'They could be. But they're not. I'm convinced of it. This all fits the pattern. I think I'm out of the denial stage now.'

'Straight into anger?'

'I think I'm past that.'

Marcia raised an eyebrow. 'A bit of fire in the belly can help if he decides to fight dirty. You might need to roll up your sleeves. The evidence I've gathered will help with property division and spousal maintenance. But his assets are significant, and he might dig in.'

Rebecca screwed up her face. 'My main concern is custody.'

'Evidence of infidelity won't help with that. Unless you can show his behaviour and lifestyle might put the children at risk. But it will help your lawyer with an overall legal strategy and provide a basis for settlement discussions. You never know. He might just go limp and meet you halfway.' She finished her coffee. 'What's this "pattern"?'

'Sneaking around. Going out at weird times. A few strange phone calls.' Rebecca held the rim of her cup to her mouth, then moved it away. 'And he's disengaged in the bedroom.' She checked herself. 'Well…'

Marcia frowned. 'Do I need to hear the details?'

'Probably not.'

'I'm happy to listen in confidence, Rebecca, but I'm not a psychologist.'

Rebecca drained her cup. 'He's always had some… things. A little strange, but I played along.' She took a breath. 'He doesn't like me to make any noise.'

Marcia nodded. 'Okay. Not everyone wants a running commentary.'

'No. I mean… Nothing. Just silence.'

'Even when you—'

'Yes. And that's not easy. Sometimes, I cover my mouth. Sometimes, he does it for me. He also wants me to keep perfectly still.' She held Marcia's gaze. 'And he can't stand me looking at him.'

'Eye contact?'

'Yes. Out of the question. I once caught his eye in the mirror of a hotel room, a suite, and he slept on the sofa.'

Marcia nodded slowly. 'A question comes to mind.'

Rebecca waved her away, tearful now. 'It's always consensual. But lately, even all this isn't working. I found a wonderful couples counsellor, but he always finds a reason not to go. Too busy. Too stressed. I love Lyndon dearly. He's the father of my children. But I can't go on like this. I'm still young. Relatively. I can't escape the feeling that there's a better life for me out there. With someone I can be myself with. Where I don't need to play this game. It's obvious that he's already found others who are meeting his needs better.' She searched her bag, frustrated. Marcia handed her a napkin and she dabbed at her eyes. 'I'm going to tell him tonight.'

'You should do it in public, Rebecca. It's a dangerous moment. Many men react badly to being presented with evidence of their secret lives. Coupled with the rejection—'

'I won't mention that I hired anyone. For now, I just want to see his reaction. Set things in motion. Please send me your report, with photos and time logs.'

'Of course.' Marcia took away the napkin and pushed it into her empty cup. 'But promise me this, Rebecca. I want a phone call. The moment you've finished talking to him.'

Chapter Forty-Three

WESLEY PEYTON SAT low in the back seat. He raised the brim of his baseball cap and looked out through a gap in the trees that lined the lane parallel to the house. Abadi had parked the shabby old Ford Focus in a potholed passing spot at the bottom of the lane, concealing it behind a dry-stone wall overrun with wild grass and weeds.

He tilted his head and surveyed the pallid moon, shrouded by low, lurking cloud. 'The gods are with us tonight, boys. You can't see a thing. Now, we've had a bit of rain, so you're gonna get dirty. But let's make this nice and clean. It's not Call of fuckin' Duty. Right, then. Give us the brief.'

Abadi nodded at the man in the passenger seat. Tarek El-Masri was in his late thirties, with sun-weathered skin and a long, equine face underscored by a jutting jawline. A well-healed scar ran across the base of his chin.

He pushed a tight black beanie over his shaven head and turned to face Peyton. 'Two bedrooms, both downstairs. Kitchen and bathroom and sitting area upstairs for some reason. Two cars in the front driveway. There's a small storage outbuilding, septic tank. The garage is doorless and full of junk.'

'Where's the girl?' said Peyton.

'I've seen her at the front bedroom window. No sign of the man. He must have taken the back room. The grounds are too open to get a sight on it without risking discovery.'

Peyton scowled. 'Why are the fuckin' bedrooms downstairs?

'Usually, it's the age of the occupants,' said Abadi. 'More accessible.'

'Sometimes it's for the views in the living space,' said El-Masri. 'There might also be energy concerns.'

Peyton looked between the two. 'You don't need Google with you two bastards about. Let's get moving. Girl first. That gives us leverage with her dad.' He pointed to them both. '*Don't* fuckin' kill her. I get first dibs. Cocky little bitch. Now, we've all got two-ways. I'm staying here and I'll follow you in when you've got the girl, and her dad is under control. If I don't hear from you in reasonable time, I'm history. Yeah? Remember, Daddy's gonna watch while I teach his daughter some manners. Then I get to put his lights out.' He pointed at Abadi. 'You're filming that bit. How are we doin' for tools?'

Abadi raised his Glock. El-Masri reached into the footwell and showed his compact black submachine gun.

Peyton leaned forward and studied the weapon with the light from his phone. 'Is that a Heckler?'

El-Masri nodded. 'MP5.'

Peyton sat back, smiling. 'Go on. What's your logic?'

El-Masri glanced at Abadi with the hint of a smile. 'Reliable. Perfect for close-quarter fighting. Accurate with low recoil. You miss with one shot, it's easy to get another away quickly. And, anyway...' He shrugged. 'Eight hundred rounds a minute. You would need to be blind not to hit *something*.' He glanced at Peyton's eye-patch, held up a hand. 'Sorry.'

Peyton shook his head. 'Don't worry about it. So, are we loud?'

El-Masri nodded. 'The barrel is threaded so I could use a suppressor, but there's not much point out here. If you want to save the man for yourself, I can shoot out his knees or ankles. No problem.' A broader smile. 'He'll be helpless, but you won't be able to tell on your video.'

Peyton grinned and screwed on his baseball cap tighter. 'We're using this lad again, Farouk. He thinks the way I do.'

'Of course, I would prefer to have night-vision goggles,' said El-Masri.

Peyton sniffed. 'You won't need 'em once you're in close. Just get to the girl, smoke out her dad. You've both got decent built-in night vision, anyway. It'll kick in as you approach. This is one fella, remember. And his soppy fuckin' daughter.' He looked between them both, sniffed. 'Chocks away, then.'

Abadi and El-Masri opened their doors.

'Oh! One more thing. It is not part of the plan to fuck this up, yeah?' He stared out of the window at the house silhouette. 'I've known Billy Rice since I shat my pants in his garden when I was six and his mam helped clean me up. Fletcher killed him like he was swatting a fly. He's not getting such an easy way out.'

ABADI AND EL-MASRI moved along the edge of the field adjoining the house, staying low. El-Masri took point, MP5 levelled. They used dim lapel-mounted torches to navigate the soft ground, then rested by a wall at the far side of the house, letting their eyes adjust.

El-Masri adjusted his beanie and peered over the wall. All was calm. No sound but rustling grass and chirping crickets.

He whispered to Abadi. 'Front room light is on. Can't tell about the back room light from here.' He looked through a small monocular. 'Sash window. Open a few inches. I get in. You hang back and wait for any sign of response, then follow.'

Abadi nodded. 'We gag the girl. Kill the man. Call Peyton.' He made a slash sign across his throat. 'I distract him. You do it. No hesitation.'

Masri shrugged, unconvinced. 'He is *hemar*.' He raised his index fingers to the side of his head, mimicking donkey ears.

Abadi put a hand on his arm. 'Don't write Peyton off, Tarek. Assume the worst. There's no value in being over-confident. We clean up, exfil at the car. I have a spare key.' He leaned closer. 'Go.'

El-Masri vaulted the wall and crouch-walked to the foot of the window. He listened for a moment.

Rushing shower water from the ensuite bathroom.

He reached up, and slowly raised the window, then climbed into the room, illuminated by a soft bedside lamp.

He looked around: a collection of women's clothing hanging in the open wardrobe; female cosmetics on the dresser. He sniffed a mug, steaming on the bedside table; it smelt of strawberry.

Downtempo music played from a portable speaker on the dresser.

The shower water stopped.

El-Masri turned to face the bathroom door, but the

MP5 muzzle caught the edge of the blanket, and he overcorrected the movement, nudging the mug of herbal tea with his elbow. He tried to catch it, but the hot water upended over his hand, and he cried out as the mug clattered on the wooden floor.

Loud footsteps charged to the bathroom door, and it swung open.

Sadie Fletcher stood in the frame, wearing a loose T-shirt and joggers.

El-Masri raised the MP5. 'Scream and you die,' he hissed. He raised a finger and pressed it onto his lips, cradling the MP5 in the crook of his arm. 'It's okay. We're not here for you.'

Sadie stepped towards him, but he gripped the gun in both hands.

She froze and pointed to the window. 'Get out of my fucking bedroom.'

El-Masri smiled and reached into a pouch on his jacket. He tossed a pair of handcuffs onto the bed. 'Put one cuff on your wrist, attach the other to the radiator pipe there.'

Sadie picked up the cuffs, looked down at them, up again at El-Masri. She threw them back; they landed on the floor and spun away to the corner. '*Get.*' She shouted, loud and clear. '*Out.*'

El-Masri turned the MP5 and fired two rounds into the pillow. The muzzle flash lit up the small bedroom, the sounds fierce and explosive. She cried out and leapt back. He levelled the gun at her face. 'Your father is going to die tonight. But now I think you will, too.'

Sadie ducked back into the bathroom and tried to slam the door, but El-Masri covered the ground and shouldered through. He grabbed Sadie by the wrist and dragged her back into the bedroom. As he hauled her towards the bed, she launched a powerful front kick that connected between his legs.

El-Masri roared in pain and swung his fist towards her. But she sidestepped it and faced him.

He backed off, aimed the MP5. She cried out again and fell to the floor, covering her head with her arms.

At the window, a Glock cocked.

El-Masri turned, wincing in pain.

Abadi held the gun on him. '*Tarek*. What are you fucking doing?'

El-Masri doubled up, holding his crotch. 'That bitch. I'm going to—'

'*What the fuck's going on in there?*' Peyton's voice came over Abadi's two-way radio. '*Who's shooting?*'

'Tarek fired to scare the woman,' said Abadi. 'It's under control.'

'*Sounds like it! Have you got 'em both?*'

'Just the woman,' said Abadi.

'*Right. Well, keep it under fuckin' control, yeah? I'm coming in.*'

PEYTON OPENED the car boot and took out a sawed-off single-barrel shotgun and a small carry pouch with a Velcro fastener that he fixed to his lower body.

He hurried up the lane, staying low. He slowed, looked around for signs of movement, then ran through the main gate and dived into a dense patch of wild grass by the low dry-stone wall.

He peered over the top, watching the movement behind the open window of the front bedroom.

Lesser opposition.

He looked up into the night sky as the clouds cleared

and the moon—full-circle and blazing white—slid into view. The second of the month.

Peyton grinned. 'No fuckin' way.'

He knew it was cheesy, but his team's song ran through his head. '...*you saw me standing alone...*'

And a memory flash: Eddie stepping in after a post-match scrap down in Gorton after City had given the Rags a sound beating. 2002 to 2003 season.

Fighting his battles for him.

'Not a fuckin' puppy no more, eh?'

He was about to vault the wall and head for the front bedroom when he caught movement through the small window of the outbuilding. He watched, saw the movement again.

The sneaky bastard had seen him.

He was waiting for him to go in.

Using the dry-stone wall as cover, he crouch-walked back to the near side of the outbuilding where the wall had crumbled, and he could see inside.

A large figure crouched in shadow at the opposite end, beneath a door with a broken window, shoulders rising and falling.

Peyton smiled. He took a grenade from the Velcro pouch and stepped forward, slowly, soundlessly.

He squatted by the outbuilding, pulled the pin, and rolled the grenade inside, then ran for cover, diving into the wild grass.

He turned, watching as the explosion ripped away the building's makeshift roof. Flames reared up and vented through gaps in the brickwork, and the front door flew away, tumbling through the air.

Peyton pushed up out of the grass and sprinted for the

front bedroom window, feeling the heat from the burning outbuilding. He vaulted into the room.

Abadi stood at the side of the bed, aiming his Glock on Sadie Fletcher, who sat glowering in the corner, holding her knees up to her chest, wrist cuffed to the radiator pipe. El-Masri sat crumpled in a corner chair, MP5 at his side.

Sadie glared up at Peyton as he entered. 'Just as I thought the evening couldn't get any worse. I was hoping I'd never see your ugly mug again.'

'What's going on out there?' said Abadi, keeping his eyes on her. He shifted around as Peyton entered and stood with his back to the window.

Peyton shot a crazed grin at Abadi. 'The big man is toast. Caught him spying on us from the outhouse.'

Abadi frowned. 'You killed him?'

Peyton walked over to Sadie. 'Have a look. I don't fancy his chances, do you?'

El-Masri hauled himself to his feet, grimacing. 'This man. You say he's a British marine. He would know the sound of a grenade landing. He wouldn't stick around waiting for it to go off. You might only have flushed him out.' He lifted the MP5, aiming it at the bedroom door.

Peyton crouched by Sadie. 'Call him.'

She held his eye. 'What?'

He looked up at Abadi and nodded. Abadi took out a narrow-bladed boning knife and handed it down to Peyton.

'Call for your dad,' said Peyton, raising the knife to Sadie's cheek. 'Or I'll make you call for him.'

Sadie replied without hesitation. 'Fuck.' She leaned closer, pushing her cheek into the flat of the blade. 'Off.'

Peyton sighed. 'Eyes on me, boys. A good friend of mine taught me this. He held the blade up close to Sadie's eye. 'You don't make threats you're not prepared to carry out.

First, you threaten to cut out their eye. Then, if they still won't talk, you cut it out and you threaten to do the same with the other one. That's the part where they weigh it up. Do they give you what they want or accept being blind for the rest of their life? You've already carried out the first threat, so that's usually the bit where you get what you need.'

Sadie sneered at Peyton. 'Is that what happened to you? You wet your pants after they cut out one eye. Squealed like a little piglet.'

A thick spray of fresh blood spattered onto her face.

She cried out and turned away.

Peyton felt the warmth on his neck. He stumbled away from Sadie, twisted round in time to see Abadi topple forward on the blood-spattered bed, bounce back, and tumble off the side onto the floor, exposing a large hole punched into the back of his head.

Movement outside the window.

Peyton dropped low and El-Masri snatched up the MP5. He stumbled to the window and blind-fired.

'Woah!' shouted Peyton. He put a hand on El-Masri's shoulder, and he stopped shooting. 'Stay here with her.' He cocked the shotgun and charged out of the bedroom door, through a small sitting room. He pulled back the window curtain and paused, checking outside. The outbuilding fire spat and crackled, lighting up the house grounds, catching a heap of tools and junk stacked up by the gate.

No sign of anyone.

Peyton raised the shotgun, then opened the front door and stepped out, scanning for movement.

He turned and scouted around the side of the house, keeping his head low, checking his rear. He turned and sprinted for the outbuilding, pegged back by the heat of the fire.

He squinted through the smoke, looking in at the blasted hole where the front door had been.

The building was empty.

Gunfire back in the bedroom.

Sadie screamed.

Peyton ran, away from the main house to the back of the grounds. He crouched behind the two cars, near the external piping and drain field of the septic tank, grimacing at the faecal reek. He covered his mouth and nose with his hand.

Through the smoke, he could just about make out a figure running from the house, out to the field beyond.

He coughed and wheezed, desperate to clear his airway. He keyed his two-way radio and shouted into the mouthpiece. *'Tarek. Fuckin' talk to me!'* Silence. He keyed again. *'What's going on?'*

Still nothing.

He lay there, catching his breath.

Peyton pushed away from his hiding place and ran for the front bedroom window, his system supercharged by adrenaline.

He crouched, peered over the edge, then climbed into the room.

In here, the smoky smell had sweetened, and Peyton realised the aroma came from the huge man slumped against the dresser.

His scraped-back blond hair was streaked with soot and ash, and he was bleeding from a gunshot wound in his side, and another at the base of his neck.

Austin Fletcher's hand hovered close to a suppressed

Glock that lay at the foot of the bed. But he didn't have the strength to shift position and take it.

Peyton raised the shotgun and approached.

'Please,' said Fletcher.

Peyton frowned. 'Didn't have you down as the begging type.' He checked around the room, keeping his distance from Fletcher.

Abadi lay face down in a puddle of blood, just beyond the base of the window.

El-Masri lay near the open bathroom door, on his back, a single gunshot wound in the centre of his forehead. His MP5 had skidded across the floor and lay at the far side of the bathroom.

Sadie had gone. Her cuffs lay open, attached to the radiator pipe.

Peyton raised the shotgun at Fletcher.

'Please,' he said again.

Peyton caught a sound on the air. He paused, listened.

A distant siren.

He smiled. 'Oh! *Police*. Right, right. Yeah, fuck it. Cavalry on its way.'

He poked the barrel of the shotgun down at the Glock and scraped it away from Fletcher. 'You've done well, big lad. But you've ran out of road now.' He held the shotgun on Fletcher. 'You killed a good friend of mine. So, now I'm gonna kill you.'

Fletcher's body twitched. He kept his head down as Peyton crouched and edged his face close.

'And I'll be back for your daughter, yeah? I don't want you meeting your maker thinking she'll get away with this shit.' He lowered his voice to a hissing whisper. 'Hey. We could be related one day. You might end up as a posthumous grandad.'

The siren grew louder.

Peyton aimed the shotgun at Fletcher. 'I need to get going now.'

At last, Fletcher raised his head and pinned Peyton with his hollow eyes, holding his gaze, unwavering.

The look sent a streak of ice through Peyton's stomach, and he took a step back. When he spoke, he couldn't conceal the tremor in his voice.

'Billy Rice's family send their regards.'

Chapter Forty-Four

SAWYER DROVE his forearms into the mid-level struts on the wooden man dummy. He focused on his fundamentals: blocking, parrying, absolute efficiency of movement. The flow drill developed his sensitivity to contact and his ability to react swiftly and appropriately.

He paused.

Engine outside. The vehicle crossed the private driveway bridge, over the thin stream of reservoir run-off, then stopped.

He pushed on with the form: one hundred and ten techniques in total, flowing into each other in perfect integration.

Footsteps outside, then three taps on the door.

Sawyer always trained topless; he towelled off and slipped on his tatty grey Bruce Lee T-shirt, then padded into the sitting room, barefoot.

He opened the door, then turned and walked into the kitchen.

Shepherd stepped in, out of the darkness. 'You know

that's borderline reckless. Not checking who's on your doorstep this late at night? I didn't see the blind twitch.'

Sawyer poured out a glass of Diet Coke, held up the bottle. Shepherd shook his head.

He headed to the sofa. 'I recognised the old Rover engine. Although it's sounding a touch—'

'Arthritic?' said Shepherd, taking the armchair.

Sawyer nodded, watching Shepherd, reading him. He set down his drink on the coffee table and sprawled across the sofa. 'It's nice to see you. But late is never good.'

'There's nothing good at the moment. Did you get that visit from the NCA?'

'Yes. They're more concerned with actually finding Peyton than what caused our…'

'Altercation?'

'I'd go for *unpleasantness*. NCA are more about the bigger picture. They're up to their elbows in Peyton's role in the Manchester crime gangs. He'll want revenge on me for the beating, so I suggested a sting. But there's still pressure to get answers about the station attack. They don't want Peyton killed in a high-risk op.'

'Is there any heat on Strickland?'

'There will be if they bring Peyton in.' He sipped his drink. 'Anyway. I had a look through your casework. Sorry about that. Someone accidentally left their HOLMES log-in lying round.'

'And?'

'I watched the interviews with Gray. Including the Farrell shitshow.'

Shepherd scoffed. 'Farrell looks like a man under mortar fire armed with an old twig.'

Sawyer leaned forward. 'It's what Gray says to you when

you ask him if he knows where Phoebe is. "You're wasting time." Not wasting *your* time.'

Shepherd frowned. 'Go on.'

'You missed something. It's a tiny something. And, as you say, nothing is good at the moment. And your SIO is a world-class idiot.'

Shepherd sat back. 'Just give me the theory. Try not to be too smug about it.'

'I think Gray knew Phoebe was alive at that point. *You're wasting time*. It's a strange thing to say, given she's been missing for three weeks.' He reached into a tin on the coffee table and took out a boiled sweet. 'The video feels like he's addressing someone directly. At first, I thought it might be Gray who was abusing the bodies to order and filming it for a third party.'

'How lovely.'

Sawyer unwrapped the sweet and slid it into his mouth. 'But... And here's the thing you missed. It was only added to the casefile by one of Sally's team two days ago. Gray doesn't have a latex allergy. He said he did. But he doesn't. So, why are there traces of latex-allergic condoms on the mortuary bodies?'

Shepherd shook his head. 'Maybe he prefers—'

'Think it through. Why would he *pretend* to have a latex allergy?'

Shepherd stared into Sawyer's blank TV screen for a moment. His eyes shifted back. 'Because... he didn't abuse the bodies himself...'

'No. But someone else did. Someone with a latex allergy. And Gray wanted to make it look like it was him. Which is why he told us he was allergic.'

'But why would Gray be so keen for us to link him with the abuse? Or divert attention from the real abuser?'

'Because he's not a master criminal. And he was desperate and not thinking straight. He was out of options. So, he tipped off the hospital authorities, and got himself caught.'

'Intentionally?'

Sawyer narrowed his eyes. 'Well, yes. Hence the anonymous tip-off.'

Shepherd scrubbed at his beard. The lights were coming on now. 'So, he was desperate because... his daughter was missing...' He stalled, looked across to the kitchen.

Sawyer followed his gaze. 'The answer isn't in the cat bowl.'

'I give up.'

Sawyer smiled. 'Orlando Gray isn't a necrophile. He didn't abuse any bodies. He's not The Vulture. A necrophile abducted his daughter to get leverage over a not particularly bright man who could give him access to fresh bodies.'

Shepherd nodded slowly. 'A necrophile with a latex allergy.'

'Yes. There's a sentence I never thought I'd hear in this house.'

'Brad Singleton?' said Shepherd.

'No. Again, nothing in his history. No necrophilic or paedophilic tendency. Just a past association with Gray. And no latex allergy. I mean, Gray wasn't a complete idiot. He thought through the latex thing, knowing police would find evidence of the real abuser's non-latex condoms. But he thought that if he could get himself removed from the hospital, forcibly, through seemingly no fault of his own, then the real abuser would lose his leverage and—'

'Would have no use for his daughter any more. Jesus fucking Christ. But—'

'I know. Like I say, you can see the faulty logic but he's

not a master criminal. All it did was force the real abuser to kill Phoebe, to get her off his hands. It's a desperate plan by someone who doesn't have the intelligence to see that it will fall apart. But he didn't reckon for a Rottweiler like Farrell to snatch up the ball and run with it.'

Sawyer took a drink. 'Hannah Lewis. Post-mortem abuse. Strangled with a ligature. Uma Leary. Similar type to Hannah Lewis. Strangled with a ligature. And I assume you're here because you've just found out initial forensics show she suffered similar post-mortem abuse.'

Shepherd nodded. 'Drummond is pulling an all-nighter with O'Callaghan. He says it looks like Uma Leary's body experienced some kind of rare spasm, and Sally's team have found new trace evidence. They're putting it together now.'

'The killer strangled Phoebe Gray,' said Sawyer. 'He didn't use a ligature because he didn't need to, on a relatively weak nine-year-old girl. Drummond's report on Hannah Lewis notes the finger pattern bruising around the neck, along with the ligature marks. He tried to use his hands, realised he wasn't strong enough, then improvised with the vacuum cleaner cord. I don't think you'll find finger pattern marks on Uma Leary.'

'Why not?'

'He's learning. Getting better. Escalating. And there's an urgency now. An arrogance. Certainly a recklessness.'

Shepherd pondered. 'But if dead bodies get you off so much, why not just break into mortuaries? Or rob graves?'

'There's a pattern. Freshness. He is someone who can only get what he needs through the sexual abuse of a recently deceased young woman. One who broadly fits the look of Hannah Lewis and Uma Leary.'

Shepherd nodded. 'That's why he didn't bother to abuse Phoebe.'

'Not his type. This is someone who connected to Orlando Gray, then took his daughter to make sure he stayed quiet about his illicit access to the mortuary.'

'No cameras in there, anyway.'

'But someone could have seen him if he just broke in. He needed Gray to get him in and out when the coast was clear. We should check entry points. Timings. Approach routes. Cameras near the hospital that fit the timings. Also, pull up HR files at local companies. Any jobs that involve proximity to bodies. Anyone who's applied but been rejected. History of inappropriate behaviour around dead bodies. People who've been dismissed from jobs related to work with bodies.'

'I'll get the boy wonder Walker on all that.'

Sawyer checked the time. He opened his laptop on the coffee table, typed something. 'Your timing is good. I have a meeting. Zoom.'

'What, now?'

'From the States.' Sawyer patted the seat next to him. 'You should join me.'

Shepherd took the spot and watched as Sawyer emailed a Zoom meeting link. 'But... What about Brad Singleton? The hair on Phoebe's body.'

Sawyer eyed him. 'Isn't that obvious?'

'No. Sir. It isn't obvious.'

Sawyer waved a hand. 'Cross-contamination. Singleton had contact with the killer, not Phoebe. We need to double down on his car and phone data. Like I said, match with any locations where Phoebe might have been held. We don't know how Singleton connects, but I'm pretty sure he didn't kill Phoebe. Maybe he helped the killer in some way. Or it could be a wild coincidence and the contact is purely random.'

Shepherd nodded to the laptop. 'So, who are we talking to?'

'I sent him a request earlier and briefed him with the details.' He anticipated Shepherd's protest and held up a hand. 'I know. But he's a trusted contact who's worked with police before. I met him a couple of years ago when I was working the case in London. He's a wise old Spanish psychiatrist who specialises in paraphilias. Bit of an odd sense of style. Not too socially elegant.' Sawyer caught Shepherd's eye. 'You'll like him.'

DR GUILLERMO CABRERA took a moment to stir his coffee. He stared into the cup, nodding. Sawyer had introduced Shepherd, and briefed Cabrera on the latest development with the Uma Leary post-mortem abuse. They watched him on-screen as he sprang to his feet and walked out of the Zoom window. He wore an emerald-green velvet blazer over a high-collared cream silk shirt.

After a moment, he arrived back in shot and sat down, thumping a weighty-looking hardback onto his desk. 'My colleague here in Portland is on vacation. I've taken his office for this part of my lecture tour.'

'Western USA?' said Sawyer.

'Correct. Starting here in this copycat 'Frisco. My San Franciscan colleagues hate that term, of course.' He smiled, revealing a set of brilliant white, porcelain-perfect teeth. 'Which is why I keep using it.' He slipped on a pair of round-framed glasses and patted the book cover. 'Bedside reading. *Sexual Deviance: Theory, Assessment, and Treatment.* Latest edition. The students here carry this round like their lives depend on it. In many ways, that is true. I insist on rigorous citation. It might not stop them googling but at least it forces them take a look inside the library.' He looked between Shepherd and Sawyer. 'I'm aware of your proclivities, Detective Sawyer. But, Detective Shepherd, I trust you are of a robust constitution?'

Shepherd nodded. 'Detective Sawyer has helped me along that road, yes. But he's more of an inspiration than an aspiration.'

Cabrera laughed. 'Well, for me, gentlemen, you've found yourself quite an exciting and rare specimen.' He patted the book again. 'What the SexDev editors call a true necrophile. That is, a necrophiliac. The most famous previous examples are Kemper, Christie, Dahmer.'

'How many types are there?' said Sawyer.

'Oh, many. Role players, romantics, fantasists, fetishists. If Detective Sawyer's assessment is correct, then there is a clear escalation pattern, up to homicidal, or true, necrophile. That is, an individual whose need for sexual gratification is so urgent and defining, he is willing to kill to satisfy it. He's no opportunist.'

Shepherd glanced at Sawyer. 'So, an opportunist necrophile doesn't kill?'

'Ah. Yes, he does. And I'm afraid we are talking about a *he*. Female necrophiles are so rare they're hardly worth talking about. Opportunists are killers, usually sexual sadists, who *indulge* in post-mortem abuse. The killing or infliction of pain is their main course. The necrophilia is like…' He searched for a word. 'Dessert. They might only indulge once, out of curiosity. But the true necrophile is exclusively killing to service his needs. He'll be self-confident, with good social skills.'

'Is he a psychopath?' said Shepherd.

'Oh, there's no scenario in which this guy isn't a psychopath. He's higher up the chain than, say, Jeffrey

Dahmer, who didn't have the social skills. He's a little bit Ted Bundy, but he mainly reminds me of John Christie, who took advantage of Timothy Evans, as he was… mentally impaired. Your gentleman…' Cabrera looked at his notes. 'Gray. He would be the Evans figure in the scenario laid out by Detective Sawyer. Low status. Controllable.' He laughed. 'He's more of a sparrow than a vulture.'

Sawyer tapped notes into his phone. 'So, what kind of character might our man be? What work could he be in?'

Cabrera ran a hand over his bald head. 'I'm reluctant to go any further with profiling, Detective Sawyer, but his psychopathology points to a cold necrophile. That is, someone who prefers to have sex with the body when it's been dead for a while, but not too long. This is why robbing graves will not serve him. He's a preserver. Warm necrophiles are more destructive. Many of them mutilate and eat the corpses, for some reason. He will probably be seduced by the idea of stillness. The lack of agency will be important. He may have a history of sleep rape. This might have begun with somnophilia, a fascination with watching people sleep. Possibly pygmalionism.'

'Mannequins,' said Shepherd.

'Indeed! Again, it's that lack of agency. The stillness. But true necrophiles tend to prefer the reality of humans, rather than simulacra.'

'Could he have a history of drugging partners?' said Sawyer. 'Rendering them unconscious to remove the agency?'

Cabrera nodded vigorously. 'Oh, absolutely. Bundy used to go into bedrooms at night and club his victims unconscious. And there are accounts of necrophiles paying sex workers big money to take cold baths, place ice cubes into their orifices… You could talk to local sex workers and see if they've encountered any clients who were into that. But I feel those days are long behind him.' He looked down at a tablet screen. 'The young girl. Phoebe. She wasn't sexually abused. Again, the sign of a true necrophile. They tend to stick to a demographic, a type. They rarely dip down into pre-pubescents. Psychopaths are good at compartmentalisation. It's a mistake to assume that paraphiliacs are weird loners. They can often have a normal-looking outside life with their fetish kept secret or indulged in some relatively benign way.' Cabrera took a sip of coffee.

Sawyer scrolled through his notes. 'What do you mean by "preserver"?'

'Ah! The experience will be so heightened for him, that he will want to indulge in private, and he will feel a strong need to relive it. Perhaps through photographs or video.' Cabrera looked at his watch, returned to his coffee.

Shepherd rubbed his eyes. 'So... How did he get this way?'

Cabrera smiled. 'That's a big question, Detective Shepherd. I have a long day ahead, and I don't really have the energy for a debate on *tabula rasa*. But this psychopathology is so distinct, so specific, he will surely have experienced something extreme that planted a seed in his mind. I suppose that's for you to discover, once you have a suspect.'

AFTER SHEPHERD HAD LEFT, Sawyer showered and lit a stick of incense. He dressed in loose underwear and a thin vest and settled on a floor cushion in the corner of the bedroom.

He began with mindful breathing, focusing on the sensation of the air entering and leaving his body, releasing the tension and calming his mind.

His mother, screaming and shouting.

He knew the usual thoughts and images would drift into view...

Running back to the grass verge.

But he had learned to gently acknowledge them and return focus on his breathing.

The sun flaring. Bright red blood dripping off the grass.

Sawyer eased into a loving-kindness meditation: *metta bhavana*. He spoke out loud.

'May I be happy.'

Caldwell's voice. 'You think you're enlightened...'

'May I be healthy.'

His mother's face, smiling at the gate.

'May I be at peace.'

The same face, obliterated by Caldwell's hammer.

He extended his wishes outward: to loved ones, acquaintances, those he had difficulty with, and to all sentient beings.

The sound of his father's knees as he stood up.

He visualised their receipt of the good wishes, tuned in to their happiness and peace.

The shotgun thundercrack.

As he began his reflection on the day, his phone vibrated with a message on the bedside table.

He gently redirected his thoughts back to moments of kindness he had experienced that day, things he'd learned and how he could carry the lessons into the next day.

His mother's voice. 'All shall be well.'

He contemplated his sense of gratitude: for both significant events and simple pleasures.

Caldwell again. 'But you're still in the dark.'

After a minute of mindful breathing, he slowly opened his eyes and rose to his feet.

He checked his phone.
Text.

Jake,
I miss you.
Mags X

Out in the kitchen, the cat flap sprang open.

Sawyer walked through and stared down at Bruce, who sat in the centre of the floor, washing himself. He spotted Sawyer and stared up at him.

'You're home early, big man.'

As Sawyer crouched and reached out to stroke the cat, he caught an unfamiliar sound from the side of the house.

Someone was swishing through the grass, making no effort to stay quiet.

They moved onto the wooden decking. Pausing at the back door.

Sawyer ran a hand across Bruce's back. His fur was stiff and taut, his muscles rigid, his tail fluffed out.

Breathing outside. Panting.

He stood up, switched on his phone light, and walked slowly to the back door.

He raised the light to the window, saw who was there, and opened the door.

Bruce bolted and tucked himself under the coffee table, as Sadie Fletcher stumbled inside.

Chapter Forty-Five

LYNDON WILDE ROSE from his padded chair and stepped forward into a pool of lukewarm light cast by the LED strip overhanging his mask gallery.

He walked along the line, admiring his private exhibition. The faces gazed down on him sightlessly, their wall mounts tilting the chins upward, giving the impression of repose. Wilde ran his fingers along the cheekbone contours of Lydia Wilkes, one of the Cavendish mortuary women. Three spaces along, he compared the finish of Hannah Lewis's gauze mask to the porcelain-like purity attained from the cheesecloth he'd used on Wilkes. Lower detail on Wilkes, but grainy on Lewis.

From a distance, he preferred the cheesecloth. But up close, the gauze revealed a subtlety of texture that would sustain him, deepen his desire. As he added more gauze masks, he would take down the cheesecloth versions and store them elsewhere as curiosities. Prototypes.

All the great artists had faced the same journey: from

the fumbling solipsism of their early experiments to the eternal majesty of their later masterworks.

He smiled, thought of *The Potato Eaters* to *Starry Night*.

Henry VI to *Hamlet*.

'Piano Sonata No.1' to the ninth symphony.

'The Laughing Gnome' to 'Heroes'.

He startled, as the studio walls rattled to a loud knocking sound from the main room out front.

'Lyndon!'

Rebecca.

They had a strict understanding: his studio was Lyndon's exclusive domain. Rebecca had agreed that if their marriage was to survive, they would each need distance, privacy. She would never bother him here, and Milo and Jamie were careful to not even step onto the winding path that led from the front garden.

The knock came again: violent and urgent.

'Lyndon. I need to see you.'

'Need' was not good.

He checked his watch: just gone 11pm. On the nights he came out to the studio, she would normally be settled in their bed with her audiobook or watching some true crime documentary on the sofa bed in her own private room.

Was there a problem with the boys?

He closed the mask gallery panel, flicked off the light and stepped out into the main studio space, activating the recessed lighting.

Rebecca stood outside, in her pink La Perla silk pyjamas, hands cupped around her eyes as she pressed her face into the window glass.

He had forgotten to close the blinds.

She hammered on the window with her palm.

Wilde sighed and swiped the biometric panel, unlocking the door.

She pushed through and stepped inside, then tried to slam the door shut behind her. It stopped a few inches from the frame, then eased closed, engaging the automatic lock.

Rebecca stared at him. She was flushed, and her eye make-up had pooled around the lower lids, then ran down her cheeks in oily smudges, carried by tears.

He reached for her, but she shoved him back.

'Rebecca,' he said, quietly. 'What is it?'

She wiped her cheeks with the back of a hand. 'I know.'

'Know what?'

'Cole Lane,' she said, her voice cracking. 'In Hayfield. That place near Chatsworth.'

He studied her, frowned, then laughed. 'What? I don't understand. What do you know?'

She steadied herself. 'I wanted to try. You didn't. You made this happen. You thought you could just sit back and let me arrange counselling. Carry on accommodating you. Trying to understand.' She moved in a step. 'But I've been *watching* you.'

A lurch of nausea, deep in his core.

He lowered his eyes, stayed silent.

Four in, six out.

'I have evidence,' she said. 'Of your secrets.'

He looked up. 'I don't have any secrets.' Now she was close, an arm's length away, he could smell the alcohol. 'You're drunk. You've worked yourself up into a state.'

She pointed. 'What's in that room back there? I saw you coming out, through the light from the window. I didn't even know there was a room—'

'It's private,' said Wilde, his expression blank. 'We agreed.'

She sneered. 'We agreed to have our own spaces. Not hide things from each other.'

Three in, three out.

Rebecca held her head in her hands. She shuddered, gasping for breath, choking back tears.

Wilde reached out to her, and she let him caress her tear-matted hair. He tucked a stray strand behind her ear and shifted his tone: soft, sympathetic. 'What do you know, Rebecca? What's this "evidence"?'

She shook her head. 'Lyndon… Tell me what's in that back room and I'll tell you what I know.'

He pulled her closer. 'It's nothing. But I'll show you if you like.'

'Yes,' she said quickly. 'Show me.'

He took her hand and swiped his thumb across the second biometric panel.

Chapter Forty-Six

SADIE FLETCHER SAT cross-legged on the sofa, cradling a mug of steaming tea in both hands. She wore Sawyer's padded running top over her branded black hoodie, and a pair of his winter socks.

Sawyer dragged the armchair around to face her and took a seat. On cue, Bruce crawled out from under the coffee table and settled next to her.

She sipped her drink, laid the mug on the coffee table.

'You're privileged,' said Sawyer. 'He normally assumes the worst of visitors.'

Sadie looked up. 'An incurious cat.'

'Keeps him alive. Are you ready?'

'What for?'

Sawyer studied her. 'Bedtime story. You're telling.'

Sadie sighed, reached a hand to Bruce and stroked his back. 'Dad insisted on sleeping in the shed outside. He said he'd get a better early warning of intruders than he would in the bedroom.'

'He was right,' said Sawyer.

She steadied herself. 'I was in the shower, so I didn't hear a thing. They cuffed me to the radiator.'

'Peyton?'

She nodded.

'Who else?'

'Abadi, and another guy I haven't seen before. Abadi called him Tarek. Middle-Eastern looks. Abadi had his Glock. The new guy had a bloody machinegun. When I wouldn't cuff myself, he fired a couple of shots into the pillow to make me. He got a kick in the bollocks for that. Not my most elegant move, but… Y'know. Low-hanging fruit.'

Sawyer smiled. 'Then what?'

'Peyton comes over their radio, wanting to know who's shooting, says he's coming in. Then, there's an explosion outside. I'm terrified about Dad, hoping he's okay.'

'Grenade,' said Sawyer. 'Peyton's a fan. Go on.'

'Peyton comes in with a sawed-off shotgun, says he's killed my dad.' She shrugged. 'I didn't believe him.'

'Neither would I. Keep going, Sadie.'

She took another drink, winced. 'How much sugar is in this?'

'Sorry. Force of habit. Carry on.'

'Peyton threatened me, tried to get me to call my dad. But Abadi was standing by the window.' She grimaced. 'I got a face-full of the bastard's blood. Dad must have shot him from outside. Tarek sends a few rounds through the window. Then, Peyton goes out the front with the shotgun. Soon after, Dad lobs a bottle in through the window, distracting Tarek. Dad gets him in the head, but he fires off a few rounds and catches Dad.'

'Where?'

Sadie held his eye. 'In the neck. And side.'

Sawyer's head dropped. 'Then what?'

'I... I heard a siren. Dad uncuffed me, told me to run. I said no, but he said he was too hurt to defend me and either I left or we'd both die.' Her eyes glinted. 'I grabbed my hoody and phone and got away across the field. Flagged down a car...' Her voice wavered. 'Sirens behind... They must have...'

Sawyer moved over, lifted Bruce onto the floor, and sat beside her. He rested a hand on hers. 'Sadie...'

Tears came now. She shouted, in anger and anguish. 'He killed two of those bastards.'

Sawyer nodded. 'He did. He saved your life.'

She dropped her head. 'Yeah, but —'

'Listen. The sirens might have spooked Peyton. He would have been waiting in a car, probably parked away from the house. He'd have to run. He's already wanted for murder.'

Sadie's head shot up. 'What?'

Sawyer sat back. 'He couldn't risk coming back for your dad.'

'You didn't see him. He was in a bad way.'

Sawyer got up and walked over to the kitchen, perched against the sink. 'Where was this place again?'

'Near Wetley Rocks. Staffordshire.'

He pondered. 'Someone probably heard the shooting. Or explosion. The call would have gone to Staffs Police. They'd probably send ARUs and a few locals for back-up. How did you find your lift?'

'The car stopped for me on the main road up through Leek. The driver was a woman, heading for Bamford. Coming from her sister's house in Stoke. She wanted to take me to the police, but I said I'd just got lost after a party.'

Sawyer nodded. 'Lucky.'

'I don't believe in luck.'

'Don't tell me you're a determinist.'

She gave a pained laugh. 'I'm not sure this is the time for a debate about free will. But this woman was like a guardian angel. We stopped at a garage, and she got me some tea.'

'You'll look her up someday and find that she died ten years ago.'

She shook her head, wiped her eyes. 'Fuck off.'

Sawyer took a loaf of bread out of the cupboard. 'Are you hungry?'

'Yes,' she said quickly.

'There's not much in.'

She nodded to the bread. 'Toast would work. Maybe a bit of almond butter.'

He smiled. 'Would peanut butter be acceptable?'

Sadie took an elastic band from a set of Blu-rays under the TV and tied back her hair. 'It's not ideal but I'll cope.'

Sawyer slotted the bread into the toaster. 'So, how did you know where to find me?'

'When you were back in the psych unit, Dad gave me a few options, including this address.'

'He put a tracker on my car, another life ago.'

'Ah...' She took out her phone and navigated to an app called TracePulse. 'Dad had this EMP tracker. A tiny magnetic thing. He wanted me to carry it round after they came to my flat.' She opened a map and pinch-zoomed to show a blinking red dot.

Sawyer took the phone and studied the map. 'Lancashire. Appley Bridge.' He looked at her. 'Did you go there with him?'

She shook her head.

He thought for a moment. 'Your dad shot Abadi

through the window to draw them away from you. But Peyton left the other guy there, came out after your dad… He doubled back to the house…'

'Dad could have put the tracker on Peyton's car.'

Sawyer nodded and handed back the phone.' Or this location could be where your dad managed to get to if he got away.'

She sank back into the sofa. 'You didn't see him. It was bad.'

The toast popped up. Sawyer put it onto a plate and took it to her, with a knife and a pot of peanut butter. 'I know a DCI at Staffs. I'll get the details from him later.'

Sadie ate for a while, head down. 'Dad had this thing. I got it into the mission statement for the self-defence club. *Train sport, practise art, think street.*'

Sawyer raised an eyebrow. 'That's good. Does he… communicate with you in the way he talks to everyone else?'

She smiled. 'Oh, yes. I used to get moments where he opened up, but they were rare.'

'I admire the efficiency,' said Sawyer.

'His communication?'

'Yes. I understand that, from my JKD.'

'I get that,' she said. 'Direct, fluid, adaptable. Minimise wasted effort. Maximise effectiveness…'

Sawyer stood up. 'I'll take the sofa. Don't worry. I washed the bedsheets the other day. You should stay here until the picture is clear. Peyton will come for you. He'll probably do it himself.'

'He has to. He's running out of fucking cronies.'

Sawyer laughed. 'Get some rest. I have a motion-sensor camera I can set up. It'll alert me if anyone comes near the house. I'll check on your dad early tomorrow.'

'Thank you.'

'I'll get some bedding.' He turned to go, paused. 'Last question. Why come here at all? Why not just go to the police, with the woman who picked you up?'

'One… They were already on their way. That was obvious from the sirens. Two… Before I left, Dad said something. Just one word.'

'Which was?'

Sadie sighed. '*Sawyer*.'

Chapter Forty-Seven

FRAZER DRUMMOND and Sally O'Callaghan sat side by side at the far end of the conference room table.

Drummond watched as O'Callaghan sloshed around her oversized vacuum mug and drank from the spout. 'Jesus Christ. That thing is bigger than my head. If you've got coffee in there, you'll be awake for a week.'

O'Callaghan yawned and rubbed her eyes. 'It's a YETI Rambler. And not coffee.'

'Vodka?'

'Ginger tea.'

Farrell barged in, shoving his way through the lower-ranked detectives huddled near the door. His suit was crumpled, and his hair was unkempt, with mottled grey roots. He hurried to the top of the table and took a seat by Shepherd and Walker. 'Right.' He looked around the table with sunken eyes. 'Okay, people. We have a serious case of a large pile of crap hitting a giant fan. Who wants to start the show?' He leaned back in the chair and rooted a finger around in each nostril in turn.

Shepherd got to his feet. 'Thanks, everyone, for coming in so early. I know many of you were working through the night.'

Farrell leaned forward and slammed a hand on the table. 'Let's lose the love and kisses and get on with solving this case.'

'Cases,' said O'Callaghan.

Farrell squinted at her. 'What?'

'Five enquiries and counting. The abduction and murder of Phoebe Gray. The arrest and subsequent suicide of Orlando Gray. The Cavendish mortuary abuse. The murder of Hannah Lewis. The murder of Uma Leary—'

Farrell raised his hands and gave a slow burst of sarcastic applause. 'Full marks for paying attention. DI Shepherd, carry on.'

Shepherd tried to catch O'Callaghan's eye, but she'd lowered her gaze, sipping from her mug. 'No progress on the murder of Phoebe Gray. We have no sightings of Brad Singleton, but plenty of ANPR detail on his movements over the past couple of weeks. Rhodes is working through it now, trying to match with places where he could have been holding Phoebe.'

'If indeed he's the murderer,' said Walker. 'And it's a big *if*.'

'There's little to add on Orlando Gray's death, although there are several internal enquiries…'

Farrell raised his hand and twirled his fingers around in a gesture of impatience.

Shepherd swiped at his screen, and the image on the main screen changed to a grainy night image of a car parked among trees. 'Silver, or grey, Porsche Cayenne.' He tapped his screen several times; the image refreshed with each tap, showing the same car in the same location but from a slightly different aspect. 'Rhodes caught this vehicle on several occasions near the hospital perimeter road during the time when the mortuary abuse would have taken place. Can't see the plates. There's been no sign of it since Gray's arrest.'

'Your conclusion?' said Farrell, cracking out a breath mint.

'I'll return to that later, sir.' He swiped the screen, showing recent images of Hannah Lewis and Uma Leary. I strongly believe these two young women were murdered by the same person, and that person also perpetrated the Cavendish mortuary abuse. Strangulation with ligature. Post-mortem sexual abuse. Sally's team have found traces of Plaster of Paris on the face and neck areas of both victims, which tallies with the victims in the Cavendish mortuary abuse.'

'So, we're looking for a painter and decorator,' said Farrell. 'Who somehow framed Orlando Gray for shagging the stiffs at Cavendish.'

Shepherd took a breath, caught O'Callaghan's eye, and her subtle nod. He swiped his screen; the main screen switched back to the image of the Porsche Cayenne. 'We have a witness sighting of this car in Hannah Lewis's road. No direct link with Uma Leary yet.' He nodded to Drummond.

'But Uma has left us something terribly interesting,' said Drummond. 'I hope we've all digested our egg and bacon butties.' He swiped through a series of close-up images showing detail from Leary's post-mortem. 'From working closely with my delightful colleague here throughout the night,' he gestured to O'Callaghan, 'I conclude that Uma Leary was strangled with a ligature and sexually abused post-mortem.'

'Same MO,' said O'Callaghan. 'Non-latex condoms. Non-latex gloves. No prints. No DNA. But we have new evidence of compounds and polymers from around the top of Uma's face, around the eyes. Also fibres.'

'And...' Drummond swiped to a close-up image of Leary's eyelid, with her open eye visible. 'She lost a few of the lashes from her right eye. Bruising and capillary damage around the lid, so I'd say they were torn out by hand. I couldn't see any evidence of tool marks. Tweezers, whatever. Sally's findings suggest gaffer tape. So, here's the terribly interesting bit. At the moment of her death, Uma suffered a rare form of muscular stiffening known as a cadaveric spasm. It's a sort of instantaneous rigor mortis, usually seen in violent deaths, and caused by the sudden depletion of adenosine triphosphate, the chemical energy within muscle cells.'

Farrell laughed. 'Frazer. Is there forensic significance here, or are you just gathering material for the next pathologist coffee morning?'

Drummond lowered his head. 'I know four-syllable words might be stretching the limit of your intellectual capacity, DSI Farrell, but do try to keep up.'

'He tried to close her eyes,' said Walker.

Drummond pointed at Walker and grinned. 'Someone's getting it. Cadaveric spasm would have kept Uma's eyes open.'

Shepherd nodded. 'And when he couldn't close them, he covered them with tape.'

'We found a match for the DNA under Hannah Lewis's fingertips on Uma Leary,' said O'Callaghan. 'And it tallies with one of the rogue profiles found at Cavendish. It has to be the same killer.'

Farrell sat back in his chair, mouth hanging open. 'This

doesn't add up. Why would Orlando Gray effectively confess to the mortuary abuse if he had nothing to do with it? And please don't say he was under mental duress because of his missing daughter.'

'He knew where his daughter was all along,' said Shepherd.

All eyes turned to him.

Farrell looked up at Shepherd. 'Do go on.'

Shepherd took a breath, nodded towards Walker. 'We believe that Hannah and Uma were murdered by the person responsible for the abuse in the Cavendish mortuary. And also for the murder of Phoebe Gray.'

Farrell squinted. 'Brad Singleton?'

'No,' said Walker. 'Singleton knew her father, and so there's been some kind of cross-contamination. That hair has been leading us in the wrong direction.'

Shepherd continued. 'The killer, the driver of the Porsche Cayenne, took Phoebe Gray as leverage. He kept her somewhere and forced her father to give him access to the mortuary. All the CCTV of the Porsche near Cavendish tallies with Gray's night shifts. Quiet, nobody around. Singleton doesn't own a Porsche. He drives a Volvo SUV.'

'Gray was desperate,' said Walker. 'He wanted it to look like he'd been forcibly removed from access to the mortuary. That way, in his mind at least, the killer would lose his leverage and have to let Phoebe go. Instead, he killed Phoebe.'

'And dumped her in the open,' said Myers. 'Maybe out of anger.'

Shepherd nodded. 'Makes sense.'

'Makes *sense*?' said Farrell, throwing up his hands.

'It did to Gray,' said Shepherd. 'It could explain why he told us that we were wasting time, given that Phoebe had been missing for weeks at that point. And he would be scared to give us direct information because of what the killer might do to Phoebe if we went storming in.'

Farrell looked around the room, casting for support. Not finding it. 'So, we're looking for a fucking plasterer who drives a Porsche. He has a history of necrophilia, but not paedophilia. He indulged himself with fresh corpses at first, but then progressed to murder.'

'Pretty much,' said Shepherd. 'Apart from the plasterer bit. He might work with models.'

'Do we have anything that might identify this man, from all the cross-referencing?' said Farrell. 'Plasterers don't drive Porsche Cayennes, for one. Could he be a dentist?'

'Dentists do use plaster for modelling,' said O'Callaghan, 'but it tends to be more refined.'

Walker swiped his screen back to the image of Hannah Lewis and Uma Leary. 'We've been looking into people with records, applying for jobs that would get them close to bodies, but that's one hell of a rabbit hole. We should look at victim acquisition. As far as we know, Hannah and Uma didn't know each other. So, how did our man encounter them?'

'Rhodes is working through CCTV and ANPR for both locations and the surrounding area,' said Myers. 'Uma had been house-hunting with her husband, Elton. He was in Prague on business when she was murdered. He checks out. Hannah Lewis's bank card shows her last purchase in a branch of Boots in a retail park near Hathersage on the day of her death. We have CCTV. Nothing remarkable. She buys some make-up, leaves, gets in her car. No sign of anyone else with her. No joy from house to house in her street.'

The room fell silent. They sat with heads bowed,

beneath the screen, under the expectant gazes of Hannah Lewis and Uma Leary.

'Sir?' DC Beverley Swift spoke up from a group standing at the far wall.

Farrell and Shepherd spoke in unison. 'Yes?'

'DS Walker asked one of the intelligence cells to flag any calls related to women of similar physical description to Hannah and Uma.' She checked her notepad. 'We had a late-night call from a Marcia Stillwell. She's a private detective. She mainly does divorce, low-level fraud. Stillwell says she's been surveilling the husband of a client who suspected he was having an affair. The client, Rebecca Wilde, fits the type. Stillwell says Rebecca was preparing to tell her husband she wanted a divorce and made her promise to check in with her after the conversation. She didn't call, and Stillwell has been to the address and there's no sign of Rebecca or her husband.'

Chapter Forty-Eight

SAWYER FED BRUCE and set the coffee machine running. His limbs ached from the sofa half-sleep, and his thoughts were too febrile for morning meditation.

He forced himself through a few stretches then slumped onto the sofa and checked the latest HOLMES casework on his laptop. New CCTV and forensics... Plaster of Paris on all victims... Silver Porsche seen near the hospital and at the Hannah Lewis scene... Still no sign of Singleton and none of his DNA at either of the women's scenes...

He studied Drummond's Uma Leary report, noting the detail about the spasm and the attempt to close the eyes.

'Have you heard anything?'

Sadie appeared at the bedroom door in a pair of Sawyer's joggers and T-shirt.

'Come and sit down. There's coffee.'

She hurried over and sat in the armchair. 'Just tell me.'

He closed the laptop. 'I spoke to the Staffs DCI about the farmhouse. They found two bodies. Neither match your dad's description.'

Sadie leaned forward. 'So, he got away?'

'Why so surprised?' Sawyer got up and brought over coffee, with milk and sugar. 'I don't know any more. It's not my case, and I had to ask really nicely to get that detail, so I can't be definite on ID. I only know this much because I'm helping the DCI with another case.'

She added sugar to the coffee and stirred, holding Sawyer's eye. 'He'll contact me if he's okay.'

'He won't. Not yet. But…'

Sadie sipped the coffee. 'Oh, God. Please. I can't take any *buts* now.'

'Well. You've had all the good news. I gave my contact the tracker location in Appley Bridge. There's no car there and no sign of Peyton. Someone was living at the location and he's in custody, but it looks like Peyton has been holed up there. There's lots of his stuff lying round. Check the tracker app.'

Sadie took out her phone. 'It's in the same place.'

Sawyer took a slug of coffee. 'He's checked and found the tracker, then left it somewhere and taken the car.'

'But the guy they've arrested—'

'Peyton would know they'd come for him. But he doesn't care anymore. Whatever happened at the farmhouse with your dad, it's kicked him onto another level. There's a lot of history between Peyton and me.' He stood up. 'I'll fill you in on the way.'

'On the way where?'

'I have a job up in Padley Gorge. You'll have to come with me. Until they find Peyton, I can't leave you alone here.'

Sadie stood up. 'I'll take a quick shower and be ready in five minutes. But I'm not sitting in the back of your car all day. You can drop me at the S&G school in Castleton.

That's on the way to Padley.' She finished the coffee and turned back to the bedroom. 'I'll be okay there. The place will be busy with contractors and my team, and it's right in the centre of town. I'll let you know if Dad gets in touch. You can pick me up later.'

'What about clothes?'

'I have stuff in my office at the building. In the meantime, I noticed you have decent taste in underwear. The fit isn't quite right for me, but I'll make do.' She walked through into the bathroom and turned on the shower, calling back. *'Toast would be nice.'*

Chapter Forty-Nine

SAWYER PARKED the Mini by the café at Grindleford Station. Bentley's team had set up a wide cordon around the north end of Padley Gorge, a lush, wooded valley on the eastern fringe of the National Park. He could just make out a group of detectives and the two prison officers beyond a clutch of dense oak trees off the side of the road. An officer in a Hi-Viz vest guarded the scene tape at the entrance to a walking track.

He sat back, wallowing in the final track on his playlist: Mazzy Star, 'Into Dust'. Hope Sandoval's drowsy vocal coiled around him like a lover's embrace.

Flash to a clink of beer bottles.
Maggie's face.
'I think I'll talk to you.'

The music slipped away. He turned off the engine and opened the windows, letting his senses feast on the natural sounds and aromas. Fresh earth, damp moss, sweet and pungent wildflowers. Jays chattered overhead, and he caught the frothy murmur of Burbage Brook drifting up from the base of the valley.

It had flowed this way for thousands of years. For all of Sawyer's trials and terrors, his existence was barely a single drip from a tap in comparison.

He closed the windows, then his eyes.

He spoke out loud.

'May I be happy.'

His father's voice. 'There is nothing in darkness that will not be disclosed.'

'May I be healthy.'

His mother's shout. 'Run, my darling!'

'May I be at peace.'

He startled, at the sound of knocking on the car window.

Bentley stood there, smiling, holding up a hand. DC Boateng stood at his shoulder.

Sawyer held up two fingers, mouthed, 'Two minutes.'

Bentley nodded and retreated with Boateng to stand near the cordon officer.

Sawyer made a call; it connected instantly.

'Sir.' Shepherd sounded weary and rattled. 'Walker's in my office with me.'

'What if there's a reason we can't find Brad Singleton?' said Sawyer.

'The reason being?' said Walker.

'He's not on the run. What if he's dead? If Orlando Gray knew his daughter's abductor drove the silver Porsche, he might have asked Singleton to follow it. Try to find where he was holding Phoebe. Singleton is ex-army. He'd be bold, familiar with surveillance principles. So, he tracks the abductor but only sees him drive back to his home. Maybe he watches him do normal domestics, realises he can't be keeping Phoebe there. Gray, desperate, follows through his alternative plan of getting himself arrested, removing the killer's leverage.'

'Wait, wait,' said Shepherd. 'Why doesn't Singleton just expose the abductor if he's followed him?'

'It's too risky,' said Walker. 'He needs to know where Phoebe is first.'

Sawyer continued. 'But then, with Gray already arrested, Singleton gets lucky, and our man goes to the place where he's keeping Phoebe—'

'But our man clocks him,' said Shepherd. 'Kills him?'

'That's one explanation for why Singleton has vanished. And, if he had to get rid of Singleton and Phoebe's bodies, that could explain the presence of Singleton's hair on Phoebe. It also adds up with why there's no Singleton DNA at the Hannah Lewis or Uma Leary scenes.'

'So,' said Walker, 'why hide Singleton's body somewhere but dump Phoebe out in the open?'

'He's angry,' said Sawyer. 'Angry at Gray, for taking away his access to the mortuary. It's a rebuke. You should triple-down on where the abductor might have been holding Phoebe and match it with ANPR detail for Singleton.'

'There's something new,' said Shepherd.

'What?' Sawyer looked out to the cordon. Bentley held up an arm, tapped his watch.

'Could be related. A new missing woman. Rebecca Wilde. Fits the Lewis and Leary type. She's been working with a private detective, Marcia Stillwell, building a divorce case against her husband. Stillwell says that Rebecca was about to tell her husband she wanted the divorce and agreed to call Stillwell after, to check her husband's reaction.'

'It might be nothing,' said Walker, 'but we're leaving soon to meet with Stillwell.'

Sawyer opened the door. 'Send me your location when you're done. Oh, and take another pass at that Hannah Lewis CCTV. I had a look this morning.'

'Why?' said Shepherd.

'She pays for her items on a self-checkout till, then leaves. But the guy next in the queue picks up something from the till. The video cuts and I can't see what he does next, but you need to get a longer version. Looks to me like Hannah Lewis left her purse behind.'

Chapter Fifty

DALE STRICKLAND FINISHED his Peloton programme and walked across the top floor landing into the open-plan wet room. He took extra time over his shower, running through the permutations and scenarios, as the vast rainfall showerhead engulfed him, and steam billowed up from the marble floor.

Chess was not his game, but he knew enough to analyse his current position. After a long, turgid period of thrust and parry, the middle game was over. The board was simplifying.

With Peyton Jr out of the way, he would be free to rebuild from the ground up, using his political reach and the deeper connections of Peyton Sr. He had a side project: keep Stokes on side, but squeeze him out to the fringes, while transitioning the younger, deadlier Eddie Peyton into the role of his key general.

And then, with a seasoned cop-killer at his call, he would push forward with his main goal: Sawyer. It would be easy to sell as an ugly loose end from the attack on Peyton Jr.

It would take time. But all good things…

As long as he kept that desire running hot.

He dried off and dressed for work, then checked his phone.

Still nothing from Abadi.

Permutations. Scenarios.

Dead Fletcher then dead Peyton, as ordered. Abadi and El-Masri downed in crossfire.

Dead Fletcher then dead Peyton. Abadi and El-Masri lying low, without phones.

He didn't want to telegraph specific interest, but he should call Oliver. Get him to check police activity around the location.

Strickland hurried down to the ground floor hall and entered his office.

Wesley Peyton sat in a chair on the back garden porch, head down, beside a bright blue New York Knicks backpack. He saw Strickland's movement then rushed to the window, pointing to the door.

Strickland took a breath.

Permutations. Scenarios.

Dead Fletcher. Dead Abadi and El-Masri.

But not dead Peyton.

He unlocked the door and Peyton stepped in.

Strickland closed the blind. 'What the *fuck* are you doing at my house?'

Peyton took off his backpack and crashed down in Strickland's padded office chair. He tipped back his head, pulled down the brim of his baseball cap. 'Nobody saw me. I waited until your missus and son had left. I didn't come down the fuckin' garden path and ring your doorbell.'

Peyton was flushed, slathered in sweat. He held a bloodied bandage against a deep gash along his jawline.

'You're injured. You've got an eyepatch. People will remember you.'

'I told you. Nobody saw me. I went back to my place. My man Remmel did a sweep and found a fuckin' tracker under the car.'

Strickland spun away. 'Jesus Christ.'

'Keep your hair on. Remmel took off. I got a few things and scarpered. Left the tracker.'

'What happened at the farmhouse?'

Peyton bared his teeth. He groaned with frustration, spraying saliva as he spat out the name. '*Fletcher.* I had the bastard. He was injured. Looked bad. But he suckered me in. Grabbed the shotgun barrel. I got a shot off, but he'd pushed it up. Brought down half the ceiling. Then, he stuck this on me.' He pointed to his chin. 'Nearly laid me out cold. By the time I got my head straight, he'd legged it. Dibble were on their way, so I had to do the same. The shottie's in my backpack.'

Strickland stared him out. 'The others?'

No answer from Peyton. He stepped closer.

Peyton shook his head. 'No good. He had 'em both.' He sprang up out of the chair and walked to the window, peered round the edge of the blind.

Strickland reached a steadying hand out to his desk and eased himself into the chair, head whirling. 'The daughter?'

'Gone. We had her cuffed, but Daddy must have unlocked her.'

'What did you leave at the scene?'

Peyton waved a hand. 'Nothing that could link to you.' He shrugged. 'The feds will find two dead Egyptians.

Assume it's some kind of ethnic bullshit. Or drugs or whatever.'

Strickland tipped back his head, stared up at the ceiling. 'Abadi is a known associate of mine.'

'I admit it's not great, but there's still no evidence he was acting on your watch.'

Peyton stepped in, too close. Strickland winced at his rancid breath.

'You know what, though, Dale? I'm done chasing that maniac around.' He lowered his voice to an angry hiss. 'I'm calling in one of my lads. Technically, he's one of our kid's, but he gets it, yeah? Speaks English, for one.'

Strickland shook his head. 'We've been here before. You still need Eddie's sign-off—'

'Hey!' Peyton waved his arms, paced back to the window. 'You know what? *Fuck* Eddie. Right back when we were kids. Eddie this, Eddie that. Always first refusal for Eddie, then whatever's left for little Wesley. Toys, toffees. Cast-offs. Hand-me-downs. Everything second hand, after Eddie had done with it. Fucked it up. He always licked the bowl *and* got the last helping.' Peyton beat a palm against his heart. 'Not anymore. You're looking at *Wes Peyton 2.0*, yeah?' He waved his fingertips through the air. 'If you want to keep your hands in all the sweetie jars, you'll get used to working with me, not him.' He dropped the volume and leaned in close, speaking into Strickland's ear. 'Cos we're in it together, Dale, aren't we? Joined at the hip, yeah? Invested in each other's success.'

Strickland held a beat. 'What does that mean?'

Peyton stepped back. 'Hey. You can help or you can leave me to it. Your shout.' He pointed to his eyepatch. 'But I'm all done with "sign-off". I'm calling in what's fuckin' owed. *Now*.'

Chapter Fifty-One

WILLIAM CALDWELL DUCKED under a low hanging branch and stopped at the edge of a vast tract of flat, open moorland overlooked by heather-covered hills.

He shielded his eyes from the sun and pointed to the far side of the moor, towards a vast Gothic-looking lodge with pointed arches.

'Longshaw. They shipped dozens of injured troops here during World War One. Treated them there. The moss round here was made into wound dressings.' He turned, regarded Sawyer with his deathly eyes. 'Sphagnum moss.' Caldwell pointed to the opposite edge of the moor, a short walk away. 'There's a patch down there. Springy green stuff. I think that's where I put the last one. In the woods near there.'

'Julie Saltwell,' said Sawyer.

Caldwell grinned, flashing his yellowed teeth. 'The moss didn't do much for her wounds.'

He hobbled on, along the edge of the moor.

Sawyer checked behind. Bentley and Boateng were

keeping a judicious distance, with the two prison officer escorts.

'Your father was a good detective,' said Caldwell. 'He could have gone far, if he hadn't filled his head with all that religious claptrap.'

'And you hadn't murdered his wife.'

Caldwell paused mid-step and squeezed out a wheezy laugh. 'There is that, yes.' He carried on, almost bent double now. 'I do have a stick, but I wanted to do this by myself. Sort of a pilgrimage.'

Sawyer kept back a few paces. 'Do you feel anything?'

'Hardly. I'm out of my fucking mind on morphine.'

'I mean for the people you hurt. Killed. For the people who loved them.'

Caldwell leaned to the side and rested an atrophied hand on his knee. He barked out a few coughs, then spat something into the grass. 'Look at the fucking state of me. Do you really think I give a shit about some silly tarts who didn't have the brains to get proper jobs? Who had to open their legs to keep themselves in hair dye?' He moved off. 'Jess was different. At first. Before she started to get guilt trips. She was pretty confused, though. Giving it away to that teacher.' Another wheezy laugh. 'What do they call it? An overlap? She was on an overlap from an affair with another affair.' He looked over his shoulder, found Sawyer's eye. 'She couldn't get enough.'

'They reminded you of your mother, didn't they?'

He waved a hand, turned again. 'Oh, *Little Jake*. Really?'

'Dark black hair. Strong-willed. Needed putting in her place…'

Caldwell held up a hand and wagged his finger. 'My mother wasn't violent, though. The usual cliché. She left that to my father. He gave me the belt. Made me hate him. She went the other way.'

Sawyer quickened his pace slightly. 'No love.'

He scoffed. 'Yes. That woman wouldn't have known love if—'

'It had hit her in the face with a hammer?' said Sawyer.

Caldwell laughed again. 'She used to wash out my mouth with carbolic soap when I swore. Actually did that.'

They walked without speaking for a few minutes, then Caldwell pushed aside more branches and entered a wooded clearing.

Sawyer checked behind. The detectives and escorts had emerged from the trees onto the side of the moor.

He followed Caldwell into the wood. 'Julie's father is also ill. Lung cancer. He still keeps his vigil at the family church. After all this time.'

Caldwell waved the bony hand again. 'He can survive lung cancer. Pancreatic, though…'

'It killed Steve Jobs.'

'Yes. But that stupid bastard only had a neuroendocrine tumour. Mine is more aggressive. Adenocarcinoma. He could have had surgery, but he went for all the bullshit, thinking it could save him. Acupuncture, herbals.' Caldwell sat down on a tree stump, panting. He looked around, then dropped his head. 'This isn't the place. It's similar, but not here. Maybe round the other side. Near the brook.'

Sawyer watched him. 'Maybe not.'

Caldwell nodded. 'I'm done for today. Too fucked. I haven't got the energy.'

'What happened at Bolehill Wood, Bill?' said Sawyer. 'With Sharon Wright.'

Caldwell kept his head down. A swirl of wind caught his

white hair, holding it above his head like a suspended twist of smoke. He raised his eyes, letting his gaze drift.

Sawyer walked over and crouched by Caldwell. He kept his voice low. 'I know what you want.'

Caldwell's eyes shifted to Sawyer. 'I want to rest.'

Sawyer nodded, shuffled closer. 'I know what you want, Bill. Tell me about what happened at Bolehill, and I'll give it to you.'

Caldwell closed his eyes. 'Next time?'

'Next time.'

Chapter Fifty-Two

LYNDON WILDE EASED the Porsche into a patch of shade at the back side of the courtyard. He switched off the ignition and got out of the car, then walked to the foot of the external staircase and sat on the bottom step.

He slapped his cheeks with both hands, shocking himself into the moment.

Focus on process, not emotion.

Rebecca wouldn't be missed until early evening.

Milo and Jamie had school football and were due to be picked up by Rebecca's sister for a birthday party near her house. Rebecca had arranged to collect them from the party.

He had time.

His left foot tremored, sending his leg into spasm. He clamped a hand down on the knee, opened his mouth wide, and drew in a lungful of air.

It tasted metallic, tainted.

Six in.

Hold for four.

He replayed the scene at his home office.

Six out.

Rebecca had known about the first woman. She'd named the street.

'I have evidence of your secrets.'

She had been overwhelmed by emotion. Loaded with alcohol.

Had she already gone to the police?

No. They would have arrested him.

So, what about the second woman?

'I know…'

How? How did she know?

Four in.

He would report her missing.

Six out.

Worst case: she had spoken with her sister about her suspicions, about confronting him.

But surely she couldn't know the full story.

Nausea reared up, and he leaned to the side, dry-retching.

He slapped himself again.

Process.

He would calm her down, find out how much she knew.

The situation was serious. Out of control. But he could make her empathise. Once she connected to the depth of his pain, his sickness, she would understand his actions, become his advocate.

She would be on his side, if only to keep the boys safe and shielded.

Flash of the girl's wide, twitching eyes.

He would lay out the full picture. The whole story.

The purity of her hatred.

Wilde froze, as a car passed down the lane alongside the house, then turned away towards the main road.

He inhaled: sudden and sharp. He had been holding his breath.

He slapped himself, spoke it out loud.

'Four in. Six out.'

He shuddered, tears welling.

He ground his teeth, biting back the urge to scream.

Wilde stood up and paced the perimeter of the house, checking for anything unusual. He'd been forced to pursue vacation notices on squatters before, and this property was a prime candidate.

No signs of forced entry. No makeshift window covers. No rubbish bags.

He had the place to himself again.

He walked over to the car and looked inside.

Duffel bag and wheeled suitcase on the back seat.

He opened the boot.

Rebecca lay on her side, hands in front of her face as if in prayer, wrists tightly bound.

Wilde had pushed her knees up to her chest and bound her ankles, then secured her upper legs to her lower body.

Her hair, splayed across her shoulders.

Her teeth, biting on a multi-layered gag.

The bruise had bloomed across her forehead and gathered at the bridge of her nose.

It was the first time he'd hit her. But it had been necessary. Only to subdue.

Wilde stared down at his wife.

She stared back, her eyes widening, imploring.

Chapter Fifty-Three

SAWYER STROLLED into the Insomnia coffee shop. He stood at the door for a moment, scanning the customers, then fell into a padded green chair at a back window table overlooking the Hope crossroads.

A young woman in a striped apron came out from the back and hovered while he studied the menu.

'Earl Grey and blackcurrant cake.' He looked up. 'Is that a combo or a cake flavour?'

She smiled. 'Cake flavour.'

'Sold. Regular latte, too, please.'

She nodded, turned to go.

'Oh... Were two men in here earlier? Shifty looking. One large, the other not so large. Probably talking to a third.'

The server hesitated, turned to the counter for help. Nobody there. She looked back to Sawyer.

He held up his warrant card, smiling. 'The answer is yes. I just wondered if you could tell me how long they've been gone.'

'Oh. Okay. Not long. Half an hour or so.'

'Thank you. And no fork with the cake, thanks.'

'Right.' She nodded and left.

The place was quiet, in a late morning lull, with most customers favouring the sun-baked seating area out front.

Sawyer's phone rang. Shepherd.

He answered. 'Lime.'

'Sir?'

'Your shower gel. This is a coffee shop with many competing aromas, but your essence remains.'

Shepherd sighed. 'How was Caldwell?'

The server bought the coffee and cake.

'I'd go for *loathsome*,' said Sawyer.

'We couldn't stay.'

He broke off a chunk of cake. 'Go on.'

'Rebecca Wilde. She's missing, along with her husband, Lyndon. The private detective saw him visit Uma Leary's house and spotted him in Hannah Lewis's street. Timings fit. Walker's on speaker with me.'

'Lyndon Wilde runs a high-end property agency,' said Walker. 'Elite Estates International. I called the property manager who said he was due to have breakfast with Wilde this morning. He called in sick. But—'

'He's not at home.' Sawyer munched on the cake, slurped some coffee. 'And his silver Porsche isn't there.'

'Are you eating?' said Shepherd.

'Cake. It's incredible. Is Rebecca a similar type to Hannah and Uma?'

A pause. 'Yes,' said Shepherd. 'But... she's his wife. Surely—'

'She confronts him about the detective's findings. He realises she could connect him to the murders. He panics.'

'She might already be dead,' said Walker.

Sawyer thought for a moment. 'It won't be as easy for him to kill his wife. And we might have an advantage.'

'What?' said Shepherd.

'Time. He might not know about the detective. He certainly doesn't know about the detective contacting us. So, he probably thinks Rebecca's absence won't be noted for a while.'

'Rhodes has been busy,' said Shepherd. 'He's narrowed down ANPR and phone data for Singleton, and he has corresponding CCTV and ANPR for Wilde's Porsche. But no potential places linking up yet.'

Sawyer looked out at the crossroads. 'He might know a route with limited ANPR coverage. It's not difficult to find out. Have Rhodes run fresh ANPR and CCTV for the Porsche's movements today. Try to match up with areas that feature properties on the agency's books. Narrow it to places that are open or for sale. What about Rebecca's family?'

'We've contacted her sister, Kayla,' said Shepherd. 'She's due to pick up their two children after school. We have a team at the Wilde house. He has a custom-built garden studio. Rhodes has the computer. Wilde's last phone ping was a mast close to the house.'

'He ditched it,' said Sawyer. 'I bet he didn't take it to the place he kept Phoebe. Probably has a burner there.'

Walker spoke up. 'The CCTV from Boots. The guy is clearly Wilde. We watched a longer version, and he checks out Hannah Lewis's purse, then hands it in. ANPR puts Wilde's Porsche in that area on the day.'

'He got her address,' said Sawyer. 'Probably from her driving licence. Have you spoken to Uma's husband?'

'He's in transit from Prague,' said Shepherd. 'He says he's willing to talk later.'

Sawyer finished his coffee. 'You're close. Find that property. It will be on Wilde's books. Somewhere he feels safe, where he has easy access. Singleton's ANPR will be the key. Whatever's happened to him, and it doesn't feel good, he might help us in his absence. Don't go charging in, though. You have to assume Rebecca is still alive. And dig deep into Lyndon Wilde. You might unearth something that helps us find him or throw more light on where his head's at. That could help if you need to convince him to give himself up.'

Sawyer turned, and the sun flared through the window. He leaned back, into the shade, but it was too late.

Flash of the bloodied hammer, raised.

'Uma Leary is someone else who's helping in her absence.'

'How do you mean?' said Shepherd.

'The cadaveric spasm, how the killer tried to close her eyes.' He took a breath. 'Caldwell said something... I asked him why he used the hammer. Why he attacked the women's faces. He said it was the shame. He couldn't stand them looking at him, judging him. Maybe there's something similar here. Trying to close Uma's eyes, then giving up and covering them with tape instead.'

'So he couldn't do the deed while being watched,' said Shepherd. 'Even by dead eyes.'

Sawyer got up. 'I need to go. I'm due back at the day job. There's another chat with my NCA chums scheduled. Listen. Good work. Although it's not my case, of course.'

'Of course,' said Shepherd.

Chapter Fifty-Four

SADIE FLETCHER FINISHED LOADING the dishwasher and placed two deep wine glasses on the coffee table.

She opened the fridge. 'You really don't drink?'

Sawyer looked up from browsing the streaming channels. 'I've tried. I really have. It never goes well.'

'It's not compulsory. Even for a northerner.' She brought over a glass bottle of red and a plastic bottle of Diet Coke. She nodded to the Coke. 'I'd say that's the worst of those two evils, though.'

'Evil is my middle name.'

She laughed, poured the drinks. 'Here you go. You can drink your fizzy pop from a grown-up glass. Might make it taste better. So, what *is* your middle name, then?' She held up a hand. 'Wait! Let me guess...' She studied him. 'Marvin?'

'No.' He took a drink. 'Marvin is incorrect. But more interesting than the reality.'

She grimaced. 'Oh, don't tell me you're one of those boring no-middle-name people.'

'Afraid so.'

Sadie sipped her wine. 'So, what happened in that psych unit? Must have been pretty intense. Did you have things like birthday parties? Did you celebrate with people when they got out?'

'That's problematic.'

Sadie sat on the sofa next to Sawyer. She pulled her knees up to her chest and pivoted to face him. 'Why? Because you're not supposed to make an event out of anything?'

'Because it implies the end of something. That's too much pressure. Of course it's progress when service users move on, but readmission rates are high."

'So, apart from the pressure thing, you're basically celebrating before the game is over.'

His eyes held hers. 'There's never an "over".'

'Yeah, yeah. It's a work in progress. I had all that when I was a kid.' She took a big breath. 'My stepdad abused me.'

'I know.'

She took a big slug of wine. 'Sorry. Failing to keep it light. Yeah, he was foul. Didn't end well for him, though. You know that, too, I'm sure.'

'Oh, yes.' Sawyer got up and drew the blinds, shutting out the dusk. He scrolled through Spotify on his phone and set some music playing on his smart speaker. Hazy synths. Reverb-drenched guitar.

'What's this?' said Sadie, angling her head.

'A new band called Harp. Well, not really new... The singer used to be in Midlake. They've been around for a while.'

She smiled. 'You think I don't know who that is. Actually, you've hit my sweet spot. Folky but a bit strange. Fleet Foxes. Iron & Wine. Bon Iver. All that.'

He sat down again. 'I know that, too. I researched your social media.'

She shoved him. 'You'd better be joking.'

Sawyer just about saved his Coke from spilling. 'You remind me of someone.'

'Who?'

He shook his head. 'No one you know. You were telling me about your stepdad.'

Sadie winced. 'Let's not go back there. Nothing else to say about him really.' She looked round. 'Where's Bruce?'

'He keeps strange hours. Sometimes, he turns up late. Sometimes early.'

She got up, browsed the shelves behind the TV. 'I love that you've got actual CDs. Oh, I forgot to say…' She sat down again. 'Thanks for looking after me.'

'I assume you can generally look after yourself.'

'You assume right. The Strength & Grace Academy is really taking shape. I just wish Dad wasn't such a bloody outlaw. I'd love to have him there for the opening.' Her eyes widened. 'Oh! You should do a seminar. JKD. You know. The principles of efficiency. The shortest route to the target. All that.'

'Sign me up. But my main concern now is keeping you alive to open it. Until your dad gets in touch, we don't know what he did to Peyton.'

She scowled. 'Will you catch him now he's surfaced?'

'He'll be picked up soon. Staffordshire CID are working with GMP. There's a warrant, fresh intelligence gathering. They will have circulated his ID in the national databases, and they'll watch ports and airports. He'd just better hope your dad doesn't find him before we do.'

'So, how long can I stay in your humble abode?'

He shrugged. 'As long as it takes.'

'Thanks. Your fridge contents need work. I'll get on it.' Sadie fidgeted, jogging one leg then the other. She got up again, looked through the DVDs and Blu-rays. 'Do I want to know why Peyton was after my dad?'

'Probably not.'

She didn't turn around. 'Tell me anyway.'

Sawyer sighed. 'Your dad was in custody. Suspected of involvement in an unrelated case. When Peyton and friends attacked the police station at Buxton, he got a gun from the evidence room and fought his way out. He shot one of Peyton's men. Billy Rice. Presumably he was close to him, given the trouble he's going to.'

Sadie came back to the sofa. 'But why attack the station? To get to Dad?'

'To get to me. It was complicated. Then it got even more complicated when a close friend of mine was injured in the attack. When I realised Peyton was involved, I reacted badly. I wasn't well at the time.'

'And you're better now?'

'You can't say that in the unit, because you're never the first to know.'

She frowned. 'If you're getting better?'

'Yes. They prefer you to say you're ill, but hopeful. Hasn't your dad talked to you about any of this?'

'Of course not. We don't *talk*.' She finished her glass. 'What did he mean when he said you'd know who was pulling the strings?'

'You'll find out soon.'

She scoffed. 'What are men like? Settling your little scores. Passing them on. Not caring who gets hurt in the process.'

'We'll get Peyton and his puppet master soon. Then the cycle ends.'

Sadie closed her eyes. 'I'm exhausted, Jake. But I feel bad about taking your bed.'

'Get some rest. And I'm fine with the sofa. It's comfier than the bed in the unit. I'll clear everything away before I crash.' He grinned. 'Or maybe in the morning.'

She yawned, stared into space. 'My dad got caught up in that nonsense, too. Revenge. Settling a score.'

'With your stepdad?'

'Yeah. My parents split up when I was five. So, I only really knew Austin as my dad for a short time. The man who was always around, who lived with us. But my memory of him is so strong. I know it's hard to believe now, but he used to be so lovely. Loving. It's like... he got poisoned by the separation, by what happened in the army. He tried to carry on by wearing this mask of acceptability. But he couldn't keep it up.'

'I suppose some people just learn to get good at hiding the pain. Or they take on a persona that can bear the pain for them.'

Sadie got up, headed for the bedroom. 'Yeah, but the mask slips eventually.'

SAWYER SETTLED ON THE SOFA, zoning out to the sound of light rainfall outside. But his eyes wouldn't stay closed, and as he gazed across the dark room, the outline of the front window formed a backdrop for his churning thoughts. Faint patterns of light swirled and formed images, each morphing and blending into the next: Caldwell's yellow-toothed smile; his father's head popping round the corner of his childhood bedroom; his mother smiling at the gate; Hannah Lewis and Uma Leary; Caldwell's victims.

He projected his father's abstract paintings into the

space, the colours marked by multiple shades of light and dark, shifting and cycling: purple, green, blue, pink. And the work in progress he'd seen in the studio: the jagged lines. Blended browns, reds and blacks. Blurred at the centre.

His father's terrors laid bare in lurid primaries.

And another shape formed in the window space: an oval, with two curved lines forming at the top. Horns.

Scott Walton's animal mask. The veil for his pain.

He heard Walton's question. *'Who are you?'*

Sawyer sat up and turned on a lamp. He checked his phone: just gone midnight.

He called Shepherd, pressing the phone to his ear, keeping it off speaker. He walked to the corner near the front door, far from the bedroom.

Shepherd answered. 'Good evening, Sir.'

'You mean morning.'

'Well. Just about.'

Sawyer kept his voice low. 'He's making masks.'

'Okay—'

'Plaster of Paris. Cabrera talked about necrophiles being "preservers", and that he would want to take photos or video. But he goes for fresh victims. He doesn't rob graves. As Cabrera said, his pattern is freshness. Recently deceased. As recent as possible. Close to the living version.'

'Sir—'

Sawyer paced. 'He wants that… proximity but without agency. Without awareness. And that's why he strangles. No facial injuries. He's casting the victims into death masks. Capturing them at the freshest possible point after death. When they're closest to life—'

'*Sir*. We're way ahead of you.'

Sawyer's phone buzzed with a notification. 'Ahead in what way?'

'Walker dug through Wilde's computer history. He recently ordered two books. *Plaster of Paris: Techniques From Scratch* and another general book on mask-making. He also visited a site called *Instructables* that gives specific instructions for making a death mask.'

A door closed at Shepherd's end.

'Are you still in the office?' said Sawyer.

'Yes. Walker's with the team at Wilde's home. We have a possible location for Wilde. ANPR and phone mast data is pointing to an area in the Dovestone Valley up on Saddleworth Moor. GMP territory but we're liaising because of the scenes inside our manor. Wilde's agency has a property there. A big farmhouse. Elton Leary confirmed that he and Uma viewed the place a few days ago. They met Wilde there.'

'Are you getting an assault team together?' said Sawyer.

Shepherd hesitated. 'Yes.'

'Not my case, I know. But... Priority of Life, remember.'

'I know. You said. We can't go charging in. She might be alive. We're waiting on a negotiator. And gathering intel on the layout. They've got drones up already. Wilde's Porsche is there. We can isolate and contain the perimeter, try and talk him out.'

Sawyer saw a reflection in the oven door. Movement behind, at the bedroom door.

He turned.

A tall, top-heavy man stood behind Sadie Fletcher, guiding her into the sitting room. He had a beefy arm around her throat and a hand across her mouth.

Wesley Peyton followed them in. He wore his sky-blue baseball cap and held his single-barrel shotgun at his side.

'Sir?' said Shepherd.

Peyton pointed to Sawyer's phone. He held a finger over his lip, then dragged it across his throat.

Sawyer looked at the phone screen, swiped, and saw the source of the notification: the motion sensor camera rigged outside.

They had come round the side.

Sadie must have opened the window for some fresh air.

Sawyer spoke into the phone. 'I'll call you back.'

He set the handset on the kitchen surface, face down.

Peyton held the shotgun on Sawyer and walked into the kitchen. He jabbed the gun towards the window and Sawyer moved away.

Peyton picked up the phone. The call to Shepherd was still open. He disconnected, then dropped the handset onto the floor and stomped the screen with the heel of his boot.

'Worth a try,' said Peyton. 'But do I look like a fucking idiot?'

'Maybe Long John Silver.'

Peyton laughed. 'Nice one.' He looked down at the pillow and bedding on the sofa. 'Someone's in the fucking doghouse, eh?'

Sawyer stayed by the front window. 'Did you dig two graves, Wes?'

Peyton frowned. 'What?'

'Surely you know the old saying about seeking revenge. A well-read type like yourself.' He nodded to the big man. 'So, who's this?'

'This is Mason. Good mate of mine. Well, more my brother's but I've known him for a good many years.'

The big man moved Sadie further into the kitchen. He passed into a pool of light from the lamp, revealing his heavily lined bald head, grey stubble and greying monobrow.

'I thought you'd brought your dad for a minute,' said Sawyer. 'Have you run out of fresh recruits?'

Peyton hissed a laugh, nodding. 'Jesus Christ, Sawyer. A year in the nuthouse and you're still fucked in the head.' He held up a hand. 'Before we get started, let me have a quick look around.' He made a quick show of surveying the room: up, down, left, right. He pushed his face close to Sadie's. 'Nope. No sign of Daddy this time.' He walked across the kitchen, keeping the shotgun trained on Sawyer. 'Let's get on. I've been over a few ideas, Sawyer. Can I run them past you? I thought I could go for a proper eye for an eye thing and take one of yours.' He half-turned to Sadie, grinned. 'Do that after I've given her one, though. It'd put her right off, yeah? But, y'know what? I think I'll just get this debt paid off and be on my way. A close-up blast from this baby will take off your whole fuckin' face. Even if they do put you back together, you'll be a walking nightmare. I once saw—'

Mason shoved Sadie forward. She stumbled to the floor then scrambled towards Sawyer at the window.

Before Peyton could react, Mason had raised a silenced handgun to his temple.

'Don't turn, Half Pint.' His voice was gruff and angular. Broad Mancunian.

Peyton froze, keeping the shotgun on Sawyer and Sadie. 'What the fuck, Mase?'

'Eddie says he's sorry it worked out this way,' said Mason. 'But he's been away too long. You're more trouble than it's worth now. Business first.'

'Over fuckin' *family*?'

Peyton ducked, tried to spin with the shotgun, but Mason corrected his aim and shot Peyton in the side of the head before he could pull the shotgun trigger.

The shot tore away Peyton's eye-patch, sent his baseball cap flying.

A fine mist of blood spattered over the fridge door and Peyton dropped hard onto the floor, face down.

Sadie shouted out in shock. Sawyer gripped her shoulder, keeping her near the front door.

Mason kept the handgun on Sawyer and Sadie as he leaned forward to retrieve Peyton's shotgun.

He gave a sheepish grin. 'Don't move. It won't work. You're both just a few feet away. I could miss from a few feet, but if I were you, I wouldn't fancy it.'

Sawyer caught his breath. 'So, we either stand here and let you shoot us. Definitely dead. Or rush you and *maybe* survive? Have you really thought this through, Mase?'

Mason smiled, shook his head. 'Hey. It's your call. And in case you're wondering, I don't give two shits who you are. Coppers killed my lad when he was on a job a couple of years ago.' He jabbed the gun towards Sadie. 'And Billy Rice was a good fucking mate of mine. So, you'll do. Until we get—'

A loud crack from the back door, as the cat-flap flew open.

Bruce scampered in, thought better of it, then crashed back through the flap again.

Mason spun around, aimed the gun high, anticipating a human intruder. He saw the cat exit, turned back.

But Sawyer had moved at the cat-flap sound. He snatched up the empty wine bottle from the coffee table and reached Mason just as he raised the handgun, adjusted his aim…

Sawyer smashed the bottle into the side of Mason's head. He cried out, staggered, dropping the shotgun but keeping hold of the handgun.

Sawyer stayed in close, gripping Mason's gun wrist firm. But he was strong and hauled it up and around, grunting with the effort, until the barrel had almost lined up with Sawyer's face.

Mason twisted away, wrestling for an angle to get a shot off. Sawyer spotted the opening and caught him bang on the bridge of his nose with a fierce headbutt.

Mason skittered backwards, almost toppling, but somehow holding on to the gun. Sawyer caught him with a heavy body blow, but it was like punching solid brick. Mason leaned back, winding up a punch of his own, but Sawyer pivoted, hitting him with an elbow strike into his chin, cracking bone. He howled, dropping the gun.

'Jake!' Sadie's shout.

The shotgun cocked, and Peyton rose onto his knees, the seal of his uncovered eye smeared in blood from the gunshot wound to the other side of his head.

He spat, wiped at his face with his aiming arm. Mason's bullet had ripped through his cheek and scored a bloody furrow in the side of his head, but it hadn't penetrated the skull. The furrow steamed with heat from the bullet.

Peyton lifted himself off his knees, aiming the shotgun at Mason, now with a bloodied and broken nose, and clutching at his fractured jaw with both hands, groaning in agony. 'You dirty fuckin' shit-out.' He drew in a juddering breath which turned into a sick laugh. 'You had one job, you useless cunt, and you fucked it up.'

He raised the shotgun, aiming at Mason with his good eye.

Sawyer dived away, dropping to the floor as Peyton fired. The gun boomed, the muzzle flash flooding the darkened room. Shot peppered the back wall, shattering a stack of plates on a high shelf. The blast caught Mason square in the chest and face, hurling him into the corner by the back door. He slumped there, oddly upright, then slid down, his skull a mush of blood and bone.

Peyton stared at his body, half-dazed, then broke open the shotgun barrel, exposing the chamber. The spent shot fell to the floor.

Sawyer got to his feet and took a step towards Peyton, who looked up, squinting. He reached into his pocket with trembling fingers, slick with blood, fumbling as he pulled out a fresh shell.

Sawyer stopped, standing a few feet from Peyton. He kept his voice low and calm. 'It's time to stop.'

Peyton dropped the shell, wiped his fingers on his leg, picked it up again.

'Cut your losses,' said Sawyer. 'Your own brother just tried to have you killed. What's next? You go after him? Then more of his people come after you?' He reached out a hand to the shotgun, but Peyton twisted away, trying to load the shell. 'You've lost an eye, Wes. Half your face. It's done. Time to stop. Time to break the cycle.'

Peyton slotted the shell into the chamber.

'For fuck's sake.'

Sadie Fletcher charged at Peyton. She gripped him by the shoulders, stepped in close and delivered a powerful knee strike to his groin. He roared in pain and reeled back, dropping the shotgun. She hit him with a bludgeoning haymaker punch, smashing the back of his head into the fridge. He fell to the floor, out cold.

She turned to Sawyer, puffed out a sigh. 'There you go. Efficiency.'

Chapter Fifty-Five

LYNDON WILDE BARGED through the door at the end of the connecting hallway and stumbled into the kitchen. He closed the door behind him and flicked on the main light.

Too harsh.

He switched it off and opened the fridge door wide, muttering to himself.

'Four in.' He inhaled.

'Six out.' He exhaled.

Wilde gripped the edge of the central island and tipped his head back, repeating his ritual, over and over, always out loud now.

He stared up.

This majestic farmhouse conversion boasts soaring ceilings and exposed original beams.

Vehicle noise outside, close to the house.

A breathtaking blend of rustic charm and modern elegance.

Multiple vehicles.

The ceilings enhance the sense of space and light.

'Four in... Six out.'

He scrambled to the window, staying low.

Three unmarked SUVs sat at the far end of the courtyard, alongside a large van with blacked-out windows.

Wilde yanked a chopping knife out of a wooden block by the sink. He threw open the connecting door, then charged down the stairs that led to the open-plan ground floor.

They would see the light from the fridge, assume he was still on the first floor. He had also left a lamp on in the upstairs bedroom.

He switched on his phone light and hurried through the main hall to the utility room at the back of the house. The door was ill-fitting, and he winced at the loud crack as he eased it open a few inches.

He peered through the gap to the small window overlooking the deck and back garden.

No sign of movement. No lights. No sound.

He whispered his ritual to himself as he inhaled, exhaled.

Wilde slid into the room and closed the door. He cast his phone light around. Stone floor. Stacked shelving, cabinets.

A practical and spacious area equipped with ample workspace.

He paused, listened.

A low buzzing sound. Water pipes? Heating?

No. It was outside, overhead.

The upstairs lights would make them cautious, giving him time to get away. But a drone might spot him, alert them…

The darkness would save him.

He could make it to the shelter of the wood beyond the back garden. Then out to the moor.

The buzzing sound receded. Wilde took a small key

from a box on a high shelf and let himself out of the back door.

He ran across the deck to the edge of the garden, head down.

'Lyndon Wilde.'

As Wilde emerged from the garden onto a scruffy track that blended into the wood, he spotted a short, slight man standing at the base of a birch tree. The man spoke into a handset which he slipped into his inside pocket, then stepped forward, barring the way.

Wilde slowed and stopped, keeping the knife behind his back.

The man walked forward and halted a few paces ahead. He held up a police warrant card. 'DS Matthew Walker. Where is Rebecca, Lyndon? Is she safe?'

Wilde stood firm. As his eyes adjusted to the dark, he noticed a burly man had stepped forward and taken a position at Walker's shoulder. It was clear from the man's silhouette that he was cradling an automatic weapon, aimed at the ground.

'You're all done, Lyndon,' said Walker. He shrugged. 'I bet it feels like a relief.'

Wilde held up the knife.

The man behind Walker raised his rifle. 'Armed police! Drop the weapon.'

'If you run,' said Walker, 'we'll track you and capture you in next to no time, and you get a bonus charge of resisting arrest. If you try anything with that knife, you'll be dead before you hit the ground.' He touched a finger to the faint scar at the base of his Adam's apple, then took two slow steps forward. 'I found your mask room, Lyndon. And I know what happened to you in Matlock. You were barely a teenager. You were bullied. You were broken, and you grew without healing properly. But you can be treated. Helped. We can't bring back Hannah Lewis or Uma Leary, but you can choose to keep Rebecca safe. You can give yourself a chance to heal, and you can give Rebecca a future, along with Milo and Jamie.'

The buzzing sound grew again, overhead.

Four in.

Wilde stared up into the black sky.

Six out.

He lowered his gaze, held Walker's eye. 'I'm not a *vulture.*'

Walker shook his head. 'You're a victim.'

Chapter Fifty-Six

SALLY O'CALLAGHAN GESTURED to the front door and stepped outside. Sawyer followed, edging around three CSIs in white Tyvek suits loading Mason's body into a heavy-duty vinyl bag.

DC Myers sat on the sofa talking to a support detective writing on a clipboard form. He nodded at Sawyer and forced a smile.

Sawyer found O'Callaghan sitting on the edge of the wooden decking, watching the activity to and from the Scientific Services van, parked just over the driveway bridge. At the far side of the road, a squad car sat next to an unmarked BMW.

She looked up to the sky, blushed with a faint shade of sunrise. 'I had big plans for yesterday evening, Sawyer. A red hot eight-hour date with my eye-mask and white noise app.'

'I could make you a cup of tea, if that would help.'

'Peppermint?'

'PG.'

She sighed, stripped off her latex gloves. 'I'll hold out for a caffeine mainline. All good with the scene exam. We'll ship your luckless, faceless visitor into the care of the good Mr Drummond. The first-responder bobbies got your companion home safe.'

'We offered her an FLO,' said Myers, joining them. 'She said she was fed up with being babysat.' He stuck out his bottom lip, glanced at O'Callaghan. 'You've found yourself a toughie there.'

Sawyer stared him down. 'Peyton?'

Myers winced. 'Cavendish ICU. Not pretty.'

'I have to talk to him.'

'You won't be doing that tonight,' said O'Callaghan. 'He's going to need some work done.'

'A few shots of Botox at least,' said Myers, earning a glare from O'Callaghan.

Sawyer rubbed and stretched the skin at the edge of his eyes. 'What happened with Shepherd and Walker? Peyton smashed my phone.'

'Ah!' said Myers. 'The Dynamic Duo. They caught The Vulture. Not much of a catch, really. They set up around the farmhouse. And out he came. His wife was inside. Bruised and petrified, but otherwise fine.'

'Didn't quite live up to his tabloid billing,' said O'Callaghan. 'The next job will be patching her up mentally, and keeping those poor children supported.' She smiled. 'If only we knew someone highly talented in the field of psychology and family liaison.'

Sawyer got to his feet. 'Are we all done here? I might get my head down for a couple of hours.'

O'Callaghan gaped at him. 'Christ on a trampoline,

Sawyer. A home invasion by a one-eyed maniac. A near-decapitation by shotgun blast. How are you going to get to sleep? Rohypnol?'

He yawned. 'No choice. I need the energy. The fun might be finished, but the games aren't over yet.'

Chapter Fifty-Seven

THREE DAYS LATER

FARRELL SAT BACK in his office chair and propped his feet up on the desk. He flapped open a heavy-looking folder and skimmed through the documents, shaking his head.

He let Shepherd and Walker stand for a moment, then jabbed his finger towards the two chairs, keeping his eyes on the documents. They both sat down.

Farrell closed the folder and tossed it onto his desk. He screwed his eyes shut, opened them again. 'Psych reports, yes?'

'Yes, sir,' said Shepherd. 'Wilde's brief is pushing for a full evaluation.'

'Hoping for an insanity defence,' said Walker.

Farrell nodded, popped a breath mint out of his canister. 'But only if the shrink says he's a psycho.'

'M'Naghten legal standard,' said Shepherd. 'The court won't accept it unless they establish defect of reason. Disease of the mind.'

Farrell scoffed. 'He knew exactly what he was doing. Same old story. Trying to get his time in a cushy psych hospital instead of a Cat A. What about all the planning? Stalking the women? And what's this secret room?'

'We found a hidden room in his home office with death masks of the mortuary victims,' said Walker. 'Also Hannah Lewis and Uma Leary. He took his mask-making equipment with him to the farmhouse when he kidnapped his wife. So, it looks like he was planning to do the same for her. We got to him before he could bring himself to kill her, though.'

'It all connects,' said Shepherd. 'We were right. There's also evidence he was keeping Phoebe Gray at the cottage, as leverage over her father.'

Farrell slapped a palm on the table. 'And then Orlando Gray had this ridiculous idea about getting himself arrested.'

'He was desperate,' said Shepherd. 'He'd asked Brad Singleton to follow Wilde and locate his daughter, but he wasn't having any luck.'

'And there's still no sign of Singleton?' said Farrell.

Shepherd shook his head. 'We believe Wilde encountered or spotted him, which is what caused the cross-contamination of Singleton's hair on Phoebe's body.'

'Wilde probably dumped her out in the open through sheer petulance,' said Walker. 'He's staying quiet on Singleton, but I expect he'll give us a steer once his options run out.'

Farrell opened the folder again, skimmed through a few more documents. 'What the hell drives someone to want to do this? He's married, two kids. He runs a lucrative business.'

'It's more like he needed to do it,' said Shepherd. 'He was involved in a pretty awful home invasion back in 1995 when he was thirteen. Three older boys took Wilde with them when they got into a house down in Matlock. The oldest, Jasper Waterhouse, had a previous arrest for rape of a minor, but it was thrown out due to lack of evidence. A couple lived at the house with their fourteen-year-old daughter. The family had been in a car accident a few weeks earlier. The man died, but the woman survived relatively unscathed. The daughter, Melanie, suffered from spastic quadriplegia. The boys beat the woman badly, tied her up, then took turns raping Melanie. There's no evidence that Wilde joined in, but, according to Melanie's testimony, they made him watch.'

Walker took over. 'She would have been helpless, immobile. With necrophiles, there's often an obsession with lack of agency. So, Wilde's developing healthy sexuality might have been warped by the intensity of the encounter, by the sight of her. Creating a fetish. And that's not a want. It's a need that has to be fulfilled, regardless of morality.'

'According to his wife,' said Shepherd, 'Wilde struggled to perform sexually if she made eye contact or showed any awareness. She once caught him spiking her with sleeping pills. His search history shows he was looking for harder stuff.'

Farrell frowned at him. 'So, that progressed to stiffs?'

Shepherd glanced at Walker. 'That's one way of putting it, yes.'

Farrell slapped his hand down on the desk again, making them both jump. 'Well... Whatever's going on in his head, he won't be murdering anyone else to get what he *needs*.' He crunched his mint. 'You know, some might find it a little inappropriate to celebrate in these circumstances, but I think I might open something special tonight. A toast to taking the real Vulture off the streets.' He stood up. 'Now, with the greatest of respect. I need you both to fuck off. I have a meeting.'

Shepherd and Walker stood up and exited Farrell's office, passing two tall stern-faced men in good suits with leather bags slung over their shoulders.

Shepherd nodded to Walker, and they took a small meeting room opposite, with a clear view of Farrell's office. The two men entered, greeted Farrell and closed the door behind them.

'I wish we could hear it all,' said Walker as they watched through the window: Farrell shaking the men's hands, sitting first, keeping them standing for a moment.

Shepherd smiled. 'I wish we had some popcorn.'

The two men sat, took documents from their shoulder bags.

'What's their rank?' said Walker.

'Good question. IOPC is a civilian oversight body. They're senior investigators.'

A third man, older, followed the other two into Farrell's office. They watched as Farrell waved a hand, directing the others to pull up a third chair.

'Observer?' said Walker.

'Sort of. He'll be the Police Federation rep.'

'So, is this an informal hearing?'

Shepherd shook his head. 'That comes later. This is serving notice. My confidential complaint over Farrell's conduct in the Orlando Gray interview held more weight than normal because Gray's brief backed it up. The IOPC enquiry into Gray's suicide will have connected the two, and his parents have also lodged a protest. They can't hold Farrell directly responsible, but, from what I hear from my IOPC contact, they might suspend him ahead of the formal hearing with the Chief Constable.'

Farrell slammed his desk again, stood up, pointed at the men.

Walker gripped Shepherd's arm, grinning. 'Please let him have a pop at them.'

'On top of the circumstances leading up to Gray's suicide,' said Shepherd, 'most of the team have lodged complaints about Farrell's conduct in briefings, including Frazer Drummond and Sally O'Callaghan. That's more a matter of professional standards, but along with the other issues, it backs up the suspension and the need for a hearing.'

Farrell shouted something, paced to his window, arms flailing.

'I don't suppose this reaction helps, either,' said Walker, unable to contain his glee.

Shepherd smiled. 'There's also complaints from families of some of the mortuary victims, and, worse, the families of Hannah Lewis and Uma Leary. They'll be looking at whether their murders would have been preventable if Farrell had handled Gray's custody with more care. If we had managed to gain Gray's trust with a softer approach and get the truth out of him about Wilde, then there's a good chance we would have located Wilde before the other murders.'

'So, what's going to happen to Farrell at the hearing?' said Walker.

Shepherd pondered. 'It could take weeks to get to that. Until then, probably suspension at full pay. If they uphold everything, it would be the Chief Constable's call. Farrell might even be dismissed or put out to pasture somewhere. Running a grotty CMU like the one where Sawyer works.' He patted Walker's shoulder. 'Hold on. Here he comes.'

Farrell crashed out of the office and hurried down the

corridor towards the lift, leaving the three men behind. The Federation rep closed the door and sat in Farrell's seat, in conference with the IOPC investigators.

Shepherd and Walker watched as Farrell hammered the call button, his face beetroot red.

'Won't he go running to the mayor?' said Walker. 'After all, he was appointed on Strickland's insistence, after the post-Keating revamp.'

Shepherd laughed. 'Let's see how that works out for him.'

'What do you mean?'

Shepherd gave Walker an incredulous look. 'Do you really think that Sawyer has been dutifully tidying up old casework on an out-of-town industrial estate since he got out?'

Chapter Fifty-Eight

DALE STRICKLAND GAZED into his right-hand monitor, rearranging the solitaire cards. The left screen showed his workspace desktop, cluttered with files and folders. The number in the corner of his email icon read *137*.

A young man in a tailored navy suit sat cross-legged on the curved, silvery grey sofa. He swiped and pecked at an oversized tablet.

'New glasses, Oliver?' said Strickland.

Oliver adjusted the thick octagonal frames. 'Yes. Cutler and Gross. I'm worried they're a bit too *statement*.'

Strickland pushed out a smile, tapped his wedding ring against the glass desk. 'I'm anticipating a social week, given your attention to appearance.'

Oliver grinned. 'We're crossing over soon. From incumbent to second-term campaigner. I'm getting you busy pressing the flesh outside the fundraising circuit. It's time for community outreach.' He held up a hand. 'Don't worry. I'll hold back the door-to-door until the last few months. You might need to show your face at a few town halls, though.

Hyper-local visibility boosts the man-of-the-people vibe.' He gave a theatrical slump of his shoulders. 'Before the voter engagement, though... I'd welcome a bit of general engagement.'

Strickland closed the solitaire game and turned to look out of his open window, up into a pristine blue sky. 'Guilty as charged. I'll give you my full attention for the rest of the month. At least. Then I might take you up on the fact-finding trip idea.'

'Study visit,' said Oliver. 'I'd recommend Silicon Valley for tech partnerships. Tel Aviv for start-up ecosystems. Seoul for digital governance and smart city initiatives.'

'Just keep me out of the fucking Nordics. And let's at least time the trips so I'm getting sun on my face when the heavens open round here.'

A knock at the office door. Strickland turned. A small group of formally dressed men had gathered outside. One of them peered in through the window overlooking the open-plan office floor.

Strickland caught Oliver's eye. 'Is this scheduled?'

'No,' said Oliver, getting to his feet. 'It is not.' He opened the door. 'I'm sorry, but Mr Strickland is currently—'

The lead man—slim, forties, trim greying beard—stepped around Oliver, trailed by two younger colleagues.

Strickland stayed in his seat, regarding the intruders with calm curiosity.

'Good morning,' said the bearded man. 'Dale Strickland?'

Oliver stepped in between the man and Strickland's desk, held up his hands. 'Look. Whatever this is about, you can't just walk in here without an appointment.'

The man flicked his eyes to Oliver then returned to Strickland. 'Actually, we can.'

'It's okay, Oliver. Yes. I'm Dale Strickland. And you are...?'

'My name is Spencer Mullin. I'm a Senior Officer with the National Crime Agency. With me, I have Field Agents Emmett Webb and Victor Millard.' He turned his head to check as another man entered. 'Also present is Detective Inspector Jake Sawyer, from Derbyshire CID.'

Sawyer stepped in and stood near the office window. He wore a fitted navy blue suit with white shirt and orange tie. He was clean shaven, with trimmed and tidied hair.

Strickland lifted his head and locked his blue eyes with Sawyer's green.

Mullin showed his ID, and his colleagues followed.

Sawyer stepped forward and showed his warrant card. His eyes never wavered from Strickland's. 'Mr Strickland. You are being arrested on suspicion of conspiracy to commit murder, money laundering, two counts of assisting an offender, and conspiracy to commit terrorism under the Terrorism Act 2000 and subsequent legislation. You do not have to say anything, but it may harm your defence if you do not mention when questioned something which you later rely on in court. Anything you do say may be given in evidence. You have the right to legal representation. Do you understand the charges against you and your rights as I have explained them?'

Oliver gaped at Strickland. He felt for the arm of the sofa and guided himself down. '*Terrorism?*'

Strickland laughed. 'Is that it? Are you sure there's nothing about killing puppies and kittens, Sawyer?'

'We'll find it if there is.'

Strickland looked around the faces in turn, receiving no

solidarity. 'I understand the charges and my rights, yes. The charges are idiotic, but I understand them. I can't wait to see where you're getting this rubbish from.'

A flicker of a smile from Sawyer. 'I had plenty of time to work it all through.'

Strickland nodded. 'Not just lifting weights and taking your medication, then.'

Sawyer took out a pair of handcuffs. 'My favourite thing about you, Dale, is your little obsession with a military strategist who probably didn't even exist. And you mis-read his most popular advice... *Know the enemy and know yourself.* You put plenty of effort into knowing the enemy, but you could never quite put eyes on yourself, could you? That fatal combination. Too much self-confidence, not enough self-awareness.' He stepped around the desk, inches from Strickland. 'I'll afford you the dignity of front-cuffing you for the walk of shame past your undeserved minions.'

Strickland sighed. 'Really? Handcuffs?'

Sawyer nodded. 'Really. Handcuffs. You're a bad guy, Dale. Listen to those charges.'

Strickland shook his head and held out his hands.

Sawyer clicked on the cuffs. 'I should let you know that we've obtained search warrants for your home and office. There's an unmarked vehicle outside, waiting to take you in for booking, fingerprinting, interrogation.' He waved a hand. 'But you know that drill. If you go quietly and quickly, you might slip away without any press interest. Unless some unkind soul has already tipped them off.'

Strickland got to his feet and stood face to face with Sawyer. 'So, you're the good guy after all, Sawyer.'

Sawyer shook his head. 'I have my faults. But you've done the damage. You've caused the suffering.' He shrugged. 'Sometimes, bad guys finish last.'

Chapter Fifty-Nine

SAWYER PICKED up the takeaway coffees and followed his brother out of the Yondermann Café.

'Christ,' said Michael. 'I used to work here.'

'A million years ago.'

Michael took his coffee cup. 'The scary thing is that it hasn't changed. I think I threw that banana skin into that bin back in 2004.'

They headed past the Three Stags' Heads Inn, climbing the steep path that snaked up to their home village then blended into the heather-clad hills of Longstone Moor.

The day's heat was reaching a midday peak, and as they trudged on, the incline set the sun glaring full in their faces. Sawyer looked back at his brother, trailing a few paces behind.

Michael had dropped a couple of kilos since their last meeting, but he had retained his usual walking pace: slow, steady, measuring each step. Despite the gait, he seemed brighter, lighter, more in tune with his surroundings. He wore large, aviator-style tinted shades and he'd lost his neutral normcore look in favour of bolder colours: white trainers, pastel-blue shorts, a light pink tie-dyed T-shirt carrying a loud legend: *LOVE IS THE FING.*

'Idles,' said Sawyer. 'Proper band.'

'Compared to some of your R2-D2 music, you mean?'

Sawyer laughed. 'Your musical taste has improved a lot. I remember you used to love the Butthole Surfers.'

'I still do.'

As they approached the block of grey-stone semis at the edge of the village, Sawyer crossed onto the walking track that connected to the fringes of farmland, and the lane and verge where their childhood world had fallen apart.

'Are we not going past the old house?' said Michael, catching up.

Sawyer caught his eye. 'Do you want to?'

Michael pondered, took a sip of coffee through the lid. He shook his head. 'Not really.'

Sawyer took point, and they walked on, grateful for the shade as the path dipped into lush woodland.

'Is Butthole Surfers the worst band name ever?' said Sawyer.

'What the hell are you talking about? It could be the best.'

'And the worst?'

Michael slowed, as Sawyer matched his pace. 'I'd go for Sixpence None The Richer.'

'Fuck,' said Sawyer. 'You win. I can't top that.'

They moved on, climbing a stile into a vast pasture.

Michael held up a finger. 'One of the developers who works with us... He said his student band was called Sigmund Freud and the Motherfuckers.'

'That's actually pretty good,' said Sawyer. 'Good luck with daytime radio play, though.'

The field levelled off as they reached the far side. A warm breeze fluttered up from the lane below, and they sat on the grass and gazed down at the verge, sipping coffee.

'Dad would say this was an inappropriate drink for the weather,' said Sawyer.

Michael laughed. 'He'd be right. What were we thinking?'

'Didn't feel as warm back at the café.'

They fell silent, tuning in to the birdsong. Michael dug the base of his coffee cup into the earth and lay back, while Sawyer kept his eyes on the verge.

'Do you know the Ship of Theseus thought experiment?' said Sawyer.

'Yes. That's the one about the ship having all its parts replaced with new ones over time. So, if nothing remains of the original, is it still the same ship?'

'You can look at it in lots of ways. But it's only a puzzle if you subscribe to externalism.'

Michael sighed. 'Jake. I don't think I can cope with philosophy and painful memory at the same time.'

'It's not that complicated. It's the way we assume that what is true in our minds is also true in the world. But think of human intuition. That's fluid, fallible. Some people wouldn't even consider the ship to be a subjective idea in the first place. It's more a collection of objective parts.'

'But it has… perceptual continuity.'

Sawyer raised an eyebrow, paused. 'Yes. What happened here… Down at that verge. Think of all the changes since. The objective parts being replaced. The environment. Us. Our cells. And you could say that back then, we were on a journey, and we were interrupted. We lost our way. We lost the sense of who we were, and that displacement became the source of our pain. In the unit, we talked about the idea of finding your way back to that. Doing the self-work. Improving. Upgrading. But also rediscovering yourself. The version before the displacement. When you get lost in snow, you can retrace your footprints, even if most of the snow has long since melted.'

'How come?'

'The compacted snow caused by the footfalls melts at a different rate, and your prints stick out. That's what we're doing here. Despite all the changes from time passed, we can still follow those old prints back to ourselves.'

Michael sat up, slurped his coffee. 'I see what you're saying, Jake, but I was hoping we could just talk about this woman I've met.'

Sawyer smiled. 'I thought you seemed a bit… loved up.'

Michael winced. 'Don't say that.'

'I'm happy for you,' said Sawyer, turning back to the verge. 'Tell me more, in horrible detail, on the way back. How do you feel, though?'

'About her?'

'About this.'

Michael took in a breath. 'I feel close to Mum here. Closer than I do back at her grave. Is that bad?'

Sawyer shook his head. 'The grave is a symbol. This is where we lived it. Lost her. Lost ourselves. I feel close to her now, too. Here. It doesn't feel like a pain anymore, being here. It's a way of getting close to her again. After all, this is the place where we both last felt her love. What happened after that had nothing to do with you, me or Mum. It was all down to Caldwell.'

Michael lay back again. 'Let's keep coming here. Making that feeling stronger.'

'Tracking those footprints.'

Michael nodded, went back to his coffee.

'By the sound of the way you're talking about your new woman,' said Sawyer, 'you'll be bringing your kids here soon.'

Michael laughed. 'Also, it's the third act of our relationship.'

Sawyer looked at him. 'The third act?'

Michael held up a hand. 'Sorry. We're working on a new game. Single-player story thing. I've been getting into *arcs* and *acts* with the producer.'

Sawyer ran his hand through the grass. 'Speak of the devil…'

'Dominic isn't that bad. Maybe a bit earnest.'

'I mean the other devil. The one I just spoke of.'

Michael swallowed, steeled himself. 'Are you not done yet? Is that bastard not dead yet?'

'Soon. Also, I was thinking about Dad. About his art. There's so much of it. We'll have to clear it out of storage. I'd like to hire a dealer. Sell off most of it. Hold on to the key works. Maybe open a gallery in his name.'

'I like that. But what do you mean by key works? They all look the same to me.'

'That's because your idea of art is videogame posters. There's one painting that stands out for me. The one with deep red at the centre. Lighter round the edge.'

'I know that, yeah. Abstract. Like the others.'

Sawyer shook his head. 'Dad once told me that *there's nothing in darkness that will not be disclosed.*'

'Bible nonsense.'

'No.' Sawyer lay back, savoured the heat on his face. 'I think I know what he meant. It's linked with that painting. I just need to confirm it.'

Chapter Sixty

WILLIAM CALDWELL STEPPED AWAY from the trail walkway and inched onto a shallow but rugged slope that led down to the base of the Padley valley. Sawyer followed, working his way around Caldwell and arriving first at the edge of Burbage Brook.

Caldwell stumbled down from the slope and rested on a moss-covered rock, panting.

Sawyer looked up to the tree canopy, the densely knitted oak branches diffusing the mid-afternoon sun. Behind them, the slim path followed the brook through thinning woodland at the eastern side of the Longshaw estate.

'I think there's another one through there,' said Caldwell, waving a hand. 'That clearing just off the main track. I remember it because I came back the next day to check I'd buried her properly, and I looked up the slope and there was an ice cream van parked there. Can't remember her name.'

Sawyer looked behind, up to the top of the slope, where Bentley waited with Boateng, with the two Nottinghamshire prison officers hanging back near a parking lay-by. He nodded to Bentley, turned back to Caldwell. 'Shall we stop this now, Bill? Finish up.'

Caldwell raised his head to Sawyer. His eyes seemed to have retreated deeper into the sockets, and Sawyer found himself staring into shifting shadow. He lifted a gnarled hand from the rock, pushed himself forward with the other, then shuffled along the trail in front of Sawyer.

'You tried to stall us,' said Sawyer. 'Bentley's team used ground-penetrating radar at the spot where we last talked, round by the old veterans' hospital. They found Julie Saltwell's remains. Skull smashed like the others.'

Caldwell hesitated for a moment but kept walking.

'They also found her watch, identified by her father.'

Caldwell half-turned. 'What made you look there?'

'You were lying. Psychopaths do that. Take us to the actual spot, draw us away. For the fun of it.'

Caldwell stopped, faced him. 'Why the fuck would I want to string you along? I'm trying to get compassionate release, remember?'

'No. You're not. Even now. At this late hour. You can't resist a bit of evil. Misdirecting. Hoping to leave some of your pain behind after you've gone.' He leaned forward, sneered into Caldwell's face. 'Your fucking *legacy*.' Sawyer looked back at Bentley. He was talking to Boateng, turned away. 'You're out of time. Out of victims. Out of leverage. You're done.'

Caldwell turned again, walked on. 'You said you'd give me what I want, Sawyer.'

Sawyer followed him over a short stone bridge. 'That's why we're down here, isn't it? It was too open up by the hospital. Down here, though. It's harder for the others to step in so quickly. Gives me time to do it. There's no *another one*, is there, Bill?'

Caldwell staggered to a low, flat chunk of stone at the far side of the bridge and sat down again. He dropped his head, tried to steady his breathing.

Sawyer took another look back to the top of the slope. Crossing the bridge had put them out of Bentley and Boateng's sightline. He leaned to the side and saw Bentley craning his neck, hand above his eyes, peering down through the trees.

He walked to Caldwell, stood over him. 'You don't want compassionate release, do you, Bill? What are you going to do with that? See out an agonising few weeks in your old bed, delirious on morphine, with Sheila bringing you soup? What you *want* is Julie Saltwell's father to keep carrying his pain. The pain you gifted him. And you want me to be the one who takes your pain away. To give you the satisfaction of knowing the consequences I'd face.'

Caldwell raised his head again as Sawyer crouched at the side of the path and dug a large rock out of the earth, weighing it in his hand.

'Maybe you didn't believe I'd take the opportunity. So, you planned to goad me with a few final details. Push me over the edge.'

A smile curled at the edge of Caldwell's lip. 'You're doing well. Here's one for starters. When I was DCI at Buxton, I made sure your idiot father saw Jessica's scene photos in all their glorious gory detail. He should never have had access, of course, but I made sure they were accidentally left out for him.'

Sawyer shook his head. 'I know. He worked that into his art. I saw it in one of his paintings. I have photos of my mother in life, and my dad immortalised her in death.'

Caldwell's breathing quickened. 'Imagine, though. Seeing your wife like that. The mother of your children.

Her pretty face smashed to pieces. It was almost worth him keeping me in that fucking basement.'

Sawyer shifted the rock from left hand to right. 'You're wondering if I can do it, aren't you?'

'Bash my head in with a rock?' Caldwell lowered his voice to a hissing whisper. 'It would be fitting, eh? Don't you think it's what Jess would have wanted, *Little Jake*?'

Sawyer stood upright. 'I'm sorry, Bill.'

'For what?'

'Sorry that you managed to get so much life yourself. Life you denied those women. Once I've given you what you want, I'll do my best to make sure you aren't cremated. Releasing your foul essence into the air would be bad for the environment. I'm going to lobby hard for alkaline hydrolysis. Water cremation. Boil you away to nothing.'

'*Sawyer?*' A shout from Bentley, back at the top of the slope.

Sawyer took a step back, holding the rock at his side.

Caldwell closed his eyes, turned his head away. He was whimpering now: a wavering moan of terror. And trembling. A mortally wounded animal, bracing for mercy. Waiting for the death blow.

Sawyer scoffed. He leaned down, close to Caldwell's ear. 'I wouldn't have thought you had it in you, Bill. Fear.' He lowered his voice. 'Calm yourself. I'll make it quick. Painless. We have a couple of minutes before they find their way down and get here. I'm going to give you what you want. I promise. I'm going to finish up. But first, I need you to tell me a story.'

Caldwell opened his eyes, stared up at Sawyer. 'What story?'

'What happened with Sharon Wright? What happened at Bolehill?'

Chapter Sixty-One

IVAN KEATING CROUCHED beside his vintage wicker fishing basket and flipped open his waterproof fly box. He pressed a finger into the foam insert and popped out a Mayfly Dun: an imitation of the adult stage of the mayfly. He held it up to the first rays of sunlight filtering through the riverbank willows. The Dun was meticulously crafted in olive and brown, designed to tempt the brown trout in the limestone-rich waters of the Wye.

'Caught much?'

Keating turned and looked back along the riverside path and the iconic five-arched stone bridge that led into the centre of Bakewell town.

Sawyer strolled over and perched on a raised section of riverbank, gazing out at the flowing water.

Keating refocused on the fly, threading a few inches of line through the eye of the hook. 'Just about to start. You're looking well, son.'

'I'm ill, but hopeful.'

'That's good to hear. I think.' Keating sat on the fishing

basket, angled towards Sawyer. The basket creaked and cracked as he rested the fly on his knee. He pulled off his tweed poacher's hat, scrubbed at his white hair, then replaced the hat and set about tying the bait to the line. 'I assume you fancied a morning stroll and just happened to bump into me.'

'I knew you usually fish up at Ladybower. But then I remembered you'd bought a retirement place in Sheldon and thought this would be the most likely spot. Bit of fishing. Maybe a Full English at the Farmer's Feast… Also, I called your wife and asked.'

Keating smiled, kept his attention on the fly. He pinched the standing line and tag end between his thumb and forefinger at the eye of the hook, then wrapped the tag end around the standing line. 'Big news about Strickland.'

'NCA directed it all. I was a sort of Executive Producer.'

Keating nodded. He threaded the tag end through a small loop near the eye of the hook, creating a larger loop. 'He'll fight it hard.'

'Of course. On one level, a corrupt politician is hardly news. Farrell is out, too. But that's more about him being a shit copper. At least Strickland had brains and balls. Farrell had neither.'

Keating laughed. 'He always struck me as one of those types who got an undeserved promotion somewhere back in the dark ages, then used it to impress the old guard in performance reviews.'

'They wouldn't fall for his type, these days,' said Sawyer. 'His status says a lot about the culture of the force, back when he was lower status.'

Keating threaded the tag end through the large loop. 'So, is this your plan now? Take down your enemies?'

'Just weeding out the bad actors.'

Keating eyed Sawyer's attire: walking boots, blue-and-white softshell jacket. 'You don't look dressed for an arrest.'

'You're deflecting. You're more concerned about the early hour. How there's nobody around.'

Keating touched the tip of his tongue to the loop and tightened the knot. 'Clinch knot. The moisture stops it weakening from the friction.'

'I saw Caldwell.'

Keating glanced at Sawyer. 'In person?'

Sawyer nodded. 'He's terminal. I've seen healthier corpses. He made a play for compassionate release. Offered to show us the location of the bodies of two women he killed before he came to Buxton. You know how that normally goes. A sadist's final act of power and cruelty. Promising hope for the family, then snuffing it out. I played along for a while, but then I realised what he really wanted. Suicide by cop. He killed my mother and, indirectly, my father. He wanted to goad me into putting him out of his misery, which he knew would ruin me once and for all.'

'Has he given up the locations?'

'Yes. He tried a bit of misdirection on one, but the DCI cross-reffed with old case notes and we realised what he was doing. The families have their remains. They can go through their rituals. Close the loop.'

Keating looked up from the fly. 'You don't believe in closure.'

'No. But if they do, then whatever helps.' He got up and walked over to the river's edge, near Keating. He sat on the grass. 'I played Caldwell at his own game. I promised him a quick end, but then backed out of the deal, once he'd given us what we needed. I reminded him of what I said to Dad in that basement. *It's better that he lives.* Continues to suffer.

Rots away. I told him how I dwell in possibility. How he failed to deny me and my brother a future. And now we have one, and he has nothing to look forward to but pain. I also told him I looked forward to passing water on his grave.'

Keating squinted. 'Isn't that from *Blackadder*?'

'It is.' Sawyer watched as Keating trimmed the line with a small nail clipper. 'He also scratched a personal itch for me.'

'Which was?'

Sawyer squatted down, level with Keating. 'Bolehill.'

Keating set down the clipper and tugged on the fly, ensuring the line was secure and the bait solidly attached. He closed the fly box and placed the fly carefully on the lid, then looked up. 'What do you want from me, Sawyer? My version?'

'You knew my dad had Caldwell in that basement, right from the start. It's why you told the AFOs to stand down when I was about to shoot him. Let me do it. Cut the final link to Bolehill.'

Keating shook his head. 'I didn't know he had him down there. I knew Harold had something to do with Caldwell's disappearance, but I didn't pursue it.'

Sawyer held his eye. 'Because it helped you both. It was my mum's journal that got me thinking. She wrote an entry in June 1984. "Ivan was here, with Harold... Ivan said they can't just 'let the thing with Bill go away'."' He edged closer. 'What I want from you is for you to accept your role in my mother's death.'

'He was a fucking monster, Jake. You don't know.'

Sawyer nodded, his stare flat and unyielding. 'Here's what I do know. In 1986, after killing three sex workers down in Stoke, Caldwell was promoted to DCI and moved to Buxton, commanding you and my dad. The following year, the three of you stayed in a cabin in Hathersage, near Bolehill Wood.' He waved a hand. '*Fishing*. Caldwell brought a woman. Sharon Wright. He probably said she was his girlfriend, but he'd hired her services for the trip.'

Keating held up a trembling hand. 'We... We heard noises from his room in the night. Your dad told me he heard Sharon go out early the next morning. He said he heard Bill... Caldwell go out soon after her. He woke me...'

'And you and my dad followed.' Sawyer moved the fly box and fly to the side and sat next to Keating on the fishing basket. He leaned forward, facing him. 'And what did you find, Ivan?'

Keating lowered his head, stared down at his boots. 'He'd killed her. Smashed her face in with something. She was lying there in thick grass. There was so much blood it had pooled, half-submerging her skull in a pocket of grass. He swore he hadn't done it. He said he'd found her like that. We wanted to call it in, but he said we couldn't, because she was a sex worker, and it would end his marriage. Your dad was about to leave, and Caldwell took out a gun, held it on us. Then we heard kids shouting nearby. He said we had to go, saying we didn't want to get caught close to the body as we'd be implicated. He insisted we go back to the cabin. It was a long walk. The first responders called in CID, and Caldwell ended up leading the investigation.' He looked up at Sawyer, eyes glazed with tears. 'Your dad and me... We were both tied up in it. He threatened us, said he would twist the story, pull us both in. You saw a version of Caldwell yesterday, but you've no idea how scary he used to be. We were younger. I'd never seen a bloody gun in real life back then. The woman was already dead, and it would only have ruined our careers, marriages... We did the wrong thing, for the right reasons.'

Sawyer gave Keating a sick smile. 'You enabled a killer. A monster, as you say. To save yourself. Your *career*.'

'We didn't know what he was back then.' He leaned forward. 'Remember what your dad said to me in that basement? He asked me to look after his boys. That's what I've been doing. Think of all the times over the past few years when I've helped you, rooted for you, tried to steer you. And all the time it was clear you were so unwell.'

'You did nothing. Nothing to stop him. And it made him more confident. And the next year, he murdered my mother. The ripples from your inaction flowed out into the future. And now here you sit, indulging yourself. Pitting your wits against unsuspecting fucking trout, while my mother and father lie in the cold ground.' He got to his feet. 'But you're lucky today.' He patted his stomach. 'I've had my fill of revenge.'

Keating opened his mouth, about to say something.

Sawyer held up a hand. 'Please don't insult me with an apology. Any idiot can express their regret. Obsess over what happened yesterday. The hard bit is holding all that regret inside you and still living for tomorrow. The really hard bit is knowing that you can't unburden your guilt by stepping up and expressing the regret now there's nothing at stake. You left it too late.' He smiled, giving Keating the dimple. 'Enjoy your retirement.'

Chapter Sixty-Two

SHEPHERD OPENED THE GLOVEBOX. He looked across at Sawyer, smiling.

Sawyer glanced over. 'What?'

Shepherd pulled out a large bag of Haribo Goldbears. 'Okay, so we're eight years old now?'

'You need to get over this. Everyone has sweets in their car.'

'Yes. For long journeys. Not as a staple of their diet. What happened to the lemon sherbets?'

'Second attempt, but I think I might have kicked them this time. The Haribos give me the sugar hit but they're kinder on my teeth.'

He eased off the accelerator as the broad Castleton Road narrowed into Hope Road. Shepherd gazed out of the window.

'You're silently judging the music,' said Sawyer.

Shepherd didn't turn. 'I like it. Radiohead.'

'Close. It's a band called The Smile. With Radiohead's singer.'

'Walker listens to rap.'

'What kind?'

Shepherd shrugged. 'It honestly all sounds the same to me.'

'That's because the subtleties are lost on your ageing ears.'

'Theo will be onto it soon. I should educate myself.'

'He'll see through that. Let him find his own thing. I assume you've already poisoned him with Everton indoctrination?'

Shepherd turned. 'I tried.'

'Don't tell me—'

'Man City. I know. Wrong kind of blue… That reminds me. How's the mad bomber?'

'Peyton? He's in a bad way. They're saying he might lose his hearing. Also, nerve damage on one side of his face. He's spilling the lot, though, on the association with Strickland, selling out his Manchester crew.'

Shepherd whistled. 'I suppose they sold him out.'

'More than that. His own brother tried to have him killed. Can't really blame him for taking a protection scheme. He'll need to go all-in, though. It's being managed by NCA and CPS.'

'Relocation?'

'Need to know. And I don't want to. He's a Yankophile, so he'll probably go west. If you tally up the potential convictions, including Strickland, he's quite the supergrass.'

Shepherd took out a Haribo, waggled the packet at Sawyer who shook his head. 'Do you really think the Strickland case will stick?'

'I put enough work into it. I was meeting NCA contacts during my runs in the park near the unit. Proper spy stuff. Covert park bench meetings. I helped them connect up the threads that led back to Strickland. Your location for the graft phone he used with Curtis Mavers was the glue that held it together.'

'How many counts are there?'

'I've lost count. On top of his entanglement with the Peyton crew, which is backed up by NCA financial forensics, they have several murders of associates, county lines drug trafficking, laundering through various front businesses, a shitshow of creative accounting. I also obtained direct audio of him ordering the Buxton station attack and my murder. His lawyers are claiming it's an audio deep-fake, but we have Peyton's testimony to back it up, and masses of ANPR, CCTV and phone data that tallies with the allegations.'

'I wish I'd seen his face in his office. Did he come quietly?'

'Yes. But he lost his cool when our old friend Dean Logan doorstepped him with a photographer on the way to the car.'

'I wonder who could have possibly leaked news of the arrest to Logan?' said Shepherd, grinning.

'Oh, that was me.'

Shepherd sighed, chewed his Haribo. 'And what about the guy from the Manchester crew? Stokes.'

Sawyer nodded. 'He was running the Peyton operation in Eddie Peyton's absence. But he's also gone for protection. He got us the Strickland audio and he's testified to Strickland's dealings and doings.' He held up a finger. 'Here's the bit about Stokes I really love. He had a micro camera in the frame of a painting in his sitting room. An Auerbach.'

Shepherd shrugged.

'British. Expressionist. Anyway. There's plenty of Strickland footage on there, backing up the circumstantial and the audio. Oh, and Eddie won't be getting out anytime soon.

We linked his comms to the guy who tried to kill Peyton, making him an accessory to attempted murder. I was thinking of arranging a cell share with Strickland once it all goes down, but... Y'know. That would just be vindictive. Anyway. Enough about me. You did a fine job yourself, on Mr Farrell.'

'It wasn't just me.'

Sawyer scowled. 'Don't go humble on me now. He's basically toast, right?'

Shepherd allowed himself a smirk. 'All the breath mints in the world couldn't freshen him up now. We have an acting DCI in place. Sonia McBride.'

'I remember her. Nottingham. She was with us on the Bowman case.' Sawyer smiled at Shepherd. 'Oh, thank Christ. A grown-up at last.'

He swung the Mini away from Hope town centre and joined the straight, hedge-lined road up to Thornhill village.

'I feel bad for Strickland's wife and son,' said Shepherd.

'They'll be a lot better off without him. Luka's a tough one. I taught him a few tricks. Eva might have to make a few lifestyle adjustments, but she'll manage.'

'She won't be short of interest on the dating apps.'

Sawyer narrowed his eyes. 'You'll need to moderate the casual objectification now you have a woman in charge.'

He parked the Mini at the top of Shepherd's cul de sac and switched off the engine. They got out of the car and Sawyer squinted at the sleek, bright-red SUV sitting at the end of the drive.

He gaped at Shepherd. 'This is a fabulous new sensation. I'm jealous of your car.'

'It's a Range Rover Evoque,' said Shepherd. 'I was going to hold out for the new electric. But there's a waiting list.'

'And you can't wait?'

'Could you?'

Sawyer thought for a moment. 'No.'

'There you go. I'm blaming your influence.'

'Your buyer seemed a lot farmier than you. That boxy old monstrosity will serve him well.'

Shepherd sighed, rolled his neck muscles. 'Well. Sir. Thanks for the lift. I'll have to love you and leave you. I promised to take Theo for a drive in the fresh new car, then I have to help prep a serious dinner party later. Three couples, including Walker and his missus.'

'Tell him I said good work. On the Wilde thing.'

Shepherd laughed. 'You couldn't have solved our case without us. Are you still at the CMU?'

Sawyer shook his head. 'Didn't really suit me. I'm taking Occupational Health's advice for once. A bit of time off. Mike and I are sorting Dad's art. Then I might have a rethink. Do some travelling. Broaden my horizons.'

'Write your memoirs in Lanzarote.'

'Not enough material yet. I like to think there's more ahead of me than behind.'

Shepherd pushed away from the Mini and headed off. 'Yeah, that's good thinking.' He winked. 'Don't look back.'

Chapter Sixty-Three

SAWYER TAPPED in a phone number and pulled away from Shepherd's road, heading back down into Hope.

'Jake.'

Sadie Fletcher's voice was thin, and she was short of breath. 'Before you say anything, I've just finished a training session.'

'How are you doing?'

She sniffed, composed herself. 'Oh, I'm alright. Had a hectic few weeks, as you know, but things are calming now. I actually think we're a little ahead of schedule with the S&G school. I've been hammering social media. We've had so many sign-ups I might need to put a cap on it. I'm workshopping sessions, auditioning staff. Hey—'

'I know. JKD. I was thinking maybe I could come over tomorrow. Talk about how I can help.'

'That would be wonderful. Nine sharp?'

He winced. 'On a Sunday?'

'What's your excuse? I know you're not due at church.'

She took a drink of something, spluttered. 'Listen. You've caught me at a bad moment. I'm busy with some staff. But I need to tell you something.'

'Your dad called.'

'Yes.'

'Is he okay?'

She scoffed. 'Of course he is.'

'What did he say?'

'Not much.'

Sawyer laughed. 'Did he say where he was?'

'Of course he didn't. He did have a message for you, though. Again, just the one word.'

'Go on.'

'*Thanks.*'

SAWYER DROVE SOUTH, through the central Peak villages, the road signs echoing place names from his childhood: Coldeaston, Sheldon, Milldale. He stuck to country lanes, wallowing in the invincible beauty of the rolling landscape, so easily relegated to backdrop in the relatively brief lives of its inhabitants. It had been a warm summer so far; not oppressive. But the pollen was rising, and he sensed the heat stealing in over the Dove Valley hills.

He opened all four windows, regaling the sheep with the dream-pop drone of his favourite album: *Loveless*. The sun roared down from a pure cerulean sky with no whisper of cloud.

Sawyer pondered the *metta bhavana*.

He was happy, healthy, at peace.

He was no longer in the dark.

All was well.

And, as the meditation suggested, he contemplated his sense of gratitude.

He still had thanks of his own to give.

Chapter Sixty-Four

THE HOUSE WAS A PICTURE-POSTCARD CLICHÉ: a two-storey stone cottage set in modest grounds in the shadow of Thorpe Cloud hill. The front side was partially veiled by a generous and unmanicured spread of ivy, its green tendrils framing the windows, reaching up to the eaves. The small front garden was adorned with multiple pots and planters in full bloom: deep pink roses, creamy white daisies, velvet red geraniums, all basking in the sunlight.

Sawyer walked up the narrow front path, edged with weathered stones, and rang the doorbell.

No answer.

He waited for a while, then walked around to the far side of the house, where a metallic grey Toyota Prius sat at the end of a short gravel drive.

'Can I help?'

Sawyer turned. A stout man in his early sixties stood in the front garden. He had a bright, open face with weathered skin, lightly tanned, and a full head of silvery brown hair, thin enough to be tousled by the breeze from the field behind the house.

He took off a pair of gardening gloves and dusted down his hands. 'Are you looking for the stepping stones? You're a bit off course, I'm afraid.' He checked his watch. 'And you won't be able to park now. It gets popular on weekends.'

Sawyer walked back around and stopped by the front door.

He offered the man his warrant card, held up his hand. 'Don't worry. Nothing's happened.' He smiled. 'I'm not a tourist.'

The man took the card and studied it for a moment. His forehead creased. *Jake Sawyer...*' He handed back the card, studied Sawyer. 'Do you need help with something?'

Movement inside. The sound of a small dog barking.

'Sorry to disturb your Saturday,' said Sawyer.

The man waved a hand. 'Oh, don't worry. Hugo is a neurotic old sausage. Our dog, that is.'

The front door opened and a slim, elegant woman, around the same age as the man, stood in the frame, with a wriggling dachshund under her arm. She had honey-blonde hair, softly curled at the neck. The dog whined, its paws scrabbling at her loose-fitting floral blouse.

She angled her head, regarding Sawyer with kind, enquiring eyes.

The man stepped through from the side and scooped up the dog. He crouched, setting him down on the floor and holding his collar. Hugo strained forward, sniffing Sawyer and wagging his tail. 'You're privileged. Hugo isn't usually this good with visitors.'

Sawyer stooped down and fussed the dog, who wagged his fluffy tail and licked at his fingers. 'He can probably smell my cat.'

'He'd have your hand if he could,' said the man. 'I don't think his nose is so keen these days.'

Hugo settled at the man's feet, and Sawyer stood up, looking from the man to the woman. 'I'm so sorry to drop in on you like this.' He showed the woman his warrant card. 'It's not a police matter. More of an impulse, really. Look... If you're busy now, maybe we could talk another time?'

The woman slowly raised her widened eyes from the card. *Jake?*'

The man watched her. 'What is it, Fran?'

Sawyer smiled. 'Please don't ask me to come in. I just... I just wanted to...'

Fran gazed up at Sawyer. She put a steadying hand on the door frame. 'Oh, my goodness. Duncan, do you know who this is?'

Sawyer dipped his head. He took a sharp breath, felt his eyes fill with tears.

Duncan squinted at Sawyer. His mouth dropped open and he gaped at Fran, then back to Sawyer. 'The boy? From the lane?'

Fran shook her head, tears coming for her now. 'Oh... Look at you, Jake. *Look at you.*' She reached up a trembling hand, shifted Sawyer's hair to the side. She stepped back, reached to a side table and pulled out a handful of tissues, gave a couple to Sawyer.

He smiled. 'Look at me? Look at *you*. It's so good to see you both. Still together.'

'What happened to you, Jake?' said Duncan. 'And your brother?'

He smiled, sniffed, wiped at his eyes. 'You don't read the papers, then?'

'God, no,' said Fran. 'It's all bad news. We just keep ourselves to ourselves. Duncan works for the Trust. I have a little catering business, and a small bakery in Ashbourne.' She dabbed at her eyes. 'We've been married for thirty-six years, Jake. We had two wonderful girls. They have lives of their own now.' She rested a hand on his arm. 'Won't you come in?'

He shook his head. 'Maybe another time.' He looked at Duncan. 'To answer your questions, a lot has happened to me. Mike, my brother, is doing well.' He crouched, fussed Hugo again. 'I know this is a bit of a shock, but I've had it in my head for a while.'

'How did you find us?' said Fran.

He shrugged, stood upright. 'I do that a lot. Find people. I looked through the old case notes. Your statements.'

She nodded, beaming up at him. 'You're a *detective*.'

'I try to be.'

'On the side of the angels,' said Duncan.

He grinned, sheepish. 'I think that's the idea.' He took a breath. 'My... father. Was an artist. He passed away a few years ago. Left me—'

'Oh, no.' Fran gave a sympathetic smile. She reached up again, stroked Sawyer's hair. 'No, no, no. Don't say you've come to offer us money, Jake.'

'I wanted to—'

'Thank you for thinking of us,' said Duncan. He smiled. 'But... we have everything we need.'

Fran found Sawyer's eyes again. 'Can I at least hug you before you go?'

He nodded, and she moved in for a deep, warming embrace. 'What a wonderful, wonderful surprise, Jake. It means so much to see you. To know that you wanted to see us. Oh, why would we want your money? It's enough to know you're still here. That you survived.'

Sawyer hugged her back, braced for the flashes: the lane, the verge, the blood, the sun flare.

But nothing came. Just more tears.

'I just wanted to thank you,' he said. 'I didn't think it would be like this. I'm sorry.'

Fran squeezed him tight. 'It's alright. There's nothing to be sorry about. Just let it out.'

Sawyer dug his forehead into Fran's neck and cried, loud and hard. Without shame.

Hugo whined in sympathy, and Duncan crouched to settle him.

Sawyer recomposed himself, stepped back from Fran as she handed him more tissues.

He looked between the two of them again, smiling. He held Fran's eye. 'You said I'd be okay. It took me a while. But I got there in the end.'

Chapter Sixty-Five

MAGGIE SPARK CLOSED down her client management software and used the cane to help herself up from the desk. She walked past the chocolate-brown futon and out through the hall into the kitchen.

Two burly German Shepherd dogs lay curled on their beds at either side of the open French windows that overlooked the back garden. They spotted her and their tails twitched, holding back on full-blown wagging until Maggie's intentions were clear.

She switched into dog voice: shrill, reassuring. 'Almost done, boys. I have to shut you in for now. Won't be long. Be good for me.'

Maggie backed out and closed the door behind her, then turned towards the front door. She sighed, took a moment. She would need to streamline the Saturday clients, possibly cut them out altogether. The two back-to-back online patients had been a slog, and she would need her full energy reserve to handle the face-to-face: her last consult of the day. Thankfully, he was a new patient, so it would mostly be an unchallenging fact-gathering exercise.

Engine outside.

She headed down the hall.

Behind, the dogs scratched and scrabbled at the base of the kitchen door, whining.

'Rufus! Cain!' she shouted. 'Settle down.'

But the whining continued.

She could soothe them with a treat, but that was bad training. Better to apologise to her patient and hope they calmed down once he was in the sitting room.

The doorbell rang. Maggie reached the door and swung it open.

Sawyer stood a few paces back from the door, hands in the pockets of his softshell jacket. 'Mags.'

She glared at him, shook her head. 'Mr *Robbins*?'

'I was worried you wouldn't see me.'

She tucked a curl of rust-red hair behind one ear. 'I still might not.'

He smiled. 'Am I your last patient today? I assume so, as I saw your cut-off time and booked for the hour before.'

She shook her head, narrowed her eyes. 'You expect me to honour the booking? After this blatant—'

'Subterfuge?' he said.

She wrinkled her nose. 'Chicanery.'

'Nice word.' He gazed at her. 'It's good to see you. I'm sorry I had to—'

'It's fine.'

Sawyer looked up. A light aircraft whirred across the sky. He peered around her into the hall. 'Who's home?'

'Just Rufus and Cain.' She glanced at her watch. 'Justin, Mia and Freddy are due back in half an hour.'

'The dogs can cope with that. Let's go for a drive.'

'JAKE. THIS IS RIDICULOUS.'

Sawyer planted a walking boot in place, making sure of a solid footing, then pushed himself up onto the next rugged stone step.

Maggie wrapped her arms tighter around his neck and gripped his shoulders. He hitched her legs higher up his back and held them steady, crossed at the ankles.

'It's worth the journey,' said Sawyer, taking another couple of steps. 'And you're surprisingly light.'

'I'll remember to add that to my dating profile.'

Sawyer stepped aside to let a young couple pass on their way down to the Manifold Valley trail below.

The woman smiled and nudged her partner. 'We're doing that next time.'

'What, you carrying me?' said the man, laughing.

Sawyer pushed on, leaning forward to balance Maggie's weight, centring himself after each step.

'So, I hear you're a Buddhist now,' said Maggie.

'I'm trying to apply the principles, at least. Following the teachings. Mixing in a few ideas of my own.' He stopped, caught a breath. 'Can we talk about this later?'

'It's a good look for you. I think of stoicism as the theory and Buddhism as practice. And if you can't think or meditate your way out of a problem, you can always use your fists and feet.'

'I'm trying to move on from that. I'm sure you've heard of the *ahisma* concept. Causing harm to others is bringing harm to yourself.'

Maggie pulled herself up higher onto his shoulders. 'But you have the tools in the box if you ever meet people who don't share the idea.'

'As long as it's minimal and proportionate, yes. But even

that can have karmic payback. I've spent a few days calling in consequences.'

As they neared the top of the crag, the sunlight dappled and flared through the trees. Sawyer resisted his instinct to turn away.

At the top, a small family group—father, mother, two young boys—had gathered at the point where the path split: one route leading up and around to the top of the crag, the other into the cave.

Sawyer waited while the father led the way from the cave onto the summit route.

'Did Thor used to live there, Dad?' said one of the boys.

'Yes. A long time ago, though.'

The second boy, older, gave his brother a shove and they carried on up the trail.

Sawyer carried Maggie to the ten-metre-high mouth of the cave and stopped to rest, setting her down on the ledge.

'The previous version of you would have had to correct that,' said Maggie.

'My therapist in the unit called that my "infantile self". The version who chose to suffer.'

He leaned forward and stayed low, clambering up the smooth rock away from the sun and into the cave's earthy embrace.

'I spoke to Alex,' said Maggie. 'She asked after you.'

'What did you say?'

She laughed. 'I didn't know where to start. She's well. She sends love.'

Another couple exited along the other side of the slope as Sawyer's muscle memory guided him into the main chamber. He crouched and lifted Maggie onto the flat stone that overlooked the valley and treetops far below. She rested a hand on his shoulder as he eased in beside her, catching his breath.

'Well, this is alright,' said Maggie, peering out of the natural window at the bright green valley, the patches of fields, the snaking river.

Sawyer puffed. 'That was easier in my mind.'

'And you've got to get me down yet.'

He laughed, and they sat there, basking in the view.

'You missed a big case,' said Maggie. 'Nasty.'

'I heard. Shepherd nailed it, though.'

'I had lunch with Patricia. She told me about Farrell. And I read about Strickland getting nabbed by the NCA.' She looked at him. 'Are you going back?'

He shook his head. 'Trying to stick to forward only. Taking time off. I might do some consulting. Private work. I'm helping out at a new women's self-defence school.'

'Oh, Mia is into all that. She's been doing judo. And she's working with her boyfriend, Joshua. They've set up an online therapy group to help traumatised children. Jake, I'm so proud of her I could explode.'

He grinned. 'I'll introduce her to the woman who runs the martial arts school. I think they'll get on.'

'We should head back for a proper catch-up. Mia has gone full Nigella with her baking. She'd love to see you. And feed you something sugary. She made blueberry muffins last night.'

Sawyer looked down to the valley, pondered for a moment. 'I think coming here is still healthy.'

'How do you mean?'

'It's a reconnection. Not a regression. I've learned that healing is about holding on to the thread of who you are. Using it to pull yourself back into the world. My therapist said that I have to rewrite my story, while keeping the sense of who I was and how I've come to be.'

Maggie watched him. 'Address old feelings in new ways.'

'Yes. I'd always been haunted by the way I ran ahead and distracted Mum. And then I couldn't help her. Couldn't save her. We did a session that seemed corny at first, but it changed everything. I relived the attack. And she encouraged the adult me to step in and speak directly to my six-year-old self. I *consoled* him.'

Maggie rested a hand on Sawyer's hand. 'Told him it wasn't his fault.'

He nodded. 'It made me realise that I was looking for forgiveness from my mother. But I could never have saved her, anyway. I replaced that craving for her forgiveness by finding a way to forgive myself. It's not that I wasn't good enough or strong enough to *save* my mother. That's just the story I've told myself.'

'Yes. As you say, you need to rewrite that. Make it a more hopeful narrative, instead of seeing yourself as weak, blameworthy, deficient.' She leaned in. 'Therapists can't provide answers. They listen and help the patient find their own answers. Jake. As you work on this rewriting, you'll relearn. Reconnect with yourself. Open up new pathways of self-experience. Rediscover the old ones. You'll gradually move away from the old version of your story as you experience more of the new. The old traumas will stop replaying in your mind. You'll pick up that thread. And you won't feel the need to look back. Your Buddhism has given you a way to be calm and focused. Now you need to learn how to keep that calm and focus in the face of triggers, events and people that send you back to the old narrative. You can't create something new if you're reacting to something old. Think of your Buddhism. The dharma. The guide away from the dark towards enlightenment.'

She sat back.

'I think I'll always do dark,' said Sawyer. 'But now it doesn't do me.'

He took out his new phone, and started a Spotify playlist, keeping the volume low.

Dub bass, shuffling drums. Male vocal with a soft Jamaican accent.

Sawyer turned to Maggie. 'I think I made you a mixtape.'

'You think?'

'Well. A playlist. The modern equivalent.'

She lifted her hand from Sawyer's and slid it around his shoulders. 'So, is this a date?'

He nodded to the view. 'Beats the multiplex.'

They were silent for a while, listening to the music. The cave acoustics deepened the sound from his tinny phone speaker. Maggie closed her eyes and rested her forehead on Sawyer's cheek, and he felt her body swaying slightly, in time with the beat.

'You said you thought you'd talk to me,' said Sawyer. 'The year we first heard this album together.'

She smiled. 'And you said, "You've made a wise decision."'

'You must have thought I was an arrogant idiot.'

Maggie lifted her head, opened her eyes. 'I thought you were a challenge.' She reached back and threaded her fingers through the hair at the base of Sawyer's neck. 'So, what did you think of me? The first time we were alone, you got stoned and passed out. I tried not to take it personally.'

Sawyer turned to her again. 'I thought you were too good for me. I thought you were perfect.'

She laughed. 'Well, I can finally confirm that isn't true.'

Voices from below. A new group of walkers had reached the top of the steps.

Maggie shifted her hand to Sawyer's side, pulling him closer. 'If you're going to kiss me, you'd better get on with it. We're too old to be caught necking like teenagers.'

He did. And, again, it was easy, mutual.

The kiss lightened something inside him. Lifted a weight.

'It's fucking massive!'

They broke away, laughing at the shout from below.

'I think they mean the cave,' said Sawyer.

Maggie picked up a small rock and scratched at the stone they were sitting on. It formed a faint line white line in the limestone, and she drew a small looping figure.

'Eight what?' said Sawyer.

'Not a number. Infinity symbol. Think of it this way.' She tapped the stone at the left side of the symbol. 'Depressives are stuck here, in the past.' She tapped the right side. 'Neurotics are here. In the future.'

Sawyer tapped the centre of the symbol. 'So the trick is to live here.'

'Exactly. Don't look back or forward too much. Because that acknowledges both as oppressive.'

'Today's not yesterday.'

'Okay. Is that Buddhist?'

Sawyer grinned. 'Stevie Wonder.' He stood up. 'Well, I'm going to allow myself to look forward, to those blueberry muffins.' He crouched and reached for Maggie, ready to lift her onto his back again.

She held up a hand. 'I think I can manage. Stay close, though. If I go, I'm taking you with me.'

They edged down the slope, out of the cave.

At the stone steps, Sawyer stayed alongside Maggie. She took each step slowly, using the trees for support.

Around halfway, they stopped at a passing spot to take a drink of water. Maggie sat down to rest on a flattened tree stump.

Sawyer stepped onto the far side of the path where the overhanging branches thinned. He raised his face to the sunshine and looked up to the cave entrance at the top of the steep crag.

'So, you're absolutely sure, then?' he said.

'Sure of what?'

'That you're not perfect.'

Maggie raised a hand, shielding her eyes. Sawyer stood silhouetted against the fiery midday sun, head tilted, his features lost in the golden light. From this angle, it was hard to tell if he was facing her or turned away.

'Neither are you,' she said.

He moved back onto the main path. 'No,' he said, holding out a hand. 'But we might be perfect for each other.'

She laughed, let him help her up. 'Now, I know that one. *Good Will Hunting*. Mia loves it.'

They pushed on, over the wooden bridge that crossed the river back onto the Manifold trail. Sawyer sat on the peak of a trailside verge and lay back, settling his head in a cushion of long grass.

Maggie flopped down beside him. 'I think the muffins can wait.'

'Definitely. It's a glorious day. We're adults. We can do what we want.'

He looked at her. 'Did you message home?'

'Yes. Mia knows who I'm with.'

Sawyer turned onto his side. 'We can start with lunch.'

'Nut Tree?'

'Naturally. And then... I can get started on showing you that you really did make a wise decision.'

'Okay.' Maggie lay back, suddenly serious. 'But you have to promise me something.'

'What's that?'

'Jake, when you feel the triggers dragging you back to the old traumas, when the future seems oppressive, just promise me you'll keep the image of that infinity symbol in your mind. Go back up to the cave and look at it again if you have to. Stay in that central sweet spot. In the present. Rewriting your story.'

He thought for a moment. 'I promise to try.'

More by Andrew Lowe

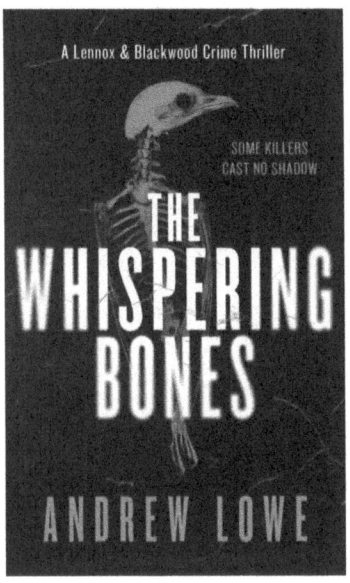

vinci-books.com/whispering-bones

Like a python after a meal, he had rested. But now the hunger was rising again…

A killer stalks North London, draining victims and leaving eerie bone displays. DCI Lennox has chased him for seven years—but now insomnia and memory lapses cloud his mind.

Turn the page for a preview…

The Whispering Bones Preview

Prologue

He stepped out into the North London twilight, into the human herd. Vendors, vapers, screamers, streamers. Elbowed by power walkers, grazed by e-scooters.

He glided over it all like a phantom.

He slid into the driver's seat of a black BMW 3 Series, the leather's texture sparking an orange flare in his mind's eye. He started the engine, its purr a soothing aquamarine that washed away the bar's lingering cacophony of reds and yellows.

He had drunk a bottle of lager, and his thinking was a little dampened. But he navigated the streets with care and grace, counting the turns, threading slowly through patches of congestion.

No drama.

That came later.

The city's rhythms conceded to the quieter pulse of the

suburbs. Here, the street lights were sparse, the shadows deeper.

He lowered the driver's side window. The sound of the sliding glass was mint-green, sharp round the edges.

He crawled the car along the perimeter road of a new-build estate, past modular red-brick homes with baize-like lawns and upscale SUVs parked side by side in dual driveways. Further in, the houses tapered to scruffy development sites set in buffer zones: prepared foundations marked out with orange plastic fencing and half-finished timber frames.

He turned into an unmarked track that led to a row of private lock-up garages shaded by a canopy of oak and beech trees. He pulled up, killed the engine, and sat still for a while, basking in the silence, broken only by the fading tick of cooling metal.

He waited, watching the garages. Listening.

Nothing.

He raised the window and got out of the car, gravel crunching underfoot: a spark of white against the night's blackness. At the end garage, he pulled on a pair of nitrile gloves and swiped an access card over a wall pad, which issued a soft double bleep: a burst of lime green.

Inside, he flicked a switch and the dark gave way to low fluorescent light. He blinked, adjusting. A silver-grey Vauxhall Insignia sat waiting. He ran a hand along its metal flank, closed his eyes, savouring the familiar bloom of purple and vermillion.

He walked back out to the BMW and retrieved a small but heavy canvas holdall from the boot. The items in the bag clinked and rattled as he moved, setting off a psychedelic surge behind his eyes, strong enough to send him down to his haunches. He took a few slow breaths and rose again. Back inside the garage, he set the bag down carefully on the Insignia's back seat.

A smile tugged at the corners of his mouth. He was in dire need of nourishment, but tomorrow the ritual would take place again. The prospect filled him with a warm pulse: honeyed gold.

He stood by the door, waiting.

A faint sound caught his attention.

A bump. Muffled, but distinct, from the Insignia's boot.

He paused, head tilted. Another bump followed, then silence.

He waited for a few moments, then switched off the light, stepped back out onto the gravel, and secured the door behind him.

The Whispering Bones Preview

Chapter One

The command vehicle's interior lights cast a sallow glow across DCI Oswald Lennox's face as he hunched over the tactical display.

His voice crackled on the secure channel. 'Control to all units. Radio check.'

A chorus of affirmatives.

Lennox's eyes flicked to the dashboard clock. 4:55.

Five minutes to breach.

He lashed his tongue round his mouth, trying to mop away the tang of scorched coffee. 'Final confirmations. Team target is Keane residence on Finsbury Park Road. Suspected armed presence.' He winced, spat. 'Christ. You don't boil coffee water. A child would know it.'

'Sir?'

'Never mind. Alpha lead?'

'Copy that, Control. Set for hard breach on your go.'

Lennox ran through the brief in his mind.

Two teams. One front, one back...

'Sir?'

'Copy that, Alpha. Beta team, you're covering the rear. Stay lively.'

Beta acknowledged.

Alpha team to breach. All officers were aware of Keane's history of violence and the firearm threat.

It was his girlfriend's flat. Limited intelligence on her but not perceived to be—

'Sir. Beta lead.'

'Copy.'

'Increased activity at rear. Light on in the basement room. Suggest we expedite entry.'

4:57.

Lennox recalled the scene in the briefing room, observing as it unspooled in his memory. The three men in the Alpha team sat on the right-hand side of the second row. Their faces triggered their names, records, honours.

He switched to a new track: reading through the documents as the teams assembled. The words re-formed in his mind as clear as the images on the tactical display.

One man, Braybrook, had grown up in the US. He was comfortable with guns but hadn't applied for firearms teams. Level head. Not a cowboy.

Lennox slipped a pellet of chewing gum into his mouth. 'Negative. Alpha team lead?'

'Sir.'

'DC Braybrook to take rear. Beta team, join Alpha and breach on my signal.'

A pause.

'DC Braybrook solo at rear, sir?' said the Beta lead.

'That's my order. SCO19, this is Control. Status?'

Radio crackle.

'Sir. Armed assets standing by.'

Lennox chewed his gum, pondering.

4:58.

'Sir. Beta team in position.'

Something was loose, hanging. Keane was a career toerag who'd notched up a cumulative five years for GBH and drug supply before his twenty-first birthday. But now he'd evolved, leaving a DNA-soaked beanie next to the body of a rival dealer.

Slash wound to the vic's throat.

Fourteen stabs to the chest. Zombie knife.

T-shirt sleeves torn. Two others holding him.

4:59.

'All units,' said Lennox. 'Stand by.'

'Sir.' Alpha team lead again. *'Suggest we—'*

'Stand by.'

'Sir. DC Braybrook reporting. From the rear.'

Lennox smiled. *Reporting.*

'Copy.'

'Figure at rear basement window. Light off again.'

'Don't deviate. Stay focused.'

Lennox savoured the moment, rolling the gum around, freshening his mouth.

Keane was probably expecting the attention. He'd have his girlfriend on watch. Maybe swapping with her when the hour got more sociable. But probably not.

5:00.

'Execute.'

A crash. Shouts.

Lennox leaned in, squinting at the shaky bodycam footage.

'Alpha and Beta team. Entry successful. Hall and sitting room empty. Ground floor clear.'

'Copy that,' said Lennox. 'Split between first and basement. DC Braybrook. Update.'

More crashing and shouting from the Alpha and Beta teams as the bodycam footage showed them sweeping the rooms.

Lennox took the gum from his mouth and stuffed it into his empty coffee cup. 'DC Braybrook. Update.'

'First floor clear.' Alpha team lead.

A woman's voice. Squealing, berating.

'Sir.' Beta team lead. *'Basement clear. We have Keane's girlfriend, but no sign of Keane.'*

Lennox detached the radio. He slid open the side door of the command vehicle and barrelled out onto the pavement. He ran across the road, past the entry point, shouting into the radio. 'Beta team. Suspect is away. Rear exit. DC Braybrook, confirm your position.'

Radio crackle.

Braybrook's voice came through. *'Sir.'* He was panting, snatching at his words. *'Suspect is unarmed but mobile... In pursuit... Of suspect. Heading east down Stroud Green Road. Towards the estate. Came out of fucking nowhere!'* A clattering noise. *'Sir.'* He grunted, then cried out.

'DC Braybrook?' said Lennox. 'Report status.' He slowed and stopped at the far end of the road. He peered through the half-light, across the scrubland that separated the converted town houses from a low-rise cluster of crumbling flat blocks.

Braybrook was on the floor, trying to haul himself up. Three officers caught up to him. Two kept running, while one crouched, trying to help him to his feet.

Ahead of the two, a hefty man in underwear and T-shirt sprinted across the scrub at half the speed of the pursuing officers.

Lennox bent double, catching his breath. He watched as the officers gained on Keane. One got alongside and felled him with a side tackle. They wrestled for a few seconds, but the other officer suppressed and cuffed him, then hauled him upright.

Braybrook was up but needed support from the other officer as they shuffled back to the road.

Lennox lifted the radio to call for reports and stand down the AR team.

He hesitated. Hooked the handset into the clip on his vest and raised his right arm.

The hand was trembling.

He stepped forward, into a pool of light from a street lamp, and stared at the hand, splaying the fingers.

Not trembling.

Shaking.

Chapter Two

Olivia Blackwood was up and moving, lurching between dresser and wardrobe. She dived into a neutral blouse, tugged on a pair of fitted black trousers.

There was a body in the bed, half-covered by the duvet.

Blond, with a scruffy burst-fade haircut. Too young for him.

Arm hanging down, fingertips on his phone.

Nasty calf tattoo.

She shook him. 'You've got to go. Landlord's coming in half an hour.'

The window pane rattled with raindrops. Blackwood flung the curtain aside, unveiling a dirty-grey pall over the distant spire of Harrow School Chapel.

She stamped into a pair of low-heels, then kicked them away, peeled off the trousers. Replaced them with dark jeans, scuffed brown boots.

'Hey!' She yanked the man's foot. 'I need you gone.'

He groaned. 'No breakfast?'

Blackwood half-tucked the blouse. 'It's not included. I'm afraid you only booked the One-Time Hook-Up special. That's a cup of instant coffee, one round of vanilla sex and a bed for the night.' She checked the dresser mirror, smoothed down her hair, grabbed her phone. 'No eggs. No pancakes. No Coco Pops. And check-out time was fifteen minutes ago.'

She crashed out of the room and jogged across the landing into the poky bathroom. Sink, toilet, wash basin, narrow bath with detachable shower head over the taps.

Blackwood segued through the rituals, barely finishing the last before starting on the next: face-wash, moisturise, few dabs of make-up. She brushed her teeth—toothbrush in one hand, scrolling the socials with the other—then used the toilet. She washed her hands, then smoothed shea butter through her dark curls before pinning them up, revealing a subtle tattoo behind her left ear. She leaned in close to the mirror, eyeballing herself.

Already, the thoughts crowding in. Tumbling over each other like a scrum of toddlers.

She stared herself down, blinking slowly. Her thick lashes wiped then renewed the image: wide, upturned eyes; glossy hazel irises.

A shout from the bedroom. *'Where's my fucking trainers?'*

If only she had a bouncer trained to clear them out at daybreak. Soundlessly, without fuss. Without waking her.

Or a chute that slid down from the ceiling and sucked them up and far away.

Or they could turn into pumpkins at midnight.

Or, better still, pumpkin pie.

No.

Apple pie. With cinnamon...

'Fuck's sake.'

She jerked away from the mirror, back into the bedroom.

He was up at least, and dressed, sitting on the edge of the bed, hunting around underneath it.

'Out, out, out,' she said. 'I mean it. I'm late for work.'

He sniggered. 'Not so submissive now, eh?'

Blackwood glared out at the rain, then bent down to pick up her brown leather shoulder bag.

His hand slapped her hard on the arse and she cried out. It stung, even through the jeans.

She turned, found him grinning. 'Didn't notice the purple streak in your hair last night.'

Bad teeth.

Oily skin.

Horsey face.

She returned his grin, then swung her open hand round in a wide arc, slapping him across the cheek.

He reeled, holding his face. 'Jesus Christ! What the fuck is your problem?'

She pulled the door wide. 'I've told you my problem. My landlord is due. He gives us shit if guests stay over.' She reached for the far side of the dresser, threw his trainers onto the bed. 'Last night was wonderful. Together, we scaled the holiest heights of ecstasy. But now you're just my guest.'

He pulled on the trainers, scowling at her. 'An unwanted guest.'

Blackwood smiled. 'Now you're getting it.' She gestured to the open door. 'You have officially outstayed your welcome.'

The man got up. He was shorter than her by a few inches.

He stepped in close, his grin fading to a frown, trying to stare her out. She held his eye.

He cracked first, smirking, rubbing his reddened cheek. 'Gave me a proper knock. What the fuck do you do, anyway? You're not a cage fighter, are you?'

He hissed out a laugh, leaned in closer.

Morning breath.

Rancid, with a sickly undertone.

Vape or gum or—

'You know what?' he rasped into her ear. 'I don't mind

it. I'm up for the rough stuff. But it goes both ways, eh? How about one for the road? Make it quick, like.'

Blackwood smiled. 'How rough are we talking?' She pivoted and pushed open the window. Rainwater splashed over the sill, into the room. The man stepped back. 'We're on the first floor, above the front garden. It's quite overgrown, so it'll be a soft landing. But you'll probably break something. Particularly if you go out head-first.' She nodded to the door. 'I'd take the smooth way out if I were you.'

Chapter Three

Lennox eased into the tilting backrest of his Herman Miller office chair. But after a night of patchy sleep, the incline was unwise, and he forced himself upright, tapping the base of his desk lamp to boost the brightness.

He'd stacked the report templates on his PC desktop in order of urgency: Incident, Use of Force, Post-Incident Procedure. There would be a formal debrief, and probably a Professional Standards interview.

Personal Statement.

Risk Assessment Review.

Possible IOPC referral.

Welfare Check.

Action Plan.

He sighed, then stood up and headed for a low shelf in the corner of his glass-walled office. He bent forward, pushing his face close to the chrome-fronted Jura coffee machine. His contorted reflection glared back.

Ambient 1: Music For Airports wafted around him as he pressed the power button. He lifted the lid, inhaled the aroma, then scooped out a measure of single-origin beans from an airtight ceramic container and poured them in. He closed the lid of the machine, set his favourite ultraviolet Le Creuset mug into the holder, and tapped the *ESPRESSO* icon on the colour touch screen.

Nothing.

Lennox turned away, gazing out at the vast, open-plan operational floor of the Hendon Major Investigation Team. One hundred and twenty-five souls. Sixty detectives.

Twenty-five uniforms. Forty civilian staff: analysts, researchers, admin.

Rows of light grey desks sat in clusters, each equipped with dual-monitor computers and modesty panels.

Along the far wall, a series of plasma screens displayed real-time information—London crime maps and stats, key CCTV feeds—above a row of whiteboards with timelines, suspect photos, flowcharts. In the near corner, a group of detectives sat huddled in a glass-walled briefing room, viewing a projected presentation.

Still nothing from the machine.

Lennox studied the display. He tapped the *ESPRESSO* icon again, caught a movement at the office door.

A short middle-aged woman had entered without knocking. She wore an immaculately draped deep-teal *hijab*, the fabric complementing her complexion. DSI Aisha Khokhar closed the door behind her and strode over to Lennox with confident, measured steps. She tucked the loose edges of the hijab under her chin and smoothed the fabric over her shoulders, then rolled up the sleeves of her white shirt.

Khokhar studied the display, then reached out a finger and tapped the *BREW* icon. The machine whirred into action.

'User error.' She smiled and took a seat facing the desk.

Lennox opened an app on his phone and silenced the music.

Khokhar caught his eye, holding her smile.

'Coffee, ma'am?' said Lennox.

She shook her head. 'On the wagon at the moment. I was shifting my last cup further forward in the day, but still couldn't switch off for sleep. So I'm retraining myself with matcha latte. Apparently, it's rich in antioxidants.'

'And a more sustained energy boost,' said Lennox. He brought his cup over and sat down. 'Tastes awful, though. Like drinking a lawn.'

Khokhar laughed, then rolled her eyes in pleasure. 'My God, that smells so good.'

Lennox nodded, took a sip. 'Just a glitch, ma'am.'

'The coffee machine?'

'The Keane op.'

Khokhar crossed her legs. 'A glitch on your watch, Oz. Collector's item. A double-tick for the apprehension and appropriate force, but a big red *SEE ME* for stationing a single officer at the rear.'

Lennox smoothed out his closely trimmed salt-and-pepper beard with the palm of his hand. 'I'm struggling with sleep too at the moment. Judgement is off.' He forced a smile. 'Braybrook picked up a sprain. Nothing big.'

Khokhar fixed him with a searching stare. 'I hear you asked a DS to "refresh everyone's memory" at the briefing.'

Lennox drained his cup. 'My homework on Keane was shaky. That was lazy. Won't happen again.'

Khokhar gasped. 'Oh, Christ. This isn't a bollocking. Really. I was genuinely curious.' She left some space for him to speak; he didn't fill it. 'Do you need a break?'

'No,' said Lennox, too quickly. 'It's just... Maybe I'm human after all.'

'I wouldn't go that far.'

'The date's coming up.' His eyes drifted to the photo frame on his desk, but he dragged them back to Khokhar. 'That's probably getting into my head, too.'

She nodded. 'Of course.' She wagged a finger. 'Don't tough this out, though. If you need time, you need time.' She sat back. 'Any more thoughts on the thing I mentioned?'

Lennox wrinkled his nose. 'I'd rather focus on the current generation. I just need to pace myself better now I'm—'

'Don't you dare say "over the hill".' Khokhar stood.

He grimaced as he got to his feet. 'Feeling it today. I'll sharpen up.'

'Again, Oz. Not a bollocking. Just checking in. For most people, I'd wait for three or four glitches. But for you, I'm here at one.' She spun and headed for the door. 'Here to help. But I can't do much if I don't know what you need help with.'

Lennox lowered himself back into the seat. 'Appreciate the offer, but no help needed.'

She stopped, turned. 'Plenty of magic left in the wand yet, eh? What are you now? Sixty-odd? That's young, these days.'

He grinned. 'Fuck off. Ma'am.'

Grab your copy...
vinci-books.com/whispering-bones

About the Author

Andrew Lowe was born in the north of England. He has written for The Guardian and the Sunday Times, and contributed to numerous books and magazines on films, music, TV, video games, sex, and shin splints.

He lives in the south of England, where he writes, edits other people's writing, and shepherds his two young sons down the path of righteousness.